THE Brothers

No.1 *Sunday Times* bestselling author Kimberley Chambers lives in Essex and has been, at various times, a disc jockey, cab driver and a street trader. She is now a full-time writer.

Join Kimberley's legion of legendary fans online: www.kimberleychambers.com

/kimberleychambersofficial
@kimbochambers
@kimberley.chambers

THE Brothers
KIMBERLEY CHAMBERS

HarperCollins*Publishers*

HarperCollins*Publishers* Ltd
1 London Bridge Street
London SE1 9GF

www.harpercollins.co.uk

HarperCollins*Publishers*
Macken House, 39/40 Mayor Street Upper
Dublin 1, D01 C9W8, Ireland

First published by HarperCollins*Publishers* Ltd 2024
1

A catalogue record for this book is available from the British Library

ISBN: 978-0-00-836604-9 (HB)
ISBN: 978-0-00-836605-6 (TPB)

Typeset in Sabon LT Std by Palimpsest Book Production Ltd,
Falkirk, Stirlingshire

Printed and bound in the UK using 100% renewable electricity
at CPI Group (UK) Ltd

In memory of my mum's wonderful cousin, Lynne Croft
1946–2002
Thanks for all your support, Lynne.
We all love and miss you, sweetheart xxxxx

ACKNOWLEDGEMENTS

Massive thanks to my great HarperCollins team. There are too many to mention individually, but I know how hard you all work to help sell my books, and I'm truly grateful.

Special mention to my lovely agent Tim Bates, Rosie de Courcy (always grateful) and the irreplaceable Sue Cox.

A big shout out to my brilliant editor Kimberley Young. Thanks for everything, darling. Gonna miss you big time, but I'm so grateful for all that you've taught me, Kim. You'll smash your new role 'cause you are simply the DOG'S BOLLOCKS!

And last, but certainly not least, I'd be sodding nowhere without me readers. I can't thank you all enough for your passion for my books and also your patience while waiting for this one.

God bless you all,

KC xxx

PROLOGUE

The room was sparsely furnished. It smelled musty, apart from a hint of lavender.

The woman was old. Her weather-beaten skin leathery and crinkled, her once shiny black hair now limp and grey.

Coughing profusely, the woman spat a mouthful of phlegm into an already filthy handkerchief before turning her attention back to her crystal ball. She was only doing this as a one-off, a favour.

Evie Tamplin's heart was beating nineteen to the dozen. Everything Psychic Lena had told her so far had been spot on, especially about Jolene and that no-good gorger boyfriend of hers.

'Ooh. Hmmm. Oh dordi!'

'What! What can you see?' A mixture of excitement and trepidation pumped through Evie's veins.

'The blond lad, he has a dark soul. There's another mush, not as tall, very handsome. He's kinder. That's her soulmate.'

1

'Is he a Traveller?' Evie asked hopefully.

'He looks like one. Dark features. I sense she's met him in the past, perhaps as a young child.'

'Ooh, that's good news. Is there anything I can do to stop her making the mistake of marrying the blond lad first?' Beau Bond was the gorger who her precious daughter was currently dating. Tall, blond, with brown eyes, Evie could see straight through those good looks of his. She hated him with a passion.

'No. I sees a journey. Your daughter will marry first, before meeting her true love again.'

'Oh,' mumbled Evie, the wind taken out of her sails. 'Can ya see how long this sham of a marriage lasts?'

Lena's wrinkly hands hovered above her crystal ball. She closed her eyes, muttering some gibberish Evie could not understand.

'I see chavvies. Lots of chavvies. And I feels heat. A burning, vicious heat.' The reason Psychic Lena had stopped using her crystal ball in the first place was because of her ability to feel the pain due to others. It had caused her some scary moments over the years, hence her decision to quit the spiritual talent God had given her.

Evie was startled as Lena began making a weird kind of howling noise, then began clawing at her arms and face. 'Whassamatter? What did you mean by heat? It ain't a fire, is it?'

Lena was too busy coughing to reply.

Realizing the old woman was struggling for breath, a frantic Evie leapt off her chair and thumped her on the back. 'You want water?'

Gasping, Lena fell to the floor of her ancient rundown trailer.

Cursing herself for allowing her sons to drop her off on such a desolate piece of land, Evie found Lena's landline and, hands shaking, dialled 999.

It was all in vain though. At eighty-nine years old, Psychic Lena had taken her last breath. And with it, she'd taken her terrifying premonitions of what was to become of Evie's family to the grave with her.

PART ONE

There are two things in life for which we are never truly prepared: Twins.

Josh Billings

CHAPTER ONE

Twins. A shortish-simple word. But what does it really mean? To anyone who ain't one, it just means two people who look alike, or if you're not identical, another sibling, like an ordinary brother or sister. Only an actual twin could understand the true meaning of the word.

Bond by name and nature, that's us. We never needed friends growing up, 'cause we always had each other. We even spoke in unison at times, like our brains were wired as one.

Inseparable, closer than close, I think you're getting the gist now. But even though we never spoke about it, we both knew there was gonna come a time we would have to venture our separate ways. Spread our wings, so to speak. Meet a woman, get hitched, have kids. That's what was expected of us, wasn't it?

Sometimes in life, though, things don't go to plan. Also, living up to expectations can prove to be difficult. Especially if you've had a fucked-up childhood like we had. Issues from the past can fester in your nut, like a rapidly growing brain tumour, which results in you acting impulsively and doing silly things like hurting people very badly.

Anyway, enough waffling on. Our names are Beau and Brett Bond, and this is our story . . .

Summer 1993

'Stop mucking around. This ain't funny now. You're scaring me.' Jamie's face had fear stamped all over it, his eyes a look of disbelief.

'This ain't no joke,' snapped Beau. 'Someone has to pay the price for Tammy's death. I won't be allowed to be with Jolene otherwise. It was you who got the pills off your so-called mate. Therefore, if it weren't for you, Tammy would still be alive. Get it?'

'But I was doing you a favour,' argued Jamie. 'You asked me if I knew anyone who sold 'em. I was just being helpful. How was I to know Tammy would keel over on one?'

'Well, helpful you weren't. Tape his mouth up, Brett,' ordered Beau. 'Let's get this over with.'

I begged Beau once more to reconsider. This was beyond awful. It was cruel, sadistic.

'Just fucking do it. Now!' hissed Beau.

'It was an accident. I'm sorry, OK? Please don't hurt me. It's madness. You're my brothers and I love you,' pleaded Jamie.

Beau glared at me, so I shut Jamie up with masking tape. He struggled and wriggled while begging for forgiveness, *even fell off the metal garden chair at one point. But Beau had tied his wrists up, so there was little he could do to stop me.*

'We ain't related by blood. We're stepbrothers,' spat Beau. 'And blood's thicker than water,' Beau added, tying Jamie's feet to the chair. The garden was totally secluded and the neighbours were away anyway.

Jamie's eyes looked sad, yet startled, like a petrified animal who knew it was about to die. I pleaded with Beau once more, to no avail.

'We gotta do this. You know we have. Man up, for fuck's sake. Ready? On the count of three. One, two, three.'

I looked into the swimming pool, expecting Jamie to drown, but then he resurfaced, and his head burst open, covering me and Beau with his brains, blood and gore.

'You not up yet?' Beau Bond lifted his arms in exasperation. 'Didn't you hear me calling you? Your breakfast is getting cold.'

Brett sat up and put his head in his hands. 'I must've finally dozed off and I wish I hadn't. I dreamt about *that* day and it was so real. Apart from the end bit. Jamie's head sort of blew up and his brains flew all over us. It was proper horrible.'

'You need to get up and pull yourself together. Have a cold shower.'

Brett glanced at his unfeeling twin, then shut his eyes to blank him out. Sixteen years old, they were identical in most ways. Tall, lithe, brown eyes and straight blond hair which they both kept in place with gel, overall good looks. They dressed well too; often went shopping for designer clobber. It was their personalities where they differed. Their humour and tastes were alike, but Beau could be heartless, disassociated from any kind of feelings, almost. What they'd done to Jamie hadn't affected Beau one iota, yet he was still having nightmares and feeling terribly guilty.

'Come on then. Chop, chop,' ordered Beau.

Brett put the quilt back over his head. The distinct smell of fried bacon was making him feel nauseous. He was dreading the day ahead, didn't have the energy to put on the facade expected of him. 'I really don't feel well. Told you yesterday I thought I was coming down with something. I had the shits and I've been sick in the night. You'll have to go without me. Just say I'm ill.'

Beau ripped the quilt off Brett's body. He wasn't silly, anything but. He also knew when his brother was trying to pull a fast one. 'You've gotta come. It'll look odd if you don't. One more day, that's all, Brett. Then we can put this tragedy behind us and move on with our lives. That's what our brother would've wanted.'

Brett glared at his twin before reluctantly getting out of bed. How could Beau even say that? This was no tragedy. It was murder, pure and simple.

'You look nice. I mean smart.' Donny Bond paused. He'd been treading on eggshells for days now, knew whatever he said would be deemed as wrong. 'You feeling OK? I know you're not OK. But you know what I mean.'

At first, Tansey had cried a river over the untimely death of her eldest son. Consumed with grief, she'd made excuses to cancel the funeral twice, so she could spend more time with Jamie at the chapel of rest. When the tears dried up, they were replaced with bitterness and anger.

'Got to be OK, I have no other choice. Jamie's not going to suddenly jump out of his coffin with a big grin on his face, is he?' Tansey spat. She pointed a finger. 'You just make sure you keep your precious twins away from me today, Donny, only I'm really not in the mood for 'em. I know my own son and I know he was in a good place. He was happy with Clare, had loads to look forward to. He would never have taken his own life without good reason, and only your conniving sons know the answer to that.'

Donny held his temper and left the room. None of this had been easy for his sons or him either. Jamie might not have been his flesh and blood, but he'd always raised and treated him as such. Tansey knew full well why Jamie had committed suicide. He'd explained his reasons in the note he'd left her. He'd got hold of the pills that had killed Tammy Tamplin. Why couldn't Tansey just accept that?

Cursing the way his life was going, Donny filled the kettle up and smashed it against the kitchen counter. Things had better improve soon as he was nearing breaking point.

The head of the Bond family was fifty-year-old Kenny. Five foot eleven with craggy features and copper-coloured hair, Kenny had plenty of aura and charm. He also had a reputation as a geezer not to be messed with.

Those close to him though, were more liable to describe him as a loveable rogue.

Like most men, Kenny had a secret side to him. A dark side that sometimes led him to make wrong decisions. He'd spent the whole of the 1970s in prison after being given a fifteen stretch for manslaughter after accidentally killing a copper. But even that hadn't been enough to make him go on the straight and narrow. Unbeknown to his loyal wife Sharon, Kenny had since been up to his old tricks again. For good reason, mind. Money had been running a bit low and there was no way his daughter was having a pauper's wedding. So, he'd got into the business of making ecstasy pills, setting up a factory with his pal Tony. The money soon rolled in, and his Sherry got married in true Bond style.

'All right, Gramps? Is my tie on straight?' asked Beau.

Kenny checked the knot. 'Where's Brett?'

'Putting his suit on. He weren't feeling great earlier, but he's perked up now.' Gramps had told him and Brett not to talk openly indoors, just in case the Old Bill had the place wired. You could never be too careful. Especially in Kenny's case, having killed one of their own.

Kenny gestured for Beau to follow him down the bottom of the garden. As far as they were aware, the police didn't have a clue that there was anything suspicious regarding Jamie's suicide. It did seem all cut and dried. 'Look, I know Brett's struggling. D'ya think he'll be all right?'

'Yeah. Course. He's gonna have to be, seeing as we're all in this together.'

Kenny lit up a cigar and took a deep drag. It had been his idea that the twins get Jamie to write notes, pretending

12

they were from them, before drowning Jamie and making it look like the lad had topped himself. It was a shitty situation all round and not one Kenny was proud of. He'd personally had nothing against Jamie, but the lad wasn't his flesh and blood, and somebody had to pay the price for Tammy Tamplin's death. Otherwise, the gypsies would come for them.

'What you thinking?' asked Beau. He idolized his grand-father, wanted to be just like him in years to come.

'Nothing. Just keep an eye on your brother. I'll be bloody glad when today's over.'

'Me too,' lied Beau. He was secretly looking forward to studying Tansey, watching her deal with the raw grief of it all. She'd always had it in for him and Brett. In his eyes, today was all about payback.

By the time they reached Ockendon Road, the sky was dull and the rain teeming down. A thoroughly miserable day, which matched Brett's mood.

Beau nudged his sibling. 'You all right?'

'Yeah,' Brett mumbled. He wasn't, but he was a Bond and that meant keeping a stiff upper lip. Visions of Jamie tormented his mind. Images of them as kids, getting up to no good, carefree, racing their quad bikes. Then there was that final vision. Jamie begging him and Beau not to drown him. The haunted expression of disbelief in Jamie's eyes. Brett shuddered as the limo pulled up outside the chapel. Tansey hadn't wanted them in the first funeral car, so Gramps had hired another.

Sensing his discomfort, Sharon Bond squeezed Brett's knee. 'You OK, love?' She had no idea that her husband

and grandsons were responsible for poor Jamie's death. She'd have disowned all three of them had she known.

'We're very sad, but we're determined to be strong, Nan,' piped up Beau.

Kenny gave his grandson daggers. He was sure Beau was getting a kick out of this and that really wasn't normal. Did the lad fancy himself to win an Oscar? Or did he have a massive fucking screw loose?

It was a boat party down the Thames that led to Jamie's demise. What should have been a joyful evening celebrating the twins' sixteenth birthday turned sour when Tammy Tamplin started to convulse, then later died in hospital after taking an ecstasy tablet.

Having purchased the pills off an old school pal, Jamie was the obvious scapegoat. The travelling community held grudges and would've been baying for blood had Kenny not devised a cunning plan. What nobody else knew, other than Kenny and his business partner Tony, was that *they* were actually to blame for Tammy's death. The contaminated pills were from *their* factory and had killed numerous other youngsters too. They weren't actually responsible for producing the pills themselves, but the bastards they'd employed were. Half a dozen or so Chinese geezers, who had since done a runner.

The factory was dust now. Kenny and Tony had burned it to the ground, and they'd had the luck of the gods on their side when the Old Bill had arrested a little firm out of Southend for the deaths after raiding their factory. It turned out the mugs had copied the crown stamp on the pill that had been Kenny and Tony's trademark.

'Dad, I need a word,' Donny said, grabbing his old man's arm and leading him away from listening ears.

'What's up?'

'It's Tansey. She ain't well, like. Not ill, but obviously today is a tough one for her. She don't want Beau and Brett carrying the coffin.'

'You what! Well, who's meant to carry it then? There's only us. And what about your sons? You can't tell 'em they can't carry their own brother's coffin.'

'I thought it might be better if you talk to 'em. Explain that Tansey's having one of her funny turns.'

Having felt an awful pang of guilt when originally asked to be one of the pallbearers, Kenny rubbed his son's arm. 'Why don't we all step back and let the funeral directors do the honours? That way, it saves any arguments.'

'Yeah. I'll speak to 'em now.'

When Donny walked away, Kenny breathed a huge sigh of relief. It wasn't every day you had someone topped, then was expected to carry them on their final journey.

'Baggy Trousers' by Madness was the first song Tansey had chosen. It was the earliest song she could remember her wonderful boy dancing to. Jamie had only been a nipper back then, but as Tansey closed her eyes, she could see him jumping up and down in his denim dungarees as though it were yesterday.

'Clare's here. She's sat right behind you,' Donny whispered in his long-term fiancée's ear. Clare was Jamie's only girlfriend and she'd made him so happy.

Tears of relief in her eyes, Tansey swung around and grabbed Clare's hand. 'Come sit next to me. It's what

Jamie would've wanted. Please,' she urged. Because of the complex circumstances, Tansey had been worried Clare wouldn't come.

'You want me to move?' whispered Donny.

'Yeah. Go and sit with *your* sons,' Tammy hissed. She knew she was being a bitch but couldn't help herself. Life was so bloody unfair. Her Jamie had been such a caring lad, unlike Donny's horrid twins.

As the song ended, the vicar cleared his throat. 'Today, we are here to celebrate the life of Jamie Turner.'

Tansey stared dismally at her son's coffin. She didn't want to celebrate his life. She wanted to hold him, touch him, talk to him.

Sensing eyes burning into the side of her head, Tansey glanced to her right. She'd given strict instructions that the twins weren't to sit anywhere near her at the service. It was Beau staring at her from across the pew. She stared back and clocked him smirk.

The tears returned then. Fast and bloody furious.

'Page seven,' Penny Turner prompted her daughter.

Tansey turned the pages but was unable to concentrate on the prayer being read. How dare that evil little shit smirk at her, today of all days. To say she was livid was putting it mildly. If there truly was a God, it would be Beau lying in that coffin, not her beloved blond-haired blue-eyed boy.

Tansey's relationship with the twins had been difficult since day one. Raised by an alcoholic drug-addicted mother until Donny had literally dumped his sons on her one not-so-fine day, they'd been insolent, feral, and bloody hard work.

Her idyllic life shattered to pieces overnight, Tansey tried her best to cope, but she'd spotted evil in the twins from early on, especially in Beau. Not only did the pair of them bully poor Jamie at first, they also purposely knocked her off a ladder while she was pregnant with hers and Donny's second son, which in her opinion resulted in Alfie being born prematurely and having behavioural issues ever since.

When the vicar called Donny up as pre-arranged to give the eulogy on her son, Tansey took deep breaths to calm herself. Unfortunately, it didn't work.

As his father began spouting his heart-felt speech, Beau Bond glanced around. His nan and Sherry were dabbing their eyes, but other than that there were no hysterical bouts of emotion being shown. Even young Ricky wasn't bawling. And most importantly, Brett seemed to be holding up well, better than Beau had expected.

Beau turned his attention to the opposite pew and stared at Tansey again. He was actually quite enjoying himself. Today was much more fun for him than your average boring day out.

Brett turned to his brother. 'Stop it. Leave her be,' he ordered.

Beau clasped his hands together and looked down at his lap. He knew Brett felt guilty, but he felt nothing. It had been the same when they'd set fire to their school in their youth. Brett had felt responsible for ages about the school caretaker who'd perished, but Beau hadn't blamed himself. If the silly old sod hadn't made himself busy and run inside a burning building, then he wouldn't have got burnt to a cinder. Therefore, Jamie paying the price for Tammy's death was no different. He had made himself busy too. Ever the people-pleaser, Jamie had fallen over backwards to be the big hero and sort the pills out, even though he didn't want one himself. Well, more fool him.

Unable to stop revelling in her misery, Beau glanced in Tansey's direction again. She clocked him and leapt up. 'I want to say something. In fact, I've got lots to say,' shrieked Tansey, interrupting Donny mid-flow.

Tansey's mum and friend Lucinda glanced worriedly at one another. 'Are you sure, love?' asked Penny.

Tansey ignored her mother's question, lunged towards her fiancée and grabbed the microphone off him.

'I've got your back,' Donny said, putting a supportive arm around Tansey's shoulders.

Tansey shoved Donny's arm away. 'Sit down, you,' she snarled.

'Shit!' Brett nudged Beau, then lowered his eyes to the floor. Tansey was glaring directly at them.

Tansey took a deep breath. 'My Jamie was a good boy. Not saying he was an angel, but nobody knows their own son like a mother does. Before his death, Jamie was the most settled I'd ever seen him. He liked his job, was content in himself and had found love with Clare, whom he adored.'

Tansey fiercely wiped the tears away with the cuff of her jacket. 'I know what everyone is thinking here but believe me; I'm telling you the truth. My Jamie was never into drugs, let alone spiking anybody's drink. He wasn't even into alcohol, let alone bloody ecstasy pills. But you see them two over there.'

18

Everybody glanced awkwardly at one another as Tansey pointed directly at the twins. 'Those two fuckers are into everything. And no way did my Jamie kill himself. They killed him and I swear to God I'll—'

Tansey didn't get to finish her sentence. Kenny Bond leapt up and swiftly grabbed the microphone.

Reverend Harris had conducted hundreds of services in his years as a clergyman, but never one like this. In a state of shock, he quickly wrapped it up with a final prayer that everybody seemed to be arguing over, then played the song Tansey had chosen for the congregation to walk out to. He was dreading the actual burial, wished it had been a cremation instead.

Once outside in the fresh air, Tansey was led away by her mum and friend to allow her to calm down. Penny Turner could tell the Bonds were furious over her daughter's accusations. She didn't know what to say or do other than appease Tansey.

Thankful that they'd told the Old Bill their presence wasn't needed at the funeral, Kenny glanced at his grandsons. Beau was fine, but Brett looked as white as a sheet.

'Fancy standing up and saying something like that. I know she's grieving, but Jesus, so are the twins, Kenny. Thank God there weren't many people here. Can you imagine if those kinds of rumours got back to the bloody Tamplins?' Sharon said to her husband. She rued the day her grandsons had got involved with that gypsy family.

Kenny had been horrified by Tansey's outburst, even though every word she'd uttered had been true. She was a lot cleverer than he'd ever given her credit for. But Kenny knew how to blag it in an awkward situation and blag it he would. He poked Donny hard in the shoulder. 'She's out of control that woman of yours. Why didn't you stand up and defend your sons, eh? As if they had sod all to do with Jamie's suicide. Madness!'

'Yeah. Gramps is right,' added Beau. 'Tansey needs sectioning. She's off her trolley.'

Kenny gave Beau a sharp kick in the ankle, then turned back to Donny. 'Man up, son. You need to sort this before we bury poor Jamie. The least the lad deserves is to rest in peace.'

The travelling community were a loyal breed, stuck by one another through thick and thin. Obviously, they had issues amongst their own. But they had their own way of sorting disagreements, usually culminating in a bare-knuckle fight. What they wouldn't tolerate was one of their own being harmed by a gorger, hence the Brown brothers sitting in a beige transit tipper truck watching events unfold.

'Why's it taking so much time?' asked Jack.

'Looks like they're arguing among themselves. Typical gorgers,' replied Davey. 'Can't even respect their dead properly.'

'I wish they'd hurry up. Giving me the heebies sitting 'ere.'

'Shut up, you tart. Just think of the lolly we're getting paid.'

'Don't like the look of those twins. Whatever was Jolene thinking, going with one of them? She's a pretty girl an' all,' stated Jack.

'We're getting paid extra if we hit *him* too. Trouble is, I don't know which one's which.'

'Best we aim for 'em both then. Two for the price of one.'

At five foot two, Sharon Bond was a short-arse in comparison to her strapping husband, yet what she lacked in height she made up for in punch, especially when it came to her family.

'That's enough, Beau,' ordered Sharon. 'And you.' Sharon poked Kenny in the chest. 'You three stay here and I will speak to Tansey and her mum. This is neither the time nor the place for a falling out and none of you are to say anything else to Donny. Understand?'

'Yeah. We got ya,' replied Kenny. He'd first met Sharon at a party when he was sixteen years old. She was a buxom blonde with a big personality and beautiful face; Kenny had fallen head over heels and they'd got engaged soon after. Even when he'd spent years in prison, Sharon had been his rock and he always let her rule the roost when it came to family matters. Well, the matters she knew about anyway.

Sharon returned a couple of minutes later. 'Tansey's calmed down, well a bit anyway. But she don't want Beau and Brett at the graveside.'

'That's bang out of order,' argued Beau. 'What have we done wrong?'

Brett stayed silent. It suited him not to watch Jamie's coffin being lowered into the ground.

'She's out of order, Shal,' stated Kenny.

'Yes. I know. But, it's her son, so if that's what she

wants, then so be it. Beau and Brett can always visit the grave afterwards to pay their respects.'

'I ain't happy,' spat Beau. He was more gutted about not being able to witness Tansey's heartbreak as Jamie was put six feet under than anything else.

A worried man, Reverend Harris approached Kenny. 'Are we ready to proceed with the burial now? I am sorry to rush you, but my next service is running extremely late.'

'Yeah. As ready as we'll ever be.'

'Oi, oi, we got movement.' Davey Brown turned the ignition. Dressed in hard hats and yellow high-visibility vests, nobody had taken any notice of them. Their aim had been to blend in, like a couple of workmen taking a break from whatever.

'They're bringing him out.'

'Hold tight.' Davey reversed back, changed gear, then awaited the perfect moment.

Kenny Bond was usually very astute, had a sixth sense of anything amiss, yet even he hadn't taken a blind bit of notice of the tipper truck parked nearby. Not until it came towards him anyway. 'Fuck! Move,' he shrieked, pushing Sharon and his daughter Sherry out of harm's way.

With the coffin on their shoulders, the funeral directors had two options, either drop it or get run over. They dropped the coffin.

Having moved away from the front of the chapel so she didn't have to look at Beau and Brett, Tansey dashed towards it to see what all the commotion was about.

She was greeted by a partial sighting of her son's corpse, then a truck reversing over him and his coffin.

Overcome by shock and horror, Tansey promptly passed out.

Everything happened so quickly, then the tipper truck sped off. For many, including the reverend, it would leave a lifelong memory. There were shouts, screams, all sorts, as the funeral directors tried to shove Jamie's corpse back inside the smashed-up coffin. They'd been ordered to never drop a coffin under any circumstances, but nobody could have prepared them for today.

Having unsuccessfully chased the truck towards the exit, Kenny and Donny returned to the chaos. 'Is everyone OK? Did anyone get hit?' Kenny panted.

'We nearly did. I think they aimed for us, but I managed to push Brett out the way, then we legged it,' replied Beau. He was worried. This had to be to do with the gypsies, so what did this mean for him and Jolene? What hope did they have for the future?

Relieved they hadn't allowed any of their younger children to attend, Donny went over to where Tansey lay. He couldn't believe what had happened. It was too awful for words. How the hell was his beautiful fiancée meant to ever get over this?

'Treacherous bloody lot, those pikeys. Told you not to get involved with those girls, didn't I?' ranted Sharon.

'Don't blame them.' Kenny protectively pulled Beau and Brett close to his chest. 'I'll speak to Bobby. No way did he know about this. He wouldn't have allowed it to happen.'

'How do you know?' snapped Sharon. 'Thick as thieves that mob are. You don't see that girl Jolene any more, Beau. Do you hear me?'

'I thought I was gonna die. I thought we were all going to die,' blurted out Ricky. Being born with Down's syndrome was yet to hold Ricky back in his life. But he did have a tendency to say things exactly as he saw them.

Sharon gave the lad she referred to as her and Kenny's 'adopted son' a motherly hug. Ricky had moved in with them shortly after his real parents had died in a car crash. His father, Alan Davey, was Kenny's close friend. They went back donkey's years.

Beau glared at his nan. 'None of us are hurt and neither is any of this mine or Jolene's fault. You can't stop me and her seeing one another. We love each other.'

'You don't even know what love is at your age,' retaliated Sharon.

'No point arguing among ourselves. It's getting us nowhere,' snapped Kenny. 'I'm going to speak to the funeral directors, see if they can sort us a new coffin. The lad can't get buried in that one. His body'll get eaten by insects.'

'You all right?' Beau slid down the wall and sat on the pavement next to his brother.

'Not really. No way am I coming back here to go through all this again.' The funeral directors had taken Jamie back to the funeral home.

'We ain't gotta come again. Tansey don't want us at the burial anyway.' Tansey had been carted off in an ambulance. Their dad had gone to hospital with her.

24

'Did you see their faces? What type of scumbags run over a dead body and a coffin?' said Brett.

'I got a glimpse of the one in the passenger seat. But I didn't see either clearly. It all happened so quickly. It wouldn't surprise me if Jolene's brothers were behind it though,' said Beau.

'Not Sonny, surely?' Sonny was lovely. Brett secretly had the hots for him and was sure Sonny felt the same. The way Sonny looked at him sent shivers down Brett's spine.

'Nah. The two older arseholes. Billy and Johnny. Mad, weren't it? Did you see his arm fall out the coffin? I heard his bones crunching too.'

Brett retched. 'Shut up. I don't even want to think about it. Jamie didn't deserve any of this, God rest his soul.'

'There you are!' shouted Kenny Bond. 'Get in the car. We're leaving now.'

'You rung Bobby yet?' enquired Beau.

'No. I will speak to him face to face, sort this shit out once and for all.' Kenny's jaw twitched furiously, a sure sign he was seething. 'What happened today was a diabolical liberty. They must think I'm some mug or something if they think I'm gonna suffer stunts like that. Nah, they want a war, they'll get one all right. I'll blow their fucking brains out.'

25

CHAPTER TWO

'You're still shaking, Mum. Go get her a brandy,' Billy Tamplin ordered his brother, Johnny. At twenty-eight and twenty-six respectively, they were the eldest two sons of the Tamplin clan. They'd been shocked to see their mother in bits when they'd arrived to pick her up and even more shocked to see an ambulance and Psychic Lena's corpse.

Evie pushed her plate away. They'd stopped at a local pub which was a popular haunt for the travelling community, but Evie had barely touched her fish, chips and mushy peas. It wasn't the shock of Lena's croaking it in front of her that had upset Evie. It was her dying words, *that* premonition. The horrified expression on the old woman's face as she'd keeled over had left Evie chilled to the bone.

Billy squeezed his mum's hand. 'She had a good innings, didn't she? And it's a godsend you were there. Better than her dying alone.'

Evie clenched her eldest's hand tightly. 'You don't understand. I know your father forbid me, but after losing our Tammy, I needed hope. Something to cling onto, to look

26

forward to. So, I asked Lena for a reading. She saw something bad; I swear she did. Then she died. I think whatever she saw might've killed her.'

'Crikey, Mum! You know what our people say about Lena. She's a curse. No good's ever come from readings with her. Even Aunt Rose said so. Don't you remember the time she told her she saw twisted metal, then Uncle Denny had that bad accident in his motor? I was only a lad back then, but was frit to death of her from that moment on. Please don't tell me you had a reading with her before Tammy died an' all?'

'Of course, I didn't. I ain't seen her for years, until today.'

Having returned from the bar, Johnny asked, 'What's up?'

'Don't ask,' snapped Billy.

A proud man from humble travelling roots, Bobby Tamplin had achieved a lot in his forty-six years. A good amateur boxer, he'd turned to bare-knuckle fighting to provide for his wife and young family. Undefeated, he'd earned a nice few bob, retired while he was at the top and plunged his money into buying land and two salvage yards.

Five foot nine, stocky with dark unruly hair and a wonky boxer's nose, Bobby's proudest achievement in life was his family. His wife Evie had always been his rock, the beauty behind his brawn; and between them they'd had six wonderful kids. Even when their youngest, Bobby-Joe, had been diagnosed as Down's syndrome, it hadn't fazed them as a family. Bobby-Joe would be loved, wanted, taught skills so he could work like his brothers. He'd be fine. He was a Tamplin.

No parent expected or wanted to outlive their chavvies and the day his Tammy had died, part of Bobby had died too. She'd only gone to Beau and Brett's sixteenth birthday party, on a boat along the Thames. Kenny Bond's boat. There hadn't been any alcohol allowed, yet that silly little fucker who was being buried today had put ecstasy in the drinks and his beautiful Tammy had drunk one. Jolene was there, said Tammy had collapsed while convulsing. She'd been taken to hospital, but it was all too little too late. She'd never come out of the coma and would have been left brain dead even if she had. Hence the heart-breaking decision to turn off her life support.

If Jamie hadn't topped himself, Bobby would've throttled him with his bare hands. He and his two eldest sons had got some retribution by doing away with the dealer who'd sold the pills to Jamie. He'd ended up in an industrial cement mixer over in Dartford. But nothing was going to bring Tammy back, which is why Bobby had told his sons, 'No more retribution. We don't want a war. Enough is enough.'

If Billy and Johnny had their way, Beau and Brett would've been next on their hit list, but Bobby forbade them to lay a hand on Kenny's' grandsons. Jamie had left them a suicide note explaining it was his prank that went wrong. The spiked drinks were meant to be drunk by Beau and Brett. Therefore, they were innocent in Bobby's eyes.

'There you are! I've been calling you,' bellowed Jolene. 'Beau rang. It all kicked off at the funeral. A truck tried to run 'em all over, then it ran over the coffin.'

'Jesus fucking wept! That's all we need. Go get me my phone. It's on charge.'

Deep in thought, Evie sat in the back of her son's Land Rover, mulling over Lena's horribly cut-short reading. 'A dark soul', that's how she'd described Beau Bond, and even though that didn't surprise Evie one iota, she had to think with her head now and not her heart.

With Johnny Cash's 'Folsom Prison Blues' blaring out, Evie leaned forward and poked both her sons hard in their shoulders.

Johnny turned the volume down. His mother was yet to make her mind up whether to tell his father about her reading. 'Yes, Mum?'

'As soon as we get home, I want a family meeting. Not your wives or kids, just me, yous, Sonny, your dad, Jolene and Bobby-Joe. And you don't mention no reading, OK? 'Cause I never really got one and I don't want your father worrying over nothing.'

'Sounds serious. But don't fret, your secret's safe with us,' replied Billy. Travelling men tended not to tittle-tattle and they certainly wouldn't betray their own mother.

'Oh, it is serious, trust me. I made a decision, and I don't want no bleedin' arguments.' Evie pursed her lips. She'd already lost one of her stunning daughters. No way was she losing the other. Over her dead body.

An impatient man by nature, Bobby was raging by the time his sons pulled up outside with his wife. Kenny hadn't sounded too happy on the phone, but had arranged to meet him later at the pub.

'Billy, Johnny, I want a word. In private,' seethed Bobby.

Knowing full well what was up, Billy stupidly asked, 'What's up?'

Bobby gave his eldest a sharp clump in the ribs. 'Don't you dare mug me off. Who'd you get to do it, eh?'

'Do what?' Billy winced. Even a half punch off his father was capable of cracking ribs.

Aware his brother needed backup, Johnny jumped in. 'What you going on about?' Billy and he had made a pact to keep schtum about the Brown brothers.

'The funeral. Trashing the coffin. Nearly killing the Bonds.' Bobby grabbed Johnny by the throat. 'Dinlos, that's what you are. A pair of fucking dinlos.'

Hearing the fracas, Evie ran out from her luxurious mobile home and grabbed hold of her husband. 'Stop it. Leave 'em be. As if today ain't a bad enough day anyway. Where's Sonny and Bobby-Joe? Get 'em here. I wants a family meeting. It's important.'

Bobby glared at his two eldest. Both were stocky, dark and, apart from his boxer's nose, looked very much like him. He'd thought they had his brains too, until today. 'We'll speak about this later,' he hissed. Bobby was determined to find out the truth, even if he had to beat it out of them.

Two cups of sweet tea later, Bobby had calmed down a bit. 'You didn't say you were visiting Lena. You told me you were going to Kent to see your family.'

'I was! But that got cut short when Lena died on me, Bobby. I don't care that you never liked her. Lena and my grandma were very good friends. She was an old

30

woman on her own, God bless her. That's why I paid her a visit. She don't get many visits these days.'

Bobby gave his wife a hug. 'You didn't get her to give you one of her curse of a readings, did ya?'

'Don't be daft! The woman died before I hardly spoke to her,' snapped Evie. She hated lying to her husband, but no way was she worrying him by admitting the truth.

'I'm sorry she died. But you know she always frit me to death that woman. So, what's this family meeting you've organized about?'

'Call your sons to come inside and you'll find out. Jolene, you sits next to me, 'cause this is about you,' ordered Evie.

A stunning five foot seven brunette with big brown eyes, Jolene put her hands on her hips. 'You better not be telling me I can't see Beau any more, 'cause I swear on Bobby-Joe's life, I will run away and marry him behind all your backs.' Her mother only disapproved of Beau because he was a gorger and, since Tammy's death, she hated him even more.

Evie fired her daughter a look of hatred. Inwardly, she half blamed Jolene getting involved with Beau for Tammy's death. She'd always warned her beloved girls that gorgers were no good and they should stick to their own. 'Just sit down and shut up. I shall be doing the talking and don't you ever swear on your little brother's life again like that. It's wicked.'

Once the family was seated, Evie started her speech. She told them that she'd already lost one daughter and under no circumstances was she losing the other. Therefore if Jolene wanted to be with Beau, she had her permission.

As expected, Evie's two eldest, Billy and Johnny were furious, but she stood her ground when they threatened all sorts. 'Listen; if it's what our Jolene wants, then it's her choice. She'll soon be seventeen. She's a woman not a child. Ain't she, Bobby?'

Jolene was over the moon, couldn't quite believe her ears. Her mother had always sided with Billy and Johnny and had never liked Beau. Jolene missed Tammy dreadfully and getting married and starting a family was the only thing that could help her with her loss. Tammy had liked Beau too. It's what her twin would've wanted. 'Thanks, Mum. And you, Dad. I'm gonna be the best wife and mother ever.'

'Not so fast, young lady,' said Evie. 'I'm only allowing you to marry Beau if you lives with me and your father on this land. After losing Tammy, I need you around me.'

Beaming from ear to ear, Jolene squeezed her mother's hand. 'Of course, we'll live 'ere. Who else is gonna babysit all the chavvies I plan to have?'

As Billy and Johnny started to kick off big time, Bobby rolled his eyes at his two other sons, Sonny and young Bobby-Joe. Bobby was amazed Evie had changed her tune, but relieved at the same time. He couldn't bear to lose Jolene either and, unlike Evie, he had no aversion to her marrying a gorger. So many of the travelling lads he knew were whoremongers who strayed behind their wives' backs. They would shag any gorger with a pulse. Bobby didn't want that for Jolene, and he could tell by the way Beau treated her that he would be loyal to his daughter.

It was Johnny who picked up one of his mother's favourite china horse ornaments and smashed it against the wall. He pointed at his sister. 'If she marries that shit-cunt, me and Billy will be off this land. We won't live near him. We want no part of it. You'll be on your own, Dad.'

Bobby loved his wife more than anything else in the world. He leaned over and squeezed her hand. 'Your mother has made her decision, boys, and if you don't like it, you can lump it.'

Evie forced a smile. The quicker her daughter married Beau, realized her mistake, then found her soulmate, the better. Only, Psychic Lena was never wrong.

Family meeting over, Bobby led his boys to the barn. He'd cooled off a bit, but wasn't looking forward to hearing what Kenny had to say. Not that he was scared of Bond. Far from it. There wasn't a man born that Bobby Tamplin was scared of. He was just at an age where he didn't want any more drama in his life. A simple, quiet life suited him just fine these days. Which is why he'd uprooted his family from Kent and bought this plot in Essex. Not that it had brought them much luck.

'I think you've broken one or two of me ribs,' complained Billy.

'Don't be such a big fanny. I only gave you a little tap. Serves you right for lying to me.'

'We didn't lie. We didn't know anything about the truck running over the coffin until you told us. What exactly happened then?' asked Johnny.

Bobby swung around and gave Johnny a worse clump in the ribs than Billy had got.

'For fuck's sake.' In pain, Johnny sank to his haunches to try to get his breath back.

'To be a good liar, you need to have a fucking good memory. I never mentioned no truck, ya dinlo.'

Johnny glared at Billy and shook his head. The game was up. 'All right, we were behind it. But someone had to do something. It's sickening that they're gonna bury that murdering scumbag in the same cemetery as Tammy. It ain't right. The Bonds are taking the piss and you're letting them get away with it.'

'Who'd you get to do it?' asked Bobby.

'The Browns. Jack and Davey.'

'See that black-and-white cob out there? That's got more brains than Davey and Jack Brown put together. Now I want yous to listen to me and listen very carefully. When it comes to your wife and kids, you have every right to make whatever decision you want, 'cause you is the head of that family. But I'm telling you now, you ever go behind my back and pull a stunt like this again regarding my family, you will live to regret it. 'Cause as much as I loves you, I will not put up with no man making decisions for me. You will never set foot in the yards again. Your jobs will be finito for a start. You get my drift?'

Still winded, Johnny nodded. 'Yeah.'

Billy held out his right hand. 'Sorry if we overstepped the mark.'

Bobby firmly gripped his son's hand. 'Apology accepted.'

Jolene sat on the wooden bench in the area her dad had made as a shrine to Tammy. Jolene regularly visited her sister's grave, but it was nice to have a patch of their own land to remember Tammy also.

34

Jolene placed her hand against the enormous framed photo of her twin. It was only a small shrine, but very peaceful and pretty. Fairy lights dangled from the trees surrounding the bench. There were angel figurines, lots of candles and fresh flowers were regularly laid. Her dad had made a tarpaulin roof to keep the area dry. 'Good news today, Tammy. Mum says I can be with Beau. I am glad, but I wish you were here with me. I got nobody to share my joy with any more. Life ain't the same. I miss our banter most of all though. We used to laugh so much and now I barely laugh at all.'

Jolene paused and fiercely wiped her eyes. There was no point crying and being miserable. Tammy wouldn't want that. 'Jamie had his funeral today. I dunno exactly what happened 'cause I won't see Beau until tomorrow. But I think the Travellers turned up and caused mayhem. Poor Jamie. He don't deserve that. I wish I could tell Mum and Dad the truth about what happened, but I don't want them thinking bad things about you and they'd probably disown me. No way would Mum let me be with Beau either. Keeping quiet protects everyone and I know if it were the other way round you would protect me too.'

Jolene fell silent, deep in thought. It had originally been Brett's idea to get some ecstasy pills for the party, but it was Tammy who was egging him on to do so. Tammy also took more than anybody else. She so didn't deserve to die though. Neither did Jamie. His only crime had been to get the pills for them. He didn't even take one. A bit of fun, that's all they'd wanted. Why did life have to be so bloody cruel?

*

35

The Jobber's Rest was where the meet was arranged. 'Sorry, I'm a bit late, Kenny. Traffic was chocka. Can I get you another drink?' asked Bobby.

'A brandy. Make it a large one. Then I think you've got a bit of explaining to do, don't you?'

Hackles rising, Bobby went to the bar. Who did Bond think he was talking to? Only he wasn't a man to take shit from anybody, especially when he was grieving his darling daughter.

Kenny knocked back the large brandy in one. 'So, what happened today? And please don't say it was nothing to do with your mob, 'cause I know it was. We shook hands, Bobby, made a deal. I thought we agreed to no more agg?'

'Made a deal!' snarled Bobby. 'You made it sound like I sold you a gry. I'm the injured party 'ere, not you, Bond. I'm the one who lost a daughter. Do you know what a loss like that feels like? Well, do ya?' Bobby's voice was getting louder by the second, so much so other customers were looking around.

'Look, I'm sorry. I worded that all wrong. What I meant was I thought we'd agreed to not start some war between our families? And I am sorry about Tammy, truly sorry. But today, that truck didn't just drive at the coffin, it tried to run my grandsons over too. Beau and Brett are as innocent in all this as Jolene is, Bobby. You know that,' lied Kenny. He knew that Beau, Brett, Jolene and Tammy had all willingly taken ecstasy. Behind his back, mind. The boys had confessed to him that night, on the boat. After Tammy had collapsed.

'I don't want no war and for your information, I had no idea what had been planned for today. Travellers have memories like elephants; they forget nothing, especially when one of their own is wronged. Many think it's a liberty Jamie is being buried in the same cemetery as Tammy and, to be honest, the more I thinks about it, the more I agree. Not that I condone what happened today. I don't. But I can't control the actions of others who are upset. My Evie didn't even know where Jamie was being buried earlier. I wasn't going to tell her. She went mad. As you can well imagine.'

Kenny sighed. He'd begged Donny to have a word with Tansey to change the chapel and cemetery, but Tansey wouldn't budge. She wanted Jamie's plot as close to her as possible. In fairness, the plot was right over the other side to where Tammy's was, and it was a massive cemetery. 'I make you right as it goes. Leave it with me. The lad never got buried in the end, the coffin was too damaged. I'll speak to Donny as soon as I leave here.'

Bobby sipped his pint, well aware that Kenny's cocky attitude had left the building and he was backtracking fast. 'Wise decision. Otherwise I should imagine the lad's grave will be smashed up regularly. I did tell you originally the lad shouldn't be buried there. You're not even blood-related to him, are you?'

'No. You know I'm not. He weren't Donny's. He was Tansey's boy, but Donny raised him. Look, I get where you're coming from and I'll sort it. Other than that, we OK, like?' Kenny knew he'd backtracked. But unbeknown to Bobby, he felt the guilt kick in.

'Yeah. We're OK. In fact, we might even be family soon. Evie's given her permission for Jolene and your Beau to be together.'

'Great stuff,' grinned Kenny. 'I'll get us another drink. We can make a toast to the lovebirds.'

Kenny's smile slipped as he left the table. He didn't mind Bobby, but Beau getting too involved with Jolene was only going to end in disaster. He could see it coming a mile off. Travellers were a different breed. Today had taught him that. A tipper truck running over a dead body was the stuff of horror movies. Especially when the corpse fell out of the fucking coffin.

Kenny returned to the table with two pints and a replastered grin. He would give it to Donny straight, say if they didn't change the cemetery, Jamie's grave would be vandalized regularly. Surely Tansey wouldn't want that?

Bobby raised his glass. 'To Jolene and Beau and their future together. God bless them and any chavvies they have.'

The thought of his handsome blond sixteen-year-old grandson marrying or knocking Jolene up made Kenny shudder, but he lifted his glass nevertheless. Beau could get any girl he wanted; he had to make him see sense. 'To the lovebirds and their futures.'

Bobby's eyes welled up. 'The wedding won't be the same without our Tammy, that's for sure. But we'll make it as cheerful as we can. It can be held on my land.'

Kenny nearly choked on his beer. 'Sorry, went down the wrong hole. Yeah. Sounds great. Apart from Tammy not being there, of course.'

Bobby leaned forward. 'The day that girl got taken from us, a part of me died, Kenny. I doubt I'll ever get over it, but you gotta learn to live with it, I suppose. I tell you something, I can't wait to get my hands on those bastards who made those pills. I got all their names imprinted in 'ere.' Bobby tapped his forehead. 'The day any of 'em step out of prison, I swear to you, I'll be waiting for them. Me and a thousand other Travellers. Only, shitcunts like that do not deserve to breathe the same air as the likes of you and me, and I'll make damn sure they don't pollute it any more.'

Kenny gulped that hard he could feel his Adam's apple pushing against his skin. 'Too right, mate. Excuse me a tick. Need the loo.'

Kenny walked into the gents and splashed his face with cold water. No way were the Chinese ever going to talk and they knew nothing about him and Tony anyway. Which left only two people. One presumed dead and the other an old prison pal who was totally trustworthy and living abroad.

Yanking the hand towel, Kenny dried his face. He and Tony were well in the clear, he convinced himself.

The problem with the past, though, is it has a habit of coming back to haunt you . . .

CHAPTER THREE

Thanks to a cancellation, Bobby Tamplin booked the wedding for the beginning of September. Neither he nor Evie were religious but had wanted to marry their daughter off properly. The church was in Vange and, unable to find a suitable-sized venue to hold the reception, Jolene finally agreed it should be held on their land.

Traveller weddings were always a massive occasion, and no expense was spared by Bobby. He was determined his daughter would have the best day of her life. Even though he knew a lot of the invited guests did not agree with his decision to allow Jolene to marry outside of their community. Bobby had always been his own man, and besides, nobody would be brave enough to tell him that to his face. His reputation as a decent amateur boxer and an even better bare-knuckle fighter saw to that, though it had been donkey's years since he'd last fought.

Billy and Johnny hadn't backed down. They'd refused to attend their sister's wedding and, unable to stand the thought of Jolene living in close proximity to what they classed as sin, had moved off their father's land and returned to Kent. Relations were strained to say the very least, especially between father and sons. Both Billy and Johnny blamed Bobby for allowing the farce of a wedding to go ahead.

Evie had never felt less excitement over a wedding in her life, but with Lena's dying words firmly imprinted in her mind, tried to feign enthusiasm for the sake of her daughter. She just wanted it all to be over with, Jolene to realize she'd made a terrible mistake, then go and find her true love.

Finally, the big day arrived. A momentous occasion that would join the Bonds and Tamplins together. As one big happy family.

'Brett, you awake?'

'Yeah.' Brett was absolutely dreading his brother's wedding, so much so he'd barely slept. He'd got bladdered on the stag night and ended up in Hollywood's nightclub with Sonny. It was all a bit of a blur, but he could recall trying to kiss Sonny and getting knocked back. Whenever he and Sonny locked eyes, Brett felt as though it was like they were looking into one another's souls . . . There was a spark, a mutual connection. Knowing he needed to seize the moment, Brett grabbed Sonny's face and plonked one on his juicy lips.

For a brief second, Brett felt Sonny respond. Their tongues touched. Then, it all went wrong as Sonny shoved him against the wall and Brett lost his footing and ended up in a heap.

'What the fuck d'ya think you're doing?' spat Sonny. 'I'm not a fucking queer.'

'But I've seen the way you look at me. I ain't a queer either. I dunno what I am. I'm confused.'

'You're drunk. That's what you are. Come on. I ain't leaving you 'ere. Get up.'

Feeling suddenly scared, Brett gingerly got to his feet. 'I'm sorry. I dunno what I was thinking. You won't tell anyone, will ya?'

'Nah. But if you ever do it again, I'll punch your lights out. I dunno what you are, but I'm a travelling man and there ain't no pooftas in our community. They don't exist!'

He hadn't seen Sonny since and was dreading having to face him today.

'Can you believe in less than seven hours' time I'm gonna be a happily married man?' For the past week the twins had been sharing a room at their grandparents to allow their great-grandparents to move back into the bungalow they'd been sharing. Tansey was out of hospital but still off her trolley. She didn't want them living with her and their dad any more.

'Mad, ain't it?'

'Try and be a bit more enthusiastic, Brett. You've been as miserable as sin all week. You have done your best man's speech, ain't ya?'

'You know I have.'

'Look, I know you're bound to feel a bit weird. I would too if it were you getting wed. But I'm only gonna be living at the bottom of the lane. You can come see me and Jolene anytime, apart from when we're shagging, of course,' laughed Beau. 'And we'll be doing lots of that.' Jolene had strong morals and had refused to have sex with him until their wedding night. He was hardly experienced himself, had only had sex once with an older girl called India, and she'd given him crabs.

'Yeah. Whatever.' Brett put the quilt back over his head. Sonny couldn't have said anything. Surely if he had, he'd have heard about it? That didn't stop him feeling an idiot, though. What the hell had he done?

Another family up at the crack of dawn were the Tamplins. Bobby sat on the step of his trailer and grinned at his transformed land. He truly had pushed the boat out to ensure Jolene had the best day. It was just such a bloody shame that he would never get the opportunity to do the same for his other daughter, Tammy.

'Whaddya want, a fry-up? Or a sandwich?' asked Evie.

'A couple of sausage sandwiches with brown sauce please, love. Don't it look wonderful, Evie? The sun is shining for us too. Gonna be the proudest man alive walking our baby girl down the aisle.'

'Shame it's to that arsehole,' Evie muttered under her breath. 'It looks beautiful, Bobby. Fit for a princess,' she said more loudly.

Young Bobby-Joe ran out of the trailer. 'What time Ricky coming?'

'He's not coming before the wedding. You'll see him at the church, then he'll be coming back 'ere with all the other guests,' explained Bobby.

Evie smiled as her youngest jumped up and down excitedly. That was the only good thing to come out of her daughter getting involved with that godawful gorger family.

Ricky also had Down's syndrome and Bobby-Joe finally had a mate who was just like him.

'Who's that keeps ringing you?' enquired Sharon.

Kenny quickly switched off, then pocketed his phone. 'The geezer I've bought Beau's present off,' he lied. 'I'll bell him back in a bit.'

'Morning. I was so excited 'bout today, I didn't sleep a wink,' beamed thirteen-year-old Ricky.

Ricky was the son of Kenny's lifelong pal, Alan Davey. Alan had been celebrating Sharon's birthday on the Thames, along with lots of other family and friends, the night the *Marchioness* had sunk. Watching the horrors first-hand had been horrific. But Kenny had been handed a double whammy. Alan and his wife Julia went missing after the party. They were found days later, still inside their car, dead in a ditch. Hence Ricky now living with him and Sharon. 'Don't lie, Little Man. You were snoring like a good un when I looked in on you last night and this morning,' Kenny said.

Ricky slapped his palm against his forehead. 'What time she coming, Vera? Gonna be bang in trouble, ain't I?'

Sharon laughed. 'I wonder what her hair looks like now.' Kenny's mother was a one-off, but also a difficult woman. She'd been a rubbish mother to Kenny, which was one of the reasons Ricky had decided to take the shears to her beloved beehive at a barbeque earlier in the year. Understandably, Vera had been livid and had only recently started speaking to her family again.

Kenny rolled his eyes. 'Christ knows! I'm surprised she's even coming to the wedding. She hates the gyppos.'

'She's not the only one.' Jolene dressed tarty and was as common as muck, in Sharon's opinion. Beau could have done so much better had he waited until he was older. He was no more than a kid himself.

'I gotta pop out in a bit. I won't be long,' Kenny informed his wife.

'You can't. We've gotta get ready soon. Where the hell you going?'

'There's a slight issue with Beau's thing. Some paperwork needs signing.'

'Can't you sign it another time? Just tell the bloke our grandson's getting married today.'

Kenny kissed his wife on the forehead. 'I obviously want everything to be done and dusted if I'm handing Beau the deeds today. I'll be back as soon as I can.'

Kenny was fuming as he drove towards the house he was forking out for in Loughton. He also rued the day he'd ever laid eyes on the gold-digging bitch who lived there.

Kenny and Sharon had been estranged at the time, thanks to Abigail Cornell, the woman Kenny had been shagging while his wife was living out in Spain taking care of her mum. Kenny wasn't a womanizer, he loved Sharon to bits, but due to her going through an early menopause, they'd hit a rocky patch. In a nutshell, he had a high sex drive and Sharon's had disappeared, which along with her long absence, had made Kenny feel unloved and unwanted. Abigail had been on hand to fill the gap.

When Sharon had returned from Spain, Kenny tried to let Abi down lightly, but she was having none of it. She'd turned into the bunny-boiler from hell, stalked him and, because she was getting nowhere, the nutjob had turned up at the nursery one day, pretending she was pregnant by him, and told Shal all about their affair.

Sharon was no pushover. She threw him out immediately, cut all his clothes to shreds and trashed his belongings. Kenny didn't care about material stuff but would never forgive himself for hurting the only woman he'd ever truly loved. He'd never strayed before. Abigail was a total one-off.

For a long time, reconciliation looked impossible. Having lost his soulmate, his rock in life, Kenny went off the rails. It was around that time he met Karen Bamber.

Unlike Abigail, who on the outside had been young, fit and gorgeous, Karen was in her late thirties and slightly above average. A mum of one, she was a schoolteacher and a good listener. He'd droned on to her for hours about Shal. He'd thought of Karen as kind and stable, a shoulder to cry on. How wrong he'd been.

Drawing hope from the fact Sharon hadn't asked for a divorce, he'd persuaded her to join him for a week's holiday in Vegas to celebrate his fiftieth birthday. On their return, Kenny told Karen he and Shal were back on good terms and he was determined to make another go of his marriage. That was the first warning sign, when Karen burst into tears and slung him out of her gaff. Kenny hadn't been too alarmed, just a bit taken aback. He'd made it clear all along that they were *just* friends with benefits, and he wanted Shal back if possible.

Nothing could have prepared Kenny for what happened the following year. Karen turned up at his house and said she needed to discuss something important. Kenny visited her the following day, thinking she had some agg or needed to borrow a few bob. That was when he first laid eyes on his son, Jake.

Having always used the withdrawal method, until Karen had insisted it wasn't totally safe and forced him to wear a rubber, Kenny knew he'd been duped. She'd obviously doctored the bastard things, probably shoved big needles in them.

Ever since then, the conniving cow had bled him dry. Gone was the pleasant, demurely dressed schoolteacher and in her place was a callous hard-faced diva. Karen had no intention of ever working again; therefore, Kenny was shelling out for everything. Not just for Jake. He paid the rent, got her the new car she wanted. New furniture, decking in the garden. He even paid for her poxy beauty treatments.

Kenny sighed as he pulled up outside the three-bedroom house that was costing an arm and a leg. If Sharon ever found out about Karen or Jake, that would be curtains for his marriage. He could kick himself, as he'd once had the chance to come clean. Shal had asked him outright had there been anyone else and, not wanting to hurt her more than he already had, or scupper their reconciliation, he'd told her there hadn't. What a shitty mistake that had been.

Spotting her meal ticket, Karen yanked open the door. 'Thank God you're here. Jake's desperate for a bath and so am I. We're meant to be somewhere soon.'

'I doubt Jake knows he's desperate. He ain't even a year old yet.' Kenny marched out to where the boiler was. It was the water pressure, exactly what he'd told her on the phone. 'Now look what I'm doing, so if it drops again, you can fix it your bleedin' self.'

'I'm not a bloody plumber. I've got every right to ask you. You are Jake's father. Not that he knows that, as you rarely give him the time of day.' Karen had once been very much in love with Kenny, had hoped if her plan worked and she fell pregnant, they'd set up home together. He'd dumped her before she even knew she was pregnant, though, and not in a nice way. He'd disposed of her like a bag of old rubbish.

Knowing he had to tread carefully, as no way did he want his dirty little secret coming out, Kenny reluctantly apologized.

'I want to book a holiday, Kenny. I fancy going away at Christmas and want to take Jake abroad. The Canaries, probably. A five-star child-friendly hotel. Obviously, you're going to have to pay for it. Could you leave me some money today for the deposit?'

'No, Karen. I can't. I ain't even got any dosh on me. I rushed out just as I was trying to get ready for me grandson's wedding. Not being funny, but you're gonna have to start pulling your horns in a bit. I've got no income at present. I ain't Baron Rockefeller ya know.'

Karen looked at him, steely-eyed. 'I take it Sharon doesn't go without? I should also imagine your grandson is getting some ultra-expensive wedding gift. I'm not stupid, Kenny. Remember, we were close once upon a time. You're hardly on the breadline.'

'I ain't got time for this today. I gotta shoot.'

'Not before you've said hello to Jake you won't.

You haven't seen him for over a week. He'll forget what you look like. I'll wake him up.'

'I've not got time to play Daddy today, Karen. I'll miss the wedding if I don't get a move on.'

'You can spare ten minutes. Remember, we had a deal, Kenny? You support me and your son and also, you spend some quality time with him once a week at least. And in return, I say nothing about Jake's existence. I've kept to my side of the bargain, therefore you must do the same. Unless you want your beloved family finding out. Which I presume you don't? So, I'll ask you once more. Can you kindly pay for a holiday for myself and *your* son? Oh sorry, I forgot to say please.'

Knowing Karen had him over a barrel, Kenny's jaw twitched. If it wasn't for Jake, he'd dispose of her the same way he had the other one. By strangulation.

'Well?'

Kenny's lip curled like a rabid dog. Nobody threatened to ruin his marriage. That's how that nutter Abigail had ended up as dinner for his pals' pigs. He took a deep breath. 'You'll get your fucking deposit in the week, and I'll spend some time with Jake then. OK?'

'Fine.'

Kenny stormed out, slamming the front door. 'Cunt,' he spat. She was truly skating on thin ice was Karen.

'Morning, Mum. You look lovely. That emerald-green suit is the nuts. Where is everybody?' asked Donny Bond.

'The boys are all upstairs getting ready, apart from your father. He's had to pop out somewhere.'

'Where? He ain't gonna be long, is he? The limo will be here any minute.'

'How's Tansey doing, love?' Donny and Tansey only lived a few doors away down Dark Lane, but Tansey had barely mixed with the family since Jamie's funeral fiasco. Sharon could understand Tansey being terribly upset, but what had happened wasn't her and Kenny's fault. They hadn't even been invited to Jamie's second burial in a cemetery in Chelmsford. Tansey only wanted Donny and their kids there. She allowed her own bloody mother to be present, mind, which Sharon had thought was out of order.

'She's getting there, Mum, slowly but surely. She won't let Bluebell come today though. She's too frightened it will all kick off. Don't even let on I told you Jamie's buried in Chelmsford, will you? Tans is so paranoid his grave will be trashed, she don't want nobody knowing apart from me and her.'

'And her mother.' Sharon raised her eyebrows. She did feel sorry for Tansey. No mother should have to bury a son. But on the other hand, she was losing patience with her son's long-term fiancée. Tansey had led Donny a dog's life of late, had little time for himself or their sons. 'Once this wedding's done and dusted, you need to sort your life out, boy. It's not fair Tans is always out gallivanting with that mate of hers with only Bluebell in tow. How must those boys feel? The way she's blamed the twins for everything is despicable an' all. It's as though she's jealous that Beau and Brett are still thriving. Not their fault that *her* son chose to take his own life, is it? And Brett needs to be moving back in with you, Donny. You're his father and he's bound to miss Beau being there all the time.'

'I know. But let's not talk about it now, Mum. I want today to be a happy occasion. I will sort something though, I promise, and Tans is helping out. She's getting the boys dressed for me as we speak.'

'Big deal! Only I was under the impression they were *her* sons too.'

The appearance of Beau stopped the awkward conversation. Donny smiled, his eyes full of pride. There weren't many lads that could pull off a pale-blue three-piece suit, but with his height, physique, swept-back blond hair and dashing looks, Beau owned the outfit.

'You look so smart, so handsome,' beamed Sharon.

Dressed in the same air force blue suit, Brett appeared by his brother's side. Visions of how unkempt they'd once been when they'd lived with their mother as youngsters flashed through Donny's mind. 'Look at the pair of ya. All grown up.' He walked towards his sons and hugged them both tightly. 'I am so proud of you. You're a credit to me, lads.'

Ricky running down the stairs shrieking, 'Dave's on the phone, Beau,' ended the poignant moment.

Beau grabbed his mobile. 'Yeah, no worries. Bring him instead and wish nutty bollocks better for us.'

'Who was that?' enquired Brett.

'Smiffy. Pullen's up the hospital. Fell off a motorbike and messed his leg up bad. Alex is coming in his place.'

'Alex who?' Brett asked hopefully.

'Mariner. That posh lad who was away with us. The lads still see him.'

'Oh right,' Brett said as calmly as he could. Alex Mariner had been his first and only crush before Sonny came along. Perhaps today wouldn't be so bad after all?

CHAPTER FOUR

The wedding ceremony was a success without any unwanted drama.

Beau squeezed Jolene's hand. She looked so beautiful; it had literally taken his breath away when he'd turned to her at the altar. He knew he'd struck gold, felt like the luckiest bloke alive. They were now back at Bobby's land. He'd hired six travelling women to cook and serve the three-course meal and they'd done themselves more than proud.

'Has me mascara run?' Jolene asked. Her dad had just done his speech and she couldn't help but get choked up when he'd mentioned Tammy.

'Nah. You're fine. I'm gonna do my speech now.'

'Don't embarrass me.'

Beau stood up and said all the usual things you would expect from a newlywed. After praising Jolene and her family to the hilt, he then spoke about his own. 'I'd like to thank my dad for raising me. And my mum, who went through a difficult time when me and Beau were kids but has turned her life around completely. But most of all, I want to thank me granddad, or Gramps, as I call him. He instilled life's values into me and if I can become half the man, husband and father he is, I will be more than happy. Because that is my main aim in life from now on, to make my beautiful bride happy each and every day. I love you, Jolene.'

'So, he's planning on having an affair then?' piped up Maggie Saunders.

'Mum! Not today, please,' snapped Sharon Bond. Her father had forgiven Kenny for his indiscretion, but her mother hadn't.

Annoyed she'd got a decent mention, Donny glared at his ex. Lori might look a million dollars now, but she'd been a druggy skank in the past. A dreadful mother, whose inability to take care of the twins properly had led to Brett being raped by a nonce she'd had living at her gaff. Eric Acorn was the brother of Lori's boyfriend at the time. The paedo bastard had his comeuppance. He and his dad abducted then tortured the beast before feeding him to his dad's mate's pigs.

'What a soppy speech. He's as silly as arseholes,' piped up Vera Bond. 'And what does she look like in that bleedin' joke of a dress? I'll give it a year, tops, this sham of a marriage.'

'Can't you be pleasant just for one day?' hissed Vera's sister, Nelly. In their sixties, the sisters were polar opposites. Vera was slim with a bleached blonde beehive. Nelly was big, stout, with curly grey hair.

'I'm only saying what others are thinking. Different breed those didicoys.'

'Shush, love,' Cliff said, squeezing Vera's hand. Cliff Davey was Vera's gentleman friend. He was also Ricky's grandfather. His son Alan had been Kenny's lifelong pal before his untimely death.

'Now for the best man's speech.' Beau handed the microphone to Brett. 'And don't you dare mug me off,' he joked.

Brett felt flustered. He'd managed to avoid coming face to face with Sonny so far, but knew Sonny's eyes would be watching him as he did his speech. Beau was also very aware of Alex Mariner's presence. Beau had yet to have the chance to speak to the Compton lads, but every time he looked around from the top table, Alex's eyes had been on him. 'My brother Beau, where do I start? He weren't great at football, was a naff boxer, but was a great arsonist. So much so, he got us both banged up at an early age.'

Beau roared with laughter. 'You bastard.'

The Compton lads were in fits, as were the Bonds and their friends, but not many of the Travellers as much as smiled. Beau wasn't one of their own. They didn't like him.

Brett rattled on, told a few more funny stories before turning serious. 'Since as far back as I can remember, Beau's been there when I've gone to bed of a night and woken up in the morning and it's gonna feel weird not having him here, even though he'll only be living a spit's throw away. Having said that, I'm so happy for you, bruv.' Brett turned to the bride and groom. 'I know how much you love Jolene and she's a top girl. I couldn't ask for a better sister-in-law, and I wish you many happy years together.' Brett raised a glass. 'To Beau and Jolene.'

'It'll never last,' numerous Travellers whispered to one another.

'And last but definitely not least, I want to remember Tammy. I don't know if many of you are aware, but we dated for a while too. I miss her so much. She was a brilliant girl, funny and beautiful. I'll never love another girl like I loved her. To Tammy.' Brett raised his glass.

'She never dated him. Not properly,' Evie hissed in Bobby's ear.

'Shush.'

'No. I won't shush. Tammy would still be 'ere if it weren't for meeting those two.'

'Stop it, Evie. Not today, please,' snapped Bobby.

Pleased with himself, Brett sat back down. Surely nobody would think he was gay after that? Sonny especially.

After Donny stood up and presented his son and daughter-in-law with a gift of a week's honeymoon in a five-star hotel in Corfu, Kenny was the next to take the microphone. Nobody knew what his gift to the newly-weds was and he hoped it would go down a bit better than Donny's luxurious holiday had. Evie hadn't been impressed, 'She ain't going abroad,' she bellowed. Jolene hadn't looked pleased or acted grateful either.

'I'll keep this short and sweet,' Kenny said, before spouting a few lines of the usual sentimental crap. He then handed Beau an envelope. 'To be the best husband and father, you're gonna need dosh. Plenty of it. Kids cost an arm an' a leg – well, your father and aunt did, anyway,' Kenny chuckled. 'The deeds I've given you, Beau, are the key to your future, and Brett's. I thought it was time you worked for yourselves, so I bought a big lump of land for you to run your own garden centre.'

Still reeling from his present going down like a lead balloon, Donny was dumbfounded. 'What the hell is he doing, Mother?'

Sharon touched her son's arm. 'I'm not too sure, but your dad will explain in a minute.'

Beau's smile was that of a Cheshire cat. 'So, it just belongs to me and Brett? Where is it?'

'Just off the A127, not far from Canvey. The business belongs to the three of us: me, you and Brett. We will split the profits equally between us.'

'That's wicked! Ain't it, Jolene?' Beau grinned at his wife.

'You better spend all your money on me,' laughed Jolene.

'That's a wonderful present, Kenny,' beamed Bobby Tamplin. Like any father, he wanted the best for his daughter. His wedding present to the happy couple had been expensive too: a brand-spanking-new luxury mobile home.

'He's taking the fucking piss,' fumed Donny. 'The twins work for me. I pay 'em well enough. Talk about make me look a fool.'

'Don't start getting irate, Donny. Not here, not now,' warned Sharon. 'Your nursery was thriving long before Beau and Brett worked there. You've got lots of staff.'

Vera Bond nudged her sister. 'Kenny needs a legal business to launder his dirty money.'

'Shush. Your voice carries.' Nelly had raised Kenny in

his teenage years and knew Vera was jealous of the close bond she had with her son.

'I just say it as it is. He's as crooked as a barrel of fishhooks, my Kenny. Just like his bleedin' father.'

When it came to weddings, Travellers were showy people. A huge marquee had been erected and everything inside, apart from the masses of fresh flowers, was pure white. It looked breathtakingly beautiful.

A huge selection of food was available, including hog roasts, and only the finest whisky and brandy was served at the makeshift bar. For the entertainment, Bobby had hired a country and western band, an Elvis impersonator, and a DJ. He'd also been careful not to invite any riff-raff, including some of his own family, who had a habit of kicking off with booze inside of them. Obviously, Bobby wished his two eldest boys were celebrating with them, but Billy and Johnny had stuck to their guns, much to Evie's annoyance.

'I gotta say, Bobby, you've done the kids proud.' Kenny slapped his new relative on the back. 'Where d'ya get that magician from? He somehow took me Rolex off me wrist. I thought I was seeing things when he got it out of his pocket.'

Bobby chuckled. 'You're lucky you got it back. Sam's a Traveller. His dad's an old pal of mine. Slippery as an eel is Sam. You did 'em proud too, the kids, with that present. I'm sure Jolene will enjoy spending all that extra wonga Beau'll be earning. On a serious note though, Donny's present didn't go down a treat. Especially with Evie. No disrespect like, but we don't do planes. I've never been on one, neither has Evie or Jolene. Makes me frit to death, the thought of some bastard having your life in their hands while thousands of feet in the air. We're land people.'

'Don't worry. I'll speak to Donny and explain things.'

Bobby smiled. Ever since that evening after Jamie's funeral when things had got a bit heated between them, Bond couldn't do enough for him.

Donny Bond was having the day from hell. He was destined to lose his two finest workers to his greedy bastard of a father. Beau had married a pikey, who had spent most of the afternoon pushing her tits back inside her ridiculous oversized dress. His junkie of an ex was acting like mother of the year and Beau was all over her like a rash. And to top it all, ten-year-old Alfie had just had a punch-up with a gypsy kid and had threatened to stab the lad with a knife. Thankfully, Donny had managed to prise it out of his hand just in time.

'Alfie's OK now, love. He's won't do anything stupid,' Sharon said reassuringly. Donny's other son Harry was a smashing lad with a lovely disposition. But Alfie had mental health issues that were yet to be diagnosed properly. Even in his younger years, Alfie's tantrums had been terrible. In Sharon's opinion, Tansey was an awful mother who was partly to blame for the boy's unruly behaviour. She doted on Bluebell but had little time for Alfie or thirteen-year-old Harry. Donny was a good dad, and it was left up to him to amuse and organize days out with his boys, alone.

Seeing his father saunter over without a care in the world, Donny's blood boiled. He'd always been close to his dad, even when Kenny had been in prison, but he'd never forgiven him for cheating on his mum with that slapper, Abigail. His poor mother had been in bits, and rightly so. 'Proud of yourself, are ya?'

Kenny was perplexed. 'What you on about?'

'Taking me boys away from me. What gives you the right to do that without even conferring with me first? The twins nigh on run that nursery for me. You know that.'

'Oh, don't talk bollocks,' retaliated Kenny. 'They ain't even got a driving licence yet – and have only been working up there full-time for five minutes.'

'No they ain't. They've been working there ages.'

Kenny looked at Sharon and rolled his eyes. 'Whatever! I just wanted to give 'em a leg-up in life, Donny, like I gave you with the boat.'

'But you're taking a cut for yourself,' argued Donny.

'So what! You was happy enough when your grand-father handed you his nursery on the understanding he took a cut. What's the difference with me doing the same for Beau and Brett?'

'Dad's right,' piped up Kenny and Sharon's daughter, Sherry.

Donny turned to his older sibling. 'You've changed your fucking tune, you. I remember you glassing your beloved father when you found out he'd ruined Mum's life by shagging that whore. Oh sorry, I forgot, he spent an arm and a leg on your wedding and is now paying off your mortgage for yer, eh, Shel?'

'He's got a point,' Maggie added loudly.

Sharon leapt up. 'Right, that's it! Shut up, the bloody

59

lot of you,' she bellowed. 'And that includes you, Mother. Enough is enough!'

It wasn't often Sharon lost her rag with her nearest and dearest, but when she did, they knew not to argue back. The table fell silent.

After a lot of suggestions, Beau and Jolene decided on 'The Wonder of You' for their first dance.

Numerous Travellers looked on in displeasure, as did some of the Bond clan, while witnessing the newly-weds snogging one another's faces off while smooching on the glittery white dance floor.

Bored with watching his brother making a tit of himself, Brett turned his chair to an angle, put his Ray-Bans on and discreetly focused on Sonny's girlfriend. Mary-Ann was nothing special, that was for sure. Even if he did fancy girls, he wouldn't have poked her with Beau's, let alone his own.

Glancing at the table the Compton lads were on, Brett clocked Alex looking his way. He might have misread the signals with Sonny, but no way had he got Alex wrong. Alex wanted him, badly.

'I know you're not a fan of Beau, but look how happy he makes our Jolene,' beamed Bobby Tamplin.

'Early days, Bobby.'

'Try to be happy for our daughter, Evie. Beau's a fine young man. Please give him a chance.'

Wanting to blurt out the marriage was destined to fail, as Lena had seen it in her crystal ball, Evie instead bit her lip. Apart from the groom and his family, it had been a lovely day. A wedding to be remembered in the travelling community.

Bobby put an arm around his wife's shoulders. 'Well?'

Evie forced a smile. She loved her husband dearly and didn't want to worry him. 'Of course I'll give him a chance. Not got a lot of choice, seeing as they're bloody married now, have I?'

'That's my girl,' grinned Bobby.

'How you feeling? If you're not good, just tell me and I'll make an excuse, so we leave immediately,' said Carl Scantlin, his voice full of concern. He'd met Beau and Brett's mum in rehab. They'd been one another's saviours, had been clean ever since, and now had a beautiful baby girl, Hope.

Lori Boswell had come a long way since falling into the clutches of heroin addiction. She'd been a clean-living happy teenager when she'd met Donny and fallen pregnant with the twins. She'd loved being a mum and looking after her man. She'd truly loved Donny back then.

But Lori's happiness wasn't to last. Donny was having an affair with his first love and even though Lori was willing to forgive him and begged him to stay, the bastard walked away without a backward glance to be with that bitch Tansey. He even took on Tansey's son, just to rub salt in the wound.

That was the trigger which led Lori down the slippery slope of drink and drugs. She was lost, heartbroken and unable to cope with her sons alone, even though Donny continued to support them financially. Her life went from bad to worse and ended up in mayhem.

Recovery had taught Lori to forgive herself for her

past actions. Brett being raped by her ex-boyfriend's noncy brother was not her fault, the therapist drummed into her. However, once an addict always an addict, and today Lori was struggling. She loathed her son's choice of wife; saw Jolene as common and tacky. The gypsy community were making her uneasy too. She could feel their eyes burning into her, especially the women.

Knowing only alcohol would get her through the rest of the day, Lori clutched Carl's arm. 'Make an excuse to Beau. Tell him Hope's not well. Meet me at the top of the lane.'

'OK.'

Trembling from head to toe, Lori fled the venue.

The DJ had a karaoke machine, and it was young Bobby-Joe and Ricky who got the Travellers and gorgers clapping and cheering together. Their version of Kenny Rogers's 'Coward of the County' nigh on brought the marquee down.

The Travellers liked the sound of their own voices and sick of them taking over the event, Vera nudged Cliff. 'You get up. You gotta good a voice as any of them. Sing Jim Reeves, you sound just like Jim.'

Cliff Davey looked at his lady friend, wide-eyed. 'Leave it out, Vee. I'm not getting up in front of all that bleedin' mob.'

'Why not?' Vera nudged her sister. 'Tell him to get up, Nell. Got a lovely voice, has Cliff.'

Aware of Cliff frantically waving his hands and shaking his head, Nelly felt sorry for the poor sod. Cliff was Ricky's real grandfather and had met Vera at the funeral of his son. Nelly hadn't expected it to last, as Vera had gone through more men than she'd eaten hot dinners. But surprisingly it had. 'I don't blame Cliff not wanting to get up in front of all them gyppos. Hark at 'em. Getting louder by the second. Anyone fancy a pork bap?'

Vera rolled her eyes. Even as kids, Nell had been plain and podgy, such was her love for eating. 'No. We're fine.'

'I'll have one,' piped up Cliff.

'No, you won't!' barked Vera. 'Not until you've bloody well sung for me.'

'Have a word with our daughter, Shal. Someone's already scraped her off the grass once,' moaned Kenny. Sherry was the mother of two young children now and was a good mum. But whenever she drank, she never knew when to stop, had even made a show of herself at her *own* wedding.

'Oh, leave her alone, Ken. She's not harming anyone and it's not often she gets to let her hair down anymore. I've seen at least half a dozen of the pikey girls stack it too. It's the grass. It's not suited to high heels. Donny's gone home, by the way. I think Alfie was driving him mad, and your gift gave him the hump.'

'He'll get over it. As much as I love our Donny, I see more of meself in the twins – Beau especially. I wanted to give 'em a leg-up in life and I have no doubt that new business will benefit me and you also. It's an income for us, babe. Far more of an income than the boat was, if all goes to plan.'

Sharon squeezed her husband's hand. 'You might put your foot in it like no other, but don't ever change,

63

you nut-nut. After Abigail, I never knew if I could love you again, but we got through it, eh? Believe me though, Kenny, if you ever cheat on me again, I'd *never* forgive ya and I swear that on our kids' lives. Not saying you would, but you've been warned. I'd have your guts for garters next time.'

Even though his wife was half-cut, Kenny was aware of the sweat forming on his forehead and his balls rapidly shrinking. Should he tell her the truth? While he still could? Only, living a lie was no fun. It was torture.

Having successfully avoided coming face to face with Sonny, Brett found himself on the dance floor with Alex Mariner. 'You not much of a dancer then?' enquired Brett, not knowing what else to say.

'Sometimes. But not when I'm sober. I'm watching out for those two chasing after the gypsy girls. What's the betting they get themselves into trouble?' smiled Alex.

'Why you not had a drink? I thought you were boozing.'

'I'm the designated driver. I think that's the only reason they invited me,' chuckled Alex. 'Actually, I've had a good time. It's been great to see you again, Brett.'

'Been great to see you too.'

'I'm not a complete bore though.' Alex pulled an already rolled-up joint out of his top pocket. 'Fancy a stroll and a smoke?'

Brett locked eyes with the lad he'd had many a wank over back in the day. His heart pounding, he took a deep breath. 'Yeah, sod it. Why not?'

*

Jolene's dress was so big and heavy; as the evening wore on, she couldn't stand it any more, felt as if she was wearing the marquee she was dancing in. 'I gotta get changed, Beau. I can't breathe. I'll get Mum to help me.'

Having been desperate to see Jolene naked for so very long, Beau saw this as a taster to the night that lay ahead. 'Nah, don't bother your mum. I'm your husband. It's my duty to help ya with anything now.'

'Well, hurry then. I'm wetting meself.'

Thanks to his days of riding quad bikes, Brett knew the land around Bobby Tamplin's gaff like the back of his hand, so led Alex over to a clump of trees, well away from any possible prying eyes.

Both lads knew the inevitable was about to happen, it was obvious. But they kept their conversation normal, asking one another what they were doing in their lives, until they were finally propped against the large tree trunk.

Alex lit his joint, took a deep drag and handed it to Brett. He'd known, even back in Compton House, that Brett was the same as him. 'I take it that speech about Tammy earlier was to put your family off the scent?'

'Whaddya mean?'

Alex put his hand on Brett's thigh. 'Oh, come on. Let's not play games. I'm a year older than you and have found some great places the likes of *us* can go. I came out to my mum. My parents are separated, so I pretend to have a girlfriend to my dad and grandparents. They'd never understand.'

Still not quite ready to admit he was gay, Brett was about to deny it, until Alex grabbed his face and passionately kissed him. It felt right. Exciting. 'I weren't lying about Tammy. I did kind of date her for a while, but I was confused 'cause I weren't feeling it like Beau did with Jolene. Do the Compton lads know? About you, like.'

Alex laughed. 'No way! They think I've got a girlfriend too. I only open up to my own kind, Brett. And so should you. Unless there's a family member you can trust, like I do my mum. She's cool with it.'

Feeling unconfused for the first time in his life, Brett grabbed hold of Alex. The next moment, they were writhing around on the grass like field worms.

Helping Jolene undress, then seeing her completely in the buff apart from a white thong, made Beau's penis pulsate like a drum. 'Let's have a quickie now. Come on, please? Then we can do it properly later.'

'We should get back to the party. We don't want people to think we've been doing things.'

'Why not? We're married now. Jesus! You're just so fucking beautiful, Jolene. I feel like the luckiest geezer alive, Mrs Bond!'

'Oh, come 'ere then. Don't you dare tell anyone we've done it already though,' chuckled Jolene.

There wasn't much to tell. Beau literally rammed his penis up her and came within ten seconds flat.

Around the same time Jolene lost her virginity, Brett lost his also.

Alex Mariner was sexually experienced. However, he had no lubricant with him and was surprised by Brett's rough approach. 'Slow down, Brett. Be gentler. I'll do you afterwards, OK?'

Brett Bond took no notice of Alex's words. He was in a world of his own, banging away like his life depended on it. Then he came, or exploded it seemed. It was an incredible sensation. A hundred times better than any orgasm he'd ever given himself.

Alex sat up. 'Was that your first time?'

'Nah,' lied Brett. 'Why?'

Not wanting to admit he'd found the experience a bit unsettling and also painful, Alex smiled. 'No reason. I just wondered. My turn now.'

Brett leapt up. 'Nah. You can't do *that* to me. I'll give you a wank instead.'

Kenny held Sharon's hand as they walked the short distance to their home in Dark Lane. 'Bobby did the kids proud, eh? Must of cost him a few bob, that whole day, like.'

'It would've been the perfect day, had Beau married a normal girl. What did she look like in that monstrosity of a wedding dress? Her lils kept falling out of it an' all.'

Kenny chuckled. 'It's a Traveller thing, Shal. Oh well, it's over now. At least there weren't no trouble there. I would've bet me motor on there being a punch-up.'

Sharon had a bout of the hiccups, and they stopped walking while she regained her composure. Even though a lot of the guests had left, the reception was still going strong.

'Did your mum and dad enjoy it?' asked Kenny, when Sharon had recovered.

'Mum was tired, that's why they left early. Your mum was hilarious though. I couldn't believe it when she said to Bobby "I'm surprised there's a hog roast. I was expecting baked hedgehog in clay." I had to look the other way, I was laughing so much.'

Hearing Tammy Wynette's 'Stand by Your Man' playing in the distance, Kenny took that as an omen to change the subject. 'When you mentioned that loony Abigail earlier, it made me think. What would you have done if she actually was pregnant? Do you think, in time, you could've accepted me having another kid and we'd still've got back together?'

Sharon stopped dead in her tracks. 'Never in a million years! Good Lord, I swear if you'd had a bastard kid by that slapper and tarnished our children's names, I would've stabbed ya. I'm not joking either. Right there.'

Kenny grimaced as Sharon playfully punched him where his heart was. Coming clean about Jake was no-go.

The newly-weds lay on the bed in their brand-spanking-new mobile home in one another's arms. They'd made love again, twice.

'What a day, Beau. Brilliant, weren't it? The bestest day ever. I just wished Tammy could've been 'ere too. She would've loved it.'

Beau turned to his wife and stroked her pretty face. 'She was with you in spirit. It was such a good day. I loved every second. Can't believe Gramps is setting me and Brett up in business.' Beau propped himself up on his elbow. 'I'm gonna make a fortune, Jolene, I guarantee you that. Then I'll buy us our own bit of land and build you the house of your dreams. You can even design it,' gabbled Beau, his voice overloaded with excitement.

'I don't wanna live in no brick house. Nor do I want to move away from Mum and Dad. I'll need Mum to help me look after our kids, won't I?' Jolene grabbed Beau's penis. 'Let's do it again. Be great if I fall pregnant straight away, won't it? If I have a girl, I might even call her Tammy,' she said wistfully. 'Mum would like that. And Dad, I think.'

Beau sat bolt upright. 'You're kidding me, right?'

Confused, Jolene sat upright too. 'What about? Calling my baby Tammy?'

'*Our* baby, Jolene. And no, about not wanting our own bit of land and our own gaff.'

'No. I'm dead serious. Why would we need to move when we got this beautiful massive trailer, and we can live on Dad's land for free? Anyway, that's what I promised Mum and Dad. That's why they allowed us to get married. I would never go back on my word and leave 'em, Beau. Especially Mum. She wouldn't cope. Not after losing Tammy.'

Beau couldn't believe what he was hearing, but not wanting to spoil their wedding day, said nothing. His erection said it all though. It deflated.

CHAPTER FIVE

I'd struck gold; that's how it felt, had the whole world in me hands. A beautiful wife, a nice home, a new business to focus on. I had all that and I was still only sixteen. The world was literally my oyster.

Jolene fell pregnant quickly. I wanted to be at the birth, but Evie told me that would be 'distasteful and unnatural'. Eight hours Jolene was in labour for, while I was stood in a hospital corridor, pulling me hair out, feeling helpless.

The emotion I felt when I first laid eyes on my son was indescribable. He was absolutely perfect, with a thick mop of dark hair. It felt surreal, I'd created him. Well, my sperm had.

The new garden centre took off big time. A lot of that was down to my business brain. I had the knack of knowing what lines would sell, such as Christmas decorations and trees. We made a killing with those.

Eleven months after Rocky was born, Jolene gave birth to our second son, Levi. I demanded to be at his birth, much to the annoyance of the woman I now privately referred to as the 'Wicked Witch of the East'. Levi was blond, looked like me; so much so, I gloated at the look of displeasure on Evie's boat-race when she first laid eyes on him.

Life was good. Not perfect, as I felt like a caged zoo animal living in such close proximity to Jolene's mother. But I suffered it, 'cause I loved her. We were a team and as long as she and me boys were happy, then so was I.

It wasn't until Jolene was pregnant with our third child that the cracks in our relationship truly began to show.

I listened to my heart not me nut, convinced myself love would conquer all.

How young and naive I was back then . . .

Autumn 1996

'Rocky! Stop that now. Leave him be,' ordered Beau Bond. 'He's sleeping.'

'No. Play, Levi. Play.'

Beau laughed, then picked Rocky up and dangled him upside down. 'Don't you say no to me, ya little bleeder. I'll tell Mummy.'

'Don't care,' giggled Rocky.

Rocky was two now, Levi one. Rocky doted on his younger brother, which pleased Beau. Obviously, they didn't share the twin bond, like he did with Brett and Jolene had with Tammy. But he hoped they'd grow up to be inseparable, have one another's backs throughout life.

''Ere she is, yer mum. Bang in trouble you are, mister,' joked Beau, much to Rocky's amusement.

Apart from the horrendous labour she'd endured with Rocky, Jolene had sailed through her first two pregnancies. This one, however, had been difficult. She often felt nauseous, lethargic and just generally rotten. It wasn't easy looking after two young sons either, especially since Levi had recently started walking too. Luckily, her mum was brilliant, helped her out loads. Beau worked long hours, sometimes six days a week, but he'd agreed to take this weekend off as she was going to a christening in Kent. 'How they been? Drivin' you mad, I bet,' Jolene slung her shopping bags in the bedroom.

'Been good as gold,' grinned Beau. 'Gissa kiss then. Did you manage to find something to wear?'

'Yeah. But I look like a beached whale in it. Not much I can do about that though, is there?' Jolene picked up Rocky, who was desperate for attention. 'Let's hope you get a sister this time eh, boy? Then Mummy can stop having babies, can't she?'

Rocky pulled a face. 'No.' He then wriggled to be put down because Levi was awake.

Beau gave Jolene a big cuddle. 'You could never look anything but beautiful. Pregnant or not pregnant. Not long now until this little one pops out, then perhaps we should take a break before having any more? Give it a couple of years, like.'

Jolene had refused to learn the sex of their baby before-hand during all her pregnancies, had wanted it to be a pleasant surprise. But after having two boys, this time she craved a girl. She would dress her beautifully, like a little princess. 'I ain't joking, Beau. We needs to pray for a daughter, 'cause I can't feel ill like this again. It's all right for you, swanning off out all the time with your brother. I feel like I been permanently pregnant since we got married. I ain't a fucking robot.'

Beau was not only shocked by his wife's outburst, but also hurt. ' It was you that always said you wanted our own football team, not me. And as for me swanning out with Brett, all we do together is *work*. He's got his own life now, as have I. The only reason I work so bloody hard is to provide for you and the kids. I thought that's what you wanted?'

Jolene pecked Beau on the lips. He was a good husband and father. 'I'm sorry. I just feel so drained and not meself. D'ya think you can take the boys out for a bit? I feel I need a day off from everything.'

Beau hated arguing with the woman he loved and was glad she'd apologized. 'Yeah, course. Get your nut down and no need for you to cook tonight. I'll grab us a take-away.'

'Quiet for a Saturday, ain't it, Gramps?' Brett remarked.

'That time of year I suppose, boy. Kids have just gone back to school. People have had uniforms to buy, over-spent on holidays, now they gotta start saving for Christmas. Well, normal people anyway.'

'Not like us then,' chuckled Brett.

'You out again tonight?'

'Yeah. Going up town with pals.'

Kenny jokingly rolled his eyes. Nineteen now the twins were, and even though most of their customers couldn't tell them apart, their lives could not be more different. Brett was out partying every weekend and was obviously a player, as the family was yet to be introduced to any steady girlfriend. 'If yer can't behave, be careful. You don't wanna be saddled with a kid, neither d'ya wanna end up catching crabs like me and Little Man's dad did, when we had a two's-up round the back of the boxing gym with a couple old sloshers back in the day.'

'What you saying about my dad?' Ricky loved working full-time and earning a good wage at the garden centre. He also loved earwigging. Brett was usually the one who he travelled to work with and, even though he pretended to be asleep or totally disinterested, he'd listened to every single word spoken. Brett was always on his phone in the car.

Kenny laughed and ruffled Ricky's hair. 'Nothing important. Come on, get your act together. Them boxes won't unpack themselves. Chop, chop.'

'Kenny, I got a message for you. Bloke rung up, said it's important,' yelled Marian.

Kenny walked over to the office. A plump jolly lady in her late fifties, Marian lived nearby in Pitsea and was an invaluable member of staff. She kept all their accounts in check as well. 'Who was it? Didn't you tell him I was 'ere?'

Marian handed Kenny a piece of paper. 'I did. But he said to call him on this number. Never left a name, just said he was your old business partner. Oh, and he said ring him at three o'clock, on the dot.'

Alarm bells immediately rang in Kenny's head. What the hell did Tony want? They'd never fallen out, but after the major cock-up that had befallen their ecstasy factory, Tony had bought a gaff out in Marbella, and they'd parted ways. Both knew how lucky they'd been, could've been looking at hefty sentences, probably life in his case. The Old Bill blaming and arresting the wrong firm had not only been a godsend but also a wake-up call for Kenny. That was one of the reasons he'd bought the garden centre, to go straight. Obviously, he and his grandsons robbed the taxman blind. But other than that, these days, he kept his nose well and truly clean.

'What was that about, Gramps?' enquired Brett.

'Search me. Never even heard of the geezer.'

Over in Chigwell, Sharon was browsing through the rails of her favourite clothes shop, Debra's, helping her pal to find a suitable outfit for her son's forthcoming wedding. 'What about this? I love it. That colour would suit you, Tina.'

'Oh, leave orf, I don't do pink. I'll look like a fat fairy.'

Sharon laughed. Tina Pickett worked with her at Donny's nursery. She'd been a wonderful support and tonic to her when Sharon had found out Kenny had been having an affair. They'd since become great pals over the years.

'Sharon! It is you, isn't it? I've been looking at you for the past five minutes. You've put on quite a bit of weight, but I think it suits you. How are you? You don't remember me, do you? Pat Grainger, I used to live next door to your mum and dad when they lived in Chipping Ongar.'

Seeing the look on Sharon's face when the haggard old bat had all but called her fat, Tina was creasing up, had to walk away.

'How could anyone forget you, Pat?' Sharon's reply was sarcastic. Her mother had loathed Pat Grainger. She never had a good word to say about anyone, had been the local village gossip and an all-round unbearable bragger.

'How are your mum and dad? I no longer get a Christmas card from them. Are they both OK?'

'Fine. Currently residing and living it up in Spain,' lied Sharon. She knew Pat would ask for her parents' address, such was her inquisitiveness, so gave her the one her mother and father had just sold. 'Listen, not being rude, but I've not got time to chat, Pat. My Kenny is taking us out for a meal tonight. I'm running late as it is, and I must help my friend find a wedding outfit. That was the whole point of me coming 'ere. Lovely to see you. I'll remember you to Mum and Dad.'

'Doesn't look a day older, your Kenny. Has he kept himself' – Pat tapped her nose and chuckled – '*clean* since coming out of you-know-where? I was going to talk to him, ask how you all were when I saw him over Epping Forest with a little boy recently. Your grandson, I should imagine? But he saw me and quickly darted off in the opposite direction. Perhaps he had to be somewhere too?'

'It couldn't have been Kenny. We don't live anywhere near Epping Forest.'

'Oh, yes it was. Never forget a face, me. Especially one like your Kenny's. He's the only . . .' Pat lowered her voice, '*criminal* I've ever truly known.'

Overhearing the back end of the conversation, Tina grabbed Sharon's arm. 'Too posh for me in 'ere, these outfits. Come on, let's go!'

Not for the first time in his life, Kenny had a burner phone. This time it wasn't for any skulduggery, mind.

It was solely used to call that money-grabbing bitch a couple of times a week to check on his secret son.

Kenny took the burner out of its well-concealed hiding place and tapped in the phone number Marian had handed him.

Tony answered immediately. 'How you doing?'

'Still breathing. Battling on. What's up?'

'We got problems, mate. Can we meet? Tomorrow?'

'I've got a lot on with the family tomorrow. Just tell me on the phone.'

'The Scientist is alive and got in touch with me. He wants dosh, lots of it. I'm fucking off back to Spain on Monday. I don't need this shit.'

Kenny was gobsmacked. When The Scientist went missing, both he and Tony had assumed that the Chinese gang who'd taken over the making of their ecstasy pills had done away with their top man.

'What the hell! How much does he want? I know we owe him some, but . . . And where's he been?'

'Look, I can't talk now. Meet me tomorrow, in our old spot, at eleven. I'll explain all then.'

Sharon was flummoxed and annoyed that she hadn't asked more questions. As far as she knew, Kenny had never taken any of their grandsons over Epping Forest. Why would he when they had lots of parks and greenery on their doorstep? 'Turn the car around, Tina. I need to know more.'

'Oh, don't be daft! She was a proper shit-stirrer if I ever saw one. I bet it weren't even Kenny, and if it was, there'll be a simple explanation. You mark my words.'

'Do a U-turn,' Sharon ordered. She'd once trusted Kenny implicitly, but having been shit on from a great height, she knew this doubt would linger in the back of her mind unless she knew all the details.

Tina did as asked, then waited outside the shop as Sharon ran back in. 'Well?' she asked, when her mate reappeared.

'She's gone and Debra said she don't live in Ongar any more. She moved to Buckhurst Hill and Debra don't know her address.'

'You don't wanna be knocking at her door asking stuff, mate. She was a rotter. Get a grip, Shal. Your Kenny adores you. No way would he betray you again. When does he ever go out alone?'

'Hardly ever, unless he's up the garden centre. Ignore me. I'm probably just being a drama queen. Once bitten, twice shy, I suppose.'

By the time Kenny arrived home, Sharon had given herself a good talking to. Nosy Pat had said she'd seen Kenny with a little boy, not a woman. That's if it even was Kenny.

Running into the kitchen, Ricky excitedly emptied his pockets onto the table. 'I got all this in tips today, Sharon. I'm on my way to being rich.' Ricky loved working up at the garden centre with Kenny and the boys.

'Good! You can pay for our meal tonight then,' joked Kenny.

'No. I'm not that rich.' Ricky quickly scooped his money up and fled the room.

Kenny kissed his wife. Their marriage had gone from strength to strength these past few years. 'How was your day?'

'All right. Until I bumped into Mum's old neighbour, Pat. You been over Epping Forest recently?'

'No. Kenny felt the hairs on the back of his neck stand up. He could hardly admit he'd taken Jake over there, recognized Pat and bolted off in a different direction.

'Pat swore blind she saw you over there recently, with a little boy.'

'I don't bloody think so. Pat needs to go to Specsavers. Deffo weren't me, love.'

Having been with Kenny since she was sixteen years old, Sharon could usually tell when he was lying. He refused to look her in the eyes.

Thankfully for Kenny, for once, he managed to stare straight through Sharon's soul.

CHAPTER SIX

Parked up in a navy Range Rover in a YMCA car park were the notorious Daley brothers. Christened Derek and Barry by their doting mother, they were known throughout Essex as Mad Ginger and Baz, having built up a rather tasty reputation. 'Violent, unscrupulous criminals' a judge once referred to them as, before sentencing them to a seven stretch for GBH following a bungled robbery.

At forty, Ginger was the elder by two years and the brains behind their many achievements. Heavily tattooed with a shaven head and flattened nose, he cut a menacing figure thanks to his addiction to steroids, sparring and lifting weights. Baz looked similar to his brother, but due to his most recent stint in rehab, had lost a lot of muscle and weight.

Ginger impatiently tapped his pork sausage fingers against the steering wheel. It had been a total fluke his brother had come to this AA meeting last week and bumped into the slippery bastard they'd spent ages searching high and low for. Hopefully, today they would find out his real name at least. He'd called himself 'The Scientist' when he'd briefly worked for them making their ecstasy pills and acid tabs.

Baz glanced at his watch. 'It's ten to. Shall I go in?'

'Got your phone?' Ginger replied, his voice laden with sarcasm. It had been pure bad luck Baz had left his phone in his motor last week. Ginger wasn't one for waiting around, so had gone to see an old prison pal who lived nearby. By the time he returned to pick Baz up, The Scientist was long gone.

'That's him! In the green car,' pointed Baz. 'That's the geezer who gave him a lift. He's got some old bird with him today.' Baz had managed to grab hold of The Scientist last week and give him his phone number. The lying bastard had promised to call the following day, but hadn't.

'Off you go then. Make friends. You know what to say.' Ginger waited until his brother was inside the building before having a toot. He was partial to a line or two most days, but no addict like Baz. Cocaine helped him think straight, clarify stuff, reach conclusions.

Ginger thought of his men and what they must be going through. He'd had a pukka firm behind him, salts of the earth, worth their weight in gold. Now they were all banged up for a very long time, for crimes they didn't commit. A total piss-take.

Frustrated, Ginger smashed his fists against the steering wheel. Gone was his massive drum, set in two acres with the full-size gym and swimming pool. His bird, an ex Page Three model, had fucked off too. The only property he owned now was a modest three-bed in Stanford-le-Hope that he shared with Baz.

The Scientist had double-crossed him, Ginger had no doubt about that, but no way had he acted alone. He wasn't the type, didn't have a big enough pair of bollocks. No, the real villain of the piece was the Mr Big behind the *other* ecstasy factory, and once Ginger found out who that was, he'd make sure he paid. In more ways than one.

'Hello, Brett. Come in the kitchen and wait for His Lordship there. He's still upstairs, getting ready.'

Brett politely kissed Josie Mariner on both cheeks and followed her through her incredible property in Barnet to the state-of-the-art kitchen.

'Where you off to tonight? Alex is too busy with his social life to bother to talk to me lately,' smiled Josie.

'We're going to a party. Nothing special, like,' lied Brett. Alex had met a bloke recently who'd told him about these 'Special Parties' that were held once a month at a gaff in Hemel Hempstead.

'Well, I hope you have fun. I'm sure you will. Would you like a small glass of bubbly while you're waiting? Make sure you leave your car there if you have too much to drink as well, Brett. I've warned Alex, if he writes off this car, I will not be buying him another.' Two cars Alex had written off in quick succession. He hadn't been drinking, mind, just driving too fast.

Brett chuckled. Josie was a super-cool minted mum, who owned an art gallery. She was also the only person, other than Alex, that knew of his sexual preferences. 'Yeah. I'd love a glass of bubbly, please.'

Brett and Alex were out most nights and took it in turns to drive and pick one another up. They weren't a couple, were incompatible as lovers. Instead they'd built a solid friendship. Meeting up with Alex again had not only enriched Brett's life but allowed him to explore his sexuality too.

Alex walked into the kitchen with a big grin on his face. Being a male slag, he was totally excited about this evening. He'd never been to a gay swinger's bash before. 'Looking hot, Brett.'

'You too, mate. We ready to make tracks?'

'We sure are!'

Josie gave her strapping son a hug. 'Have fun. Behave yourself. Oh, and don't do anything I wouldn't do.'

'Mum!'

Unaware his brother was off to some dodgy party, Beau was at home with Jolene watching a film. 'He's such a dude, ain't he?' chuckled Beau. It was the second time they'd seen *True Romance*, the first being at the cinema, and Beau was loving it all over again.

'He reminds me of a dark-haired version of you, ya nutter,' Jolene replied, referring to the Christian Slater character.

When Beau wrapped his arms around her tightly, Jolene pushed him away. 'I'm parched, gonna make a cuppa.'

'You can't miss the next bit. It's brilliant, the big shoot-out.'

'You watch it. I remember it.'

Beau paused the film. 'I've been thinking about what you said earlier. I'm gonna have a word with Gramps and Brett, so I can spend more time with you and the boys.'

'No. There's no need for you to do that, Beau. Take no notice of anything I said earlier. I didn't mean it. I've just felt more knackered than ever today, been snappy, like.'

Beau got up, walked over to their kitchen area, hugged his wife from behind and kissed her neck. 'Honestly, babe, it's fine. We got plenty of staff and I want to spend more time with you and the boys.'

Jolene sighed, could kick herself for opening her big mouth. She did love Beau. *But*, there were a couple of things that had really started to grate on her. His high sex drive was one, the other was his need to constantly hug, kiss and be lovey-dovey all the time. 'Don't do anything rash, Beau. There's honestly no need.'

After a wait that seemed to go on forever, Baz finally reappeared. 'I found out his name. It's Johnny. He ain't been going there that long, apparently.'

The adrenaline that had been running through Ginger's veins instantly disappeared. 'Is that it? Please don't tell me I've sat here all this time just for that.'

'I was about to find out more, off the geezer who gave him a lift, but that woman who was with him earlier started sticking her oar in. I could tell she was wary of me, so I shut up.'

'Brilliant. Just fucking brilliant!' Ginger moved his Range Rover into the space next to the green Renault Clio.

'What you doing? We're on bail, remember?'

'Of course I remember. Another cock-up of yours.' Baz had got them arrested for kicking off with a cabbie a few months ago. They'd both been out of their nuts and he'd ended up joining in, but that wasn't the point. They had no date for their trial yet and Ginger hoped Baz putting himself in rehab might help the jury take pity on them.

'Oh, God,' Baz exclaimed as the man and woman walked towards them. 'Don't kick off, Ginge. Please.'

Ginger studied his prey. The man was skinny, forty-odd, wore glasses, a pretty nondescript nobody. The woman was older, done up like a dog's dinner with blonde curly hair. A good judge of character, Ginger just knew she was going to have some trap on her. 'All right, mate,' smiled Ginger. 'You don't know me, but you've met my brother,' he explained, pointing at Baz. 'Mind if we have a quick chat? Alone? It won't take a minute.'

'Who are you?' barked Doreen Delaney. Twenty-five years clean, she was now extremely compos mentis and had known Baz was bad news earlier.

'I ain't talking to you, darling. I'm talking to him,' spat Ginger.

'He doesn't want to speak to you, and I am certainly not your darling. Our fellowship is called Alcoholics Anonymous for a reason you know. It respects people's privacy, including the chap your brother was prying about earlier.'

'See you, ya nosy old cunt,' seethed Ginger. 'If you don't keep your trunk out, I'll shove you in the boot of my motor, pour a bottle of vodka down your neck, then make sure you have a fatal accident.'

Seeing the startled look on both the woman's and man's faces, Baz grabbed hold of his brother's arm. 'Leave it. Come on. We're going.'

*

Expecting some seedy-looking dive, Brett was a bit perplexed when Alex's map-reading led them to a road in the middle of nowhere. 'This can't be right, surely? The few gaffs we've passed look like stately homes down 'ere.'

At the sight of two expensive motors approaching from the opposite direction, Alex ordered Brett to turn his BMW around and follow them. 'I told you Gordon said it was a posh gaff. Look, see! The cars have stopped. This has to be it, Brett.'

'There's two heavies on the gate. Best you do the talking.'

The two cars in front entered the property, the gate closed and a big black bloke peered inside Brett's motor. 'This is a private party. Are you on the guest list?'

'Yes,' smiled Alex. 'I'm a friend of Gordon's. Alex Hardy, and this is my plus one, Brett Laurel.'

The man scanned his list. 'In you go, gentlemen.'

As they drove through the gate up the extremely long driveway to what did look like a stately home, Alex laughed. 'Did you pick up on our dodgy surnames?'

Astounded by the Rolls-Royces, Lamborghinis and Ferraris, Brett mumbled, 'No.'

'Laurel and Hardy, you muppet. Those can be our incognito names.'

Alex was buzzing as they sauntered into the gaff. 'Look at this place! It's wonderful,' he said, as he took a flute of champagne off a scantily dressed waiter.

Brett felt differently as he laid eyes on the other guests. Most were old, fat and bald. 'I don't know if this is gonna be our cup of tea, mate. Look at the state of 'em.'

'It'll be fine. The night is young. Have a drink.'

To say Brett felt like a fish out of water was putting it mildly. Especially when they were approached by a tanned flamboyant grey-haired man dressed in a white suit and pink shirt. 'Well, hello there, gentlemen. We haven't met before. Who invited you?'

'Gordon. Do you know him?' Alex asked.

The man laughed and patted both lads on the shoulder. 'I should say so! We've been a couple for the past twelve years. Gordon's upstairs getting ready. Be late for his own funeral that one. He has impeccable taste inviting you two though, I must say.'

Aware that the man was eyeing them up and down, Brett felt hot under the collar and not in a good way. 'We can't stay long. Unfortunately, something's cropped up at home.'

'Oh, don't be so silly. The party's not even started yet. There'll be lots of things cropping up later, trust me,' chuckled the man. 'I'm Stan by the way. This is my home. Follow me, gentlemen. I'll show you where the real party is held.'

Most Saturday evenings, Kenny took Sharon out to eat somewhere nice. But tonight, Ricky was with them, so they'd let him choose and ended up in Jailhouse Rock in Hornchurch.

'Look! There's Elvis,' pointed Ricky excitedly.

Sharon glanced to her left. There was a rowdy mob celebrating a birthday and they were already getting on her nerves. 'Do you know anyone on that table? I'm sure they're talking about us.'

Kenny had a butcher's. 'Nah. A load of pissed-up imbeciles by the looks of it. Ignore 'em.'

'She's pretty. Look,' pointed Ricky. 'I'm off to dance with her.' Ricky stuffed the rest of his half-pounder in his mouth before bolting off to the small dance floor.

'Loves a bird, don't he?' laughed Kenny.

'Must take after you.'

'Give it a rest, love. I've had a stressful enough day as it is.'

'Why? Because of what Pat said?'

'Nah, not that.' Tony's earlier phone call had unsettled Kenny, and he needed to convince Karen to move further out. He couldn't risk being spotted out with Jake again.

'What then?'

Kenny was saved from answering by a tap on the shoulder. He turned around and came face to face with a short, stocky, meathead-looking bloke with big muscles and some blonde bimbo with a pair of massive false tits. 'Yeah. What's up?'

The bloke smiled. 'Sorry to interrupt you, but I had to come and say hello. You're Kenny, ain't ya? Kenny Bond.'

'Yeah. We met before?'

'Yes. In Palms. But you was a bit worse for wear that night, so you might not remember me,' the bloke chuckled.

Kenny cringed. He'd gone through a rough time when Sharon kicked him out. That's when he'd been going up Palms and to other clubs, with Tony. 'Nah. Can't say I do remember.'

The bloke held out his right hand. 'Danny. Danny Griffin. And this is my girlfriend, Gemma. You're a fucking hero of mine, Kenny. Ain't he, Gem? I hate the Old Bill.

Gem'll tell ya. The way you did away with that copper is the stuff of legends.'

'Danny despises the filth with a passion,' Gemma said proudly. 'He went mental when they raided our house recently, had to be restrained. It took six of 'em to hold him down.'

'It was an accident, what I did. I didn't even know the geezer was Old Bill,' explained Kenny.

'Shall we order dessert?' Sharon said loudly. Kenny didn't suffer fools and she could tell the couple were as thick as two short planks.

'Danny reckons they should make a film about it,' grinned the dumb blonde. 'One of his mates is a film producer. Danny could introduce you to him, Kenny, couldn't you, Dan?'

'Yeah. As long as I can be an extra or something. I don't wanna play the dead cop. What was his name? Harry something, weren't it, Kenny?'

Aware that Kenny was about to lose it, Sharon leapt out of her seat and walked over to the couple. 'No disrespect, but d'ya mind leaving us alone, please? We're trying to have a quiet family meal.'

Meathead went bright red. 'Sorry, love. Sorry, Kenny. Enjoy the rest of your evening.'

The actual party was held in Stan's basement. It wasn't any old basement though, had been especially designed to resemble a flashy nightclub.

'Fucking hell, Alex. Whatever you brought us to?' whispered Brett in his pal's ear.

Disco music was playing and there were loads of scantily dressed young men. Some were clad in leather, some skimpy shorts, and there were half a dozen doing all sorts of upside-down acrobatics on the big silver poles that went from floor to ceiling.

'This is fabulous, Stan. I bloody love it!' grinned Alex.

His special discotheque had cost Stan a small fortune and he was extremely proud of it. 'You wait until the party starts properly. It's electric. And anything goes! See that corridor?' Stan pointed.

Alex nodded.

'If you go to the bottom of the corridor and turn right, there are rooms, you know, for a bit of private hanky-panky,' chuckled Stan. 'The bar down here is a pay bar, as I have to pay all these handsome hunks to keep you guests entertained,' Stan winked.

Looking at the eye candy, Alex felt like a kid in a sweet shop. He nudged Brett. 'This is going to be great.'

Aware of some of the lads eyeing him up, Brett gave a false smile. 'Yeah. Let's go back upstairs now, though. No point being down 'ere until the party is in full swing.'

'Swing!' Stan burst out laughing. 'There'll be plenty of swinging later. Nobody holds parties like Uncle Stan does.'

By the time they got back to Stanford-le-Hope, Ginger had calmed down.

'So, what do we do now?' enquired Baz. 'Only I can't go back to that bloody meeting no more, thanks to you.'

'I've already said sorry. Don't expect me to keep apologizing.'

'Had you taken something? Only, it looked like you had.'

'Don't be fucking daft,' lied Ginger. 'I told you I'd

support ya. While you're clean, I'm clean. Well, apart from a few beers 'ere and there.'

'Good. 'Cause you know what our brief said. With our record, we were lucky to get bail and, as much as a hint of trouble, we'd be remanded until our court case. Sod that for a game of soldiers.'

Ginger paced up and down the living room. 'I got it! There's gotta be a number for the AA that you can find out all local meetings in that area. Sod the YMCA. No way am I waiting another week to find Johnny, that's if his name ain't really Sid.'

'There's loads of meetings over that way. I overheard someone asking about them today.'

'Good. Right, get on the blower and find out where.'

Back at Jailhouse Rock, Kenny's day was getting worse. 'Go get him off that dance floor, Shal, before I smash every cunt's face in on that table.'

Sharon glanced over at the noisy birthday crowd. There was no proof they were laughing at Ricky. They were out of their seats singing and dancing themselves. 'You're being paranoid now. Stop it.'

'Nah, I ain't. Look at him, Shal. He's too old to be dancing about like that now. And too big. He needs to lose some timber. I'm gonna join him up to a gym next week, teach him how to use some weights, stuff like that.' Kenny looked over at the table full of drunks. 'And they *are* taking the fucking piss, I'm telling ya.'

Aware of Kenny's twitching jaw, Sharon marched up to the dance floor and grabbed Ricky's arm. 'Come and have a sit down now, love. You're all hot and sweaty.'

Bopping away to 'Blue Suede Shoes', Ricky wasn't moving. He liked standing in front of the make-believe Elvis and copying his dance routines. 'No, Shal. I'm enjoying meself.'

At five foot two, Ricky was the same height as Sharon. But at fourteen stone, he was three stone heavier; therefore, Sharon could hardly drag him off the dance floor. He didn't want to leave it either, was having a whale of a time, and if those arseholes were taking the mick, Ricky couldn't care less, was oblivious to it.

Kenny knocked back the rest of his drink. He'd felt edgy ever since *that* phone call, then Shal had confronted him on something that was true. Now he was stuck in a restaurant with a load of idiots. Meathead and the blonde had proper rubbed him up the wrong way. As if he wanted to make a film about his mistakes. He wanted to forget about them. Not only that, but he was also a private person, liked to keep himself and his family out of the bloody limelight. Only losers bragged. Losers and nobodies.

Sharon sat back down and squeezed her husband's hand. 'He's having a whale of a time, Ken. Please don't drag him off the dance floor. I told him we're leaving as soon as Elvis stops singing. He can't help the way he is, love, and as long as he enjoys life, that's all that matters. You've been a brilliant substitute dad to him. I bet Alan's looking down with pride.'

Kenny softened, sighed, then gestured the waitress over to get them some more drinks. A mistake in the making.

*

Stan's party in full swing was not for the faint-hearted. The guests were happily cavorting in front of everyone with the scantily dressed lads.

'He's hot, that blond with the cropped hair in the light denim shorts,' gushed Alex. 'Who you got your eye on?'

Brett was on the brandy now, needed it to deal with the shock. He'd never seen so many todgers, but unlike Alex, who was in his element, the promiscuousness of the evening was making him feel nauseous. Some of the guests were old, their manhood disgusting. Thoughts of Noncy Eric kept popping into Brett's mind. He hated fucking perverts with a passion. 'None of 'em, thanks. This ain't my thing. Let's get out of 'ere, eh, mate?'

'Oh, come on, Brett. Don't be a spoilsport. You haven't got to do anything you don't want to, but don't ruin it for me, please.'

Before Brett could respond, Alex was approached by Stan's partner, Gordon. He was then led off to a private room, leaving Brett alone.

'Kenny, please leave it. Don't make a scene. They're not worth it,' urged Sharon. The sloshpots celebrating the birthday were now all on the dance floor with Ricky.

'Look at 'em!' hissed Kenny, his jaw twitching furiously. There were eight of them in total, four women and four blokes. Each and every one looked like they'd fallen out of the ugly tree and hit every branch on the way down. Dregs of society and they had the brass neck to take the piss out of *his* boy. Because that's what Ricky was now. His own father wasn't around to protect him, so Ricky was *his* responsibility.

Sharon, who was now sitting in Ricky's seat, squeezed Kenny's hand. 'They ain't worth getting nicked for, Ken. Vermin, the lot of 'em. You sit here and I'll go and get Ricky away from 'em.'

His face burning with fury, Kenny grabbed Sharon's arm. 'Nah, you won't. I'll deal with this.'

The tempo slowed with 'Are You Lonesome Tonight' and Ricky was a bit gobsmacked when an older blonde lady grabbed him for a smooch and started rubbing her crotch against his groin.

The birthday crowd stood on the edge of the floor in hysterics. It was Lyn's birthday and they'd had a bet with her that she wouldn't be able to give the Down's syndrome lad a hard-on.

Kenny wasn't stupid, knew what the scumbags were up to. Seeing the ugly skank try to twist Ricky around to show her pals the proof was the final straw for Kenny.

'Nooo! Kenny, leave it,' shrieked Sharon, as· her husband stomped across the restaurant like a raging bull.

As much as the bird deserved a slap, Kenny didn't hit women. Instead, he took his anger out on the four geezers. He headbutted one, who went down like a sack of spuds, elbowed another in the face, gave the third a right-hander which sent him sprawling across a table and easily got the fourth from off his back, who he then kicked in the nuts.

Elvis stopped singing, women were screaming, and people were fleeing as the management and Sharon tried to stop Kenny from causing any more uproar. 'They'd been laughing and picking on our Down's syndrome son all evening. That's why this happened,' shrieked Sharon, hoping the explanation would stop the staff from involving the police.

Ricky was in bits, his erection well and truly deflated. 'Stop it, Kenny. Stop it! We was only dancing. I was having fun,' he wept.

Seeing the rough old malt who'd been dancing with Ricky pick up a bottle and lunge towards Kenny, Sharon grabbed her hair so hard, she fell backwards and dropped the bottle. 'He might not be able to hit you, but I bloody well can,' screamed Sharon. She then punched the woman straight on her wonky nose.

Feeling sorry for the lad, Elvis put his arm around Ricky's shoulders to console him. He knew the blonde had been taking the piss, had felt uncomfortable witnessing it.

'The police are on their way,' shouted the manager, which prompted the skanks to quickly exit the premises. One of the men was currently on bail for numerous burglaries. Another, the one Kenny had headbutted, was still dazed, could barely walk and was literally dragged from the restaurant by his pals.

'Go. Just go. I'll sort it,' Elvis said to Kenny.

Kenny didn't need telling twice. He grabbed Ricky, then Sharon, and dragged them out of the place they would certainly never be returning to.

After being accosted by a couple of older guests and approached by some perve wearing a leather thong, Brett took himself off to the bar area. Never would he come to another of Stan's weirdo parties, not in a million years.

Knowing he'd now be sleeping in his car anyway, Brett ordered a large brandy and turned around, leaning his back against the bar. He felt safer here, didn't have to watch any more disgusting acts taking place. Spotting that old boy, who was even older than his granddad, getting his shrivelled-up dick sucked by a bloke dressed up in an afro wig and PVC dress had nearly made him regurgitate the Burger King meal he'd eaten earlier.

Singing away to Bronski Beat's 'Smalltown Boy', Brett locked eyes with a black-haired man in a dark suit. He was older, but unlike all the other guests, fit and good-looking.

The man walked over to Brett. 'Not your scene either, I take it?' he said. He had a deep Irish accent.

Brett felt his stomach do a mini somersault. Up close, the bloke was even more handsome. He had penetrating blue eyes; a cheeky smile and that Irish accent made him even more appealing.

'Nah. Not at all. I got dragged here by a pal, who has now disappeared.'

The man held out his right hand. 'Aidan. And you are?'

Feeling hot under the collar, but for good reasons this time, Brett returned the gesture. 'Brett.'

'How do you fancy a bottle of champagne in a private room, Brett? I'm not putting it on you, I promise. I just fancy a sensible chat away from all these perverts.'

Aidan's penetrating stare said otherwise, but Brett didn't care. 'Yeah. I'd like that. A lot.'

CHAPTER SEVEN

Early the following morning, Sharon was awoken by her husband's restlessness. 'You all right? You don't think the police will turn up here, do you?'

'Nah. No one got badly hurt, did they? And apart from a chair and some glasses, there was sod all damage. I do worry about Little Man though, especially now he's older.'

Sharon put her arm across Kenny's chest. 'I know you do, but as I said last night, Ken, he can't help the way he is. He loves music and dancing. You can't stop him from enjoying himself. Let's be honest, that mob last night were spectacular arseholes. It's not often these days people pick on a lad like Ricky. And Ricky was oblivious to it anyway, until it all kicked off. I don't think he truly understood even then. He was so upset on the way home, bless him. I think he thought he'd done something wrong.'

Kenny propped himself up on his elbow. 'I'll have a proper chat with him today, man to man. And that's what he is now, Shal, a working man. I meant what I said yesterday, I'm gonna join him up to a gym. I could do with toning up a bit, so we'll lift some weights together. And if he wants to dance, I'll take him to some classes. He can learn how to dance properly there without being laughed at.'

'You're going a bit overboard. What happened last night was a one-off.'

'I want Ricky to lead an independent life, Shal. Say we ain't around one day to look after him? He's bright. So what if he's got Down's? He's got more brains than them tossers we had a tear-up with last night put together. I'm gonna teach him to drive, promise to buy him a car as an incentive when he passes his test. He'll be able to do it, I know he will.'

'I very much doubt the DVLA will let him drive, love.'

'Why not? Plenty of fucking notrights are let loose behind a steering wheel. I'll kick up a right stink if they don't give him a provisional. That'll be discrimination. I'll get a good brief on it an' all if I have to.'

When Kenny had a bee in his bonnet, Sharon knew there was little point arguing with him. 'You do whatever you think's best.'

'I will. No more takeaways. We're going on a health kick, me and Little Man. Actually, no more calling him that either. He ain't little any more, he's big. And I'm gonna turn him into a man. A proper man, who can fend for himself.'

Brett Bond opened his eyes and turned his head. Aidan was still lying next to him and Brett could hardly believe his luck. He looked just as handsome, even when sleeping.

He had the longest eyelashes Brett had ever seen and gorgeous jet-black wavy hair.

Aidan stirred. 'Morning handsome,' he mumbled, a half-smile on his lips.

'Morning.' This was a first for Brett, actually spending the whole night with a man. He'd given Aidan a blowjob too, another first for him. Feeling content for once in his life, Brett put his hands behind his head, lay back on the pillow and grinned. This was heaven. It hadn't all been about sex. He and Aidan had chatted for hours about all sorts. There was chemistry there, a true connection, and when he'd finally fucked Aidan, it had been the best sex ever. Rough, wild and spontaneous.

Recalling his orgasm, Brett grinned stupidly. Aidan was twenty-nine, originally from Dublin, now lived in Canary Wharf and described himself as 'A bit of an entrepreneur.' He was funny, edgy and far more interesting than any bloke Brett had met in the past.

'Is he awake?' Aidan muttered, opening one eye, a half-smile on his face as his hand wandered and made contact with Brett's penis.

Brett's cock immediately stood up like a flagpole. And when Aidan put his lips around it, Brett couldn't help himself. He spurted his load within sixty seconds flat.

'You look beautiful,' smiled Beau.

'Oh, leave it out. I feel like a sodding elephant. Can't wait to get me figure back, for good this time.'

'Where going, Mum?' enquired Rocky.

'To a christening. You're going to a barbecue, you two, with Dad.' Jolene gave her sons a hug and a kiss.

'Where's mine?' asked Beau.

Jolene sighed and pecked her husband on the lips. 'Have fun, the three of you.'

'You too. What time you gonna be back?'

'I dunno, Beau. But Sonny's dropping me home, so no need to worry.'

'Ring me if you need me,' Beau replied.

'Will do,' Jolene smiled but it felt forced. She knew that it was horrible to even think it, but she was so looking forward to a day out with her own people, without Beau cramping her style.

Beau was the most loving husband and father a woman could wish for. But sometimes, Jolene felt suffocated by his neediness and dependency upon her. It was over-bearing.

Kenny fed Sharon his usual load of Sunday-morning bullshit, then headed to Karen's gaff, the house he was renting for her in Loughton.

Every Sunday, Kenny would take Aunty Nelly to visit his nan in Bow Cemetery. It was the only excuse Kenny could think of to make a detour on the way home and spend an hour or two with Jake.

Jake was three now. An inquisitive and likeable kid, he deserved a proper father, something that Kenny felt guilty about. But there was no way that he was going to risk his marriage again, which was why he spent as little time with Jake as possible. Becoming too attached to the lad was something Kenny wanted to avoid. Jake could never be part of his everyday life, not even when he was older.

Kenny cursed his luck as he got out the car and bumped into Karen's sixteen-year-old daughter. 'Hello. How you doing?' he asked awkwardly. Karen knew the rules. Kayleigh wasn't supposed to be at the house when he visited.

Kayleigh ignored Kenny. 'Ring me when he's gone, Mum,' she shouted, before stomping off with a face like thunder.

'For Christ's sake!' Kenny hissed, once inside the house. 'Does she know who I am?'

'I think so. I can hardly pretend Jake was an immaculate conception, can I? Does it matter?'

'Well, yeah, it fucking does, actually. Especially if she knows me surname. She's a teenage girl, Karen. They're full of gossip.'

Karen flicked back her dyed-blonde hair that had cost Kenny a fortune. 'Oh, please! Get over yourself, Kenny. Kayleigh is sixteen, has a boyfriend of her own now. She certainly isn't interested in gossiping about an old man like you. How old are you now?'

Kenny looked with hatred at the monster he'd impregnated. She was unrecognizable from Karen the schoolteacher who had been his shoulder to lean on in his hour of need, in person and in personality.

'Daddy,' Jake ran towards Kenny, a big grin on his face.

Kenny picked up the lad and gave him a hug. 'What you been up to, boy?'

'He's getting restless and becoming a handful,' replied Karen. 'He has a lot of energy, Kenny. He also needs to interact with other children more. There are no kids his age for him to play with nearby. Which is why I did some research and I managed to find a wonderful nursery only ten minutes away. I went to view it, obviously. It truly is fabulous. Wonderful amenities and staff. It will be great for Jakey. It's not cheap, mind. But it'll be worth every penny as it will give our boy a great head-start for when he's old enough for school,' beamed Karen.

'No can do, I'm afraid. I got spotted over Epping Forest with Jake by a woman Shal knows, had to talk me way out of it. You know the score, Karen. I fork out for your and Jake's lifestyle, but in return, my marriage stays intact. Loughton's too close to home now Jake's getting older. I also know a lot of people around 'ere, or they bloody well know me. I need you to move further out in Essex. There's some lovely rural areas the other side of Chelmsford.'

'I'm not moving to bloody Chelmsford,' snarled Karen. There was no way that she was going to let Kenny call the shots on this one, Karen held the upper-hand and she knew it. 'I like it here, have made friends. And what about Kayleigh? Her college?'

'You're gonna have to move.'

'No, Kenny. I'm not your puppet. I'm the mother of your youngest son and I'm going nowhere.'

Brett felt as though he was doing the walk of shame as they came up the stairs and bumped into Stan, who insisted they stay for breakfast.

Brett would rather just leave, but Aidan agreed, so breakfast it was. It soon became clear that Stan and Aidan knew one another well, a bit surprising as Stan was quite old, loud, camp and Aidan the opposite.

The full English was cooked by a chef, served by a butler and Brett suddenly found himself ravenous. He also felt embarrassed as six other guests joined them. He recognized one, a young lad who'd been wearing leather shorts, a black string vest and a leather baker's hat. He was with a very well-spoken bloke with a loud voice and grey hair. Gordon was there too, seated next to Stan and it was clear he also knew Aidan well.

The conversation was jovial, with all saying how much they'd enjoyed the party. Then it turned to *him*. Brett could feel himself blush as his and Aidan's evening was put under scrutiny.

Aidan gently squeezed Brett's arm. 'You know me, Stan. Very choosy. But you'll be seeing more of this one.'

'He's not fibbing either, Brett. I've been trying to fix him up for years,' chuckled Stan. 'So pleased you two had a fabulous evening. Oh, and please give myself and Gordon plenty of notice if we need to buy a hat.'

Aware Brett was feeling out of his depth, Aidan laughed, then stood up. 'Thanks so much for your hospitality, Stan, but we'll be making a move now. Places to go, people to see.'

Stan leapt out of his seat and warmly embraced both Aidan and Brett. 'What a handsome couple you make, and I mean that with all my heart. Jesus wept! I almost feel like Cilla Black,' Stan chuckled. 'I'll call you in the week, Aidan. Be good, the pair of you, and if you can't be good, be careful.'

Once outside, Brett enjoyed the feeling of the cool breeze hitting his face; taking a deep breath he began to feel more like his confident self. 'Sorry if I didn't say much. But I don't know 'em. How do you know 'em so well?'

Aidan smiled. He had thin lips, but they somehow suited him, added to his sex appeal, thought Brett. 'Through business. How about I take you out for a meal tonight? I'll explain all then.'

'Erm, yeah. I'd like that.' Brett was taken aback, yet thrilled that Aidan wanted to see him again so soon.

Aidan handed Brett a business card. 'Meet me at that address at seven.' He then gave Brett a lingering kiss on the lips. 'See you later, handsome,' he winked, before turning and walking away.

Brett unlocked his BMW and sank into the driver's seat. He could not believe what had happened to him in the space of one evening. Total madness.

About to turn his ignition, Brett heard a toot and looked up. If he wasn't already shell-shocked, he certainly was now. The motor was a silver Rolls-Royce and in the driver's seat was none other than Aidan.

After some heated words with Karen, Kenny Bond wasn't in the best of moods as he parked up in his and Tony's old meeting place, a small, secluded car park, opposite the Camelot pub in Lambourne End. The reason they'd always met there, was you could be aware that nobody was following you and literally walk into the arse-end of Hainault Forest with the knowledge that there was no way your conversation could be tapped.

The first to arrive, Kenny picked up his newspaper. The front page was still full of Prince Charles and Lady Diana's divorce proceedings, even though that had happened over a month ago. Why couldn't the press just leave people alone to get on with their lives? Kenny slung the paper down in exasperation, not because he was a massive fan of Charles and Di, but he knew what it was like to be hounded by the press. Even all these years later, his name would be mentioned on certain anniversaries of the copper he'd killed. He'd even had the press contact him in the past, wanting interviews. Kenny had politely told them where to go. He'd done his time and just wanted to be left alone to hopefully live the rest of his life in peace, not that he was getting much of that recently. Drama seemed to follow him around.

Tony pulled up minutes later in a Land Rover. Mid-forties with brown-wavy hair and a penchant for lifting weights, he was the son of Teddy Abbott, a notorious armed robber back in the sixties and seventies. Tony jumped out the motor and gestured for Kenny to follow him.

'You're looking well. Suits ya, living abroad,' grinned Kenny. They'd parted ways after the ecstasy pill fiasco. They'd had such a lucky escape; they'd decided not to keep in touch, unless necessary. For the time being at least.

After exchanging a few niceties about one another's families, Tony looked around furtively before sitting on a large log. '*He* sent a gezzer round to knock on me parent's door. It weren't him 'cause the bloke was short with glasses and a bald head. Anyway, me muvver was handed a note with a phone number on it saying it was urgent I get in touch. I rang you straight after I called him. He reckons we still owe him thirty grand.'

'We don't,' Kenny interrupted. 'He was due to be paid twenty-four when he decided to do a disappearing act and leave us in the lurch, the cheeky bastard.'

105

'You ain't heard the best bit yet. People are onto us, so he says. He reckons there's big money being offered to find out who was really behind the pills that did the damage.'

'That's bollocks!' snapped Kenny. 'The Old Bill milked those convictions. As if they're gonna admit to such a cock-up now and let 'em all go. They'd make themselves look massive dicks. And what would they have on us? Jack-shit. Even if that chancer were to grass, it's his word against ours. There ain't a scrap of evidence.'

'It's not the filth looking for us, Ken. It's the Mr Big behind the Southend op. The long and short of it is, The Scientist wants two hundred grand, plus what he's already owed, to keep his trap shut.'

'Why didn't Mum want a lift with us?' Sonny Tamplin asked his sister. They'd just gone through the Dartford Tunnel, but had to pick Mary-Ann up on the way to the christening.

'Because Aunt Lydia wanted to go to Dagenham market, so offered to take Mum with her. She'll be travelling home with us though,' replied Jolene.

'Why ain't Beau coming? I thought you'd have wanted the boys there.'

'Nah. Beau's taking the boys round his granddad's. It's nice to have a break, if I'm honest. Get out on my own, with me own people.'

Surprised by his sister's admission, Sonny glanced sideways. 'Don't say that in front of Mother. She'll have a field day. You two had a row or something?'

'No. But I've been grumpy lately, 'cause I'm sick of being preggers. I've told Beau we're having no more chavvies after this one. I just pray it's a girl. Anyway, enough about me. How's your love life? Any plans to propose yet?'

'Nah. We're happy as we are, for now.'

'You might be, Sonny. But I doubt Mary-Ann is. All us travelling women want that ring on our finger so we can have our chavvies young.' As soon as the words were out of her mouth Jolene wondered if she had rushed into motherhood and marriage too quickly – perhaps Sonny was right to wait.

'I'll get round to it. When the time feels right,' chuckled Sonny. 'I haven't seen Brett for ages. How's he doing? Has he got a girlfriend yet?'

'I ain't seen much of him either. Beau reckons he's a player, got a different bird every weekend.'

Remembering their strange altercation, Sonny said nothing. He very much doubted it was birds that Brett was pulling though.

Kenny Bond was livid, his jaw twitching repeatedly, 'No way are we succumbing to a blackmailer, mate. Not on your nelly! We'll go halves, pay him what we owe him and give him six grand on top to make it up to thirty, as a goodwill gesture. Other than that, he can do one. We'll take the cunt out if need be.'

'We don't even know his real name, Ken. Or where he's from,' Tony reminded his pal.

'But we know what he looks like. You bumped into him in Lakeside that time, with a bird if I remember rightly?'

'So! We haven't got a photo of him, have we? And people travel from all over to go to Lakeside. What about your pal? The one that introduced us to him in the first place.'

Phil, AKA The Pharmacist, was a trustworthy nerd who Kenny had first met in prison. He'd been the one who'd worked for them originally, and was responsible for the finest ecstasy tablets Essex had ever seen. Phil wasn't stupid though, had earned an enormous lump of wedge and got out while the going was good. He'd retired abroad, only God knew where. 'I doubt I'll be able to track him down, but I'll try. In the meantime, you arrange a meeting with cheeky bollocks to pay him off and I'll come with ya.'

'I can't. I've booked a flight for tomorrow, to go back to Spain.'

'Best you cancel it then.' Kenny looked his partner firmly in the eye. There was no chance that he was being left to mop up this mess on his own.

'But I gotta get back. I've got a kiddie on the way, Ken.'

'Congratulations an' all that. But I ain't having no fucking stranger knocking on my front door, handing Sharon weirdo notes. We were partners, pal, still are, until this crap is dealt with. That's the old school way. Ask your father.'

The christening was wonderful, so much so that Jolene managed to forget about being heavily pregnant for a while. It was so good to see and chat with family and friends without having to worry about Beau's feelings and neediness. She felt free for the first time in ages and even though lots of family and friends had never agreed on her choice of husband, now she was carrying their third child, they respected her choice, and had stopped making snide remarks. Apart from her two eldest brothers that was, but thankfully they weren't present today, only their wives and kids were.

Turning away from her brother, Jolene locked eyes with a dark-haired lad with a child in his arms. The after-bash was being held in a marquee. Travellers always had trouble booking decent venues. Once their accents were heard, or one turned up to pay a deposit, the organizers usually found a reason to cancel. 'Who is that bloke over there, Sonny? Dark blue suit with a chavvy in his arms. I'm sure I recognize him from somewhere.'

Sonny put his arm around his girlfriend's shoulders and smiled. 'That's Mary-Ann's second-cousin. He's also the man our Tammy had set her sights on shortly before she died.'

Jolene looked at Sonny in amazement. 'Nah. That can't be right. Tammy would've confided in me. We told each other everything.'

Annoyed with himself for having said the wrong thing, Sonny gave his little sister a comforting hug. 'I'm sure she was planning to tell you. Perhaps she didn't want to curse her luck? You and Beau were inseparable back then. She might not have had the chance to tell you.'

'Don't talk rubbish! We bloody lived together. When did she tell you?'

'It weren't actually me Tammy told. It was Brett. I'm not sure if they went on a date, or were going on one. His name's Jimmy. Jimmy Dean.'

*

Exceptionally warm for autumn, it was Kenny's idea to have one last barbecue before the weather turned. It was meant to be cold and teeming down all next week. Not that you could believe much Michael Fish predicted anymore. Poor bastard had become a laughing stock since he'd got *that* hurricane back in the eighties so very wrong.

Deep in thought, Kenny prodded the lamb chops, chicken and steaks. He was yet to hear back from Tony about the 230K. The Scientist had some front, he'd give him that much. Cheeky tosser!

'Don't mind me standing with you for a bit, d'ya?' asked Cliff. 'As much as I adore your mum, her voice don't 'arf carry, especially when she's slagging people off.'

Kenny laughed. His mum and Cliff had never moved in together and were the most unlikely of couples, but their relationship seemed to work. 'Like a foghorn. Who's she slating now?'

'Charlie. She's telling Nelly what a pervert he is. I'm sure the poor sod can hear her. I wanted the ground to open up and swallow me.'

'To be fair, Cliff, she might have a point there,' winked Kenny. Charlie was Sharon's father and had always seen himself as a bit of a smoothie. Kenny had never been a fan, especially since he'd found out Charlie had cheated on Sharon's mum years ago. Shal didn't know. She'd never have forgiven that particular indiscretion and Kenny hoped to save her the pain. 'Grub's up,' bellowed Kenny.

Sharon brought out the bowls of salad, home-made coleslaw and chunks of French stick. 'Ring Brett again, Beau. I'm getting a bit worried about him now. He definitely said he was coming today.'

'I've just tried him, Nan. His battery must be dead. I wouldn't worry too much. He was at some posh party last night with Alex. The pair of 'em are bound to have woken up in some strange bird's bed with raging hang-overs.'

'No. That won't have happened,' piped up Ricky.

'What do you know that we don't then?' joked Donny.

'Alex don't like girls. He likes boys,' explained Ricky.

'You what!' said Kenny, Donny and Beau, in virtual unison.

Aware that all eyes were on him, Ricky beamed. He loved being centre of attention and knew his love of earwigging would come in handy one day. 'Alex doesn't have girlfriends. He's a poofter.'

CHAPTER EIGHT

Still in the previous night's suit, Brett arrived at an awkward moment. 'Sorry I'm late. Was at a mental party last night.'

'Was it a party for queers?' enquired Vera.

'Shut it, you,' snapped Maggie Saunders. 'All I've heard is your nasty innuendoes today. Sick of it. And for your information, my Charlie ain't a bleeding pervert.'

'Mum! Stop it,' ordered Sharon.

Brett felt the colour drain from his face.

'You gonna let *her* talk to me like that?' Vera asked her son.

Kenny stood up. 'Enough! The lot of ya. Can I have a word, Brett? In private.'

Trying to quickly compose himself, Brett followed his grandfather inside the house. 'Where you been all night?' asked Kenny.

'At a party, then round some bird's gaff. Why?'

'Ricky reckons that lad you knock around with is gay.'

Brett forced a laugh. 'Alex! You're having a laugh, Gramps. He's worse than me. He'd have a different bird every night of the week if he could.'

'That's what I thought. Come outside, speak to Ricky in front of everyone, boy. You know what your Nan's like.'

Having no option other than to front it out, Brett grabbed Ricky in a playful headlock. 'What's all this I hear 'bout you calling my mate an iron?'

'Didn't call him an iron. That's what you un-crease clothes with. But he does like boys and not girls, don't he, Brett? I heard your conversations on the phone.'

Brett burst out in false laughter while trying to think of a good answer. 'You nutter!' He ruffled Ricky's hair. 'It's 'cause he's talking from home that Alex pretends he's stayed round lads' houses. His mum worries 'cause he got a girl pregnant a few years ago. She's also a serial earwigger like you.'

'Right, now we know poor Alex ain't Larry Grayson in disguise, can we get back to stuffing our faces, please. I saved you some meat, Brett. I'll cook it fresh for ya,' said Kenny.

Vera nudged her sister. 'Never smoke without fire. Bet the lad is partial to a bit of John Thomas.'

'Can't you say something nice? Just for once,' snapped Nelly.

Beau grinned as his brother sat down next to him. 'You had a good night then?'

'Yeah. Was wild. What's Ricky like, eh? We'll have to remember to never talk about anything naughty in front of him again. He's got ears like a bat.'

Beau locked eyes with his twin. 'He kind of had a point though. I always said to you when we were in Compton that I thought Alex batted for the other side.'

'But he don't, Beau. He's a serial-shagger, of birds. I swear he is. I'd hardly be knocking about with him if he liked blokes, would I?' The palms of Brett's hands were beginning to sweat, he partly wondered what his family would say if they knew that one of his best pals batted for the other side, but he decided that now wasn't the time to test the waters.

Beau smiled. 'Nah. Course not. So what was the bird's name you ended up with last night?'

'Mandy. I quite liked her, actually. I'm taking her out for a meal tonight.'

'Jesus! It must be serious. Let me know if you need a best man.'

Brett laughed. 'I ain't getting hitched until I'm at least thirty. I like partying too much.'

Donny smiled as Levi tried to walk, fell on his bum and was helped to his feet by Rocky. It felt weird being called 'Granddad'. He was only thirty-six, his youngest child only nine. He was ever so proud of Beau though. He and his father had been very dubious when Beau had married Jolene, had thought at sixteen Beau was far too young to know what he wanted. But Beau had proved them both wrong. He was settled, happy and a brilliant dad. Much better than Donny himself had been when the twins had been born.

Kenny opened two bottles of lager, handed one to Donny and sat next to him. Even though they only lived a few doors away, they didn't see that much of one another any more. Shal did. She still worked up at the Stapleford Abbotts nursery with Donny. 'How's tricks?' asked Kenny.

'All right. Can't complain.' It had taken a while for Donny to forgive his father for poaching his sons, but at last he could see that it benefited the boys. No way would he have been able to pay Beau and Brett what they were currently earning. Like most fathers, Donny wanted his sons to stand on their own two feet and live opulent lifestyles, and if being part-owners of the garden centre enabled that, then so be it.

'How's Tansey doing?' Kenny had little time for his son's long-term fiancée. She ruled Donny with a rod of iron. What Tansey wanted, Tansey got. Donny was currently forking out on another mortgage as Tansey had wanted to move out to Blackmore. She'd taken Harry and Bluebell to live with her and left Alfie with Donny. Kenny had been livid about that. How could a mother not want her own flesh and blood just because the lad had behavioural issues?

'Tansey's good. We've been getting on really well lately. So much so, I'm thinking of selling up in Dark Lane, Dad. Tans and I spoke about it only yesterday and the time feels right for a new start. Living together, like.' Donny and Tansey had never actually split up, were still a functioning couple in many ways, but they'd not lived in the same house since shortly after Jamie's funeral.

'What about Alfie? And Brett?'

'Alfie'll live with us, obviously. As for Brett, I'll help him find a nice flat or something. He's rarely in these days anyway.' Tansey had mellowed with her attitude towards his twins, probably because she had hardly seen them for years. No way would she want either of them living with her again. Getting away from Dark Lane and all the memories it held had been the right move for Tansey, had helped her heal somewhat over Jamie's untimely death.

Kenny rolled his eyes, but said nothing. What was the point? Tansey wore the trousers. End of.

Jolene yanked her phone out of her handbag. It was Beau ringing, yet again. This time she answered it, just in case one of her sons had had an accident. 'I'm fine, Beau. You know I'm fine 'cause I'm with my mum and Sonny. I'll be home when I get home, OK? I gotta turn my phone off now 'cause you keeping on ringing has run my bloody battery down.'

'Hello. Sorry to disturb you, but I had to come over and say how sorry I was to hear about your sister, Tammy. She was a lovely girl. I was gutted when I heard what had happened. I'm Jimmy by the way, Jimmy Dean.'

Jolene locked eyes with the bloke her sister had apparently set her sights on. His dark wavy hair was in no particular style, his suit looked too big for him, but he had big blue eyes and a gorgeous smile. 'Thanks. My family were devastated. Still are. How did you know Tammy?'

As Jimmy began to explain, a thin woman with a headscarf and a baby in her arms walked up next to him. Jimmy put an arm around her shoulder and looked at her lovingly. 'This is my wife, Alicia, and our daughter, Demi. Alicia, this is Jolene, Tammy's sister, who I was telling you about earlier.'

When Alicia smiled at her warmly and started to speak, Jolene suddenly felt weird. It was clear Alicia must be ill. She had no hair. Was it that making her feel uncomfortable? Or was it that Jimmy had planned to take Tammy on a date shortly before she'd died and she'd known nothing about it? 'It's been lovely to meet you, but I must go outside, ring my husband back. He's been driving me mad, ringing me – probably thinks I'm in labour.'

Once outside the marquee, Jolene took deep breaths to calm herself. When they'd lived in Kent, she'd known all the gossip. Who was who. Who fancied who. Who was dating who. But now she knew nothing.

For the first time since moving, Jolene cursed her father. If he hadn't uprooted them to the arse-end of nowhere, she wouldn't feel like a stranger amongst her own community. But even more importantly, Tammy would still be alive.

Even though Brett had already guessed Aidan wasn't short of a few bob, he was still taken aback when he reached his destination. There was a security guard manning the gates and the cars inside put his four-year-old BMW 3 Series to shame. There were Bentleys, Lamborghinis, Porsches, plus Aidan's Rolls-Royce. The apartments looked luxurious, even from the outside, and newly built. Brett's heart beat rapidly as he pressed the buzzer and heard Aidan's sexy Irish tone telling him to 'Come up.'

The lift was one of the poshest Brett had ever been inside. It played music and Marvin Gaye was crooning 'Sexual Healing', which seemed crazily appropriate.

Once inside Aidan's penthouse apartment Brett was even more amazed. It was modern, light and airy. The decor was white, the views spectacular, and Brett couldn't stop looking at the massive snake that lay still in a tank. 'Is that real?'

Aidan laughed. 'Of course it's real.' He opened the tank, took out the boa constrictor, wrapped it around his shoulders and lovingly stroked its head. 'Alvin, meet Brett. You two will hopefully be seeing lots of one another in the future.'

Wanting a man-to-man chat with Ricky, Kenny suggested they go to the pub for a pint. Kenny wasn't the most articulate of men when it came to talking about sensitive subjects, but tried to put his point across as gently as he could.

Ricky was perplexed. 'So, I can dance in a class, but not in a restaurant?'

'Yeah. You can also dance when you're amongst family and stuff. But not out in public, like last night. Reason being, the world is full of arseholes, lad. Nasty, idiotic ones. And you ain't no idiot. Which is why I've gotten us a joint gym membership. We're gonna train together, lose some timber and put on some muscle. And if you do what I ask you to, guess what I'm gonna do for you?'

Ricky took a sip of his Guinness. He loved holding a pint glass. It made him feel like a mature man. 'Allow me more than one pint?'

'Nah. Better than that. How would you like to learn how to drive?'

'Really!' Ricky's eyes shone with delight.

'Yeah. How 'bout I take you over the cardrome next

weekend? Give you your first lesson. I'll even buy you a car if you pass your test.'

Ricky's current TV obsession was *One Foot in the Grave* and he had a habit of picking up his favourite characters' antics. He smacked his head against his forehead. 'I don't believe it!'

Kenny chuckled. 'Well, best you do, 'cause it's happening, Big Man.'

If a smile could light up a boozer, Ricky's would have. 'I love you, Kenny. And can you please always call me Big Man in future? 'Cause I ain't little any more, am I?'

Beau was fuming as he waited for Jolene to get home. She'd turned her phone off, so he'd been ringing Sonny, but even he hadn't answered his phone. His foul mood hadn't stopped him performing his fatherly duties, mind. The boys had been bathed, put in their clean pyjamas and were now tucked up in bed.

'Don't let her mug you off. Turn your phone off after work tomorrow and we'll go out. Give her a taste of her own medicine,' was Brett's advice earlier.

Flicking through the Sky channels, Beau finally heard Sonny's motor pull up. Brett was right. Kicking off at Jolene would only make him look like a saddo. Giving her the same treatment back was the answer.

'All right? Sorry me phone died. How was your day? Did the boys have fun?'

'Yeah. All good. Boys are soundo. I'm bang into this film. OK if we catch up properly tomorrow?'

A bit taken aback by Beau's laid-back attitude, Jolene

sat down and put her arms around him. 'I weren't lying. My battery really was on the blink.'

Beau forced a smile. 'I never said you was.'

The restaurant Aidan took Brett to was a regular haunt of his in the heart of Mayfair. The staff greeted him warmly and he was led to the privacy of the corner table he requested. Minutes later, the waiter returned with a bottle of champagne in an ice bucket. 'From Marco. He's not here this evening but insisted that this is on the house.'

Wondering who Marco was, but not wanting to pry, Brett asked Aidan how his meetings had gone earlier.

'Good. But I was knackered. We didn't get much sleep last night, did we? I sure needed that siesta this afternoon. How was your day?'

Brett explained he'd had to stop on the way home and have a kip in the back of his car as he was scared he'd have an accident.

'Wise move. Always better to be safe than sorry. Did you find out what happened to the pal you were with?'

'Yeah. I rung him. He's OK. He got a cab home.'

'Did you tell him about me? Or should I say *us*?'

'Nah. I like to keep my personal business to meself. It's the way I've been raised.'

Aidan smiled. 'I'm the same. We're going to roll along just fine me and you.' He lifted his glass. 'To us.'

Having never properly dated before, Brett did his best to hide his nerves. Aidan had an aura, was extremely funny as well as handsome, and as the evening wore on, Brett found himself relaxing more and more in his company.

'It's weird, you know, as soon as we met last night. I could tell you'd been a bad boy and didn't come from a normal family either. Call it Irish instinct,' grinned Aidan.

Brett laughed. It was actually quite eerie how much they had in common. Aidan was the oldest of five siblings and had been raised by his alcoholic mother, who'd turned to booze after his father had received a long stretch in prison. Aidan had also been expelled from school and been in trouble with the law as a kid. 'So, do your family know you're gay? I could never tell mine. They wouldn't understand, would more than likely disown me.'

'You'd be surprised. They might have an inkling, especially your twin. I got chucked out the church choir at the age of thirteen for wanking off Patrick O'Feeny. The priest caught me with Patrick's cock in my hand.'

'You're winding me up, surely?'

Aidan held his palms up. 'Honest to God. My mother's boozing went off the Richter scale after that little episode. She went into full "Hail Mary" mode and dragged me off to confession. She then insisted that none of it was my fault, Patrick was a pervert and I was never to mention his name or what had happened ever again.'

'This is so funny.' Brett was cracking up. 'How old was Patrick?'

'Fifteen. I never spoke to him again. He wasn't a looker. Gave a good blowjob though.'

Brett held his sides. Aidan had the most mischievous smile and eyes he'd ever seen and the way he delivered a funny story was an art. He could easily be a comedian. 'Surely your mum must know you're gay now though, if you ain't ever took a bird home?'

Aidan shrugged. 'The only one I've ever come out to is my sister, Aisling. We're really close. She's a lesbian, a total fucking lunatic, but I love her to bits.'

'Don't your family get on your case, like? Wanting to know when you're gonna settle down and bang out kids? I know mine will in time.'

'I've got a son.'

'Nah. You're having me on.'

Aidan smiled. 'I'm not. Conor's eleven now, lives in Ireland with his mum, but I get to see him regularly. He also keeps the family off my case, if you get me gist.'

'Wow! That's mental.'

Aidan winked. 'Mental, but cool. You stick with me, kiddo, and I'll teach you plenty. Living life in the fast lane certainly beats crawling along in the slow.'

CHAPTER NINE

Jonathan St Clement kissed his mother on the forehead. 'You need me to pick you up anything while I'm in Lakeside?'

'No, love. What time will you be home?' Jonathan had only been living with her again since his father died five months ago. He'd had problems over the years though, mainly with alcohol, and although he was currently in recovery and went regularly to his meetings, Geraldine still couldn't help worrying about him.

'I'll be home this afternoon. Then I'll probably go to a meeting tonight.'

'Good boy,' smiled Geraldine. 'I'll cook you a nice lamb stew.' Jonathan was her only child. She and her husband had been unable to have children of their own, so had adopted Jonathan as a baby. He was their chosen one, the apple of their eyes, a wonderful son.

Jonathan left the four-bedroomed bungalow and politely nodded to a couple of neighbours attending to their front lawn. His mother lived in a quiet cul-de-sac, thankfully. He hadn't come back here by choice, mind. He'd lost everything else that mattered to him. His lovely girlfriend, her two sons whom he'd adored, his sobriety, his driving licence . . . Then he'd woken up one day with no money left. It had all run out, just as his luck had when he'd been forced to work for those horrible bastards the Daley brothers again. He'd once made acid tabs for them in the late eighties. A pair of monsters, in more ways than one.

Hearing a car toot loudly, Jonathan nigh on jumped out of his skin. He'd been living on his nerves ever since Baz Daley had sauntered into the same AA meeting as him the Saturday before last. It couldn't have been a coincidence, they must have tracked him down. But how, he didn't know. Nobody knew his real name, he never gave that out. He wasn't even registered as living with his mother, or with a local GP. He went by Johnny at his AA meetings, and in the *trade* he'd only ever been known as The Scientist.

As Johnny weaved his way through the backstreets to get to the nearest train station, he breathed a sigh of relief when he arrived at his destination unscathed. He knew exactly what those Daley brothers were capable of. They'd been waiting outside his ex-girlfriend's flat one day in Thurrock, bundled him into the back of a car and insisted he make their ecstasy pills. He'd tried to politely refuse, but had quickly changed his tune when they'd threatened to kill his other half and her two sons. That's when he'd started drinking again.

The platform at Chadwell Heath was busy, the train came quickly, and Jonathan managed to get one of the last available seats. He'd decided to travel in rush hour for a reason: there were lots of other people around. He'd also decided to take the long route. He'd get off at Mile End, jump on the District Line to Upminster, then get the bus to Lakeside. That way he could be sure he wasn't being followed; he couldn't afford that to happen, today of all days.

Getting in touch with Kenny Bond and Tony Abbott had taken a lot of guts. But in the end, he had no choice. As they would soon find out.

Kenny Bond was counting out the dosh he unwillingly needed to pay out. When he heard his wife's footsteps, he quickly shoved it under a cushion.

'You got any money lying about, Ken?' asked Sharon.

Having had to scrape together fifteen grand at short notice, for once, Kenny didn't. 'Nah. Why? What d'ya need?'

'Five hundred. It's for Sherry, not me. I'm meeting her for lunch now, so you'll have to take Ricky shopping with you.'

'I can't. I've got lots of stuff to do today. As for Sherry, she ain't paid back the last monkey she borrowed. Or the grand before that. She's taking the piss, Shal. Tell her to ask her in-laws for once.' Kenny's relationship with his only daughter had been tainted somewhat when his affair with Abigail had come to light. Sherry had understandably sided with Sharon. But what angered Kenny was, even though Shal had forgiven him, Sherry hadn't. She rarely came to family get-togethers anymore, preferred seeing Sharon alone. Yet she'd been happy enough to allow him to pay her bastard mortgage.

'You're in a fine mood today,' snapped Sharon. 'Don't be such a tight-arse. You know Sherry's no good with money, and it's not like we can't afford it.'

'Our daughter is a thirty-three-year-old woman. She ain't our problem any more, and if we keep bailing her out when she and that tosser she married overspend, they'll never learn.'

'Don't speak about Andy like that. He's the father of our grandchildren.'

'He's also a short-arse loser, just like his father. I told her at the time, she could do better.'

'With who? She could hardly afford to be choosy. Poor cow inherited your wonky nose and curly ginger hair. Stick your money up your arsehole, Kenny. I'll borrow it off Donny instead.'

When Sharon stormed out, slamming the front door behind her, Kenny punched the wall, hurting his knuckles in the process. Thanks to The Scientist, he was stressed up to the eyeballs and the day had barely started.

Ginger Daley flexed his muscles while studying himself in the mirror. He'd spent most of yesterday down the gym and was thrilled with the results of those higher-dosage steroids. They'd bulked him up good and proper.

'You ready?' asked Baz. There were four AA meetings around Havering, Barking and Dagenham today. One lunchtime, three this evening and they planned to go to them all.

Ginger grinned, the diamond in his gold tooth glistening in the sunlight peeping through the blinds. 'I got a good feeling about today. We're gonna get some answers, I can feel it in me bones.'

'Let's hope so. What's in the sports bag?'

'Just a few tools, in case we need 'em.'

'Like what?'

'Tell you on the way. I need to stop at a supermarket, grab a cooked chicken. Hank Marvin, I am.'

Tony Abbott was gobsmacked when his old partner in crime turned up with Ricky in the motor. He pulled Kenny to one side. 'We can't take the boy with us. I promised that arsehole we'd be on our own.' The Scientist had given specific instructions that they were to meet him in the Marks & Spencer's café in Lakeside at 11 a.m. and they *must* be alone.

'It's fine. Ricky wants to go shopping anyway. He'll be mooching around while we're with the other geezer. Looks less conspicuous if we've got him with us an' all.'

'No, Ken. It's more noticeable. Two grown men and a mongol lad. What planet you on?'

'Don't fucking call him that,' spat Kenny. 'Ricky's coming and that's the end of it. Ridiculous meeting place anyway. You should never have agreed to it.'

The journey took around fifteen minutes and, once parked up near Debenhams, Kenny gave Ricky strict orders. 'Don't be chatting to no strangers and don't be doing your usual, buying stuff that don't fit ya, 'cause we won't be coming back 'ere anytime soon. Try whatever on and make sure you check your phone regularly. If anything unexpected happens, like our phones ain't working or you get lost, just ask someone to point you in the direction of Debenhams and meet me back here at half twelve, OK?'

Ricky rolled his eyes. 'I'm not silly, Kenny.'

'I know you're not.' Kenny took a wad of money out of his back pocket and rolled off two fifty-pound notes. 'Treat yourself, but you're not to tell Sharon I left you on your own ere, OK? If she asks, I shopped with ya.'

'OK.'

'Sorry for calling him a mongol, mate. I didn't mean it derogatory. It's just the wording we used back in the day, ya know. He's a good lad.'

'I know. Come on, let's head straight to Marks. Put your dosh in my bag, so we just hand him the one. I don't care what he tells us though, Tone, he won't get another penny out of us. Understood?'

Kenny hated lateness and had just started losing his patience when The Scientist walked towards them. He looked different, skinnier with a goatee beard and longer hair. He reminded Kenny of someone, but he couldn't think who.

The Scientist sat down. 'Thanks for meeting me. I didn't want to get in touch, but I was left with little choice. Did you bring any cash?'

Kenny leaned forward and pushed the bag across the table. Eric Clapton. That's who the cheeky bastard looked like. 'There's thirty in there. Twenty-four that we owe ya and call the other six a goodwill gesture. There ain't no more where that came from though. Neither do we take kindly to being blackmailed. You got an actual name, have ya?'

'Johnny. Me name's Johnny. And you don't understand. I'm no blackmailer. I didn't want to do this. You were OK guys, fair to work for.'

'Why'd you leave us in the lurch then?' growled Tony.

'I didn't want to do that either. They put it on me, insisted I make the pills for them. I couldn't say no in the end, was too afraid of what might happen. I'd worked with 'em back in the eighties, you see, used to make all the acid tabs for 'em. They're nutters, threatened to do away with my girlfriend and her two kids if I didn't play ball. What was I meant to do?'

'Who are they?' Kenny and Tony asked in unison.

'Mad Ginger Daley and his brother, Baz. They were the Mr Bigs behind that Southend firm and they weren't best pleased when they lost their stash and all their boys got banged up. They knew it weren't them the police were gunning for. They'd only been up and running just over a month.'

'You never mentioned our names to them, did ya?' Tony wanted clarification. He knew exactly who Ginger and Baz Daley were. Two nasty, violent nutjobs who'd caused a lot of mayhem in their hometown, Basildon, back in the day. They weren't exactly classed as big shots, due to their idiotic behaviour that regularly saw them banged up. They were trouble though and neither he nor Kenny needed that. Neither did they need any other bastards knowing that they'd been the ones responsible for that dodgy batch of pills. Killing a load of youngsters, even though it was accidental, was hardly something to be proud of and it was something Tony would rather nobody else ever knew.

'I'm no snitch. But they offered me money for your names. Big money,' exaggerated Jonathan.

Kenny folded his arms. 'You don't owe me and him

anything. So, why didn't you snap their hands off for a big pay day?'

'Because I don't trust them. That's why I wanted to see you two. If you can come up with enough cash, I'll disappear abroad, start again somewhere. They turned up at my AA meeting last week – well, Baz did. I managed to grab a lift home with some stranger, and I've been looking over my shoulder ever since.'

'I never knew you was an alkie. No wonder they knew you were making the pills. What did you do? Prop up bars in shithole boozers, bragging to all and sundry?' enquired Kenny.

'Of course not! I gave up drinking in my mid-twenties, have been sober for over eighteen years now.' Jonathan didn't bother explaining about the couple of times he'd fallen off the wagon. Kenny, in particular, wasn't the type to understand or care.

Tony glanced around to make sure nobody was looking. 'This is confusing. Those pills in the haul the police plastered all over the TV had our stamp on them.' When Johnny had been working for them, he'd come up with the 'Crown' stamp to differentiate their pills from others on the market, such as the 'Dennis the Menace' type and the 'Doves'.

'They made me put the crown on them,' explained Jonathan. 'They knew they were the ones currently selling like hotcakes.'

'But how did they know to approach you in the first place?' spat Kenny.

'I never told a soul what I was up to, I swear. Listen, there aren't many blokes like me and Phil around, you know, that have good knowledge of chemicals and what to do with them. I think it was just a hunch at the time, that I could be useful to them. As I already told you, I worked for them in the eighties, making acid tabs. They knew I was capable, so to speak.'

'Nah. I ain't buying this,' spat Kenny. He turned to Tony. 'Firstly, he's telling us he's been offered big money for our names. Then in the next breath, they employed him on a fucking hunch. Next he'll be telling us they're related to Arthur Daley. He's got the dosh we owed him, plus a drink on top. That's the end of it.'

With time to kill until they had to meet Ricky, Tony led Kenny to a quiet restaurant he knew. Both of them could do with a stiff drink to help decipher what had been said.

Kenny downed his whisky chaser in one. 'Tell me more about the Daley brothers. Obviously, I've heard of 'em, but they've always sounded like a pair of dickheads to me.'

'They caused mayhem in and around Basildon back in the eighties. Off their faces, running around smashing boozers up until they got paid pub protection. That type of thing.'

'Didn't they get banged up for that?'

'Yeah. Both did bird. They also shot a geezer once in a kebab shop at point-blank range, but got away with it as people were too scared to grass. A silly row over some bird. The geezer lived an' all. Whoever pulled the trigger obviously weren't a very good shot.'

'They sound like a right pair of morons.'

'They are. But you don't wanna be on the wrong side of 'em. I did hear Baz spent time in rehab to get clean.

131

Dunno if he still is. Drunk, drugged-up or sober, they ain't the full ticket.'

'I still think Johnny's making a lot up. That's if his name is bleedin' Johnny. You know what these addicts are like. He's probably a gambler as well as a drunk and got himself into a load of debt he wants us to get him out of,' suggested Kenny.

'I'm not so sure. If you hadn't stomped off, you'd have heard what else he had to say. He seemed pretty legit to me.'

'Yeah, course he did. That's 'cause he senses you're a soft touch and he's trying to wangle two hundred grand out of us. You know our world as well as I do, Tone. It's the luck of the draw who gets caught and who don't. As long as there's no grassing involved, it's fair play. Mugs, mate. They gotta be, to get their factory turned over within a month or so. Anyone with half a brain would've taken a break until all those deaths died down. Their greed is what got 'em caught. Sod all to do with us.'

Tony sighed 'I know you're right. But I don't want our names cropping up. Not after all this time.'

'And they won't. He's walking away with thirty grand, that slippery bastard. He can go plenty of places and set himself up for life with that type of dosh. He can probably buy himself a bar and a fucking mansion in Bangkok.'

'I told him I'd speak to you, see if we can rustle up another few grand between us and ring him back. Shall I not bother?'

'Never give in to blackmail, mate. Because, believe me, if you do, the blackmailer will always find a reason to ask for more. I should know. I got lumbered with Karen.'

Tony chuckled. 'I'll blank him then, in that case.'

As Kenny began jovially explaining Karen's demands to Tony, he had no idea that he had massively underestimated the Daley brothers and the damage they could cause.

After an enjoyable lunch with her daughter and grand-children in a restaurant in Billericay, Sharon decided to stop at the Stapleford Abbotts nursery on the way home. Her mate Tina had been her rock when Kenny's affair had come to light and Sharon could think of nobody better to vent the anger she was feeling today. She might even take Tina out for dinner. Let that tight-arse she'd married cook himself something for once.

'Ooh, I'm glad you popped in. Been dying to ring you since Saturday, but wasn't sure if Kenny would be in earshot,' grinned Tina.

'Don't talk to me about that tosser. Fancy a bite to eat and a bottle of wine after work? My treat, of course.'

'Oh dear! You've had a row, ain't ya?' laughed Tina. 'Don't worry; you can chew my ear off. But, let me tell you my news first. You know I told you I was gonna try out that new over-thirty's night in Chigwell?'

'Yeah. Let me guess. You met the man of your dreams again?' chuckled Sharon. Tina had no luck with men. She also had a habit of falling in love at the drop of a hat, only to find out shortly afterwards that they weren't 'The One' but yet another wrong un.

'No!' Tina's grin broadened across her face. 'But I did bump into your ex, Ray. Ooh, he's so good-looking, Shal. You were mad not to try him out for a bit of rumpy-pumpy, if nothing else.'

'Oh, God!' Sharon rolled her eyes. Ray Weller had taken her out once when she'd split up with Kenny. Sharon had made a total show of herself by getting drunk and falling arse over tit in a posh London restaurant, yet it hadn't put Ray off. He'd still wanted to date her. 'You didn't mention me, did you?'

'No. But he did. He still likes you, Shal. I can tell.'

Sharon looked quizzically at her friend, 'Don't be so silly. I've not seen him for years. We never even bleedin' kissed or anything.'

'Well, more fool you. Honest, Shal. He was all suited and booted, looked as fit as a fiddle. When I go there again, you'll have to come with me.'

'No, thank you,' chuckled Sharon. 'You can have Ray. You've got my permission.'

Beau was the first to arrive at the Indian restaurant in Upminster. He'd had a rubbish day up at the garden centre. Usually Brett, Gramps or Ricky would already be there waiting for him, but today he was on his own with just a couple of staff members. The day had really dragged.

Beau took his phone out of his pocket. Normally, he'd ring Jolene a few times while at work, but Brett's words were still firmly ringing in his mind and today he'd resisted. He smirked as he read her last text message asking if he was OK. Then he decided to put her out of her misery and call her. 'Sorry I didn't get back to you earlier. Had a bit of a manic day. You and the boys all right?' Beau would have continued the conversation had Brett not arrived. 'I gotta go now. Me battery's a bit low, so I'll see ya later. No need to wait up for me.'

'Right, let's switch our phones off,' ordered Brett. He didn't want Aidan calling him while he was out with his brother.

'Done,' smiled Beau, watching as his brother sank into his seat. 'No idea how you're more clued up on women than me, but your playing it cool advice is deffo working. So, how'd it go with Randy Mandy?'

'Who?'

'Your bird. Mandy.' Beau raised an eyebrow, and wondered how Brett could care so little about his date – this was something he needed to learn.

'Sorry, I thought you said Andy. Yeah, we had a great night. She took me to one of her favourite restaurants in Mayfair.'

'Mayfair! That must've cost you a few bob.'

'It was on the house,' lied Brett. 'Mandy was owed a favour by the owner, which is why she took me there.'

'What is she, a brass?' laughed Beau.

Knowing he would trip up on his own lies if he didn't keep to a certain story, Brett had decided earlier that he'd describe Aidan and just tweak the obvious. He wished he'd have thought of a more exotic name than Mandy though. 'She's some high-flying businesswoman. You wanna see her gaff, Beau. Out of this world.'

'What does her father do? Gotta be some Daddy's-little-rich-girl. How old is she?'

'If I tell you, it's just between us, OK? Only I bumped into Gramps on the way out of Dark Lane and he said he might pop down for a beer. I think he's had a row with Nan.'

'Sod Gramps. I wanna know more about Randy Mandy,' grinned Beau.

'She's twenty-nine.'

Beau burst out laughing. 'That's well old. You're a dark horse, you are, Brett Bond.'

Having already checked out two meetings, Mad Ginger and Baz finally struck gold at the third as they spotted Johnny, AKA The Scientist, get out of a minicab, then glance around before entering the small dowdy-looking hall.

'Bingo!' grinned Ginger, handing Baz the binoculars. He'd parked a short distance away outside some flats in case they were spotted.

'What happens now?' asked Baz.

'We wait until the meeting's over, then bundle him in the back. It'll be dark by then. I want you to drive while I get the answers out the bastard.' Ginger could feel the excitement starting to pulse through his veins. He'd been waiting a long time to get his hands on the Scientist and the bastard was finally going to get what was coming to him.

'I'm on a ban,' Baz reminded his brother.

'I know that, ya numpty. You're still capable of driving five minutes up the road though, surely?'

'What's in that?' Baz gestured towards the Head sports bag.

'Nothing too terrible.'

'Tell me,' ordered Baz. It was unusual for Ginger to keep things from him, and he was starting to think his brother had brought a shooter with them.

Ginger grabbed his sports bag and unzipped it. Inside was some thick rope, a pair of socks, gaffer tape and a large bottle of Jack Daniels. 'See. Nothing too untoward.'

'Why the booze?'

'Can you think of a better way of getting info out of a recovering alcoholic?' Ginger tried to supress a grin; tonight was going to be fun.

Overcome by another terrible shooting pain, Jolene clung on to the table to support herself. She'd tried ringing Beau, but his phone was switched off.

'What matter, Mum?' enquired Rocky. Jolene looked into her son's little eyes full of concern; she was trying to keep calm and not worry the lad but it was getting harder by the second.

It was at that precise moment Jolene's waters decided to break. 'Go get Nan, Rocky. Quickly,' she panicked. 'Tell her the baby's coming. Go on. Run!'

Unusually for Beau and Brett, the evening turned out to be a boozy one. 'Oh, leave it out, Gramps,' laughed Beau as the waiter placed three large brandies and Baileys on their table. 'Me and Brett have gotta open up tomorrow. What you trying to do to us?'

'I can't drink no more. I had too much at that bloody party on Saturday. Won't be doing that again in a hurry,' replied Brett.

'Drink up, the pair of ya. How often do we have a lad's night out, eh? It makes a nice change.' replied Kenny.

'Let's switch our phones back on. See if Jolene's been ringing me more than Randy Mandy has you.' Beau grinned as his phone began bleeping like mad. 'I got loads of answerphone messages,' he crowed, waving his new Motorola StarTAC in the air.

As Beau listened to the messages, the colour drained from his face. 'Shit! I gotta go. Me baby's coming.'

Having managed to get parked nearer to the hall, it was Ginger who spotted the same minicab that had dropped off their prey earlier, return. 'You wait 'ere.'

Baz nervously glanced in the interior mirror. The meeting would be over soon. 'What did you say to him?' Baz asked, aware that the cab had driven off.

'I paid him the fare, told him Johnny had to leave early. I also found out where he lives, I think. Geezer picked him up on a corner of a turning off Whalebone Lane.'

'Great stuff. Hang on, nope, yeah. I think they're coming out. The door's just opened.'

Ginger put the hood up on his black sweatshirt and stood back against the wall, opposite his motor, with a lit cigarette. It was dark now, not pitch black, but dark enough.

Ginger heard him before he saw him, thanks to his irritating squeaky voice. He glanced to the side, then darted forward and grabbed his prey by the arm.

'Johnny. You OK, Johnny?' shouted a man as his fellow AA member was shoved in the back of a dark Range Rover.

'Shout out you're fine, else I'll slit your throat,' hissed Ginger. I know where you live an' all. Off Whalebone Lane. Very helpful, your cabbie,' he added.

Absolutely petrified, Jonathan somehow managed to bellow, 'I'm fine,' before being driven away at top speed.

The dozen or so AA members looked at one another in bewilderment until Doreen piped up. 'Who has a phone?

We need to call the police. Those men who have driven Johnny away are the ones who threatened to kill me in the YMCA car park on Saturday. Did anyone get the number plate?'

Beau sat in the passenger seat, his head in his hands. 'I ain't taking no more advice from you. What was I thinking? I knew she was ready to drop any minute.'

'Don't blame your brother,' replied Kenny. 'Jolene's got her parents with her and we're 'ere now. Just say the battery conked out in your phone, like we said. End of drama.'

Brett pulled up outside the A&E Department of Oldchurch Hospital. 'You two get out and I'll come and find yous once I've parked up.'

Beau was in a frenzy. He'd had a couple of abusive answerphone messages from Evie. Plus Bobby and Sonny had left him some stern-sounding words. 'Don't forget. We was out on a work thing. Don't yous dare put your foot in it or Evie'll have my guts for garters. You stay with Brett, Gramps,' ordered Beau, leaping out the motor.

Brett found a parking space. 'He's gonna end up like Dad has with Tansey.'

'Tell me about it. He's always been obsessed with that bloody girl. As I said to you earlier, you stay single for as long as you can. Anything with tits and a fanny gives you nothing but grief, boy.'

Brett smirked.

His hands and feet tied up with rope and a sock stuffed in his mouth, Jonathan St Clement could barely breathe let alone speak.

'Where am I driving to?' asked Baz.

'I dunno. Somewhere quiet. If you do a right at the next lights, it'll take us towards Hainault Forest. Go that way.' Ginger opened the bottle of JD, took the sock out his prey's mouth and forced him to drink the sour-tasting liquid.

Coughing and spluttering, Jonathan twisted his head from side to side. He needed to stay sober to have any chance of survival with this pair of lunatics.

'Drink it,' Ginger shoved the bottle so hard in Jonathan's mouth it dislodged a crown, which he promptly swallowed. 'I wanna know who you were working for before us. Who was it, eh? Who stitched us up?' bellowed Ginger, before removing the bottle.

Having been sober for a while, the effect of the Jack Daniels had knocked Jonathan for six, even though a lot of it had ended up saturating his jumper. 'There were two blokes, but I only met one of 'em. Kenny. His name was Kenny,' slurred Jonathan. Tony had been nice to him earlier. Whereas Kenny was an arsehole.

'Kenny who?' shrieked Ginger, tilting the bottle to force more down his throat.

'Where shall I drive now?' asked Baz. The country park car park was shut.

'I dunno. Find somewhere quiet,' snapped Ginger. He slapped his prey round both sides of his face. 'Kenny who?' It was at that very second he heard sirens, lots of sirens.

'Shit! It ain't the Old Bill, is it?' panicked Baz. The sirens were getting louder.

'Do a left,' ordered Baz. There was an industrial estate on the left.

140

Within thirty seconds flat, the Range Rover was surrounded by a police van and three cars and forced to screech to a halt. 'Fuck! Shit! Bollocks!' Ginger cursed as he frantically tried to undo the rope.

Ginger and Baz were pulled out of the vehicle simultaneously. 'I am arresting you on suspicion of abduction. You do not have to say anything. But, it may harm your defence if you do not mention when questioned something you later rely on in court. Anything you do say may be given in evidence . . .'

After running into the hospital, then around the corridors like a madman, Beau finally bumped into Sonny. 'Where is she? Is she OK? I'm so sorry. I never go out, and me phone went dead.'

Sonny smiled. 'She's more than all right. Come see for yourself.'

''Ere he is. The wanderer. Call yourself a good husband and father? Don't make me laugh,' spat Evie.

'Don't have a go at him, Mum. Beau works hard to provide, and he never goes out alone,' said Sonny. He was quick to defend his brother-in-law and Beau was grateful for the ally.

'Well, he was tonight,' argued Evie.

Bobby squeezed his wife's hand. 'Not now, love. Let's not spoil the special moment.'

'Baby's been born and Nan says it's massive,' announced Bobby-Joe.

'Born! Nah. It can't be. Not already. I can't have missed it.'

'Well, you have,' spat Evie. 'A beautiful daughter you've got. Not that you deserve her.'

Beau felt relieved, overjoyed. 'I wanna see her. Where is she?'

'You can't go in there now. Nurses are in there, cleaning Jolene up,' replied Evie.

Beau sat down. He couldn't believe Jolene had given birth so quickly. She hadn't with the boys. 'A little girl,' he mumbled. He was thrilled, as he knew how much his wife had wanted a daughter.

A midwife appeared and Beau stood up. 'Is Jolene OK? I'm her husband. Can I see her and the baby now?'

'Yes. You have a truly gorgeous little girl,' smiled the Irish midwife.

Bobby grabbed his wife's arm. 'No, Evie. You sit back down. You've already seen the baby. Let 'em have five minutes on their own, then we'll all go in. I can't wait to meet her, hold her. A granddaughter, eh?' beamed Bobby.

Beau followed the midwife. Jolene was sitting up with a bundle in her arms. 'I'm so sorry, darling. Me phone went dead and . . .'

'Forget it. It's not important now. Come and say hello to our daughter, Beau. She's absolutely gorgeous.'

Beau had never seen such a big baby. Neither could he believe her mop of dark curly hair. His daughter was a vision of beauty. It was mad to think he and Jolene had created such perfection. 'Oh, Jo, I love her to bits. She's something else. She's even got a quiff like Elvis.'

'I know. She's perfect. We're so lucky.'

Beau kissed Jolene on the forehead. She looked so happy and radiant. 'Have you decided on her name yet?'

After Tammy had died, Jolene had vowed if and when she had a daughter, she'd name her after her beloved twin.

But as the years had passed, that no longer seemed the right thing to do. Her mum wasn't keen on the idea either. There was only *one* Tammy, after all. 'I have thought of a name and it so suits her. It ain't none that we spoke about though.'

'Go on then. Surprise me,' said Beau. 'I can't stop looking at her, Jo. She's so unlike other babies. She looks older, like she's been 'ere before somehow.'

Jolene chuckled. 'She deffo has an older face. A Traveller through and through she looks. Which is why I want to call her Romany. Do you like it?'

Beau shrugged. 'Yeah. Can I hold her?'

Beau stared in awe at the child in his arms. 'Look at you. You're such a cracker. Welcome to the big wide world, Romany Bond. Me and your mum love you so much already.'

Jolene couldn't stop smiling. It had been an awful pregnancy, but worth it in the end. Her dad had driven her to the hospital, and she'd literally given birth within half an hour of arriving. 'I love you, Beau Bond. That's our little family complete now. We gonna be so happy, the five of us. I just know we are.'

Unfortunately for Jolene, those sentiments were not destined to last.

Jonathan St Clement woke up in the early hours of the morning in the same hospital as Jolene. The police had tried to question him last night and would be coming back today. Even though Jonathan's head felt muzzy, his brain was in overdrive. He needed to get out of here, out of this situation, swiftly. Testifying against Ginger and Baz was a definite no-go.

Silently thanking his Higher Power that he'd been given the intuition to hide the thirty grand at his mother's house before attending the AA meeting, Jonathan reached out for the jug of water next to him. He'd planned to call Tony again today to beg for some more money, but he wouldn't bother doing that now. He was in a no-win situation. If he stayed in England, it would only be a matter of time before the Daley brothers or their cronies caught up with him again. And if he was to grass Kenny and Tony up, he was sure that Kenny, in particular, would want retribution. Had he given Kenny's full name to Ginger? It was all a bit of a blur, but he was sure he hadn't mentioned Tony. Or had he?

Jonathan swung his legs over the bed and peeked through the curtain. He wasn't in a ward. He was in a cubicle in A&E by the looks of it.

Seeing a nurse walking by, Jonathan ducked back inside. He'd wait until the coast was clear, then leave. Then he'd grab his money and jump on the first available flight to Spain.

CHAPTER TEN

I don't know when I first realized that I was gay. And I often wondered why I was and Beau wasn't. Was I born that way? Or was it because of what had happened to me as a child with Noncy Eric? Surely if anything, that would put me off men though? So many unanswered questions. But the one thing I soon became sure of was I was head over heels for a bloke I knew little about.

I finally let him do the deed. I didn't enjoy it, probably never would. But Aidan meant the world to me and I wanted to give my all to him.

We fell into a routine. Aidan would cook for me and I'd stay over at his. But he was often away, regularly went back to Ireland, and I was never invited. Neither was I allowed to meet any of his friends or family.

Within weeks of meeting him, Aidan hadn't just fucked me physically; he'd also fucked with my mind. He was on my nut the moment I woke, throughout the day, and before I went to sleep.

Kimberley Chambers

Was that what love was? I had nobody to ask. But what I did know was I didn't believe all the money he had came via the antiques business he supposedly ran with his father. I wasn't stupid. Gramps was a ducker and diver. Therefore, I knew a dodgy bastard when I spotted one.

I tried to talk to Aidan, but he wouldn't open up to me. So I threatened to call it a day. For the sake of me own sanity, if I'm honest.

That was the moment things seemed to shift in our relationship. For better and for worse . . .

Spring 1997

Singing along to R Kelly's 'I Believe I Can Fly', Brett Bond swung his motor inside the gates that led to Aidan's apartment. He was excited about today, yet a tad nervous at the same time. This was a big thing for him. A first.

Aidan greeted his young lover with a passionate kiss. 'You smell gorgeous.'

'Calvin Klein. Me latest bargain off the shoplifter who comes up the garden centre,' grinned Beau. 'Is she still coming?'

'She sure is,' Aidan glanced at his watch. 'We've still got time for a quickie though.'

Brett stopped in his tracks as Aidan went to lead him to the bedroom. 'Nah. Not now. I don't wanna look all dishevelled.'

'Oh, come on. I'm horny.' Aidan unzipped his trousers, flopped his penis out and smirked. 'Get on your knees and suck it.'

Sinking to his knees, Brett happily obliged.

*

'What you looking so happy about?' Beau asked as he handed Gramps his egg-and-bacon sandwich. It had been his idea to open a food van on their premises. Beau had employed two sisters, Travellers from a site in Wickford. Their grub was top drawer.

Kenny pushed the *Basildon Echo* towards his grandson. 'I was chuckling at those two on the front page. Meant to be faces an' all. Silly pair of bastards.'

Kenny had been reading about Mad Ginger Daley and his brother Baz. Two years the pair of 'em had got, for an argument with a cab driver over a fare. They hadn't even given the cabbie much of a dig, just a few slaps by the sounds of it. It was what they'd said that appealed to Kenny's humour the most. 'Do you know who we are?' Turned out the cabbie was Asian, had only been in England for six months, had no clue who they were and had a camera inside his vehicle. Hence their arrest for racially abusing the man.

Still grinning from ear to ear, Kenny sipped his coffee. He hadn't heard another word from The Scientist, AKA Johnny, since the day he and Tony had met him at Lakeside. Neither had he heard a dickie-bird from the Daley brothers. Instinct had told him they were imbeciles and, as usual, he'd been proved right. He'd done a bit of asking around at the time and found out they were on remand in HMP Brixton. Apparently, their bail had been cut short for issuing death threats to some old dear, the pair of numpties.

Beau pushed the newspaper across the table. 'Dunno what you found so funny about that. They look what they are. Pair of retards.'

Kenny laughed out loud. The Daley brothers would never win a beauty competition, that was for sure. Thick as two short planks – and ugly. What a combination.

Sharon Bond felt miserable as she drove towards Chigwell. She and Kenny hadn't been on holiday for ages, were meant to be going to Santorini in a fortnight, but her mum wasn't well again, and Sharon was worried sick that the dreaded cancer had returned.

As the news presenter banged on about England winning the Eurovision Song Contest, Sharon turned off the radio. She had about as much interest in Katrina and the Waves as they had in her.

Cursing as the car in front nicked the only available parking space, Sharon sighed as she hunted for another. She wasn't even looking forward to having a spend-up in Debra's, wouldn't have bothered except she desperately needed new outfits for her upcoming holiday. She'd put on weight too, and was bound to look like crap in whatever she tried on. Her mum's refusal to go to the doctor was a big factor in that. Why did she have to stuff her face when upset and worried? Didn't normal people feel less hungry and lose bloody weight?

A valued customer, Sharon was greeted warmly by Debra.

Sharon explained her issue. 'I'm so short, if I shove on half a stone, I go up a whole size. I'm looking for long summer dresses, preferably ones that hide the fat.'

'You're not fat,' insisted Debra. 'How's Kenny and the kids?'

About to reply, Sharon heard a distinctive voice chirp, 'Morning, ladies. Got anything new in for me since last week?' Sharon knew who it was without having to have a sneaky look around. That nosy old battleaxe who used to live next door to her parents, the one who'd thought she'd seen Kenny over Epping Forest with a little boy.

Not only did Pat Grainger have the voice of a cheese grater, she also had the eyes of a hawk. 'Sharon! I thought that was you. How's your mum now? I heard she had breast cancer and was living back in England. I saw your Kenny at the hospital last week with his young son and I was going to ask him, but the boy's mum and Kenny were bickering, so I didn't like to interfere.'

'Mum's fine, thanks,' snapped an increasingly agitated Sharon. 'And Christ knows who you keep getting my Kenny mixed up with, but I can assure you it ain't him, Pat. Last time I saw you in here, you swore blind you'd seen Kenny in Epping Forest with a young boy. Well, it weren't him, 'cause I bloody asked him and he didn't have a clue what I was talking about. Therefore, there must be some Kenny lookalike who lives your way. It's either that or you're trying to shit-stir.'

Debra glanced worriedly at her staff before attempting to lead Sharon towards the changing room. She could feel a storm brewing and didn't want all her fabulous frocks going flying.

'How very dare you!' retaliated Pat. 'I might be a lot of things, but a troublemaker I am most certainly not. I know exactly who I saw and what I heard, Sharon. My husband and I were in the next cubicle, so we couldn't fail to hear, especially when they started arguing. The woman's name is Karen and the boy's called Jake.

Jake had a head injury – looked and sounded quite bad actually. There was a gap in between the curtains, which is how I could hear and see so clearly. Kenny arrived around half past seven and was still there when we left, which was gone ten. Last Wednesday evening this was, at Whipps Cross.'

Sharon felt her heart palpitate with electric speed. It was last Wednesday Kenny had disappeared all evening, hadn't arrived home until after midnight. He'd told her he was meeting up with an old pal to discuss a bit of business and she'd thought nothing of it, even though it was a spur-of-the-moment thing.

Pat Grainger smirked as Sharon suddenly followed Debra towards the changing room. She wasn't silly, had seen the colour drain from Sharon's face at the end of their little altercation. Good! That family had always thought themselves better than the rest of the neighbours, especially that arrogant sod, Charlie Saunders.

'Take no notice,' Debra whispered in Sharon's ear. 'I'm sure she only pops in to gossip.'

Sharon could feel her hands trembling as she snatched the dresses handed to her. 'I didn't argue any more, but only 'cause I was in your shop. Off her rocker the woman is. Kenny was at home with me last Wednesday. All evening,' she bluffed.

Debra smiled, patted Sharon's shoulder reassuringly, then felt sorry for the woman as she turned away. Reason being, she'd heard via another source that Kenny had a secret son. But unlike Pat Grainger, Debra valued her life and didn't have a death wish.

*

'Finally! We thought you were never coming.' Aidan hugged the only sibling he had any time for, then led her into the kitchen, a strong arm around her shoulders. 'Aisling, meet the man I've told you lots about. Brett, meet my nutty sister who I've told you as little about as possible, as I don't want you to go off me.'

Brett chuckled as Aisling grabbed him in a warm embrace. She was very pretty, in a geezer-bird way and dressed like a rock chick.

'Aidan, go get my cases out the taxi and pay the driver while I become acquainted with this handsome man of yours.'

'Cases! You're only meant to be here one night.'

'Fell out with me flatmate. Long story, but I need a place to stay for a while and it's not as though you haven't got the room, is it?'

Aidan playfully rolled his eyes. Ever since she was born, Aisling had the capability of winding him round her little finger. She was now twenty-one, yet he still fell for it every time. Even though she was a fecker and a terrible influence on him.

'Bye, ladies. Thanks again.' Sharon's false smile slid off her face as she marched towards her car with the three dresses she looked like an elephant in. Her head had been all over the place but sod the poxy cost. Her pride was more important.

Sharon slouched inside her E-Class Mercedes and took a series of deep breaths to calm herself. Kenny having a young son? Never in a million years would he ever mug her off like that. *If* it was him up at Whipps Cross hospital, then there had to be a credible explanation. But if that were the case, why would he bloody lie about his where-abouts?

'All right. Sorry I'm a bit late. Traffic was murder,' explained Kenny Bond as he rounded the corner of the ward, his eyes settling on his son lying flat out in the hospital bed. 'How's he been today?'

'He was awake and quite chirpy until they took him down for his brain scan. We haven't got the results yet, but the doctor seemed pleased with his progress. I need to shoot home, have a shower and a change of clothes. Can you stay up here until I get back? I don't want him waking up to find nobody's here, bless him,' replied Karen.

Kenny could hardly say no. Jake was his flesh and blood, after all. 'How long d'ya reckon you'll be?'

'I don't know. Depends how the trains are running. Least you can do, seeing as his accident was all your bloody fault in the first place.'

Kenny's jaw twitched. 'I'll wait 'ere, OK? But don't start blaming me again. We've been through all that.'

When Karen left the ward, Kenny held the hand of his four-year-old son. Jake had suffered a swelling on the brain after flying off the motorized ride-on tractor Kenny had bought him a couple of weeks ago for his birthday. He'd been transferred from Whipps Cross to Great Ormond Street and was currently linked up to a ventilator to help with his oxygen supply. 'Encephalitis' was the doctor's diagnosis, but thankfully Jake's memory was fine. He was chatting as normal when awake.

Kenny smiled as Jake stirred and clenched his hand.

He'd seen Jake every day since the accident, the most time he'd ever spent with his son.

'Hello, Daddy. How long you been here?'

'Not long. Your mum's popped home for a bit, but she'll be back soon. In the meantime, you're stuck with me. So, how you feeling?'

'Happy. 'Cause I seeing you more, Dad.'

Kenny felt a wave of emotion wash over him. With his brown hair and big brown eyes, it was uncanny how much Jake looked like Donny had at a similar age. Kenny knew he could never be a proper dad to the lad, which caused a pain deep in his chest. Jake was a good kid, deserved so much better. But Kenny's priorities would always lie with his *own* family. Especially Sharon . . .

'What d'ya reckon? Told you she was off her head,' Aidan said warmly.

Brett turned around. Dressed in tight faded jeans, a ripped grey off-the-shoulder top and knee-length black leather high-heeled boots, Aisling was dancing around the gay bar she'd dragged them to in Greenwich as though she owned the joint. 'I think she's great fun, Aidan. So pretty too. I can't believe she's taller than you and nearly as tall as me though.'

'She's not. Five eight she is. But Aisling loves to stand out in a crowd, so wears fecking four-inch heels,' replied Aidan.

Brett laughed. It was so good to finally meet a family member of the man he'd fallen in love with. It was also good to go to a gay bar together, something they'd never done before. Usually, they just went out for the odd meal or stayed at home. 'I'm loving it, this bar, the music, us being 'ere together. Can we do stuff like this more often?'

Aidan smiled. 'We'll see.'

'You know that night we met, at Stan's weirdo do? 'Cause me and you got drunk, I thought you were gonna be a right party-animal. Not that I wanted you to be, 'cause I'm not. But it's good to get out and let our hair down now and again, don't ya think? Among our kind of people, obviously.'

Aidan stroked Brett's cheek. He'd vowed never to love again, not after what happened with Finlay. However, it was still too soon to introduce Brett to any associates, take him to the wild parties, let him into his real world.

'There ain't half a lot of people looking at us. D'ya reckon it's 'cause we're new in 'ere?'

'No. It's because we're special.' Aidan grabbed Brett's hand. 'Come on, let's dance, give 'em something to salivate over.'

Sharon drove straight to the nursery and begged Donny to let Tina leave early as she needed her help with something.

'Whatever's wrong?' Tina asked, as her friend drove out the gates like a madwoman.

Sharon pulled into the car park of the Top Oak, which seemed apt. This was the pub that nutter Abigail had turned up at while she was having a family lunch to inform her that Kenny was cheating on her the last time he'd been caught.

'I'm fuming. Fucking livid,' Sharon spat, before explaining all that had happened. 'He ain't at the garden centre like he said he would be today either. I didn't bother asking Beau 'cause, knowing Kenny, he would've clued him up. Thick as thieves them pair. I rung Ricky instead, didn't ask outright, but Ricky let on that Kenny's not been there since early this morning.'

Seeing tears in Sharon's eyes, Tina gave her a big hug. She'd been shit on from a great height by her own husband who'd cheated on her with a neighbour, of all people. 'Listen, once a cheat, always a cheat. That's usually my motto, but not your Kenny. He adores you and he's probably one of the only men I've ever met that I could vouch for not to make the same mistake twice. And no way would he be getting another woman pregnant. Not after the Abigail turn-out, surely? How old did that evil old witch say the boy was, Shal?'

'I dunno. I was in that much shock, I didn't ask. How I held it together, I'll never know. I'm still shaking now. Look.' Sharon held out her hands.

'Right, let's go inside the pub and get you a brandy to calm yourself down. Then we'll think up a plan. The truth will out itself, mate. It always does.'

Desperate to check any missed calls, Kenny dashed towards the car park. Three and a half hours that bitch had taken to return. On a more positive note, the doctor had given him good news. The swelling was reducing nicely on Jake's brain. It had felt odd spending hours alone with his secret son, but nice at the same time. Kenny had told the boy some stories, even played a couple of silly games with him.

Hoping that Sharon hadn't been trying to get hold of him, Kenny took his phone out the glove compartment. Not one missed call or message. He'd got away with disappearing all afternoon. Result!

Back at the Top Oak, Sharon was still agitated. 'I really don't need this shit, Tina. I got enough on my plate worrying about me mum not being well. Shall I just have it out with Kenny? Confront him tonight?'

'No. You don't want him to know you're onto him, Shal. Not that I'm saying he's done anything wrong, of course.'

Sharon took another sip of brandy. 'You know, the more I think of it, the more I reckon his Sunday-morning routine don't seem right. He never used to visit his nan and grand-dad's grave every single Sunday. He used to go quite a lot, but not like he does now. And he leaves home virtually the same time every week and gets home roughly the same time. Shall we follow him tomorrow? In your car?'

'Too dangerous. Say he spots us?'

'True. He used to be paranoid about being followed an' all. Still has a habit of checking his mirrors all the time. If only we could find out where the bastard goes without actually following him ourselves?'

'That's it! That's the answer! My cousin Steve hired this little firm to follow someone. Steve said they were brilliant, used mainly motorbikes. They got all the info Steve needed.'

'What happened?'

'I dunno. Steve's as dodgy as the day is long, so I didn't like to ask him. Shall I give him a call?'

Sharon hesitated, she couldn't help the knowing feeling that her whole life was about to blow up in smoke and she wouldn't be able to do a single thing about it. 'Yeah. Ring him now.'

Brett Bond was a bit boozy, yet buzzing. Today had been spontaneous, brilliant, and he'd loved being out with Aidan in a lively environment. Brett wasn't daft. He knew himself and Aidan made a striking couple, but he'd still got off clocking so many other gay men watching their every move. As for Aisling, she was a breath of fresh air. They'd have been sat in some boring restaurant, or Aidan would've cooked for him if it hadn't been for Aisling. 'I bloody love your sister.'

Aidan rolled his eyes yet was secretly chuffed. 'I knew you two would get on. No talking about me behind my back though,' he winked.

'I want you to meet my family. Especially Beau. It's Sonny's stag night tomorrow. Why don't you come? I'll just say you're my pal.'

'A load of drunken blokes discussing tits and pussy really isn't my thing, Brett. And it will look odd. There is an age gap between us, remember?'

'No. It ain't gonna be like that. It's just family and friends going on a bit of a pub crawl. I get what you're saying though. How 'bout the wedding reception? It's a gypsy wedding. It's being held on the land where Beau lives next Saturday. We'll take Aisling and get her to bring a mate,' gabbled Brett excitedly. 'Say yes. Go on. Please? I know you'll enjoy it.'

Aidan looked at Brett with a twinkle in his eye. 'I went to a gypsy wedding once and it was pure entertainment from start to finish. Especially when they all started fighting.'

'Is that a yes then?'

'Perhaps,' winked Aidan.

'There you are! Me and Ricky were about to send out a search party,' said Kenny as Sharon walked through the door of their home. 'Your phone ain't on.'

Sharon forced a smile. 'Sorry. Me battery was running low earlier. Turned it off and forget to turn the bleedin' thing back on. I've been out with Tina. She wanted a bit of advice.'

'About a geezer, I bet?'

'No. Since her husband cheated on her, Tina doesn't actually like men very much.'

'Did ya see that, Ricky? Sharon's in a good mood. Her mouth just snapped like a crocodile's.'

Ricky burst out laughing. 'Sorry, Sharon.'

Knowing she needed to act more normal, Sharon put her hand on her forehead. 'No. I'm sorry, love. I've got the headache from hell. You two don't mind if I don't come out with ya tonight, d'ya?'

'Oh, babe. That ain't like you,' Kenny sympathized.

Sharon tried not to flinch as Kenny wrapped his strong arms around her. 'I'm fine, honest. Just not been sleeping well 'cause of worrying about Mum.'

'Kenny, can we go to the gym? Lucy might be there,' Ricky grinned, flexing his muscles. Ricky had taken to the gym like a duck to water, especially the weight training. He also had an eye for the girls down there.

Kenny chuckled. 'Saturday night ain't for training, Big Man. It's for drinking and eating only. You name the place and I'll take you there.'

'Jailhouse Rock. I wanna see that nice Elvis again.'

'You can sod right off,' replied Kenny. 'Anywhere but there. I think we're barred anyway.'

'Harvester then,' giggled Ricky, knowing full well Kenny hated it there too.

As soon as Kenny left, Sharon switched her phone back on. There was no word from Tina. She had spoken to her cousin earlier, mind. He'd said he'd speak to the blokes involved and get back to her asap.

She was about to pop out to see how her mum was when her mobile finally rang. 'Tina. Well?'

Sharon listened intently, then ended the call. It was on. It wasn't going to be cheap. She also had to meet a bloke in the week to give him all the details on Kenny's daily routine, a photo and a deposit.

Feeling like a criminal herself, Sharon suddenly needed a glass of wine. She very much doubted that Kenny was capable of such a cover-up. But if he was, and he'd embarrassed her and her children by bringing a bastard child who was related to them into their lives, Sharon wouldn't just want to divorce him. She'd want him dead.

CHAPTER ELEVEN

Having a daughter brought out a madly protective side of me. One I hadn't known existed. Romany was precious, a gift from God, and as her dad, I vowed it was my duty to ensure no bastard ever harmed a hair on her pretty head. Don't get me wrong, I was protective of me boys too. But they'd grown up to fight their own battles, just like me and Brett had. It was different for girls, weren't it? Well, I thought it was anyway.

Jolene was as happy as a pig in shit. Business at the garden centre was booming and I was the most content I'd ever been. Not every day was wine and roses, mind. Me and Jolene still had our head-to-heads. I wanted to move off her parents' land. She didn't. I wanted our sons to go to mainstream school. She didn't. I wanted regular sex. She didn't – and so forth. But overall, we were happy. No money worries. Three healthy gorgeous chavvies. We were blessed.

But then something happened. Something totally irreversible. It was at that point, my life, hopes and dreams started to unravel. In one horrible twisty fucking mess.

'What you doing? You laughing at your dadda? Are ya?' Beau playfully tickled his daughter's belly. 'Who's a daddy's girl then?'

'She ain't a parrot, Beau, and I wish you'd stop talking to her in that stupid voice. It's so unmanly. She'll grow up to think you're a dinlo,' mocked Jolene.

Beau took no notice of his misery guts of a wife and continued to use the same voice. 'Dadda loves you. Yes, he does,' he smiled, tickling Romany once more. She'd recently turned six months. A beautiful, chubby bundle of fun, with a mass of curly dark hair, she literally melted Beau's heart. She rarely cried, loved to laugh and had already started to crawl, the clever girl.

Jolene picked up her beloved daughter. Most Sundays, weather permitting, she and her mum would take flowers over to Tammy's grave, then go shopping down Dagenham Sunday market. Romany would accompany them, all dressed up to the nines in her luxurious Silver Cross pram. 'Where you going with the boys? Round your granddad's?'

'Nah. I'm taking 'em to see me mum. Not seen her for over a month, so it'll be nice to catch up. We gonna eat out as usual later?'

Even though Evie spoke to him more civilly these days, Beau knew deep down she still loathed him, and the feeling was mutual. That's why he liked taking Jolene and the kids out to eat on a Sunday afternoon. To get away from her horrid witch of a mother scrutinizing every bite he swallowed, while probably hoping he would choke.

161

'Yeah. We'll go carvery. Right, I'll be off then. Say goodbye to your dad,' Jolene said, waving Romany's chubby arm.

'See you later, me two princesses. Love yous. Oh, and don't forget I got your brother's stag drinks later. Your turn to babysit tonight.'

Still reeling from the previous day's events, Sharon decided to call Kenny's bluff. 'I was thinking, I might come with you today to the cemetery. We could pop down Petticoat Lane afterwards. I used to love going there when I was a teenager.'

Kenny nigh on choked on his sausage. 'I'm not going over the cemetery today. I gotta shoot down to Braintree to meet a geezer.'

'What for?'

'Business. We're thinking of stocking pet food and products at the garden centre. This geezer is a supplier.'

'Oh, that sounds a good idea,' smiled Sharon, even though she was inwardly seething. 'Why don't you take Ricky with you for a ride? I'm gonna pop down to see Mum for a couple of hours.'

'Wanna come for a ride, Ricky?' Kenny asked through gritted teeth.

'Yeah. OK.'

Kenny smiled at Sharon. 'Sorted, babe.' He'd drop Ricky off at the gym and bribe him to keep his trap shut in exchange for fifty quid.

'All right. How you doing? Feels like ages since I've seen you.' Beau gave his mum a hug. She looked much younger

162

than thirty-eight, and was ever so glamorous. Her long blonde hair shone, nails were immaculate, make-up perfect and she was always clad in designer clobber. Totally unrecognizable as the same woman who'd raised him as a child. She'd been a skinny, lanky-haired, spotty junkie back then. Well, that's what his dad and Gramps reckoned anyway.

Lori smiled. 'Look at you. As handsome as ever. And look at you two.' Lori crouched down. 'You look like your mum,' she said, giving Rocky a cuddle. 'And you look just like your dad,' she told Levi. 'Now, who wants some lemonade and chocolate cake?'

'We not hungry. Come, Levi, we play in garden,' Rocky replied. He wasn't really sure of Nanny Lori. She was weird in comparison to Nanny Evie.

'I'll bleedin have some. I'm starvin',' chuckled Beau. 'Where's Hope?' Hope was his three-year-old half-sister.

'Carl's taken her to visit his mum. They won't be long. His mum's in a care home now. Her dementia got too much for her to live alone any more.'

'That's a shame.' Beau had never met the woman, but maturity had taught him it was always best to be polite and have empathy. Not that he'd had much of that when he'd drowned Jamie in the swimming pool, but he'd changed since then. Jolene had been his saviour. Marriage and fatherhood had turned him into a much better person.

'I sometimes worry Carl's going to end up like his mother. He's brain dead half the time. Let's hope he doesn't forget to bring Hope home with him,' laughed Lori. Carl Scantlin had been the lead singer of a punk band in the late seventies. He then went on to become a music producer and set up his own record company. Carl was wealthy, had a beautiful home in Epping where they both now lived. Lori had first met Carl in rehab, and he'd been the making of her ever since.

Beau sipped his coffee. 'Are you and Carl still, I dunno how to put it and I don't mean sexually, but like, d'ya still cuddle, kiss and say love you to one another and stuff like that regularly?'

'Every day. We always say how we were lost souls when we met and kind of saved one another's lives too. We still say the Serenity Prayer together every morning and evening. We do everything together really. Well, apart from all my beauty treatments. Then again, Carl does love a massage and a spa day lately,' laughed Lori.

'That's well cool. I'm chuffed you met Carl, Mum.'

Lori squeezed her son's hand. She hadn't been impressed with Jolene from the start, but had never told Beau that. What her handsome son saw in that girl, she would never know. 'I know I was a terrible mother when you were growing up, love. But I'm always here for you now. If there is ever anything on your mind that you feel you can't talk to Brett or your dad about, I want to be that person you turn to. Not that I'm trying to make up for what I put you and Brett through. The past is the past and cannot be changed. Therapy has taught me to accept that. I don't want to pry, but I take it you've asked me such a question because of your own relationship?'

Beau ran his hands through his gelled-back hair. It felt weird opening up to anybody, but his mother had such a soothing voice and way about her, she could have been a therapist herself. 'I dunno, Mum,' he sighed. 'We are happy. But she don't show me much love any more. I still feel the same about her as the day we met. She's my world, like. But she kind of pushes me away if I try to cuddle her or hold her hand or do anything romantic. It just makes me feel like she's gone off me a bit. I bet you think I'm a right soppy prick, blurting all this out. Please never tell anyone, not even Carl. I suppose I just wished that things were how they used to be between us in the beginning. Do you think it's 'cause of the kids?'

Hating Jolene more than ever, Lori chose to be diplomatic rather than brutal. 'I honestly don't know, darling. It might be because she's run off her feet with the children. Or, it could be that she's worried a kiss and cuddle could lead to sex and she's too tired. Or it could possibly be – and this makes me feel terrible saying it – but it could be you are feeling this way because I let you down as a child. Once your dad left and I spiralled out of control, I doubt I ever hugged you and your brother or showed you any love. Then you were taken to live with Tansey and she never showed you any love either. Perhaps you're craving female affection because you never had any as a child, if that makes sense? But I'm sure Jolene loves you very much in her own way. She must do.'

Unusually for Beau, his eyes brimmed with tears. He leapt off the chair and gave his mother the most genuine and tightest hug he'd ever given her. 'You are brilliant, d'ya know that? Any problems I have in future, I'm coming straight to you. Brett's busy with his own life now and Dad don't understand. As for Gramps, he'd just call me a pussy if I said to him what I've said to you.'

Lori was elated. Not only did she love Beau dearly, but she also felt her presence as a mother was needed at long last. But most importantly, she could keep an eye on Beau. Only, if Jolene ever hurt her beloved boy, she'd destroy her. Literally.

'How you feeling? I bought you some of them creamy yoghurts. I also made you a pot of homemade soup and picked you up a crusty loaf to go with it,' said Sharon. Her mum had been complaining of bad stomach pains. Well, not exactly complaining, as she seemed happy to suffer them, rather than go get a diagnosis. She'd lost a lot of weight too, had no appetite and had started to look frail.

'She was up again in the night and hardly ate a morsel yesterday,' Charlie told his daughter.

'Shut up, snitch,' snapped Maggie. 'I'd rather die than lose me hair and go through that bastard chemo again, so there you go.'

'Make us a cuppa, love,' Maggie said to Sharon.

About to put the kettle on, Sharon's phone rang. It was Tina. 'What! When?'

'What's up?' Maggie asked her daughter.

'I gotta shoot out, but I'll come back later. Tina needs me,' lied Sharon. She could hardly tell her the truth, could she?

Ricky was easily bribed, the A13 was clear, so Kenny decided to make a brief stop at the cemetery on the way to Great Ormond Street. He did often visit his grandparents' grave, usually brought Aunt Nelly with him, but didn't come as often as he told Sharon he did.

A chilly April day, Kenny put up the collar of his tan Crombie. His grandfather had been his inspiration as a child. A ducker and diver, Gramps had never been short of a few bob. Kenny had never met his real father, didn't even know his name. Whoever he was, his mother hated him for reasons only she knew.

Reaching the double grave, Kenny crouched to his haunches. He'd lived with his grandparents from an early age. Good people they were. Old school. 'What am I gonna do? Got meself into a right pickle with Jake, ain't I? The more time I'm spending with him, the more I want him to be in my life an' all. "Never lie to the woman you marry, boy. 'Cause the truth will always out itself in the end." That's what you always drummed into me, Gramps. Why the hell didn't I listen? And tell Shal that time I had the chance to?'

Kenny fell silent, then said. 'Send me a sign or something. Please.'

At that precise moment, a large black crow decided to take a crap. It landed straight on top of Kenny's head.

'Bye, Hope. See ya, Carl. Rocky, Levi, say goodbye and give your nan a kiss,' ordered Beau.

Levi obeyed his father. Rocky did not.

'Give Nan a kiss,' repeated Beau.

'Don't want to.'

'Leave him, Beau. You were worse than that when you were little,' chuckled Lori. 'When will we see you again? Don't leave it so long next time. I rarely see you or Brett these days. I miss my boys.'

'If it weren't for working together, I'd hardly see Brett either. He stays over his bird's a lot. In Canary Wharf.'

'What's she like?'

Beau shrugged. 'No idea. Never met her. I tell you what, me brother-in-law's getting married next Saturday. The nice one, Sonny. It's a shotgun wedding, so they ain't holding it in a church. It's being held on the land where I live. Why don't you, Carl and Hope come? I would love yous to be there.'

'Oh, I don't know, love,' replied Lori. 'I'd feel awkward, attending someone's wedding we don't know.'

'But you're me mum. She won't be there – Tansey. She never comes to family events. You won't even have to sit near Dad. I'll put you between me and Brett on our table. Please come? I'm always surrounded by Jolene's family and never me own.'

Lori looked at Carl, who nodded in approval. She no longer got anxious at such events, not like she had at Beau's wedding. She would also be able to see how Jolene behaved towards her son, give her more of an idea of what was going on. She was very astute like that.

'Well?' prompted Beau.

Lori smiled. She was inwardly thrilled that Beau wanted her sitting next to him on his table. She'd be getting one over on Donny as well. 'OK. We'd love to come.'

Beau grinned. 'Brilliant.'

Sharon pulled up in the Halfway House car park. Tina had come with her. The people who'd agreed to follow Kenny had got in touch with Tina's cousin. They were too busy in the week to meet her, so asked if they could do so today.

Sharon glanced around. 'Did they say what car they'll be driving?'

'No. They asked Steve what car we'd be in, so I said yours. Did you write all the info down I told you to?'

'Yeah.' They'd wanted to know the obvious: Kenny's address, what car he drove, where he worked etc. She was also to make notes of regular movements, especially any warranting suspicion. 'I'm gonna tell 'em to follow him on a Sunday. Having said that, he took Ricky with him this morning, so he can't be up to no good today.'

'I doubt you're gonna get bad news, Shal. But say the worst happens. What would you do?'

'I dunno. Probably kill him.'

Kenny was livid as he drove back towards Essex. He'd arrived at the hospital and not even got to see Jake because Karen's family were there. She hadn't even bothered ringing him to warn him, or tell him to take the day off, the heartless bitch.

Feeling the need to unburden the truth of his messed-up life, Kenny debated whether to pop into his aunt's on the way home. He'd gone to live with Aunt Nelly after his grandparents had died. She'd been far more of a mother to him over the years than his own had. But Aunt Nelly loved Sharon, and he couldn't bear to see her look at him with such disappointment. Not today anyway. He felt fragile enough as it was, with his youngest son being in hospital. A son he could never be there for the way he bloody should be. His guilt ran deep.

Kenny rang Ricky, got no answer, so headed towards the gym. Kenny didn't suffer fools gladly, or posers, which is why he'd chosen a gym out North Ockendon way. It was old school and so were most of the punters. It was also owned by an old prison pal of his, Harry the Headcase.

'All right, Arthur? Where's the boy?'

Harry's brother Arthur ran the gym. A sixty-four-year-old ex-boxer. 'I think we might have a bit of romance on our hands, Ken.' Arthur chuckled. 'My granddaughter met Ricky earlier and it were like love at first sight. They've popped down the shop, wanted an ice-cream.'

Slightly alarmed, Kenny forced a laugh. 'I can't leave him alone for five minutes, the slippery little sod.'

'Our Candy's a handful too. Her parents have only just moved out this way. They were living in Barking before. She's got learning difficulties, God bless her. She's a lovely kid and took a right shine to your Ricky, and him to her. I even caught 'em having a little grope.'

Kenny forced another laugh, then excused himself to make a business call. He rang Ricky repeatedly. He knew the lad was sexually aware as not only had Sharon caught him banging one out a couple of times, but she'd also found porn mags under his mattress and Harry Monk all over his sheets.

'They should be back soon. They've been gone ages,' Arthur said reassuringly.

Kenny's jaw started to twitch. Ricky had better of acted the gentleman, because Harry the Headcase was a lunatic. His nickname spoke volumes. Any bastard who upset him or his loved ones, he tended to shoot.

Expecting a man in a car, Sharon was somewhat astounded when a beast of a motorbike roared up beside her car, then a large woman clad in black leather lifted up the visor on her crash helmet and with a fist like Mike Tyson, smashed it against her driver's side window. 'Who's Tina?' she asked in a strong northern accent.

'I am. We were recommended to you by my cousin. He's used you in the past. We're not 'ere for me though.' Even Tina was a bit taken aback as she pointed to her mucker. 'We're here for Sharon. She'll explain all.'

Sharon didn't go into any particular detail other than the basics. She then handed over the deposit and notes she'd written. 'He's not silly, the man you'll be following. He's got eyes like a hawk,' she warned.

The woman chuckled. A big hearty laugh. 'Don't you worry, pet. I run this set-up and my boys have never been found out yet.' She glanced at the notes Sharon had given her. 'Kenny Bond's luck's about to run out, believe me. I'll be in touch once I've busted him. Laters, ladies.'

Sharon sat open-mouthed as the woman roared off on the Kawasaki Ninja, with her large deposit. She hadn't even given her a contact number.

CHAPTER TWELVE

'What the hell!' Evie Tamplin sat bolt upright. She'd had a restless night's sleep, must've only dozed off an hour ago. Now dawn had broken and she'd been awoken by a loud tapping sound.

Bobby was snoring like a pig, so Evie decided to investigate herself. There it was again. Tap, tap, tap. It was coming from the kitchen.

As Evie neared the sink, she realized the noise was coming from outside her lovely home. She yanked back the curtain and screamed when she saw it.

Dressed only in his Y-fronts, Bobby dashed out the bedroom. 'What you done? Whatever's wrong?'

'Dordi! Look, dordi!' screeched Evie, pointing to the culprit.

'It's a bird, Evie,' snapped Bobby.

'No! It's the biggest magpie I've ever seen and it's trying to get in 'ere. I told you Sonny ain't happy and I had a bad feeling about this wedding, didn't I? One for sorrow, two for joy, Bobby.'

'I'm going back to bed.'

Evie flung open the window and the horrid creature flew away. She knew it was a sign though. She didn't like that Mary-Ann. Not since she'd trapped her Sonny by getting herself in the family way. Today was going to be a disaster. She could feel it in her bones.

'Oi! Where do you two think you're going?' asked Beau Bond. He'd emerged from the shower just in time to catch his sons creeping outside.

Dressed in matching Thomas the Tank Engine pyjamas, it had been Rocky who'd put their Timberland boots and coats on. 'Bouncy castle. We wanna play on it.'

'No. The bouncy castle's for later. After the wedding.'

Rocky put his hands on his hips. 'Can't we just have a little bounce?'

'No. 'Cause it ain't been blown up properly yet,' fibbed Beau. 'You don't wanna break it, do ya?'

'No. Mustn't break it,' mumbled Levi.

Beau ruffled his sons' hair. 'Good lads. Now let's take them coats and boots off before your mum spots 'em.'

A split second later, Jolene walked out of the bedroom with Romany in her arms. 'Where yous going?'

'Nowhere. Rocky was just teaching Levi how to get dressed. Between 'em they've made a right cock-up of their laces. You might have to unknot these, Jo.'

Jolene bent down. 'Oh, I meant to tell ya, I'll have to sit apart from you after the wedding. Mum wants me to sit with Johnny and Billy on her and Dad's table.'

'You what! You're having a laugh, ain't ya?'

'Oh, come on, Beau. It's not a massive issue, is it? And you'd planned to sit with your mum anyway.'

173

'Yeah. It is an issue actually. I'm your husband, yet you would rather sit with them two morons, who not only can't stand me, they refused to set foot on this land any more, 'cause me, you and our kids live on it.'

'Don't be such a drama king. It's unmanly and don't suit ya. Mum wants me to build bridges with me brothers. It's no big deal. I tell you what, the boys can sit with you and your family for the meal. Everyone'll be up dancing later on anyway.'

'D'ya know what, you're reminding me more and more of Tansey as each day passes. She was the same. As soon as she got the daughter she'd craved, she couldn't give a flying fuck about my old man or her boys. She palmed Harry and Alfie off on me father all the time.'

'How dare you accuse me of not caring about my sons. You shitcunt. Get out. Go on! Piss off to work.'

'I'll go to work when I'm bastard well ready,' seethed Beau. He looked at his boys who suddenly seemed unsure about what to do with themselves. 'She's caused all this, your mother. She knew by making you sit with Johnny and Billy it would cause an argument between us. If anyone's a shitcunt, it's that witch, not me.'

Romany screamed as her mother dumped her on the sofa and lunged at her father.

'Stop it, Mum. Leave Dad alone,' shrieked Rocky.

Upset, Levi toddled into his bedroom.

'I wish I'd never married you. Mum was right. I should've married a Traveller,' screamed Jolene, aiming punches at Beau's face.

As a punch connected just below his left eye, Beau managed to grab her wrists. He'd never seen Jolene like

174

this before. 'Stop it. You're frightening the kids.' Part of him wanted to clump her one back, but he managed to keep his temper in check. Men didn't hit women; Gramps had taught him that.

Snapping back to reality, Jolene sank to her haunches and hugged Rocky. 'Mummy's sorry. Levi, where are you?' she yelled, before picking up Romany and holding her close to her chest.

Beau grabbed his boots, jacket and Range Rover keys. He'd rather get wet feet than spend another second near Jolene right now. They'd never argued like this before. That wasn't the girl he'd married.

'OK, love. Come over to us when you're all ready.' Evie smirked as she shut her daughter's door. She'd heard the ruckus and seen Beau drive off like Stirling Moss. Good! Blood was thicker than water and she was hoping for a reconciliation between her two eldest boys and Jolene.

Evie tapped on Sonny's door. Nobody knew their children like their mother and Evie could sense Sonny's heart wasn't in this wedding. 'OK to come in, boy?'

'Yeah.'

Sonny was sitting on the sofa, in his dressing gown, looking slightly the worse for wear. 'Are Jolene and Beau OK? I heard 'em shouting.'

'She's fine and sod him. It's you I'm worried about. What's wrong? You can tell me anything, ya know. I'll always have your back, my boy.'

Sonny shrugged. 'I dunno. Probably last-minute nerves, but it's making me feel claustrophobic. I even had a dream last night that I was trapped in a lift and couldn't get out. Did you have any worries before you married Dad? I really don't fancy moving back to Kent either. I like it 'ere. It's quiet and so much easier for me to get to and from work.'

Evie clenched her son's hands. Unlike all her other kids, Sonny had never given her a day's worry. The perfect son, he truly was. 'Now, be honest with me. You don't love her, do you?'

'I don't know. I can't wait to be a father.'

'You can still be a good father without marrying her, Sonny. Nobody's forcing you to and, believe me, neither will it darken your name. Not when people find out she got herself up the duff just to trap you. You sure the baby's even yours? She's obviously easy. Has she slept with other men before you? 'Cause you can't be marrying a slag, boy. You deserve better.'

'Don't say that about her, Mum. I'm sure she ain't no slag. I gotta marry her. It's too late to cancel it now. I couldn't leave her standing at the altar. That's cruel.'

'Well, it's up to you. And I'll have your back whatever you decide. Put your foot down though if you do go through with it. It's a man's duty to choose where you'll live. Tell her you won't be living in Kent. Be firm. And if she don't like it. Tough shit.'

Kenny Bond was paranoid. Sharon was acting out of character, had spent far too much time at work this week, or with that rough mate of hers, and he wanted to know why.

'Shal, Kenny's just pulled up,' shouted Divvy Dave.

Sharon and Tina were in the nursery office, sipping coffee and discussing Kenny being followed the next day. 'Shit! You don't think he knows, do ya?' Sharon hissed.

'Course not. How could he? Just be calm,' Tina advised.

Kenny sauntered into the portacabin. 'Hello, Tina. Shal, is Ricky up 'ere with you? Only I can't get hold of him.'

'No. He begged me to drop him into Romford, said he wanted to buy Candy a present. I told you Ricky's got himself a girlfriend, didn't I, Tina?' chuckled Sharon, in the hope she was sounding more jovial than she actually felt. The woman on the motorbike had been back in touch and they were definitely following Kenny tomorrow.

'For Christ's sake, Shal. You know I don't like him going into Romford alone, and he ain't answering his bloody phone. How's he meant to be getting home?'

'I gave him a score, told him to wait by Woolworths and he was to only get in a black cab. He's hardly a child any more, Kenny. You're the one who wanted him to man up, took him training and made him learn to drive. How you gonna cope when he passes his test?'

'He's nowhere near ready to take his test,' spat Kenny. 'You must think I'm silly. I know something's going on. Is your ex back on the scene, Shal? Raymondo.'

'Oh, don't talk so bleedin' daft. I haven't seen him since I got back with you. Nothing happened between us anyway, as well you know. Kenny's twisting things, Tina, 'cause I don't want to go to that poxy wedding with him today. He's trying to make me feel guilty when he's the only one with any marital wrongdoings to his name. Talk about pot calling kettle black.'

Glad that Sharon was acting normal, Tina squeezed her pal's knee as a sign of encouragement.

'Would it have really hurt you to come today? Just for a few hours? I don't wanna be meeting Brett's girlfriend on me own, neither do I want to be stuck next to Jolene on a table. But I'm making an effort 'cause our grandsons want us to be there, Shal.'

Sharon knew she needed to act as if nothing was wrong. 'If Tina can come with me, I'll come. 'Cause I know what you're like, Kenny. Once you get on the Scotch, you disappear chatting to all the men.'

Kenny smiled. 'You up for it, Tina?'

'Never say no to a knees-up, me.'

'Oh, and you better keep that horrible cow Evie away from me,' added Sharon. ''Cause if she starts again, I'll be giving twice as much back.'

'That's my girl,' chuckled Kenny. 'Right, I'm gonna shoot down to Romford, see if I can find Ricky. Make sure you two give yourself plenty of time to get ready. We gotta be there by half two.'

When a happy Kenny left the office, Sharon let out a huge sigh of relief. 'Did I sound OK?'

'You did brilliantly.'

'Good. 'Cause I got a really bad feeling in me gut, mate. Had it since the moment I woke up this morning.'

'That's 'cause you know what's happening tomorrow. Kenny ain't cheating on you, Shal. I'd bet my house on that.'

'Let's hope you're right. 'Cause if he's got a son by some slapper, I'll knife him. Straight through the heart.'

*

Mary-Ann's family were not wealthy Travellers, which is why Bobby had offered to hold the wedding on his land and help towards the cost. Sonny didn't want anything showy and there'd been little time to plan. Understandably, the girl didn't want to be showing in her wedding dress, hence the mad rush.

'All right, love? Got over your bird fright? Good job we got them heaters in the marquee, Evie. It's a bit taters out there,' said Bobby. He'd been out to check on his scrapyards, to make sure all was ticking over nicely.

'You need to talk to Sonny. He don't want to marry her, and I don't blame him. She's not right for him, Bobby. He could do so much better.'

Bobby looked at his wife in amazement. 'Is this some kind of joke? Only, we got over hundred and fifty people on their way 'ere, plus a country an' western band, a DJ and a load of grub and booze.'

'Of course it ain't a joke. I know you mock me, but I told you when that magpie tried to peck its way into our home to expect bad news. Go ask him yourself.'

Absolutely sick of Evie and her omens, Bobby stormed over to Sonny's trailer.

Peeping through her net curtains, Evie was surprised when Bobby returned a minute later. 'Well?'

Face flushed with temper, Bobby wagged a finger near his wife's face. 'You need to stop meddling in our children's relationships, Evie. They're old enough to make their own bloody minds up without you sticking your oar in.'

Evie was taken aback. She and Bobby had the perfect marriage. He rarely ever lost his temper with her and pointing in her face was a first. 'What the hell did he say to you?'

'He's already in his suit, said he's made his bed so he's willing to lie in it. And so he bloody well should. Surely you didn't expect him to leave that poor pregnant girl standing at the altar?'

'I didn't tell him to do anything,' shrieked Evie. 'But their marriage won't last. You mark my words.'

'You said the same about Jolene and Beau. Three kids later, Evie . . .'

'Jolene ain't happy. A mother can tell. But you walk around with your head in the sand, Bobby Tamplin. Oh, and if you ever shove your fat finger in my face like that again, I'll chop it off with the bastard bread knife.'

Instead of looking forward to the day ahead, Brett Bond wished he'd never opened his big mouth. He barely knew Aisling, had no idea who the friend was she was bringing, and was now shit-scared about introducing Aidan to his family. Say they clocked on or something?

Unable to do the buttons on his shirt up because his hands were shaking, Brett opened the drinks cabinet. He was currently living alone in his old man's gaff in Dark Lane. He liked it, it suited his secret lifestyle being able to talk to Aidan openly on the nights they weren't together, and it was only costing him a oner a week. His dad had wanted to flog the place when he'd moved out to Blackmore with Tansey, but because of the gypsies living at the end of the lane, had been unable to get anywhere near the asking price.

Brett held his nose as he downed a brandy, then jumped as his phone bleeped. It was Aidan. He was early, already in the pub in Upminster where they'd arranged to meet.

Brett buttoned his shirt and put his tie and suit jacket on. He stared at his reflection in the mirror. 'Ya can't mug yourself off. You've got this. It's all gonna go smoothly.'

Brett picked his car keys up. He had no way of knowing that the day was about to be anything but smooth.

Relieved to hear a heavy-sounding diesel engine, then spot a black cab, Sharon bellowed, 'Kenny, he's home.'

Kenny darted out the shower and ran down the stairs. He'd been unable to spot Ricky in Romford, had been worried sick about the lad. He yanked open the front door. 'Where you been? And why ain't you been answering your phone?'

Wearing the hooded grey Nike tracksuit he'd treated himself to, Ricky grinned as he strolled indoors with his old clothes in a carrier bag. ''Cause I was busy, Kenny, and you never let me do what I want to do when you come shopping with me. I wanted to try on lots of things and get my hair done.'

'Hair done!' Kenny yanked Ricky's hood off. 'For fuck's sake. What you done to yourself? This is all your fault, Shal. Told ya, didn't I? Who coloured and cut that? I'll have their guts for garters.'

'Shut up, Kenny.' Sharon demanded. Ricky had had his hair cropped and dyed blond and she could see Kenny's reaction had deflated the lad. 'I quite like it. It suits him.'

'Thanks, Shal. Candy likes blond men, so I got meself a new look. I treated meself to this tracksuit too. I've had the best shopping day ever.'

181

'I'm glad,' replied Sharon. 'You better start getting ready though. You don't want to be late for the wedding.'

'I got another surprise for you,' beamed Ricky. 'But I need money to pay the cab first. I got me sums mixed up, Shal, and accidentally spent the fare you gave me.'

Kenny handed Ricky a score. 'I'm going down to that hairdresser first thing Monday morning. I bet they had a right good old laugh at him. Cunts,' he hissed at his wife.

About to tell Kenny he was doing no such thing, Sharon shut up as Ricky reappeared with a short, plump blonde girl.

'Sharon, this is my girlfriend, Candy. I've invited her to accompany me to the wedding.'

Not one to mix his words, Kenny blurted out. 'She can't come dressed like that.' Candy was wearing pink Lycra leggings, a boob tube, denim jacket and white trainers.

'Hello, Candy. Nice to meet you,' smiled Sharon. 'Don't worry. I'm sure we'll find something nice in my wardrobe you can wear.'

'No need. Candy bought a sexy dress and shoes from the market. Show 'em,' ordered Ricky.

Both Sharon and Kenny were lost for words when Candy proudly held up her outfit. Hideous was the only way to describe it.

'Another two bottles of lager, please Mr Barman, but this time we'll have a couple of shots of tequila too,' grinned Aisling.

'Oh no! Not the shots. It's far too early,' chuckled Aidan. 'Seriously, sis, we can't get hammered before we've even got there. I do really like Brett. I don't want to balls things up.'

'Chill! I've got everything under control. How do I look, by the way?'

'Great. You always look great.' Aisling had a long black dress on with a pair of cherry-red patent boots. Because of her height, stunning looks and shapely figure, Aisling could literally wear a black bin bag and pull it off.

'How about now?' Aisling undid the buttons across her front to reveal that she was actually wearing a dress coat, and underneath was not only a skimpy black mini-dress, but her cherry red boots also nearly reached her thighs.

Aidan shook his head. 'Keep the long thing on, for God's sake. Poor Brett will have a cardiac and his fami-ly'll think you're a stripper.'

Aware the barman couldn't take his eyes off her, Aisling blew him a kiss, then threw her arms around her brother's neck to pretend they were a couple. 'Those gypsy girls will be dressed more scantily than me. But they won't be able to match my moves on the dance floor. You'll see.'

'Get off me, you nutter,' laughed Aidan.

Aisling opened her purse. 'Look what I brought with me. Want a line? I've already had one.'

Aidan rolled his eyes. 'No. I can't get messy. You do your thing and I'll do mine.'

'Don't be so boring. It doesn't suit you. No point you being with Brett if you can't be yourself. So, what have you actually told him? Obviously, you won't have disclosed how you really earn your money. But have you told him about what happened to Finlay? What about Conor? And I bet you haven't told him about Brianna?'

183

'I've told him about Conor and Finlay. But I—' Aidan quickly shut up as he spotted Brett walking towards them. 'Look at you. So handsome!' He smiled, kissing his lover on both cheeks.

'All right, Aisling? Where's your pal?' enquired Brett.

'Got off her face last night and didn't make it. But don't worry, Brett, your family are going to love me,' smirked Aisling.

Brett glanced anxiously at Aidan. He hadn't expected the two of them to come alone, neither had he expected Aisling to be dressed like Miss Whiplash. What the hell was he meant to say to his family?

CHAPTER THIRTEEN

'You two wait 'ere while I go get Nan and show her where we're sitting,' Beau told his sons.

'You and Mummy friends again?' Rocky asked innocently.

'Course we are,' lied Beau. 'All adults argue. It's normal. But don't forget, if anyone asks about my bad eye, you kicked a ball at it, OK?'

Rocky nodded. He didn't usually tell lies, but he'd do anything for his beloved dad.

'All right, darling? You look smart. What you done to your eye? It's ever so swollen.' Lori hadn't wanted to enter the venue without Beau, in case she or Carl interrupted something important.

'Rocky walloped me with a ball. It's fine, just a bit bruised. Where's Hope?'

'My friend's looking after her. We were worried she'd get bored and play up,' fibbed Lori. She hadn't wanted her daughter to come in case it kicked off amongst the gypsies.

'No worries. Follow me. You're the first to arrive apart from me. Jolene ain't sitting with us, by the way. She's on the table with her own family at the front.' At that precise moment, Beau locked eyes with Johnny and Billy Tamplin. They glared at him and he glared back.

'Who are they, love?' Lori asked worriedly.

'Jolene's eldest brothers. They're arseholes,' hissed Beau.

Lori grabbed hold of Carl's arm. 'Thank God we never brought Hope,' she whispered. They weren't even in the marquee yet, and trouble was already brewing.

Kenny greeted Beau and Lori, shook hands with Carl, then sat on the nearby table with his son, who was sitting alone. 'Pour us a drop of that wine, Donny. What a bastard of a day I've had so far. Ricky's hooked up with the granddaughter of a geezer I know. Proper nutcase family. Not to be messed with, like. Bringing her 'ere today. Obviously, the girl ain't the full shilling, but wait 'til you see the outfit she's wearing. No way was they walking in with me, they can walk in with your mother.'

'People won't take no notice 'ere. Not if she's with Ricky and she don't look right. I'm pissed off an' all. I had no idea Lori was gonna be 'ere until I walked in. Talk about make me look a fool.'

'I didn't know she was gonna be here either. Let it go over your head.'

'One of the twins must've invited her. Probably Beau, by the looks of it. It riles me, Dad. I gave them boys the bestest life. They lived in squalor with her. Yet, that all seems to be forgotten now. Talk about short memories.'

'Where's Harry and Alfie? Didn't they fancy coming with ya?' Kenny knew Tansey wouldn't be here. Or Bluebell. Neither came to family events of any kind.

'Harry's gone over West Ham with a couple of his mates, and I reluctantly dropped Alfie into Romford to see his pals. That's why I'm not drinking. Gotta pick him up later.'

'Is he still knocking about with them toerags from the Waterloo Estate?'

'Yeah. But he mainly only sees 'em at school now. He's got a fifteen-minute walk to the bus stop from where we are and the buses only run once an hour. It's been good for him, us moving to the middle of nowhere. He spends all of his time in his room playing games on his Nintendo, but at least he ain't getting himself into any trouble and we know where he is.'

'And what about you? You happy with the move?'

Donny smiled. 'Yeah. Me and Tansey are good again. Bluebell's happy. We're right near the stables where she keeps her pony, and all her friends are nice kids. I think it's been tougher for Harry than any of us, but he'll be driving soon. Can come and go as he pleases then.'

'Oh no!' Kenny said. 'The dress and boots look even worse on her than when she took 'em out the carrier bag.'

Donny swung around. Grinning like a Cheshire cat, Ricky was walking towards them while holding the hand of a buxom blonde girl. Her outfit stood out like a sore thumb. A bright green shiny skin-tight Lycra dress and white ankle books wasn't the best look for anyone, let alone one so tubby. 'What's Ricky done to his barnet?'

Kenny slapped a hand against his forehead. 'Don't ask.'

*

The ceremony was short and sweet, as were the speeches. Only Mary-Ann's dad stood up, followed by Bobby saying a few words. Sonny had insisted on as little fuss as possible, so that's exactly what he got. There wasn't even the traditional sit-down meal. Instead, there was a huge buffet, with some hot food included. Even the tables weren't named and numbered. The Tamplins were right at the front and it was grab whatever table you wanted for the guests. First come, first served, so to speak.

Seeing Donny look her way, Lori tossed back her blonde locks and gave Beau a kiss on the cheek. 'Well, that was the shortest wedding I've ever been to. I told my friend I was coming here today. She's Catholic and said it was unheard of for a priest to marry a couple in a non-religious venue. Is he a proper priest?'

'Yeah. He's the real deal. Bobby managed to pull a few strings to get him 'ere.'

'Oh right. Where's your brother? Was he only meant to be coming to the reception?'

Beau shrugged. 'Your guess is as good as mine.'

'You and Brett haven't fallen out, have you? Only you don't seem your bubbly self, love.'

'I'm OK. If you must know, me and Jolene had words this morning over her sitting with her brothers. Nothing serious, like. Marriage, eh?'

Lori squeezed Beau's hand. She'd put money on it Jolene was responsible for Beau's bruises, but didn't want to embarrass him. Sometimes it was better to say nothing.

*

Having gone down a storm at Jolene's wedding, Bobby hired the same country and western band to perform at Sonny's. Kicking off with the Charlie Daniels classic 'The Devil Went Down to Georgia', the celebration was soon in full swing. Not that Sonny looked joyous, thought Evie. He'd put on a brave face during the service but had a face like a smacked arse again now. There was no longer any point saying anything to him or Bobby. 'No use shutting the stable door after the horse has bolted' was one of her dear old mum's favourite quotes. She'd wait until she was proved right until she had her say again, then she'd rub it in, like melted bloody butter.

Bobby leaned towards his wife. 'Who's that fella Jolene's talking to, love? Over there, by the portaloos.'

Evie craned her neck to see where he was pointing and her heart skipped a beat. The young man was tall, dark, handsome, and her inner psyche told her that this was the man. The one Lena had seen in her crystal ball, just before she died.

Beau nudged his mum. ''Ere's Brett. That can't be his bird, surely? She's as tall as him. Perhaps she's the other geezer's girlfriend?'

Spotting his brother, Brett grabbed hold of Aisling's hand. 'Ready for this? Please don't mess it up.'

'I won't. Have faith in me.'

With a hint of amusement on his face, Aidan followed behind his sister and lover. He had a warped sense of humour, one which this kind of situation appealed to. 'It's my fault we're late. Well, not my fault exactly. My girlfriend fell ill, so Brett kindly offered to drop her home,' Aidan explained to Brett's brother and mother. He was then introduced to Donny and the infamous Kenny. The Irish charm came naturally to Aidan and he soon had everyone eating out of his hand. As did Aisling. She was nutty as a fruitcake, but people were naturally drawn to her.

Brett felt as proud as punch as he plonked himself in between his mum and brother. They'd turned up late because he'd needed a good drink before coming. But now they were here, it was all going great. Superbly, in fact. 'Come on then, what do you think of Aisling?'

Having never met a girl like Aisling, Beau was a bit lost for words. 'Erm, she's pretty, fun, got a lot to say for herself. Yeah, she's cool, bro.'

'Mum?' prompted Brett.

Lori smiled sweetly, included Carl in her response and said all the things Brett would want her to say. For the first time since they were little, Lori was feeling needed by her sons. Wanted, her opinion valued.

'I knew you'd like her,' grinned Brett. 'I'm gonna do the rounds now. I'll be back in a bit.'

'What d'ya really think?' Beau asked his mum. 'She's not what I expected.'

'What did you expect?'

'I dunno. Someone shorter and less powerful, if that makes sense? I wouldn't fancy a right-hander from her, put it that way.'

Lori studied Aidan. He was incredibly handsome and she wasn't easily fooled. Brett and Aisling were no match. But Brett and Aidan were a different story.

*

'Who was that bloke in the dark grey suit you were chatting to?' pried Evie.

'Jimmy Dean. He's the one Tammy supposedly had her sights set on. I felt ever so sorry for him. His wife's got cervical cancer and there's nothing more they can do. They've got a little girl as well. Demi,' explained Jolene.

'How sad. So, is she dying, his wife?'

'I dunno. I didn't like to ask the ins and outs. I barely know him. He's related to Mary-Ann, second cousins or something. He said he didn't want to come alone today, but his wife and her mum insisted he did, 'cause he needed a break. Perhaps he's caring for her?'

'Terrible. Bet he won't be on his own for long. Too handsome not to be snapped up quickly.' Evie didn't have it in her to be tactful.

'Don't be saying stuff like that, Mum. The poor bloke's in bits.'

'I didn't mean anything bad. Just that Tammy had good taste. You spoken to Johnny and Billy yet?'

'Not properly.'

'Go have a chat with 'em now. Introduce 'em to Romany properly. They love you, Jolene, have only ever had your back.'

'I know, Mum. I love them too.'

'There you are! I didn't think you were coming. What you having to drink?' asked Kenny. Every table had free-flowing wine and beer. There was also a bar serving up spirits and other drinks.

'We'll both have a white wine. You all right, Donny?' smiled Sharon. She could barely look Kenny in the eye, couldn't wait for tomorrow to be over with. Please God, she hoped he wasn't up to no good and things would return to normal in time for their long-overdue holiday.

'Wait until you see Brett's girlfriend, Mum. Where they gone, Dad?' Donny craned his neck.

'What, she got two heads or something?' chuckled Sharon. Acting jovial was tough. Thank God Tina was with her to lighten her load.

'She's really tall, like a glamour model,' explained Donny.

'Can't wait to meet her. I need a wee first though. Coming, Tina?'

'Why do women always go to the bog together? Can you imagine if geezers did that?' said Donny.

Kenny winked at his son, ''Cause they're a different species.' Jake had been allowed home from hospital yesterday, yet Karen still wasn't happy. She'd had a right go at him on the phone earlier, even though she knew he was going to a wedding today and couldn't visit Jake until tomorrow. 'I'll never understand how a female's bonce ticks, boy. They're all weirdos.'

Evie stood on tiptoes, pursing her lips. 'Bobby-Joe looks a right gooseberry tagging along behind Ricky and that thing he turned up with. Look! They don't want him there, all but ignoring him. Go get him away from them, Bobby.'

'He's all right. He was dancing with 'em a minute ago. Stop being so dramatic, Evie. Kids will be kids.'

'She ain't no bleedin' kid, her. Who is she anyway? State of her in that dress. Ain't she got a mirror?'

'She's not the full works, love. I think she's Ricky's girlfriend. I'll go and check on Bobby-Joe. I'm sure he's OK. He looks happy enough to me. Be back in a tick.'

'Brett, you got a minute?' asked Beau.

Brett followed his brother over to the bar area. 'What's up?' he asked, hoping Aisling hadn't said or done anything wrong.

'I need your advice.' Beau explained what had happened earlier with Jolene and what had been said. The only thing he didn't admit to, was Jolene laying into him. He'd feel a right mug telling anybody that. 'So, d'ya think I should make the first move? It's really pissing me off seeing her brothers chatting to her while looking at me. It's as though, she's told 'em and they think they've won. I ain't having that. I'd rather apologize to her than let those two think they've beaten me. What would you do?'

'It should be her apologizing, not you. You idolize her, graft hard, you're a brilliant dad. What more does she want?'

'I did call her mother a shitcunt though.'

'Only 'cause she said she wished she'd never married ya. Fuck her, bruv. Let her come crawling to you. Otherwise, you'll end up a pussy, like Dad has with Tansey.'

'Carl and I are going to make a move now, boys. We need to pick Hope up.' Lori had enjoyed today but was ready to leave. Her beloved boys were well on their way to being inebriated and that made her uncomfortable.

She hadn't witnessed the twins drunk before and never wanted to. She'd had enough therapy to know addiction had a tendency to run in families.

Beau hugged his mum. 'I'll call you in the week.'

'See ya, Mum. Take care,' Brett politely kissed Lori on the cheek.

Beau walked away. Nobody else was in earshot, so Lori decided to take a chance. She knew why Beau was closer to her. He hadn't been the one brutally raped as a child, due to her failures as a mother. 'Come here. Give me a proper hug, Brett.'

Brett did as asked.

'I want you to know that I'm always there for you and you can talk to me about anything, without it going any further. I know I was a crap mum to you, Brett, but I'm not that person any more. I want you to be happy, whoever you fall in love with.'

Feeling a bit like a rabbit caught in the headlights, Brett forced a smile. 'Cheers. We'll have to take you out for lunch one day, me and Aisling.'

Lori stroked Brett's cheek. 'I wasn't talking about Aisling, love. I meant you and Aidan.'

Because of the unsettling incident that morning, Evie was unable to relax. Had the wedding not gone ahead, she would've comforted herself with that being the reason. But she knew there was more drama to come. There had to be. That bastard bird trying to smash its way through her kitchen window wasn't a sign to be taken lightly. Magpies weren't God's creatures, they belonged to the devil.

'There you go, Mum. Half a Guinness,' chuckled Billy, plonking the drink on the table.

'What you two finding so funny?' enquired Evie. She was chuffed there'd been some bridges built today between her eldest two and Jolene. No mother wanted to see their children at loggerheads.

'Tell Mum. She'll find it comical,' urged Johnny.

'I spilt the first half a Guinness I got ya, all down Beau's white shirt,' grinned Billy.

'What you like?' smirked Evie. 'What did Beau do?'

'He glared at us, then stormed off,' Billy replied. 'I think she's going off him, Jolene.'

'What makes you think that?' Evie asked hopefully. 'I heard 'em arguing this morning, but whenever I say anything remotely against him, she sticks up for him.'

'I could just tell. Don't ask me how. Perhaps I inherited Nan's psychic abilities. Sometimes, pals I haven't seen for ages I thinks of, then that day, they ring me out the blue.'

'That's strange and your grandmother was a legend. Promise me one thing though, don't cause any trouble 'ere, boys. Not at your brother's wedding. Your father'll go apeshit.'

After hunting around the venue in search of his guests, Brett finally clocked Aisling up the bar necking shots with another girl. No wonder he hadn't been able to spot her easily. She'd taken off her dress coat and now resembled a stripper. He grabbed hold of her arm. 'Where's the rest of your clothes?'

Having just snorted a couple of large lines, Aisling burst out laughing. 'That was a coat. This is my dress. Want to see what's underneath, lover boy?' she jested.

'No. I don't. Did you say anything to my mum? About us?'

'Of course not. Why?'

'Where's Aidan?'

'I don't know.' Aisling linked arms with Brett. 'Come on, I'll help you find him. You've got nothing to worry about though. My brother's into you. Finlay's murder hit him hard. But, finally I think he's found love again,' she grinned.

Brett did a double-take, then tried to compose himself. Aidan had mentioned having one serious boyfriend in the past and Brett knew his name, but all Aidan had told him when prompted was 'Finlay unfortunately passed away at a young age. It was tragic. I'd rather not talk about it, if you don't mind.'

Cocaine suited Aisling. It made her more observant, although Aidan did scold her for talking too much on it. 'You all right, Brett? Aidan said you knew about Finlay.'

'I did. But Aidan still finds it upsetting to talk about it. How was he murdered? I haven't asked all the details.'

'He was shot. Of course, Aidan blamed himself, still does.'

'Why?'

''Cause he thinks the bullet was meant for him. Look, best you talk to Aidan about it. It's his business, not mine.'

If Brett's brain wasn't already in a state of confusion, his eyes felt like they were deceiving him when he spotted Aidan on the dance floor. He was canoodling with a woman. She had her hands all over him and him her. 'What the fuck!'

Aisling chuckled. Aidan was a wild one once he'd had too many drinks. 'This is great. For you. Nobody will guess you're a couple now. That's probably why he's acting up.'

'She's kissing him. How the hell can he let a woman kiss him?'

'He has got a son, Brett.' Aisling playfully pinched Brett's bum.

'Yeah, I know that. But he never actually shagged Conor's mother, surely?'

Aisling burst out laughing. 'How'd you think Conor was conceived then? I do love you, Brett. Ya nutter.'

Spotting his lover and sister, Aidan unclasped the drunken woman's hands from around his neck and, grinning, walked towards them. He'd had little interest in women for years, but still liked to wind them up, and would always enjoy them lusting after him. The thrill of the chase, so to speak. 'I attract 'em. She wouldn't leave me alone,' he laughed.

Brett didn't know if he was coming or going any more. The new information Aisling had blurted out was a mind-fuck. He'd trusted Aidan, thought he knew him. Now he felt like a fool, a complete mug. As for the thought of Aidan sticking his cock up women's fannies, that made him want to chuck his guts up.

Aware that Brett was peeved, Aidan put a hand on his shoulder. 'What's up? I was only messing with that lady. I'm a piss-taker when I'm boozy. Aisling will tell you that.'

'Oh, Aisling's told me plenty, thanks. And you ain't just a piss-taker when you're boozed, trust me. I'm off home now. Sick of this shitty wedding and the company.

I can't stand fake fucking people. Never have been able to. You take care of yourself, Aidan. And don't bother ringing me any more. We're done.'

CHAPTER FOURTEEN

'Brett! Brett, come back. Don't be daft. Let me explain.'

Brett shrugged Aidan off, then once outside the marquee, broke into a run.

Aisling held on to her brother. 'Leave him. We're all boozy. Talk to him tomorrow.'

'What the feck did you say to him?'

'Nothing out the ordinary. Although, he did seem a bit freaked out that Conor wasn't conceived via a turkey baster. He weren't happy with you dancing with that tart. I think his mum said something to upset him also.'

'I don't need this shit. I knew it was a bad idea, us coming here.'

'I've got an idea. Why don't you have a couple of fat juicy lines, I'll sort us a cab and we'll show the good people of Romford how to party. Shall we try that Hollywood's?'

Aidan shrugged. 'Whatever.'

*

Evie stood up, craning her neck. She'd kept a watchful eye on her youngest son all day, but he was currently nowhere to be seen.

Bobby was up the bar talking to Kenny. So Evie marched over to Sonny. He'd been glued to Mary-Ann's side all day, seemed to be over his earlier wobble for now, at least. 'You seen Bobby-Joe?'

'Yeah. About five minutes ago. He was with Ricky. Well, he followed him outside.'

Evie exited the marquee and began hunting around. The bouncy castle was no more. Christ knows what the kids had done to it, but it had deflated to nothing. Bobby would have to cough up for that, if the damage was proved to be intentional.

About to shout her son's name, Evie noticed a small figure with its back turned towards her and immediately knew it was Bobby-Joe. What was he doing standing by that clump of trees? Not weeing, she hoped. He'd had a habit of pissing and shitting outdoors when he was younger until she'd knocked it out of him.

As she crept up from behind, Evie heard groaning, then a female voice. She grabbed hold of Bobby-Joe, peered in the trees and shrieked. That awful girl, with the bright green dress on, was sat on top of Ricky, her fat lily-white arse on show, doing God knows what. 'What the hell's going on 'ere? Get off him. Now!'

'Mum, don't shout,' ordered Bobby-Joe.

Evie covered her boy's eyes and held him close. How dare that whore behave like that in front of her baby? Talk about giving him nightmares.

Feeling awkward and also ashamed, Ricky scrambled up. 'We weren't doing nothing bad, honest we weren't. Please don't tell Shal or Kenny. We won't do it again. I promise.'

'Don't apologize to her, Ricky,' piped up Candy. 'You're my boyfriend. We're allowed to kiss and cuddle. If Bobby-Joe was spying on us, that ain't our fault.'

'Who'd you think you're talking to?' bellowed Evie. 'This is my land and my son's wedding. Who invited you?'

Candy smoothed her dress back into its rightful position, 'Ricky and Sharon said it was OK for me to come. You need to get off your high horse, lady. Else you'll have my dad and granddad round 'ere.'

Absolutely livid, Evie grabbed hold of Ricky's hand. 'We'll see about that, you ignorant fat slag.'

Even though her grandson was married to Jolene, as a rule Sharon avoided the Tamplins like the plague. Kenny got on well with Bobby, but on the one occasion she'd been forced to be in Evie's company, it had not gone well. It was at the start of Beau's relationship with Jolene and Evie had made it clear she didn't think he was good enough for her daughter. That had been like a red rag to a bull for Sharon, who'd given as good as she'd got. In her opinion, Jolene was as common as muck and Beau could do a whole lot better than settling for some gyppo who, at the time, dressed like a lap dancer.

'What's up?' Sharon asked. They'd been discussing what she would do if Kenny did have a secret son, but Tina's thoughts were now elsewhere.

'Don't be alarmed. But I think Ricky might've done something wrong, 'cause—'

Evie poking Sharon hard on the shoulder stopped Tina mid-sentence. 'I wanna word with you. How dare you invite that ignorant filthy fat whore to my son's wedding without even asking my permission? Do you know what I caught them doing? Her and Ricky. Disgusting behaviour, in front of my son. She was—'

Sharon leapt up and pushed Evie, stopping her mid-sentence. 'Who'd you think you're berating and poking? Bloody cheek! I didn't invite anyone to your son's poxy wedding. I didn't even want to come meself, truth be known.'

'Oh no!' A thoroughly embarrassed Ricky put his head in his hands. 'Please don't fight, Sharon. I never did nothing wrong. I swear I didn't.'

Candy hugged Ricky then pointed an accusing finger at Evie. 'She's mad, Sharon. We were just having a little kiss and cuddle. Then she turns up and spoils it all.'

Evie pushed Sharon back, resulting in her flying into the table and knocking all the drinks over. 'She had her fat arse showing and was humping him. In front of my poor innocent boy. Fucking vulgar! That's what she is. And him. Your Ricky. Disgusting!'

A red mist descended upon Sharon. She lunged at Evie, grabbed her hair and yanked her to the ground. The two of them then rolled around on the grass like a pair of warring fishwives.

Alerted to the commotion by Sonny, both Kenny and Bobby ran towards their respective wives and pulled them apart.

Absolutely seething, Sharon lashed out at Kenny. The anger she felt, her being here. Everything was his fault,

202

the arsehole. 'Don't you ever fucking force me to socialize with this mob again. They ain't my cup of tea and never will be. Her especially! Come on, Tina. We're leaving.'

'Been a crap wedding in comparison to mine, eh?' Beau remarked, before downing another shot. He'd changed his shirt, was proud of himself in a way for not retaliating like the old Beau would have. But he was upset. Not only had his nan mugged him off by kicking off with Evie, Jolene had mugged him off worse. He'd been looking her way all day, yet she'd barely glanced at him. Her brothers had though and were still doing so, the pricks.

Having returned to the party half an hour after leaving, Brett knocked his tequila back. He'd changed the story to focus on his own woe, had told Beau he'd found out stuff about Aisling he hadn't previously known. 'I thought Nan having a ruck with Evie was well funny. Livened up an otherwise shitty day,' he slurred.

'You might have, but it's gonna make my life even more of a misery.'

'Man up then. Have it out with Jolene. I kicked Aisling into touch soon as I found out she'd lied to me earlier,' lied Brett. 'You don't want to end up like Dad, do you?'

'You're right. I'll have it out with her tomorrow. I ain't doing it 'ere in front of the kids and her brothers.'

'Why not? I'd show her brothers who's boss. Rocky, Levi and Romany have gone anyway. Evie took 'em with her.' Beau had always been the fieriest of the two of them and, even though Brett was pleased his brother wasn't as nutty as he used to be, no way did he want Beau to be made a fool of. 'They're looking over now,

Billy and Johnny. Go talk to Jolene. Don't apologize, like. Just be normal with her and say your piece. I'll come over there with you.'

Beau squeezed his brother's shoulder. 'We'll go over there in a bit. Shout us some more shots up first.'

Kenny didn't know who was more embarrassed, himself or Bobby. Both were taken aback by their wives' childish behaviour. Bobby ordered Evie to take Bobby-Joe, Rocky, Levi and Romany home, which, surprisingly, Evie agreed to rather calmly. And Kenny, flanked by Ricky and Candy, who were still both protesting their innocence, followed Sharon back home.

Dreading the following day and not wanting to be alone with Kenny, Sharon had already persuaded Tina to stay the night when Kenny marched in with Ricky and Candy in tow. 'I'm sorry, OK? But I can't ever be around that woman again, Kenny. She started it, didn't she, Tina? She pushed me and I went flying.'

Kenny didn't want a row in front of Tina. He shrugged. 'Shit happens. They weren't at it though. Ricky's sworn on our lives, and I believe him.'

'Tina's staying the night. She's lost her keys,' Sharon fibbed. 'You go back to the party, see if you can find 'em, and apologize to Bobby on my behalf. We'll talk properly tomorrow. Make sure Candy gets a cab home first though.'

'I can't get a cab on my own. Not this time of night,' said Candy. 'I had a bad time in a cab in Barking. The driver was a filthy pervert. He was rude to me. Got his cock out. Anyway, I told my parents I was staying with yous tonight. That's OK, isn't it?'

Having had a gutful for one day, Sharon demanded Kenny take Ricky and Candy back to the wedding reception with him. 'You met her at your gym, you're friends with her uncle and grandfather. You sort it,' Sharon hissed, giving her husband a not-so-gentle punch in the back as he left.

'Oh, Shal. And I thought my life was mental,' laughed Tina. 'Let's have another glass of wine. And we can think up a good reason why you can't be around tomorrow. You can't be here with Kenny, not while you're waiting for news. You won't be able to handle it.'

'I hope I get some answers. I couldn't stand another week like this. I feel like me brain's fried,' Sharon replied, opening the fridge door. 'Who's that ringing me? Answer it, mate. It's probably him.'

'It's your dad, Shal.'

Sharon snatched the phone. 'What's up?' her face paled. 'OK. Give us five minutes and I'll be with you.'

'Whassamatter?' asked Tina.

'It's me mum. She collapsed with stomach pains. Dad's called an ambulance.'

'Come on then.' Beau grabbed his brother's arm. 'Don't forget – be polite. We'll ruin 'em with our sarcasm. They're too dense to clock on to our humour.'

'Funny smell around 'ere all of a sudden,' Billy remarked, glaring at Beau.

'I smell gorger,' grinned a drunken Johnny.

Ignoring the two imbeciles, Beau put a hand on his wife's shoulder. 'Sorry to interrupt you, ladies,' he said to his sisters-in-law. 'Can we have a chat please, Jolene?'

'She don't wanna fucking talk to ya,' smirked Billy.

'Shut it, you two,' Jolene ordered her brothers. 'I'm not in the mood for chatting now, Beau. We'll talk later,' she coldly informed her husband.

'Told ya,' laughed Billy.

'That's it, sis. Mug him off,' taunted Johnny.

'Who d'you think you're fucking talking to?' bellowed Brett.

'Tweedle Dee and Tweedle fucking Dumb,' laughed Billy. 'Off you go, the pair of ya. Crawl back under the rock you crawled out of.'

'Leave it, bro.' Beau grabbed Brett's arm. He was inwardly seething but had plastered a smile on his face. 'We need to talk now, Jolene.'

Not wanting to back down in front of her brothers, Jolene stood her ground. 'You blind? I'm talking to Crystal and Layla.'

Crystal was married to Billy, Layla to Johnny, and when they also began to snigger, Beau decided the time was right to wipe the smiles off all their silly faces. 'Seeing as you've become so close to your sisters-in-law today, dear, I do hope you've told 'em that their husbands are partial to sticking their corys up the gorger barmaids who work in their local pub.'

'You what!' Crystal looked like she'd suddenly seen a ghost.

'That's right. "Whoremongers", that's what Jolene calls Billy and Johnny. Tell 'em, girl, go on,' urged Beau.

'Take that back, you lying shitcunt,' bellowed Billy, his face red with fury. 'Take it back before I beat the granny out of ya.'

'Nah. And next time you give out marital advice, I suggest you make sure you got your own house in order first. Come on, Brett. Let's leave 'em to it.'

As the twins walked away, Billy and Johnny grabbed them from behind . . .

Holding a packet of frozen peas across his top lip, Beau lay on the sofa in his luxury trailer.

Brett was lying horizontally on the other sofa, with a packet of frozen chicken nuggets against his right eye. 'I can barely see.'

'Did you see Crystal hit Billy with that bottle? It didn't break, just bounced off his bonce,' laughed Beau.

'You want another brandy? I'm in pain.'

'Yeah. I got a tooth loose. Worth it, though, to ruin their marriages. Who'd they think they are, sticking their oars into mine and Jolene's? We're tight-knit, close, as a rule. Our kids are our life. I would never jeopardize that by sticking me cock up random birds.'

'Well, I think you might've jeopardized it a bit after blurting all that out. Fuck 'em, though. They asked for it.'

After all hell had broken loose, Crystal had driven off in one four-by-four with Layla and their kids. Billy had chased after them in the other, with Johnny in the passenger seat. 'A bit of luck he'll have an accident and kill the pair of 'em,' said Beau.

'He was well pissed. Gotta drive all the way back to Kent an' all.'

'Perhaps we should do away with 'em, like we did Jamie?' chuckled Beau.

'Jamie ain't no laughing matter. He was well all right in comparison to them two.'

'Yeah. I know. I just meant, get rid of 'em, make it look like an accident. Obviously, I won't drown 'em in the swimming pool like I did Jamie. But I could get hold of a lorry, a ringer, run them off the road, then set fire to their vehicle. I'd love to watch those pair burn alive.'

As the twins jokingly planned the murders of Billy and Johnny, they were totally unaware they were being listened to and every word had been heard. Including Beau's admission that he'd murdered Jamie.

CHAPTER FIFTEEN

'There you are,' exclaimed Kenny. 'I thought I heard you come in early hours, then I must've dozed back off. How is she? Your mum?'

Dressing gown wrapped around her, Sharon sat up. 'The pain had eased by the time I left her, but they're keeping her in. You'll have to sort you and Ricky out for food today. I need to pop into Romford, get Mum some new nighties and slippers. Tina was brilliant last night, stayed up there with us, so I said I'd treat her to a bite to eat later. What you up to? You going to the cemetery?'

'Yeah. Unless you need me to come up the hospital with you?'

'God, no. You're the last person Mum'll want to see if she's not well.'

'How comes you slept on the sofa?'

'I didn't want to wake you, and the spare room was taken.'

Kenny rolled his eyes. 'I'll drop Candy home in a bit. She ain't coming back anytime soon either. If Ricky wants to see her, they can meet down the gym, or he can take her somewhere. We ain't getting lumbered like that again.'

'She's certainly a strange one. I thought she was all meek at the start, until she gave Evie what for. Tore into her like a savage rottweiler.'

'She'll eat Ricky for breakfast, poor sod,' chuckled Kenny.

'Good. 'Cause I haven't got time to cook her any today. I'm gonna run a bath. I need a good soak.'

'You do what you gotta do, darling.' The unexpected turn of events actually suited Kenny. Down to the ground.

Evie plonked Bobby's mug of tea on the coaster. 'What happened with Billy and Johnny after I decided to leave last night? And don't fob me off, 'cause I knows there was trouble. Rosie Brazier's been on the phone.'

'You didn't decide to leave. I ordered you to. Making a bloody show of me like that. Whatever was you thinking, woman?'

'Don't swerve the subject. I already apologized, even though it weren't my fault.'

Bobby had already spoken to his sons and agreed to play things down to their mother. Evie was a woman's woman, had no time for philanderers and would side with her daughters-in-law if the shit hit the fan. Which it had to a degree, but Bobby was sure Billy and Johnny could talk their way out of any wrongdoing. Both had the gift of the gab. 'It was nothing, Evie. The boys said something to the twins. They spouted something back. End of. Handbags at dawn.'

'You sure?' Evie lowered her voice. 'Only Jolene was acting very strange last night and is still in bed. I've had to see to the chavvies. I've fed all three. That's not like her.'

Bobby tapped on the door of the spare bedroom. 'Jolene. Time to get your arse in gear. You've got three chavvies who needs you and a husband who must be wondering where you are.'

Jolene lay under the quilt, still and silent. She needed some thinking time. Away from everyone.

'How do I look?' beamed Ricky. It had been Kenny's idea he take Candy out for a meal today. Kenny was also paying for it, which had pleased him immensely.

'Very smart. Don't you think it's a little bit over-the-top for a carvery though?' Ricky was wearing a grey suit, white shirt and black tie. Kenny would hate him to be laughed at, especially if he wasn't around to defend the lad.

'This is my first proper meal date and I want to make a good impression,' Ricky replied seriously. 'Especially in front of Candy's parents.'

'In that case, you look just fine. 'Ere's your wonga.' Kenny handed Ricky a fifty-pound note. 'You can keep any change to put towards your next date. Be a gentleman though. We don't want a repeat of last night, do we?'

'Seeing as I'm now well off, can we stop off, so I can buy Candy's mum some flowers?'

'No, we bloody well can't. Not when we own garden centres ourselves. Come on, in the motor. I'm running late as it is. I gotta pick Aunt Nelly up,' lied Kenny.

When Kenny started the ignition, Ricky turned the music down. 'Can I ask you something, man to man? You mustn't tell Sharon though. Or anybody else.'

'Go on. I won't say sod all.'

'I weren't lying last night when I said me and Candy did nothing wrong. But, me willy was rock hard, Kenny, like a brick. Is that normal when you're with a woman?'

Thinking of Ricky's real dad, Kenny couldn't help but smile. He and Alan had shagged everything and anything when they were lads. Usually round the back of their old boxing gym. If Alan was looking down, listening to this conversation, Kenny just knew he'd be cracking up.

'Well?' prompted Ricky.

'Yeah. That's perfectly normal. But, from that moment on, you have to be careful, boy. 'Cause women get pregnant easily. Your best bet is to wait until you're back home, relieve yourself under your quilt.'

'You mean wank?'

'Yeah.'

'I did that last night. Do you wank too, Kenny?'

'Of course. All men do.'

Ricky smiled. 'That's good to know. 'Cause I often wondered if I was a dirty boy in the past.'

'Nah. You're a top man, you.' Kenny felt highly amused as he put his foot down along the A127. He'd been surprised when he'd dropped Candy off earlier. Because of who her uncle and granddad were, he'd expected a bit of an awkward conversation with some big bruiser of a father, but couldn't have been more wrong. Candy's dad was a tiny little fella, dressed in a shell suit and as thick as mince. Turned out Candy's mum was Arthur's daughter.

A pleasant, yet very simple soul. No wonder Candy had been given that unfortunate name and turned out like she had, thought Kenny.

Ricky looked at Kenny inquisitively. 'Why you smiling?'

Kenny winked at his sidekick. ''Cause I'm happy. Today's gonna be a good day. I can feel it in me bones.'

Engrossed in his thoughts, Kenny was totally oblivious to the Yamaha motorcycle that had been tailing him for the past five minutes.

Still wearing his wedding suit, Brett sat up on Beau's sofa. 'Jesus wept! You awake, Beau? Do I look as bad as I feel?' Just looking at the half-empty bottle of brandy made Brett feel nauseous. As for his face, he could tell it was battered and bruised.

Beau opened one eye. 'Yeah, you do. What a day, eh? I should never have blurted all that out in front of the brothers' wives. Jolene's gonna kill me. That's if Evie don't get to me first.'

'It weren't your fault. Her brothers wanted a row, and they got one.' Brett's heart sank as he recalled his own falling out. He now regretted telling Aidan they were over. He should've at least heard him out. 'What we gonna do? I doubt Aisling will forgive me either.'

'Hardly the same, is it? You've known Aisling all of five minutes. I'm married. Or was.'

Brett stood up. 'Best you talk to your wife while you still got one then. I'm off home.'

Jolene stepped out of the shower and wrapped her mother's dressing gown around her. It was far too big, smothered her, which matched how she felt. As though she were in a broken-down stuffy lift, struggling for air, with no way out. If only Tammy were still here. She'd know what to do.

'Jolene.' Bobby Tamplin pounded his fist against the bathroom door. 'I've just seen Beau and given him what for. He was wrong to say what he did and he knows it. He wants to talk to you, in private. Don't worry about the boys, they're helping me and the men tidy up the land. Romany's with your mother. They've gone shopping.'

'I'll talk to him later.'

'No. You won't. Problems are meant to be solved, not avoided. Especially when you're a married woman with three young chavvies.'

'Give me five minutes.' Jolene opened the window to let out some steam. That's when she spotted it. A beautiful little robin, tweeting while looking her way.

Breathing in the fresh air, Jolene stared at the bird. Her mum had always insisted that robins were sent as messengers from lost loved ones. It was a sign from Tammy. It had to be.

It was at that precise moment, Jolene knew exactly what she had to do.

Gloria Charles had a hard as nails reputation. Forty-seven years old, she'd been raised in Bolton, got married young and had three sons. Then rather cruelly, she'd been dumped like a bag of old rubbish, just so her Mancunian Hells Angel husband could set up home with a girl half her age.

With three young mouths to feed, Gloria had no time to wallow and fix her broken heart. She offered her services to friends, then friends of friends, to catch out their cheating spouses. Very soon a thriving business was built. All by word of mouth.

Gloria was mustard at her job, had a natural talent and passion for what she did. She didn't come cheap, would only take cash in hand. Yet she'd never had to advertise her services. She lived in Essex now, yet people still came to her, from far and wide. Just like Sharon had.

'Here he is,' muttered Gloria, as Kenny Bond walked out the Toys R Us store with two massive bags. Talking to herself kept her sane. She clicked away with her new miniature high-tech camera. 'No way are you taking those to put on Granny and Grandpa's graves, are you now, Mr Bond. You despicable dick-led dipshit.'

Brett paced up and down the garden. The fresh air had done his hangover good, as had a shower and numerous cups of tea. Nothing could ease that horrible feeling in his gut though. Where was Aidan? And why was his phone switched off?

Desperately needing someone to talk to, Brett debated on calling his mate Alex, but decided not to. He hadn't seen Alex for months and he wouldn't understand anyway. Alex wasn't interested in true love, only fucking.

Brett tried Aidan once more. No joy. He scrolled through his phone to see who else he could call. He would have to pretend he was talking about Aisling, of course. Gramps would tell him to grow a pair. His dad was henpecked himself. Beau was a selfish prick. And his nan might tell Gramps. That left only one person. His mother. What she'd said to him yesterday was bizarre. Did she know he was gay? And even more baffling, if she did, how did she know?

Deciding there was only one way to find out, Brett took the plunge and pressed the call button.

Another one needing his mother's advice was Beau. He was on the phone to her, when he saw Jolene heading his way. 'She's coming! I'll bell you later or tomorrow; let you know how it went.' Beau's stomach was in knots as he ended the call and even though his mum had just given him advice on how to handle the situation, his mind had gone blank already.

Wearing faded jeans, black boots, a long black cardigan and her thick dark hair up in a scrunchie, Jolene looked as beautiful as the day he'd met her. He stood up. 'I'm glad you're home. I'm really sorry about what happened with Billy and Johnny, but—'

'It's caused murders, Beau,' interrupted Jolene. 'Chaos in fact. Both my brothers' wives have walked out on them today because of you. Billy and Johnny are gunning for ya, and my poor mum is beside herself. All because of your big snitchy mouth.'

'I ain't no snitch. I'll sort it, OK? I'll drive down to see Crystal and Layla, tell 'em I made the whole thing up.'

'Too late. Crystal and Layla have been down to the pub and kicked the granny out of the barmaids,' lied Jolene.

'Oh no! Were they the barmaids they'd actually been shagging?'

'I don't know, do I? But what I do know is you need to go and stay with Brett. Until things calm down.'

Beau was crestfallen. Last night was the first night Jolene and he had spent apart since they'd got married and he'd hated every minute of it. 'I can't leave you to deal with all this. And what about the chavvies? Please, Jolene, I'll do whatever to make this right. I love you and the kids. You're my world.'

Jolene looked at the snivelling lowlife she'd married and for the first time ever felt nothing for him. Travellers were by no means angels. She'd known a fair few who'd killed someone. But that had been via fights or drink driving. Not a premeditated murder that involved drowning a family member in your swimming pool. That truly was the lowest of the low. 'Just pack some stuff and go, Beau. I'll call you later.'

Beau grabbed Jolene's hands. 'Come with me. I'll pack some things for you and the kids too. We can all stay at me dad's gaff until things have calmed down.'

The feel of Beau's murdering hands even touching her own made Jolene feel nauseous. Jamie had been a nice lad with a good heart. No wonder Tansey had blamed the twins and loathed Beau so much. She obviously wasn't a nutter after all. Quite the opposite, in fact. She was clued up and could see Beau for what he actually was. 'I need to stay here. Mum needs me. She's in bits over all this,' lied Jolene.

Feeling as though his heart had been ripped out, Beau sank to his knees and grabbed Jolene's ankles. 'Please don't do this. I can't be without you and the kids. I won't survive.'

'Get up and stop acting like a nancy boy,' spat Jolene. 'You've only got yourself to blame, Beau. Pull yourself together for goodness' sake. No woman likes a wimp.'

*

'Help me get dressed, Sharon. I gotta go outside, have a fag,' said Maggie Saunders.

'No, Mum. The nurse said you can't.'

'But I feel better now. The pain's all but gone. Sudden nicotine withdrawal can cause health issues an' all, you know. I'll discharge myself if I can't have a smoke.'

Sharon glanced at her phone again. Her stomach was in bits, so much so, she'd had the runs all morning.

Maggie propped herself up on her pillow. 'What's the matter with you today? Did you hear what I just said? You haven't stopped staring at that bloody phone since you got here.'

'Sorry.' Sharon dropped the phone back in her bag. 'Tina's got problems. I've been expecting her to call me.'

'What type of problems?'

Sharon forced a chuckle. 'Man problems. What else?'

Maggie eyed her daughter suspiciously. She might have stomach issues, but there was sod all wrong with her brain. If that bastard of a son-in-law had cheated on her baby again, she'd kill him this time. With her own bare hands.

'All right? Where's Hope and Carl?' asked Brett, as his mother led him into a smaller sitting room he'd never sat in before. It was very sparse and dim. A big red leather sofa, lit candles, a stereo system and little else.

'Carl's taken Hope to visit his mum. He's taking her out of the care home for a meal today, so they'll be gone a while. How did the rest of the wedding go? Not good, if that bruised eye is anything to go by.' Lori grasped Brett's left hand. 'I want you to know that I

218

would never breathe a word of our conversations to anybody, and that includes Beau. You do know that, don't you?'

'Cheers, Mum.' Brett replied awkwardly, before reciting all he could recall about the previous evening's altercation with Billy and Johnny Tamplin. 'He rung me on the way here, Beau. He's at my gaff. Jolene asked him to leave. Just temporary, so he said.'

'I know, love. Beau rung me too. But today is about us. It's you I want to concentrate on, not your brother. Tell me about Aidan. Where did you meet him?'

Feeling awkward, Brett snatched his hand away. 'Why you talking about Aidan? I'm dating Aisling.'

Ever since leaving rehab, Lori loved a bit of therapy. She'd had hundreds of sessions with the most expensive therapists Carl's money could buy. This time, she clenched both of her handsome son's hands. 'It's OK, Brett. It's fine to be gay. I've known for years and Aidan is absolutely gorgeous, may I add. Please talk to me. Not being able to speak out is no good for the soul.'

There was a weird scent in the room. It smelled of something burning, yet was calming. Brett took a deep breath, his eyes welled up, then he began to speak. Openly and honestly.

'What d'ya mean he's moving out? What has he done to you?' asked an elated Evie. Psychic Lena was right. Not that she'd ever doubted her. It still felt joyous though.

'Nothing. But I need you to back me up if he tries to talk to you. I told him you were fuming 'cause of him, Johnny and Billy getting into an argument. If he turns up,

219

I just want you to shout and scream at him, tell him to stay away.'

'Of course I will. I've always got your back and I never liked him anyway. What has he done though, Jolene? I promise I won't tell your father. Anything you tell me will stay between us.'

Jolene wished she could tell her mum, but no way could she taint Tammy's memory in the process. Her parents would be devastated if they learned the truth. It was Tammy who'd egged Beau and Brett on to buy those ecstasy pills in the first place. The same pills that had killed her. Not only that, she'd taken half of one too and had lied to her parents and brothers on the night in question. None of them would forgive her for being so deceitful, especially seeing as she'd spouted a load of old rubbish to protect Beau, while poor Tammy was lying in a coma. She could barely forgive herself for such behaviour.

Aware her daughter was upset, Evie held her close to her chest. 'Talk to me, angel. Please.'

Tears welled up in Jolene's eyes as she finally blurted out some truth. 'You were right, Mum. I should never have married a gorger. I don't love him any more.'

'It's him ringing again,' Sharon told Tina. 'I can't answer it. Not until I've spoken to her. Say he spotted her following him?' Not wanting to go to a pub where anybody knew them, it had been Tina's suggestion to go to The Bear in Noak Hill. It was lively enough for nobody to notice them, but full of Travellers, which Sharon didn't exactly need to be around, especially after the chaos of the previous evening.

'Ring him back,' ordered Tina. 'Kenny ain't stupid. He'll smell a rat if you ignore him.'

'I can't hear meself think. Not with that mob singing. I'll go outside and do it.'

'Good luck,' smiled Tina.

Sharon returned a couple of minutes later. 'Kenny was fine. Said he spent the day with his mum and aunt and he's home now. What do I do if she's a con artist? We don't even know her name and she rung me on a with-held.'

'She's not a con artist. My cousin ain't no fool. He would never have recommended her if she couldn't be trusted,' Tina reassured her.

A split second later, Sharon's phone rang again. From a withheld number.

CHAPTER SIXTEEN

'How you feeling? Silly question, I know.' Tina sat down on the end of the bed. Unable to face going home, Sharon had stayed in her spare room last night.

'Like shit. I didn't eat a morsel yesterday. All I can taste is that wine. What did I say to Kenny? I can't even remember. Did I sound as though something was wrong?'

'No. You just said you'd had too much to drink and was gonna crash at mine. I then spoke to him; told him I'd made up the spare room for you.'

'Did he sound convinced?'

'Dunno. He didn't say much. Anyway, sod him. What we gonna do when we get this address? You still want to go straight there, check out the occupants?'

Unable to think straight, Sharon held her forehead in her hands. The woman was coming to Tina's at ten with the information and to collect the rest of her money. Sharon already knew it wasn't going to be good news. She'd pleaded for some details last night and had been told Kenny had spent hours at an unknown address before visiting his mum and aunt. 'What am I gonna do if the kid thing is true? How am I meant to tell Sherry and Donny?'

'I dunno, mate. But I'll be by your side every step of the way.'

'I still can't believe he would do that to me. Not after all we've been through.'

'Well, maybe he's innocent. But he must be hiding something, Shal. You need to prepare yourself for that, mate.'

'I need to draw money out the bank to pay her. Where's the nearest NatWest?'

'Not far. You jump in the shower and I'll cook us some bacon sarnies.'

Just the thought of food was enough to turn Sharon's stomach. Hand over mouth, she leapt out the bed and ran into the bathroom, retching.

Beau picked up his phone and frantically began texting. He'd heard nothing from Jolene other than a brief message late last night, saying she was with her mum, couldn't talk, but the kids were fine, and she'd call him tomorrow.

'You're not texting her again, are ya?' asked Brett.

'I got every right to talk to my kids. I miss 'em already. It was horrible waking up this morning without them. You heard from Aisling yet?'

'Nope. Not a word. But unlike you, I'm gonna take Mum's advice, play it cool and let Aisling stew in her own juice. As Mum said, "If a person truly loves you and you're meant to be together, you will."'

'Since when did you and Mum become best buddies?' Beau's voice was laden with sarcasm.

Usually, Brett would've bitten, retaliated. But today, he felt different. At peace with himself and his sexuality. Opening up to his mum had lifted a huge weight off his shoulders. The relief he felt to finally have an ally was immense. 'You want another coffee?'

'Nah.' Beau rattled on about Jolene again. It was lashing it down up at the garden centre, so they were holed up in the office.

The portacabin door opened and in burst Kenny. 'Poxy weather, poxy women and I've now stabbed my poxy toe. How's your day going, lads?'

'Not you an' all,' replied Brett. 'You had a row with Nan?'

'Nope! She's just acting all weird. Stayed round that mate of hers last night in Harold Hill. Not answering her phone this morning. Probably too hungover. Forget about Aisling and stay single, boy. That's the best advice I can give ya. The female species will never fail to baffle me.'

'Nan's probably just worried about Nanny Maggie. You think you've got problems. I tried to ring you yesterday, twice, but you didn't answer. I'm currently living with Brett again,' explained Beau.

As his brother rambled on about his woes, Brett's phone rang. It was Aidan.

'Come in. Shal's in the front room,' said Tina. 'What is your name by the way? You never told us it.'

'Sorry. I thought I did. It's Gloria.'

Both Sharon and Tina were surprised once Gloria removed her crash helmet at how attractive she was. Clad in leathers, she looked about a size eighteen, yet her size really suited her. She had beautiful black wavy long hair and a full face of make-up which enhanced her stunning features.

Not one to beat around the bush, Gloria got straight down to business, explaining Kenny's exact movements from the previous day. 'Here's the photos of him coming out of Toys R Us.'

Sharon was dumbstruck. They weren't just small bags her husband was carrying; they were more like bloody sacks.

'Does Kenny go out to buy the grandkids' toys?' Tina asked.

'No. Never. I do.' Sharon could barely breathe, let alone talk.

'After he left the shop, Kenny then drove to this address in Loughton. He entered the address at eleven thirty-five a.m. and left the property at two fifty-seven p.m. These are photos of him entering. With the toy bags, as you can see,' explained Gloria.

'Does he know people who live in Loughton, Shal?' asked Tina.

'I don't know. Can you get me a glass of water, please? My mouth's dried up.'

Gloria continued, reporting that Kenny had picked up an Indian takeaway on the way home before heading back to Dark Lane.

Tina returned with a pint of water. 'Was it just you following him all that time?'

'No. A team of us. Two bikes and a van. He wouldn't have spotted us, if that's what you're worried about. We know our stuff.'

'I'm sure you do. I was just being curious. Sorry if that came out wrong.'

Gloria handed Sharon a piece of paper. Having been through similar herself, she knew how crap the woman felt. 'I could tell how stressed out you were last night, so I also got the Loughton address checked out for you. It's owned by a Mr G. Singh, but he rents it out. There are three occupants currently residing there. A Karen Bamber, a Kayleigh Wood and a Jake Bamber. One adult, two children.'

'Two children,' echoed Sharon.

'Who's the adult?' enquired Tina.

'I don't know. Time ran out on me. Like it is now.' Gloria glanced at her watch. 'I have to meet another client soon.'

'You better pay her, Shal,' Tina reminded her friend. Sharon looked white, deathly white, bless her.

Gloria checked the amount inside the large envelope, then handed Sharon a business card. 'You need me for anything else, just call that number. A word of advice: don't be letting Kenny know you've had him followed, whatever the outcome. Makes our job harder if we ever have to follow him again. Good luck – and if he is cheating on you, darling, get rid ASAP. Once a cheat, always a cheat. Right, I got to dash. Laters, ladies.'

Inside her trailer, Jolene was multitasking. She had her phone cradled to her neck, while chatting to her brother Billy, leaving her hands free to pack Beau's belongings into heavy-duty dustbin sacks at the same time. 'Well, I'm glad all's OK, Bill. But promise me, no revenge tactics.

He won't be coming back 'ere to live, honest he won't. No point in starting a war though. Dad and Kenny are good pals and even though Beau deserves a bloody good clump, he's still the kids' dad. I don't want to see him hurt, Bill. It ain't right.'

Relieved when Billy agreed that there'd be no retribution unless she took Beau back, Jolene ended the call. Both Crystal and Layla were fine now, believed that Beau had been making the accusations up, so her brothers' marriages were still thankfully intact. She'd told Billy that was the reason she'd thrown Beau out. Blood was thicker than water, so to speak. She could hardly tell him the truth. That she'd married a murderer.

'Jolene,' bellowed Bobby Tamplin.

Jolene opened the trailer door. 'Shush, I've just put Romany down.'

'Get your arse over 'ere, young lady. We need to talk.'

Jolene rolled her eyes. Unlike her mother, her father liked Beau, was bound to stick up for him. 'OK. Give me five minutes.'

'Well?' Beau prompted. He couldn't help but feel peeved that Aisling was grovelling to Brett, yet he'd heard jackshit from Jolene. Perhaps his mother's 'playing it cool' tactics did actually work. His brother hadn't even answered Aisling's call straight away, had left it over an hour before ringing her back.

Beaming from ear to ear, Brett said, 'She apologized. Said she was pissed. She wanted to see me tonight, but I pretended I'd made other arrangements. Mum told me not to act needy.'

'Mum told you a fucking lot, didn't she?' hissed Beau. His mother had actually given him the same advice. She certainly hadn't urged him to cling to Jolene's ankles, begging for forgiveness, like the mug of all mugs. No way was Beau telling anyone about that, not even Brett. He could quite easily beat himself up for acting like such a numpty. 'And the outcome was?'

'Me day off tomorrow, so I'm driving over to hers. We need to talk first. Then she said she'll take me out, anywhere I wanna go.'

'Lucky fucking you.'

Tina pulled up across the road from the address. It looked a typical middle-class street with leafy trees. The house in question was semi-detached. 'What you gonna say, Shal?' Sharon had been silent throughout the journey, had turned the stereo up every time Tina had tried talking to her.

Sharon stared at number 13. Unlucky for some, she thought. Was Jake Bamber Kenny's son? There was only one way to find out. 'You wait 'ere, mate.'

'Shal, Shal.'

Sharon ignored Tina's cries, marched up the driveway and rang the bell. Her heart was pounding, her legs like jelly.

'I'll get it,' shouted a voice. Not the voice of an adult, thought Sharon. The door was opened by a cocky-looking teenage girl wearing a pink velour tracksuit. 'Can I help you?'

'Is your mum in?'

'Mum. Someone at the door,' the girl shouted out.

228

'Who is it?' yelled Karen Bamber. 'I'm in the bath, Kayleigh.'

'Who are you?' smirked the girl.

'I'm Kenny Bond's wife. Who are you?'

The look on the girl's face was priceless. She backed away from the front door as though Sharon was pointing a gun her way. 'Mum, you better come down quick. It's urgent.'

'Who is it?' asked a young male voice. As the child appeared in front of her, dressed in a pair of West Ham pyjamas, Sharon's worst nightmare came to fruition. He was dark-haired, looked about five and uncannily like Donny had at the same age.

'Mum, Mum,' shrieked the teenage girl, as Sharon grabbed hold of the door frame for support.

'You OK, lady?' asked a worried Jake.

Sharon looked at the innocent child. None of this was his fault. It was hers, for being dopey enough to take that womanizing bastard back in the first place.

'Thanks,' said Karen, as her daughter put the coffees on the table. 'Can you take Jake upstairs now, please? While we talk.' To say Karen had been gobsmacked by Sharon's arrival was putting it mildly. Meeting Kenny's wife with wet hair, no make-up on and wearing a dressing gown was not how she'd envisaged it happening. Not that she'd ever expected or wanted to meet Sharon. Quite the opposite, in fact.

Now she was sitting down, Sharon felt slightly more at ease. Karen was slimmer than her, taller, but nothing special. She had long chestnut hair, but her face was hard, not pretty. She was nothing like Abigail. She had been young and beautiful. On the outside anyway.

Karen waited until Kayleigh located her phone, then left the room with Jake before asking the vital question. 'Does Kenny know you're here?'

'No. I thought it was time you and I had a chat, woman to woman. Has my husband ever told you how much Jake looks like Donny did when he was young?'

Karen lowered her eyes, focused on her newly painted false nails. 'Yes. He did mention it once or twice. I don't want any trouble, Sharon. I know this must have been a big shock for you, but I can assure you there is nothing romantically going on between myself and Kenny. There hasn't been for years. I wouldn't do that to you.'

'How very noble of you!' snapped Sharon. She could already tell that Karen wasn't her type of person. There were lots of what she and Tina referred to as 'Barbie dolls' parading around Essex of late. Fake everything, they had. Hair, tits, teeth, eyelashes, nails, and even though Karen had obviously just got out the bath, Sharon could still tell she was a middle-aged Barbie doll. 'Talk then. I want to know everything. The whole sordid caboodle. From start to finish.'

Feeling vulnerable with her bare face and wet hair, Karen put up the hood of the tracksuit she'd quickly thrown on. She'd never been vain until Kenny had so callously dumped her. He'd made her feel like shit, totally worthless, which had started her obsession with bettering her appearance. 'You're best talking to Kenny. I would hate to cause any trouble, say the wrong thing. I can call him, if you like?'

As Karen went to pick up her phone, Sharon leapt off the sofa. 'Put that down or risk it getting shoved up your arsehole. Sideways! I deserve answers and that devious bastard ain't gonna give me truthful ones. So best you do the talking, Karen. Come on, spill your guts.'

Karen was worried now. Very worried. If she said the wrong thing, Kenny would not only go apeshit, he might also stop their financial arrangement. No way did Karen want to go back to work after all this time. She couldn't, wouldn't. 'What exactly do you want to know?'

As much as she'd dreaded learning the worst, now she had and was sat in the ageing Barbie doll's front room, Sharon felt strong and in control. She was also desperate to find out the truth. What betrayed wife wouldn't be? 'Let's start at the beginning. Where did you meet Kenny and when?'

Unable to make eye contact, Karen put on an oversized pair of sunglasses. She then began to talk.

'Sorry I took ages. Romany sicked up all over me and I had to bathe Rocky's knee. He fell—'

'Forget all that,' interrupted Bobby Tamplin. 'Sit down, girl. Take the boys outside to play, Bobby-Joe. There's a good lad.'

Jolene sat her daughter on her lap. She knew her dad wanted to talk to her about Beau. 'What's up?'

'What's up! You kidding me? I had Kenny Bond on the phone earlier asking me what's going on. I says you were gonna talk to Beau later to sort things out, then your mother tells me that you ain't happy in your marriage any more. I know Beau was a fool the other night. He was wrong and he knows he was wrong. But that can't be grounds for a bloody divorce, surely?'

'She didn't say she wanted a divorce, Bobby,' piped up Evie. 'She said she wants some time alone to think over things. I dunno exactly what Beau did or said to Billy and Johnny. But I got the gist and I don't want to know any more. 'Cause if either of them have cheated on their wives, I'd chop their bloody cories off. But Beau turned grass. Jolene's like me. We don't tolerate grasses.'

'It was a drunken spat, Evie, and as you well know, our sons started it by chucking a drink all over Beau. If they hadn't done that, nothing would've happened.'

'Nothing excuses grassing. As for you, sticking up for a gorger over your own flesh and blood? I have no words,' hissed Evie.

'Stop being so dramatic, woman. Go outside with the kids. I want to talk Jolene alone.'

Evie winked at Jolene before leaving them to it. She and her daughter had already discussed how to play the situation with Bobby. Slowly and carefully.

'What's going on, Jolene?' asked a worried Bobby.

'I don't know, Dad. But I'll try to explain the best I can.'

'There you are! Jesus, Shal, you didn't arf have me worried. I thought you'd murdered her or she'd murdered you.' Tina looked at her watch. 'Forty-five minutes you were in there. What happened?'

'Just drive to mine, quick as you like. She's promised me she won't ring Kenny and I want all his stuff packed up before he gets home.'

Tina was gobsmacked. Sharon seemed like a different woman to the one that had stepped out of her car. 'So, is Jake his kid?'

'Yeah. And not only that, he's the spitting image of my Donny. Just drive, will ya. I'll tell you all about it on the way. What a lying cunt! I want him out of my life today. For good.'

Jolene squeezed her father's hands. She and Tammy had both been 'Daddy's girls' growing up. His reputation as a bare-knuckle fighter set him on a pedestal among Travellers, yet he was such a kind man too. Their hero. 'Thanks for being understanding. Do you think you can talk to Kenny and Beau for me? Help me smooth things over. For now, at least.' Jolene had explained how suffocated she'd felt of late and how needy Beau was at times. The drama at Sonny's wedding had just been the icing on the cake, she'd told him.

'Course I will. Kenny'll be fine. He's a sensible man. You'll need to talk to Beau though and he'll want to spend time with the chavvies regularly. No matter how you feel at present, that lad is a bloody good father, Jolene. Hopefully, once you've had a bit of time on your own, you'll miss your husband. In fact, I bet you will. As much as your mother drives me mad at times, I would never want to be without her. Even though she can be an old rabbit's crotch,' chuckled Bobby.

Jolene smiled and held Romany close to her chest. She knew if she could tell her parents the truth, that her husband had murdered Jamie with his bare hands, they'd never allow him near her or her children again. But she

233

couldn't betray Tammy or Tammy's memory. That would be so wrong.

'You start with that wardrobe,' ordered Sharon. 'I'll empty the chest of drawers. Don't think we've got enough bin bags, so just carry what you can't bag up. Sling it all out on the left side of the drive.'

Tina was proud of Sharon, but also worried. Her pal had been in bits up until speaking to Karen earlier; now she was acting like Rambo. 'You not gonna cut the arms off his shirts and suits? I did my Lee's when I found out what he'd been up to with her next door.' Tina's ex-husband had been carrying on with their neighbour. A woman she'd classed as a friend before learning the truth.

'Not got time. I just want every trace of him outta *my* home before he gets back.'

'He's got a lot of shoes. Want me to take 'em down in the boxes?'

'No.' Sharon yanked open the window. 'Hand 'em to me and we'll see if they can fly. Oh hang on, I need to call Dad, make an excuse why I can't visit Mum today. No way am I worrying her while she's in hospital. Then I must ring Donny and Sherry, get 'em to come over. I want to tell them the news together.'

'You do what you gotta do, mate.' Tina's heart went out to Sharon. Her coping mechanism was in overdrive. But the stark reality of Kenny's betrayal was yet to touch the surface.

There were no designated working hours up at the garden centre for Kenny or his grandsons. The twins would usually take it in turns to open up and as long as one of them was there to cash up at the end of the day, they had other staff running the joint, so were able to come and go as they pleased. Especially on the quieter days.

By mid-afternoon, Kenny started to realize he'd dropped a clanger by telling the twins to take the rest of the day off. He couldn't get hold of Sharon and, after ringing her father to check her mum was OK, it started to dawn on Kenny that something was wrong. Shal was a creature of habit, loved her own bed, so her staying round Tina's last night had been out of character. And she never ignored his calls, would always get back to him. Until today that was. 'Ricky, leave them boxes. Go tell Trevor to write out a big sign, saying we're closing early, but will be open as usual tomorrow morning.' There were only two members of staff Kenny would trust to cash up and lock up. Both were women and neither were working today.

Bemused, Ricky stood with his hands on his hips. 'Why?'

'I ain't got time for questions now,' bellowed a worried Kenny. 'Just do it.'

Donny Bond let himself into his parents' home with his own key. 'What the hell's going on, Mum?' He'd only just avoided running over his dad's golf clubs on the way in.

Having had a rushed clear-out of anything personal that belonged to the cheating bastard she'd had the misfortune of marrying, Sharon was now sat at the kitchen table with Tina and a bottle of wine. 'Whaddya think? Your sister's on her way. I'll explain in full when she gets 'ere.

But first of all, I want you to get all his tools out the garage, Donny, and dump 'em on the drive. The tools were his favourite excuse for popping back last time. There's no way back for him this time, believe me.'

Donny was perplexed. He knew his father had messed up in the past, but no way would he make the same mistake twice. 'I dunno what's happened, Mum, but I'd put money on it that there's been some misunderstanding.'

'Nah. No misunderstanding. He's a fucking arsehole and I hope he dies in a car crash.'

'Mum! Stop it!'

Kenny knew in his heart of hearts that the shit was about to hit the fan, so dropped Ricky off round Candy's gaff. His brain was working overtime and he'd narrowed it down to two things. Mad Ginger Daley and his brother Baz were still locked up, but had they somehow got hold of his name and told Sharon that he was behind those killer ecstasy pills? No. It couldn't be that, Kenny dithered. Because even if they had, Sharon would never believe it without speaking to him first. Which left one outcome. Shal had somehow found out about Jake's existence.

Kenny's worst fears were confirmed as he swung onto his driveway, spotted his son and daughter's cars, then ran over numerous pairs of his own shoes. He walked up to the front door half expecting the locks to be changed, but was able to get in with his own key. 'Shal, what's going on?'

'In the kitchen,' shouted Sharon. Her expression as cold as ice.

'What you done, Dad?' Sherry yelled at her father.

Kenny shrugged, wishing Tina wasn't present. Whatever was going on, this was family-only business.

Sharon felt hurt, foolish, betrayed. Numerous emotions were tugging at her heart. But she was determined to hold it together, for now at least. She gave Kenny a look of evil. 'You gonna tell 'em? Or shall I?'

'If this is about what I think it is, I can explain. It's not as it looks,' gabbled Kenny.

'Explain what?' bellowed Donny.

Sharon took a deep breath. 'Sorry to drop such a bombshell, but you two deserve to know the truth. You've got a little brother. Well, a half-brother. Jake. Dirty Daddy's been unable to keep his dick in his pants again.'

'You what?' exclaimed Sherry.

'Nah. That can't be right.' Donny was in disbelief. 'Dad, surely not?'

'Dad! Please tell us this ain't true,' shrieked Sherry.

Feeling like the arsehole of all arseholes, a sheepish Kenny said, 'You gotta let me explain. I never cheated on your mother. I swear, that's the truth. I didn't even know—'

Sherry flew at her father, lashing out, hitting him as hard as she could. 'How could you do this to us? To Mum?' she cried.

Kenny grabbed hold of his daughter's wrists. 'Shal, we need to talk. If I tell you the truth, you'll understand. I promise ya, you will.'

'You tell the truth! Don't make me fucking laugh. I want you out of this house, Kenny, and this time I want a divorce. I will never forgive you for this. You're dead to me now.'

As his sobbing sister ran retching into the bathroom, Donny leapt out of his chair. He was disgusted, disappointed and so bloody angry. He grabbed the lapels of his dad's leather jacket and slammed his back against the wall. 'You heard Mum. Get out. You make me fucking sick. Never will I look up to you or respect you again. You're dead to me an' all.'

Still aware that it wasn't just family present, Kenny held his hands up, palms facing outwards. 'OK. I'm going. But this ain't over. I deserve a chance to be heard and this is still my house. I paid for every brick that built it and every fucking thing in it.'

Sharon picked up her wine glass and aimed it straight at Kenny's head. It unfortunately missed, smashing against the wall behind him. 'Get out. Get out. Get out,' she screeched.

Without saying another word, Kenny glared at the gawping Tina, turned on his heel and stormed out.

CHAPTER SEVENTEEN

Kenny woke up and held his thumping head in his hands, as the events of the previous day slowly came back to him.

With his wife and kids temporarily disowning him, Kenny had turned to Beau and Brett for moral support. They'd taken the news of Jake's existence pretty well, especially when he'd explained that he and Sharon were estranged when the lad was conceived. He'd slept at Brett's an' all. Even though Donny had rung both the twins to tell them Gramps was banned from staying there. He'd even had to hide his poxy Range Rover on Bobby's land, in case Donny came checking up. Short memories his kids had. He'd helped them out so much financially over the years, was still contributing to Sherry's mortgage now.

Kenny stood up, scratched his balls, then got dressed in the previous day's clothes. He needed to sort through all his clobber. Some of it was in his motor and the twins had helped him carry the rest indoors. Knowing Sharon, she'd probably cut half of it up an' all. Especially with that mate of hers egging her on. Harold Hill Lil, Kenny called her in private.

Feeling like death warmed up, Kenny made his way down the stairs. Brett was opening up this morning, so had gone to bed at a sensible time. He and Beau had raided Donny's drinks cabinet and had sat up until the early hours, putting the world to rights, while necking rum and Coke.

'Morning, Gramps. I'm dying.' Beau put two mugs of steaming tea on the kitchen top. 'What's your plans? You gonna talk to Nan?'

'Not sure what I'm gonna do. Your nan's probably got that mate of her's stopping there and I ain't saying another word in front of her.'

'You want some toast?'

'Yeah, go on. Then I'll get a shower; find some fresh clothes to wear. I might need to borrow some pants and socks off you if I can't locate mine.'

'Take whatever. You staying here again tonight?'

'I doubt it. I should distance meself for a bit. Give your nan a chance to calm down. I'll probably go stay at Aunt Nelly's.'

'How'd Nan find out, you reckon?'

Kenny shrugged. 'I know she bumped into some nosy old cow at a dress shop a while back, but that all blew over. I'd love to fucking know how she knows, actually. See if you can find out.'

'Will do. Ricky might be the one to get all the info though. He hears and sees more, and Nan won't tell us much 'cause she knows we're as thick as thieves.'

Kenny slapped his hand against his forehead. 'Ricky! I forgot all about him. I didn't even pick him up from Candy's last night. How's he gonna react to all this?'

'Ricky's a man, not a boy any more. Me and Brett'll look after him.'

'Tell him to ring me when he's on his own today. I don't want him to think I've abandoned him.'

Beau's phone bleeped. He read the message and grinned like a Cheshire cat. 'It's Jolene. She wants me back at home at seven tonight. Says we need to talk. I'm glad I played it cool in the end. She was bound to miss me. What woman wouldn't?' he laughed.

Kenny wasn't so sure. Beau had been rambling on about lots of stuff last night and his and Jolene's relationship sounded anything but stable. He dreaded to think what might happen if Jolene didn't want the lad back. But he kept schtum. He had enough problems of his bloody own to deal with at present.

After crying herself to sleep the previous evening, Sharon woke up in a different frame of mind. A bitter, twisted and revengeful one. She also wasn't in the mood for answering numerous questions. 'Because I don't want him back 'ere, Ricky. I already told you that ten fucking times.'

Dressed in a pair of Only Fools and Horses pyjamas, Ricky's lip wobbled. He'd thought his life had ended when his parents had died in a car crash, but Kenny and Sharon had given him a new life. One that he absolutely cherished. 'But why?'

Sharon adored Ricky, would much rather Kenny had gently broken the news to him, but her fury was now at boiling point. 'You want the truth? I'll tell you the truth: Kenny is a womanizing arsehole who can't keep his cock in his pants. Oh, and he also has a son by another woman. Now d'ya understand why I'm so angry? Sorry to just blurt it out, but you're bound to find out anyway, boy.'

'A son! By another woman! Who?'

'A woman called Karen. Which is why I'm now divorcing him. He'll still be there for you though. We both will.'

Ricky ran over to Sharon and clung to her like a limpet. He couldn't imagine life without Sharon and Kenny living together. Together they were a team. His rock. His world.

To ease any nerves, Brett spent the whole of the journey to Aidan's chatting on the phone to his mum. It felt so good to have her as his ally. Not only that, his mother spoke words of wisdom. Even the tone of her voice seemed to have a calming effect on him. 'I'm 'ere now, Mum. Thanks for the advice. I'll either call or text you later with an update.'

It was a miserable day. Windy and rainy. Brett put the collar up on his Burberry raincoat. Aidan answered the buzzer immediately and in that gorgeous Irish tone, told him to come up. 'All right. How you doing?' Brett asked, sounding far more casual than he now felt.

'All the better for seeing you.'

As Aidan tried to embrace him, instead of falling into his arms like a sap, Brett recalled his mum's advice. 'Let's not rush things. I came 'ere to talk.'

Aidan raised an eyebrow. This was more like it. He liked a challenge. Needy men never lasted long with him.

He led Brett past the sleeping Alvin and into the kitchen, and poured two large vodkas with a splash of tonic. 'Fire away. I'll tell you anything you want to know.'

'Where's Aisling?'

'I told her to make herself scarce. That all you want to know?' Aidan smiled.

Brett locked eyes with the man he loved but didn't smile back. 'No. For a start, I wanna know what you're hiding from me.'

After managing to eat a little food in the café, Sharon dropped Tina home to sort some bits out, then shot into Romford, bought some yoghurts and a book for her mum, then headed up the hospital. Keeping busy was the only way she could cope. Last time Kenny had betrayed her, she'd moped around indoors, guzzling wine and eating chocolate like it was going out of style. Fat and depressed she'd ended up, and was determined not to go down that road again. The bastard wasn't worth it. No man was.

Sharon's phone rang. She ignored it. She didn't want to keep talking about what had happened. It was too raw. Donny, Sherry and both the twins had all rung her. Beau had even had the audacity to try to explain Kenny's side of the story. She'd soon cut him short. This time it was Ricky. That poor little sod had been too upset to go to work and kept ringing to check she was OK.

Sharon put the phone in the glove compartment before dashing inside the hospital. It was time to put on her cheeriest smile and bravest face. 'All right, Mum? Any news on your test results?'

'Never you mind about me. Kenny has another son! Please tell me that ain't fucking true? And who the hell is Karen?'

'Who told you?'

'Ricky. Well? Is it true?'

Sharon dropped the M&S carrier bag on the bed and sank down beside it. She suddenly felt weary. 'I was going to tell you, but I didn't want to worry you, not while you were in 'ere.'

'Worry me! I'll kill that bastard. Get me clothes out me little case. I'm coming home with you.'

'No! You can't do that. I'm fine, honest. Tina's staying with me.'

'No. You're not fine. You weren't right all last week either. I knew there was something you weren't telling me. You ever take him back after this, I'll disown you, girl.'

'I won't. Not this time. He's already gone. So has all his stuff.'

'Good. Hand me me case, please.'

'You're not discharging yourself, Mum.'

'Oh yes, I bloody well am. You need me.' This morning Maggie had received the most awful news. Her cancer was back with a vengeance. No way could she tell Sharon. Not now. Her darling daughter had enough on her plate. But while she was still alive, she would be there for her. Every step of the way.

Watching her poorly frail mum struggling to get dressed was too much for Sharon to cope with. The tears came out of nowhere. Floods of them.

*

244

Brett stared Aidan in the eyes as he swilled his sperm around in his mouth. They'd had a good heart-to-heart. Aidan had admitted that once upon a time he'd been bisexual and had actually been in a nine-month relationship with the mother of his son. He'd also spoken about Finlay, describing him as his 'first love' and how devastated he'd been when he'd been shot. Apparently, Aidan had fallen foul of a dodgy little firm in Dublin and the bullet had been meant for him. That's the reason he'd moved to London. To leave the past behind, start afresh.

'That was so good.' Aidan squeezed Brett tightly. 'You enjoy it?'

'Yeah, course.' The sex had been as expected. Passionate, wild, spontaneous. 'What was you gonna tell me? Before we ended up at it. You said something about Stan and the night we met?'

'Not now. Let's go out, get some food. I'm starving.'

Brett propped himself up on his elbow. 'No. Not until you've told me. I wanna know now. No more lies.'

Aidan sat up and covered his now flaccid manhood with a pillow. 'OK. But I don't want you to think badly of me, because my little sideline is for friends only.'

'Go on.'

'The night we met at Stan's, I was there for a reason. I would have told you, but I knew how upset you were over what happened to Tammy and I didn't want to put you off me. To put it bluntly, I supply a bit of cocaine. But only to pals and close associates. Stan likes a bit of Charlie at his parties, so I provide it. As I said, it's just a sideline. Sometimes the antique business goes quiet, especially in the kipper season. Call it an extra bit of income.'

'I always knew that you must do something else to live where you do and have such a stunning gaff. I ain't a prude, ya know. I hardly come from a family of saints meself. You should've told me. I can be trusted.'

Pleased with Brett's casual response, Aidan smiled. 'I just thought you were very anti-drug because of what happened to Tammy. You told me all about her death on the night we met. I could hardly tell you then, could I? And I liked you, wanted you to like me back.'

'I do like you. But I also understand. I'm glad you told me. It explains a lot. Is that what you do on the nights you don't see me?'

'Some of them. I'm very careful about who I do business with. I provide to a few regular haunts, nightclubs and parties. Now you know, I can take you with me. Some good nights out are to be had at my friends' parties.'

Feeling like he was finally part of Aidan's life, Brett grinned broadly. 'Yeah. I'm well up for that. When can we go to one?'

Amused by Brett's enthusiasm, Aidan chuckled. 'Soon. I promise.'

'Do you ever take it yourself?'

'Sometimes. Cocaine is a social drug. Makes you happy, talkative, and you don't get drunk so quickly. It's not dangerous. Especially the stuff I get. Mine's kosher, hasn't been cut with shitty chemicals. In fact, Aisling was on it on Saturday. It wasn't mine she took to the wedding with her, mind. She actually offered me some and I refused. I would've felt disloyal to you. In hindsight I wish I had taken a couple of lines. It would've stopped me getting so pissed, then we wouldn't have argued in the first place.'

Feeling closer to Aidan than ever, Brett forgot about his mother's 'play it cool' advice. He looked at Aidan with big puppy eyes and stroked his face. He looked incredibly handsome today, had grown a bit of stubble. 'Sometimes things happen for a reason. If we hadn't had a bust up, then we wouldn't be having this conversation now. You got any cocaine indoors?'

'A little bit. Why?'

Desperate for Aidan not to think of him as some boring little boy, Brett smiled. 'I wanna try it. But only if you take some with me.'

Aidan laughed and pinned his young lover to the bed. 'You're a bad influence on me, Mr Bond. Give us a tick and I'll get us some.'

Kenny Bond was in a furious frame of mind as he drove towards Loughton. He'd rung Karen for the first time since all the drama had unfolded and she'd calmly informed him she'd left messages on his burner phone, asking him to call her back, because Sharon had turned up at her house. Kenny kept his burner hidden up at the garden centre.

Jaw twitching furiously, Kenny thumped his fist against the door of the house he rented.

It was opened by Kayleigh, Karen's stroppy teenage daughter. 'Don't be having a go at my mum. She's upset enough as it is.'

'Daddy,' shrieked an excited Jake. He flung his arms around his father's waist, just like his mum had ordered him to.

'Hello, boy.' Kenny picked up his son. Jake was much better now, thank God. 'I need you to go upstairs with your sister while I talk to your mum. I'll give you a shout in a bit, yeah.'

'OK. Then can we play with my new toys?'

'We'll see. Go upstairs first.' Kenny slammed the door behind Jake. 'I told you in an emergency to ring me on my other phone,' he hissed. 'How is my wife turning up at your door not a fucking emergency, Karen?'

Kenny's eyes were blazing, which would have scared Karen had the children not been in the house. 'You told me I was only to phone you if Jake was taken ill. I was too scared to ring you on your other phone. What was I meant to do but wait for you to ring me? You was the one that banned me from bloody phoning you.'

Needing to take his anger out on something, Kenny smashed his fist against the wall. It turned out to be plasterboard and his fist all but went through it.

'Don't smash the house up! What about the kids? I said all the things you would want me to say, Kenny. Honestly, I did. Sharon already knew. I don't know how, but she did. She knew the exact amount of time you'd spent here on Sunday and she knew you brought Jake all those toys.'

Kenny sank to the sofa, head in hands. 'Sit the fuck down, Karen. I want to know exactly what was said. And when I say that, I mean every single paltry fucking word.'

'Bye, Trev. Enjoy your day off,' grinned Beau, as he locked the gates to the garden centre. He couldn't wait to see his wife and kids, had missed them terribly. Credit to his mum, she'd been right about not pestering Jolene.

He'd only left her alone for twenty-four hours and now she was begging him to come back.

Full of beans, Beau literally leapt inside his Range Rover. He started the engine and the plush leather interior was soon filled with the sultry tones of Dolly Parton. Dolly was one of Jolene's favourite singers.

Turning the volume up on 'I Will Always Love You', Beau sped down the road. This song could have been written for him and Jolene. Well, parts of it.

Unusually for Jolene, she was dead nervous. She'd known for a while Beau was a complex character. He was needy and, when he didn't get the attention he craved, unpredictable. He'd never lashed out at her or the kids. If anything, he was too loving and soppy. That's one of the things that had put her off him. Finding out about Jamie was just the final nail in the coffin.

Wiping down the kitchen top again, Jolene peered out the window. The kids were in her parents' trailer. But she'd let Beau see them after their chat. She had to. He was their father. Sonny was also around, doing odd jobs to his trailer. He'd convinced Mary-Ann to move onto the land with him. Jolene wasn't sure if that was a good or bad thing. She missed her brother a lot but couldn't connect with his wife. She would try though, for Sonny's sake. He had a sweet soul, did Sonny.

Jolene looked at the clock: 6.30 p.m. Roll on half an hour, she thought. Apart from when she'd had to tell her parents that Tammy was in a coma, this would be the most difficult conversation of her life. She would have to pretend she'd had a different conversation with Beau to her family. It was mad to think how she'd got herself into such a mess. But she was determined to get herself out of it. It was a mother's duty to protect her children from evil, after all.

Kenny was slouched on a seat at the Eleanor Arms in Old Ford Road. The boozer wasn't far from Aunt Nelly's gaff. He needed some Dutch courage to tell his beloved aunt the truth. She was going to be so disappointed with him, especially for not confiding in her about Jake. She'd raised him in his teenage years and, unlike his mother, Aunt Nelly had always had his back. He would've told her, should've told her. He just hadn't wanted to worry her unnecessarily. She wasn't getting any bloody younger after all.

Kenny downed his brandy, then slammed the glass against the table. He'd wanted to ring Sharon today and Donny, but guessed it might be best for the shock to sink in a bit first. Karen had told him her version of the conversation with Sharon. Whether it was true or not was another matter. He'd find out in time though, had a knack for wheedling the truth out of people.

'Kenny. There you are! Mavis rung me, said Sid had seen you in 'ere. You all right?' asked Aunt Nelly. She already knew something was up, just by looking at him and by what Mavis had said on the phone. 'Sid saw your Kenny in the Eleanor. Looked like he had the weight of the world on his shoulders,' were Mavis's exact words.

'What d'ya want to drink, Auntie?'

'Nothing. I just popped in to make sure you were OK. Obviously you're not. I can tell.'

'Have a drink with me and I'll tell you all about my latest cock-up,' slurred Kenny.

Nelly felt choked up. Kenny had endured a terrible life as a young child living with her selfish sister. After being beaten to a pulp by one of Vera's men friends, he'd gone to live with his grandparents, her mum and dad. Then when her dear mum had died, she'd taken him on. He'd lived with her right up until he'd married Sharon, and nobody was more proud of the man Kenny had become than Nelly. She had no children herself; therefore Kenny had become the son she'd never had.

Nelly pursed her lips and grabbed Kenny's arm. 'I've got drink indoors. Come on. Too many earholes in 'ere and people are looking at you, boy. We're Bonds. We don't discuss our private business in public. Your grandfather never did.'

The mention of his granddad, his hero, was enough to make Kenny see sense. 'You're right. Let's go. Me motor's round the corner.'

'We'll walk. Get some fresh air. Will do you good. You look peaky to me.'

'Nah. Gotta drive. All me worldly goods are in the motor. Well, most of 'em anyway.'

'Bye, everyone,' Nelly shouted brightly, as she linked arms with her nephew and left the pub. 'Where is your car?'

'Down 'ere.' Kenny stopped dead in his tracks. 'Ya gotta be kidding me. Fuck. No!' He angrily yanked open the Range Rover door. The interior was empty; all his expensive clobber nowhere to be seen. 'I've been robbed. All me stuff's gone. Cunts! I'll kill 'em.'

Nelly walked around the vehicle. 'There's no broken windows. You sure you locked it?'

Kenny's jaw twitched. He'd been so angry when he'd left Karen's; he'd stopped at the local offie, brought half a bottle of brandy and downed it while driving. How the hell would he know if he'd locked the thing or not?

'Come on, lovey. Let's walk. I'll ask around tomorrow. We'll get your stuff back.'

It was at that point Kenny completely lost the plot. Using every expletive he knew, he kicked seven bells out of his motor and did not stop until the bastard thing was undriveable.

Unable to wipe the smile off his face, Beau handed Jolene the flowers and chocolates. 'God, I missed you. And the kids. Where are they?'

'With Mum and Dad. We need to talk, alone. You can see them afterwards.'

'OK. Come 'ere.'

As her husband hugged her, Jolene stood rigid. She had to play this carefully and cleverly. 'No, Beau,' she snapped, as he tried to kiss her. 'Sit down. What I've got to say to you is serious.'

Beau did as she asked. 'I am sorry, ya know, what I said to your brothers. Have they sorted things with Crystal and Layla yet? 'Cause if not, I'm willing to own up to anything, to make things right for 'em.'

Heart beating nineteen to the dozen, Jolene sat on the opposite sofa. The further away she was from Beau, the better. 'Forget my brothers. This isn't about them. It's about you. Or more precisely, what you did to Jamie.'

'You what! What d'ya mean?'

'I heard you, Beau, talking to Brett on the night of Sonny's wedding. I know what you did.'

Realization kicking in, Beau's face drained completely of any colour.

Aidan's pad was like no other Brett had seen before. Every time he visited, he'd be introduced to some whacky gadget or piece of technology he hadn't been aware of.

Today was no different. Brett previously had no idea that the spotlights on the ceiling could flash all different colours. What with the surround sound, it was like being in a discotheque. 'This is the nuts!' Brett leapt up and down, punching his right hand in the air to Gala's 'Freed from Desire', which was blasting out the speakers.

'I think I'll get Alvin out of his tank. He likes to have a roam around. You all right with that?'

Brett was that happy, he wouldn't have cared if Aidan's snake bit him. 'Yeah, sure. Let's have another line first though, eh?'

Aidan couldn't help but laugh as he chopped away with his credit card. For somebody who had never taken cocaine before, Brett was hoovering it up like a fucking Dyson.

Beau had never felt any emotion over Jamie's death. Brett had, but Beau modelled himself on Gramps. As hard as nails. However, he was feeling something now. Not guilt. Regret at opening his big mouth and how poxed his luck was that Jolene had overheard the conversation. 'I'm sorry. Really sorry. But I did it for us. We would never have been allowed to be together otherwise, not properly. Your family wanted answers and a scalp. And don't forget it was Jamie that bought those pills. They came from a pal of his. Not mine.'

'Only because you asked him to get them.'

'I didn't. He offered.'

'It doesn't matter. None of what happened was Jamie's fault. Me, you, Tammy and Brett were the instigators. It was *us* who decided to get the fucking things in the first place.'

Beau shook his head in despair. Although he'd never told Jolene the truth about Jamie, he'd have thought she would be more understanding and realize why he'd done it. It was for her. For them. So they could get married. Couldn't she see that? 'If only me dad had allowed us to take or drink any booze on the boat. Then none of this would've happened and Tammy would still be alive.'

'Don't you dare blame your dad for Tammy's death,' hissed Jolene. She wanted to punch him, chuck him out and tell him never to come back. But for numerous reasons she couldn't. The kids being the biggest. 'Tell me about the suicide notes. How did you pull that off?'

The one thing Beau was thankful for, was Jolene had no idea about Gramps' involvement in Jamie's death. Thank fuck he hadn't blurted that out as well. No way was he drinking heavily again. Alcohol must make him loose-lipped. 'That was Brett's idea, the notes, and to send one to your mum and dad,' Beau lied.

'And whose idea was it to drown him?'

Beau suddenly felt uneasy and paranoid. This wasn't exactly the homecoming he'd had in mind. He leapt up, paced up and down the huge mobile home. 'I don't wanna talk about that. I can't. I was young back then. Naive. I wouldn't do it now, ya know. I so wish I could turn back time, Jolene, but I can't.'

'I get that.'

'Thanks.' Beau sat back opposite his wife. 'So, what happens now? You haven't told anyone, have ya?'

'No. But it's disturbed me, Beau. Which is why I need some time alone.'

'Nah, nah, nah. Please don't do this to me, Jolene. I want to be here with you and the chavvies. I need to be. I feel lost without you.'

Knowing the only way to get rid of him without a massive scene, for now at least, was to let him down gently, Jolene moved sofas and held Beau's hand. 'You can see the chavvies whenever you like. You're a good dad and husband, Beau. I just need some time on me own to process all this. Hearing what you said on Saturday brought everything back to me, especially Tammy's death.'

Beau cupped his beautiful wife's face in his hands. 'I'm so sorry about everything. I'll make it up to you in time. I swear I will.'

Jolene moved Beau's hands. 'I know you will. But for now, I need space. I do still love you,' she lied. 'And if you love me, you'll do as I ask.'

'OK. I'll do whatever it takes to make us right again. I love you so much.'

As Beau leaned in for a snog, Jolene leapt up before she threw up. 'The chavvies ain't arf missed their dad. Let me go and get them.'

*

255

'Whatever's going on?' Aisling was amazed to arrive home to find her brother dancing around with Alvin around his shoulders, alongside Brett, who looked equally as off his face.

Aidan put an arm around Brett's shoulders. 'He likes my snake, Aisling. We've been having our very own private party.'

'I can see that. I need a word, Aidan, please.'

Aidan put Alvin around Brett's neck. 'You take care of my big snake, while I go get a scolding. On the naughty step, me,' he sniggered.

'What the fuck, Aidan!' Aisling pushed her brother against the wall of his bedroom. 'You're off your tits and so is he.'

Aidan smiled. 'I know. Usually me saying this to you, isn't it?'

'Don't fuck with me, Aidan. What has he taken? What have you said to him?'

Aidan grabbed his sister's arms, swung her around and placed her against the wall. 'Please don't treat me like the village idiot, Aisling, because I'm not one. It turns out Brett is rather partial to a bit of Charlie after all. As for what I've disclosed – let's put it this way: I told him enough to keep him happy, but not enough to make him knowledgeable. Not even in the slightest.'

PART TWO

Revenge, the sweetest morsel to the mouth
that ever was cooked in hell.

Walter Scott

CHAPTER EIGHTEEN

I was gutted when Jolene asked me to move out for a bit, but I wasn't a quitter. Only losers quit. Therefore, I was determined to regain her trust.

I did everything right. I grafted like a Trojan, looked after the kids for a couple of hours every day and had them longer at weekends. Well, the boys. Jolene was like a mother hen with Romany, wouldn't let her out of her sight. But I didn't complain. I didn't want to upset the apple cart any further.

It wasn't easy living back at me dad's, especially in the evenings. Brett was hardly ever there, and I was no fan of me own company. I'd overthink things, get paranoid. But I was determined not to go off the rails, mentally or physically. There came a point where me balls felt they were about to burst. But I would never consider cheating. I chose to wank instead. Me, a wanker! Unbelievable, when I look back.

As winter turned into spring, I started to become more and more concerned. I'd played it by the rule book, done everything I could to show how sorry I was, and I was worthy of another chance. Yet, whenever I asked about moving back home, Jolene would make an excuse, usually that she needed more time.

By the end of March, the agitation had set in and I became angry. I'd always been a bloody good husband. Loving, kind, hard-working, generous. I was running out of ideas. I was also starting to feel like me father. A right mug.

Then I found something out. Something that boiled my piss so bad, I wanted blood, was baying for it. Me anger then turned to fury. A red mist descended.

I vowed there and then if I couldn't have Jolene, I'd make sure nobody else could. And I meant every fucking word of it.

What I didn't realize at that point, was the lengths I would go to to protect what was rightfully mine . . .

Spring 1998

Kenny Bond chucked the *Sun* newspaper onto the chair next to him. He was sick of reading and hearing about the poxy millennium. They were building some massive dome now. All at the taxpayers' expense, you could bet your bottom dollar on that.

'Morning, Gramps. You all right?' Beau slammed the door of the portacabin and warmed his hands near the heater. It was a chilly morning for the end of March, the wind was bitter.

'So-so. Did you talk to Jolene?'

'I'm getting pissed off with it all, if I'm honest. I asked her if I could come back home again and she's still saying to give it more time. It's been six months now. I mean, how much more time does she need?' Beau had never told Kenny that Jolene had overheard him and Brett discussing Jamie's murder. Aside from the fact he'd go ballistic, Beau couldn't bear it if Gramps thought of him as some loudmouth moron. He wasn't. It had been a one-off and he'd barely touched alcohol since. It obviously didn't agree with him.

'I ain't faring no better with your nan. I wouldn't mind if she'd listen to reason, let me explain things properly. I'm sick of living in that fucking rabbit hutch of a flat.' After spending a few weeks living with Aunt Nelly, Kenny had found a two-bedroom flat in Wickford and taken out a six-month rental on it. It was close to the garden centre, which was where Kenny now spent most of his time.

'What we gonna do, Gramps?'

'Dunno. But I know what would do us good. Cheer us up, like.'

'What?'

'A holiday. Somewhere hot. It'll recharge our batteries and it'll give Shal and Jolene something to think about. Whaddya reckon?' grinned Kenny. He hadn't had a proper holiday for ages, had been looking forward to Santorini until it had all gone Pete Tong with Shal.

'I'm not sure. I like seeing the kids every day – and who's gonna look after this place? Brett's hardly reliable of late.'

'About time he pulled his socks up, your brother. Flakey little fucker he is lately. It won't hurt him to have a bit of responsibility for once. As for the kids, you're dancing to her tune, Beau. Becoming the glorified babysitter that your father always was with Tansey. Jolene might want you back if you start acting out of the ordinary. You're playing into her hands at present.'

Desperate for Jolene to want him back under any circumstance, Beau shrugged. 'OK then. Let's do it.'

Sharon flopped to the ground, belly first. I'm done. I can't do no more.'

'Come on. Ten more burpees,' bellowed Scott Harrison, the personal trainer Sharon had hired on a whim.

Sharon did as ordered, then collapsed on the ground once more. 'I'm dying.'

'No pain, no gain,' chuckled Scott. 'Let's stretch it out. Then you're done.'

When Scott left, Sharon lolloped on the sofa. She'd vowed not to put on weight after kicking Kenny out, but she had. Not through over-indulging with the booze, although she did enjoy a couple of glasses of wine before bed. It was more her addiction to American TV series that had caused her weight gain. She'd become that engrossed in the likes of *Friends*, *Law and Order*, *Ellen* and *Twin Peaks*, she hadn't realized how much chocolate and nibbles she'd been scoffing at the same time. Until she'd clocked a recent photo and hardly recognized herself, that was. Hence her hiring Scott.

Sharon's phone rang. Seeing it was Kenny, she blanked it. She'd stuck to her guns, wanted nothing to do with him whatsoever, and she'd started divorce proceedings. Kenny being Kenny though, was yet to sign anything.

He still harped on about explaining things to her, whether that be by text, voicemail, or on the odd occasion he had the brass neck to turn up at her door. Sharon didn't want to listen to any more of his bullshit. She'd had enough, would and could *never* trust him again.

Hearing the bleep that meant an answerphone message had been left, Sharon rolled her eyes as she listened to it. Did *he* honestly think she'd be bothered he was going to Tenerife? He could go to Timbuktu for all she bloody well cared.

Sharon recalled her last holiday. At her mum's insistence, she'd ended up going to Santorini. Not with Kenny, obviously. She'd gone to Thomas Cook and changed his name to Tina's. It had been a much-needed break. There'd been laughter, tears and far too much food and alcohol consumed. It was only on her return to England, Sharon learned the awful truth from her mum. That her cancer was back and had spread to her stomach. Her mum had since had chemo, which had knocked the stuffing out of her again. All Sharon could do now was hope and pray it had worked.

'All right, Shal? Kenny's given you lots of money.' Ricky handed Sharon a fat envelope. 'He's booked a holiday to Tenerife with Beau and he says if he likes it, he might stay out there longer.'

Sharon opened the envelope. There was a thousand pounds inside. Typical Kenny, a grand as a grand gesture. Ricky had decided to continue living with her. Kenny had continued sending home a couple of hundred quid a week for Ricky's keep and to help out with the bills. The house was mortgage free, but the bills were expensive, so Sharon still took the bastard's money. That was the least he owed her.

'I'm taking Candy to the Harvester for a meal at teatime, then we're going to snuggle up in my room at Donny's and watch a film together,' beamed Ricky. He liked the nights Candy stayed over and he loved the sex. Or 'bonking', as Kenny called it.

'You be careful. Remember what I told you? You got enough rubber thingies?' Sharon was pleased Ricky was living a good life, but obviously she worried about him. Getting Candy knocked up was the last thing any of them needed.

'Shal!' Ricky went red. He didn't mind discussing sex stuff with the men, but not with Sharon.

'We all bonk, love. Or in my case, did.'

'Shal! That's man's talk,' giggled Ricky. 'You still going out tonight?'

'Meant to be. Don't fancy it much and I'm aching from me personal training.'

'Go, Shal. You need to start getting out more. You might even meet a nice man.'

'Oh, leave it out, Ricky. I'm off men. For life.'

Heart beating nineteen to the dozen, Jolene rang her mother. 'Can you pop over? I need you for something.'

'Course. I'll be about half hour. Just about to cook your father ham, egg and chips for his lunch.'

'Mum, pop over first. Please.'

Evie dashed over to her daughter's trailer. The boys were always playing outside and getting cuts and bruises. 'Who's hurt now? Nurse Nanny to the rescue.'

'Nobody. Jimmy Dean wants me to go out for a meal with him tonight and I don't know what to do. I want to go, but Beau's picking the boys up for a few hours and he's bound to wonder where I am if I ain't 'ere.'

'Sod Beau. You go out and enjoy yourself, sweetheart.'

Feeling anxious, Jolene paced up and down. Jimmy's wife Alicia had only passed away four months ago. 'What if we get seen by a member of Alicia's family or someone who knows Beau? It'll look bad, Mum. You know what gossipmongers people can be.'

'But you ain't doing nothing wrong, Jolene. Jimmy needs someone to share his grief with, to talk to, and you understand what it's like to lose someone close to you better than anyone. You've been meeting up with him for weeks now and having a bit of lunch together. I don't see how going out with him for a meal tonight is any different.'

'Grabbing a coffee and a sandwich after going to the cemetery is a lot different from going out for a meal of a night, Mum. This feels like, ya know, a proper date.'

'Well, it's about time you moved on from the other thing. You need to start being straight with Beau though, Jolene. You can't keep him dangling for ever. It'll only make things worse when he finds out you don't want him back. Best to be honest, but kind. Let him down gently, like.'

'I will. I'll tell him soon. I promise.'

Evie felt a chill run down her spine. If Jimmy Dean turned out to be Jolene's soulmate, then all of Psychic Lena's predictions had come true. Apart from the end bit.

'Heat. A burning vicious heat' Lena had seen in that crystal ball of hers. And that was the part that terrified Evie the most.

'Oh no! You're having a bleedin' laugh. No way am I going in there,' exclaimed a disgruntled Sharon. 'Cabbie, cabbie. Hold on a tick,' she yelled.

As the Peugeot 406 did a U-turn leaving Sharon stranded, Tina grabbed hold of her pal's arm. 'I promise you, we'll have a right laugh, and the music's great. All the good old soul stuff we grew up listening to. You'll love it. I promise.'

Sharon sighed. No wonder Tina had pretended they were off to partake in some pub music quiz, because there was no way on earth she'd have agreed to go to what she referred to as a 'Grab a Granny' night.

'Come on,' grinned Tina.

Sharon allowed her pal to link arms with her and lead her into God only knew what. The venue was the Prince Regent Hotel in Chigwell, and it was 'over thirties night'.

'What you drinking?'

'Something strong. Best you get me a white wine. A large one.' Sharon glanced around. The inside of the venue was actually nice, if you took away the people. Ugly as sin were the words that sprung to mind regarding the men. Mutton done up as lamb, for the women.

'Get that down your hatch. You'll soon liven up. We'll have a dance once we've had a few.'

Sharon rolled her eyes. In fairness, the music did seem decent. You had to go some to better George Benson, The O'Jays and Luther Vandross as the first three artists you heard walking into any gaff. 'I thought you didn't come here no more. Because of that stalker.'

'I didn't. Well, I haven't. But it's been over two months since I last heard from that notright. Only me, eh?' chuckled Tina.

Sharon didn't reply. She was kind of fixated on a good-looking man in a trendy pinstriped suit. 'Oh my God! Where's the toilets? Quick, we need to go. He's clocked me.'

'Who? What you going on about?'

Before Sharon had a chance to move, he'd already sauntered over to her. She'd only been out with him the once and had made a complete tit of herself. But he'd still wanted to know her, see her again, and if she hadn't got back with that bastard she'd married, who knew where their relationship might have gone?

'Hello, Sharon. Long time no see. How lovely to see you again.'

Feeling like a rabbit caught in the headlights, Sharon squirmed. 'You too. Need a wee. Be back in a jiffy.'

'Can I get you anything else?' enquired the waitress.

'You sure you don't want a dessert?' asked Jimmy Dean.

'No, thanks. I'm fine,' replied Jolene. It had been a struggle to eat anything in front of Jimmy. Every time she looked into those big blue eyes of his, her stomach did funny things.

Jimmy smiled at the waitress. 'Just the bill, please.' He chucked a wad of money on the table. 'Be back in a tick, Jolene. Can't get no reception in here and I need to make a work phone call and ring my sister to make sure Demi's OK.'

When Jimmy went outside, Jolene glanced around. They'd driven out to Navestock, found a quiet country pub. There was certainly nobody she recognized. Not that many people would recognize her anyway. Not in a pub. She'd only passed her driving test last week and was yet to tell Beau, as he'd been insistent on buying her first car. She didn't want anything off him. If he could drown poor Jamie with his bare hands, who's to say he wouldn't tamper with the brakes so he could raise their children alone? She wouldn't put anything past him, even though he was being nice to the point of sickly at present. She knew his persona would change the moment she told him their marriage was over, a conversation she was literally dreading, but could avoid it no longer.

Turning her thoughts to Jimmy, Jolene smiled. He was lovely. And being a fellow Traveller, they had so much in common. People, places, upbringing. It felt good to be among her own once again. She would never fully recover from losing Tammy, but being around Jimmy gave Jolene comfort. He was a good man who'd loved his wife. She understood his grief and he got hers. Unlike Beau, who thought the answer to Tammy's death was to blame, then murder his own stepbrother. What a shuddering thought that was.

Jolene paid the waitress, then glanced out the window. Jimmy was strutting up and down while talking on the phone, his tall frame clear to see. She'd thought he was lanky when she'd first met him. His suit had been hanging on him, but he'd since explained he'd lost weight due to his wife's illness at the time. At twenty-two, Jimmy was a couple of years her senior, but he acted far older and wiser. The total opposite of Beau, who would sulk like a child if she wasn't in the mood for him groping her. Jimmy was a gentleman, had tried nothing on with her whatsoever. Although, she wished he would in a way. Even a kiss would be proof he felt the same way about her as she did him, that what they had wasn't just a convenient friendship.

Jolene was snapped out of her daydreaming by Jimmy's reappearance. 'Sorry I took so long. Been an issue on a job.' Jimmy and his brother owned their own roofing company.

'Nothing serious, I hope?'

'Some dinlo thinking we're trying to rip his mother off, 'cause we're Travellers. I would never do that, neither would Mikey. We gave the old girl the best price we could. They won't get it cheaper elsewhere. Anyway, enough about work. Let's go sit on the comfy seats over there and have another drink.'

As Jimmy reached for her hand, Jolene's heart skipped a beat. This was their first intimate moment.

Once Sharon's nerves subsided, she found out more about Ray Weller than she had in the past. At fifty-one, Ray was three years younger than herself. He was a property developer who lived in Chigwell and had a second home in Spain. Sharon remembered he had a daughter. Carly worked for a Dutch bank and was now twenty-seven. She also recalled that he'd been married to an older woman called Sascha who'd cheated on him with a so-called friend.

'I'm really sorry to hear Kenny let you down again, Sharon. I know how much you loved him and how that must've hurt.'

'It did, but nowhere near as much as when I found out about Abi. I was more worried about Donny and Sherry this time. Them finding out they had a half-brother. I think once you've been shit on from a great height by a person you trusted, you're half expecting it to happen again, aren't you?'

'God, yeah. Once that initial trust has gone, it's gone for good in my eyes.'

The mention of his eyes compelled Sharon to check Ray's out. They were brown, same as Kenny's, yet had sincerity about them. Ray was a very good-looking man, Sharon had to admit that. Even more handsome than she remembered. His wavy mousy-brown hair was slicked back with what looked like Brylcreem. He had a strong jawline and a kind smile.

'How did your kids take the news, Sharon?'

'Better than I thought. Both have disowned Kenny, mind. I knew my Sherry would, but I was expecting Donny to forgive his dad at some point. Not that I wanted that to happen, Ray. I'm not a vindictive person. If either of them wants to make up with their dad, then that's fine by me. For all Kenny's faults, he's always been a good father.'

'Not knocking Kenny, but I think you need to take your rose-tinted glasses off, Sharon. I remember everything you told me in the past, every single word. It was you who raised those kids, almost single-handedly, while Kenny was banged up. No wonder they've disowned him now. I should imagine they've lost all respect for him.'

'D'ya know what, you're bloody right. Kenny's a selfish arsehole and there's no going back for me this time. I want a divorce.'

Ray smiled. 'Glad to hear it. You deserve better, Sharon. Much better.'

'Stop 'ere, Jimmy. I can easily walk the rest of the way. Me dad and brother might spot you otherwise.'

Jimmy turned the lights off and the ignition. 'I had a really nice evening, Jolene.'

'Me too. It's so nice to talk to someone that understands me.'

'What you doing tomorrow? If you're free, we could take the kids out somewhere? That's if you want to, of course? I don't want you to think I'm being pushy, 'cause I ain't like that.'

'I would love to, but the boys are bound to blurt something out to Beau. He's gonna flip a lid as it is when he gets back off holiday and I tell him our marriage is over. I don't wanna add fuel to the fire.'

'I get that. Sorry for putting you on the spot. I didn't think it through properly.'

'Don't be daft! I'm sure my mum would have the boys so we could take Romany and Demi out.'

Jimmy's face lit up. He had truly loved his wife, Alicia. He missed female company and being part of a couple. 'That sounds great. You wanna ring me in a bit? Or in the morning? Let me know what your mum says.'

'My mum'll say yes. I know she will.'

'Shall I pick you up in the same place? At say, eleven?'

Jolene smiled. 'Yeah. Perfect. My dad's gonna buy me a car next week, so it'll be easier to meet up then.'

'I like the sound of that.' Trying to find the right words, Jimmy fingered the stubble on his chin. 'I know this is awkward, like, for both of us. What with me only losing Alicia last year and you still being legally married to Beau. But I want you to know, I truly value your friendship. You've helped me through some dark times and one day I hope we can be more than friends. But only if that feels right for both of us.' Jimmy put his head in his hands. 'I'm so shit with words. Sorry if I'm rambling.'

'You're good with words and you're not rambling.' Jolene removed Jimmy's hands from his face. 'And I want us to be more than just friends too.'

What followed was the best kiss that Jolene had ever received. Beau had always had a habit of trying to shove his tongue as far as he could down the back of her throat. Jimmy didn't. His kiss was soft and gentle. It was perfect, just like him.

Ray put the drinks on the table and sat back down next to Sharon. 'Bar's shutting now and I'd be a liar if I didn't tell you I'm kind of gutted this evening is coming to an end.'

Sharon smiled. She felt a bit light-headed now. Not drunk, more chilled. 'It's been really good to see you and have a catch-up, Ray. I still can't believe you want to talk to me after I embarrassed you in your favourite restaurant that time.'

Ray chuckled. 'Please don't feel you've got to keep apologizing for that. I knew you were nervous and out of your comfort zone. It was my fault for taking you to such a gaff and picking you up in the Rolls-Royce. Believe it or not, I weren't trying to show off. I knew I liked you from the start and I dunno, was just trying to spoil you, I suppose.'

'Don't you dare apologize. You were a gentleman. I hid under the quilt for days after that night ya know. Was too embarrassed to face anyone, especially you,' laughed Sharon.

'How about we go out again? Nowhere poncey. Somewhere simple.'

'Erm. When?'

'Your call. Whenever you're free. What you doing Sunday?'

'Erm, nothing I don't think.'

'How 'bout I pick you up and we take a drive somewhere random. I'll surprise ya. I'll even pick you up in the three-wheel Reliant Robin, if ya like? Please say yes. You know that you want to,' grinned Ray.

Sharon laughed. 'Go on then. Pick me up in true Del Boy style. Or else!'

CHAPTER NINETEEN

Is it possible to get addicted to something immediately? Only, my relationship with cocaine took off like a jumbo jet. It made me feel confident, euphoric, and ballsy, like I could conquer the fucking world if I put me mind to it. I couldn't get enough of the stuff.

Whenever I was with Aidan, life was exciting, fun, worth living. So, much so, I started to resent my other life. Especially my job and me brother. The garden centre bored me shitless, as did Beau, with his constant Jolene jibber jabber. I'd always looked up to Beau, but he was so obsessed with his wife, I now saw him as a melt. No longer respected him as a man.

What I didn't realize back then was that I was exactly the same. Equally as besotted with Aidan. The only difference being, I was unable to speak out about my relationship for fear of being deemed a wrong un, a pansy, a queer.

I should've known once Beau's life crumbled mine was bound to follow suit. Telepathic twins, that was us, and

*we'd never been destined to be happy, no matter how hard
we tried. Misery tended to follow us around. As did trouble.*

*Nothing could have prepared us for the catalogue of
disasters heading our way though . . .*

'Don't stand there like a stuffed dummy, boy. Help the
man load the van,' barked Cormac Neary.

Dressed in a black hooded tracksuit, Aidan did as he
was told. His father was in a foul mood and Aidan just
hoped he wasn't the cause of it. 'You want these straight
in the van?' The van was a Peugeot Boxer with cleverly
fitted false panels.

'Give them 'ere.'

Aidan handed the firearms to the thug with the beard.
The IRA wasn't particularly active anymore, but even
so, Aidan hated dealing with the Northern Irish. Father
Adam, back in Ireland, would have a cardiac arrest if he
or his father ever confessed their true sins to him. No
doubt about that.

Aidan returned to the lock-up and came out with
another armful. Fifty-eight pieces, the Protestants had
bought today, which included AKMs, Uzis, Carbines,
M240s and grenade launchers. The bulk of their purchase
was your average street-gun, mind. The bloke dealing
with his dad was apparently an extremely well-respected
man among the underworld. At least, that's what his old
man had told him.

'Aidan! Hurry the fuck up with that,' bellowed Cormac.

Seeing the bearded wonder smirk, Aidan felt like the
lackey boy. He had no doubt now that it was indeed *he*
who his father had the hump with and was dreading

finding out why. It could only be one of two things. Brett? Or his lucrative little sideline?

'You've lost weight, love.'

'You reckon? Not noticed it meself.'

'Still as handsome as ever though,' smiled Lori. She hadn't seen Brett for a while, hence her decision to drive over to the nursery and surprise him. He certainly hadn't sounded his usual bubbly self on the phone recently and Lori was keen to find out why. 'How's Aidan?'

Brett handed his mother the menu. It had been his idea when she'd showed up unexpectedly that he treat her to lunch at a local pub. 'Dunno. Ain't seen him recently.'

'Since when?'

'Since before Beau and Gramps went away. I'm really pissed off with him, if I'm honest. I always stay at his overnight, but obviously I couldn't this week as I had to open up really early. I all but begged him to come down and stay at mine for even a night, but he just made excuse after excuse. D'ya reckon I'm wasting me time with him, Mum? I've missed him proper badly this past week, but he can't be missing me, else he'd have visited. I sometimes think I'm the only one with any deep feelings.'

'I'm sure he has deep feelings for you too. He wouldn't be seeing you for this length of time if he didn't. *But*, don't beg, son. Never beg. I remember begging your father to stay when I found out about his affair with Tansey. I still cringe when I think about that now. You and Beau were only young, but you were there when I made a total fool of myself. It didn't work. Your dad just walked out without a backward glance at all three of us.'

'Bastard! And he's got the front to blank Gramps over Jake, even though Gramps weren't with Nan when Jake was conceived. Talking of kids, that's another thing that grates on me. I really wanna meet Aidan's son. He's always flitting off to Ireland and I'd love to go with him one day. Not as a couple, obviously, I'd stay in me own room and stuff. He could just tell Conor that I'm a pal from his gym and he's showing me round Ireland or something. I mean, I hardly look camp, do I?'

Seeing the emotion in Brett's eyes, Lori squeezed his hands. 'You need to have another heart to heart with Aidan by the sounds of it. Explain all what you've said to me to him. True love is a wonderful thing, but you can only experience the beauty of it if two people are on the same page. You deserve to find true love. We all do. I should know. Carl has been my absolute saviour.'

'But what if he still won't let me go to Ireland? What do I do then?'

'Call his bluff. Tell him perhaps he has too much baggage to be with a younger man such as yourself. If he loves you as much as you love him, no way will he let you walk away. Then, you'll have your answer.'

Kenny Bond sipped his ice-cold lager. It had been just what the doctor ordered for himself and Beau, a week away in a sunnier climate. They'd ended up, via a last-minute deal, in a quiet, relaxing resort called Puerto de Santiago. They'd hired boats, messed around on jet skis, ate at some fabulous restaurants and drank until merry. But most importantly, they'd had a good rest, both mentally and physically.

Kenny sat up on his sunbed and swung his legs over the side. They were all packed and ready to fly home tonight. 'Well, I suppose it's time to talk about the inevitable.' Beau had driven him doolally on their first day, constantly rambling on about Jolene. So, Kenny had put a block on it. He'd explained that the whole point of this break was to recharge their batteries, chill out and have some fun. 'Think and plot in silence. I'll do the same. Then we can discuss what we've come up with on our last day,' were his exact words.

Beau lifted his Ray-Ban sunglasses onto his forehead and propped himself up on an elbow. 'You go first.'

'Firstly, I'm gonna force your nan to hear me out. Even if that means breaking in and tying her to a chair. She owes me that much at least and I'm sure, if I explained things to her properly, she'd understand. But whatever the outcome, I intend to move back into me own gaff. The lease is up on the flat soon and I ain't signing up for another six months. What's your plan?'

'Pretty similar to yours. I shall go see Jolene tomorrow morning and have it out with her. I ain't being ballsed about no more. I also intend on moving back home. Bobby bought that gaff for *us* as a wedding present, not just for her, and I wanna be with my kids. I'll sleep in the spare room if she wants to be arsey.'

'Great minds think alike eh, lad?'

'They sure do. Nan and Jolene need to see the light, 'cause they ain't gonna find better men than us.'

'Too bleedin' right,' chuckled Kenny. 'That's the spirit.'

Sharon was in the middle of a personal training session when Ricky bounded up the garden like a dog with two tails. Relieved to give her aching arms a rest, Sharon dropped the battle ropes on the grass. 'What's wrong? Why aren't you at work?'

'Nothing's wrong and I was never going to work today. I just pretended I was 'cause I didn't want to disappoint you if things went different.'

'Tell her. Just tell her,' shrieked Candy, jumping up and down, her huge unsupported breasts bouncing like footballs in the horrid skimpy white top she was wearing.

'Hurry up and tell me then, Ricky,' urged Sharon. ''Cause Scott needs to finish our session off.' Christ knows what the fit, handsome Scott thought of Candy, she cringed.

'I did it, Shal! First time. Or should I say, we did it?' beamed Ricky, putting a proud arm around his girlfriend.

Sharon immediately feared the worst. 'Candy's not pregnant, surely?'

'Nooo. I passed my driving test. And Candy helped me lots, with the Highway Code. Didn't you, babe?'

'I did. I helped him loads.'

'That's amazing! Well done you,' congratulated Scott.

Sharon gave Ricky a big hug. 'I'm so bloody proud of you. Kenny's going to have to buy you that car he promised you now – and you make sure you pick the one that costs the most. Have you told him yet?'

'No. Not told anybody. I wanted to tell you first because you're like a mum to me, Shal.'

Sharon's eyes welled up. Because of his Down's syndrome, she'd never truly believed that Ricky would be capable of passing his test and driving alone. But he'd defied the odds yet again. Just like he had when he'd started working at the garden centre and took to weight training like a duck to water. 'You're a little superstar. You really are.'

Dreading the inevitable, Aidan was sat at a table in the pub that his father had ordered him to meet him in.

Cormac Neary arrived twenty minutes late and approached his son with a stern expression.

'I got you a Scotch. Where did you have to go?'

Cormac sat down. 'Don't be worrying about me. It's you we need to talk about. Who's the boy?'

'What boy?'

Cormac studied his eldest child. He wasn't stupid, had heard the Chinese whispers over the years. Especially when Aidan was younger. However, he refused to believe such idle gossip. His son was not only his protégé, he was a man now and a father himself for feck's sake. 'The young blond boy. You know exactly who I mean.'

Having had a bit of time to prepare for an interrogation, Aidan grinned. 'I think you're referring to my mucker, Brett. He's hardly a boy. He's a businessman like myself. I'm allowed to have friends, aren't I?'

'It depends who they are, Aidan. Let's be honest, it's not a good look, a man your age running around with a lad half his age, is it? You stand out like a sore thumb, which means people get curious and then, you know, they talk.'

'Talk about what? Bejesus! Some people must lead very boring lives. So, what are you trying to say to me? Are you telling me you don't want me hanging about with Brett? Only, he's good craic. He's also sound, comes from decent stock, if you know what I mean. A bit like meself.'

280

Not liking Aidan's jovial attitude one little bit, Cormac leaned forward, a steely glint in his cold-dark eyes. 'Oh, I know exactly who your little friend is, Aidan. I know who his grandfather is too. All I'm asking you to do is tone it down. Only, as I've already told you, running around in public with young lads raises eyebrows and poses questions and risks. For instance, what does young Mr Bond know about you? Or me? How much have you told him?'

Shocked that his father had indeed done his homework, Aidan gulped. 'I'm not stupid, Dad. Brett knows nothing. I don't even see him that bloody often. We just go to the gym and out clubbing sometimes. That's it. I swear.'

'Well, best you make sure it stays that way, son. Only, it would be awful if your friend Brett ended up in the firing line like your other friend, Finlay, wouldn't it now?'

'All right, Mum? I wondered if you fancied going bingo tonight?' asked Sharon. Since finishing her chemotherapy, her mum had barely been outside the door and Sharon knew how worried her dad was about her. The chemo had knocked her for six. She'd lost her lovely hair and looked a shadow of her former self.

'No thanks, love. I couldn't think of anything worse,' replied Maggie Saunders. She loathed going out looking the way she did, hated the way people would look at her with sympathy in their eyes once they clocked her head-scarf. She felt as though she had 'cancer victim' stamped on her forehead.

'Have you eaten? I thought we might get a takeaway.' Sharon wasn't hungry, had been right off her food since meeting up with Ray again, but was keen for her mum to start eating more.

'No. I'm not hungry, thanks. I tell you what I do fancy though. A Baileys. I really fancy a glass with ice.'

'We've got an unopened bottle from last Christmas in the garage. I'll go get it,' said Charlie Saunders.

'Ricky passed his driving test today. Can you believe it? We didn't even know he was taking it,' smiled Sharon.

'I know. He rung up to tell us. He's a remarkable young man, he really is. Come on leaps and bounds since Kenny moved out. You got a good heart, taking him on.'

'I dunno about that. I think it's Candy that's changed his life. She's an odd one, but she certainly makes Ricky happy.'

'You look happy. Radiant in fact.'

'Probably the personal training sessions. He don't half make me work hard that Scott.'

'Nah. It's more than that,' replied Maggie knowingly. Ricky had slipped up, informing her that Sharon had been talking to a man on the phone lots.

'Shush. Dad's coming back,' hissed Sharon. It wasn't that she didn't want to tell her mum about Ray. It was just such early days; she didn't want to build her mum's hopes up, only for them to be swiftly dashed.

'You look gorgeous, darling,' beamed Evie Tamplin. Jolene was off out for another meal with Jimmy Dean and Evie couldn't be more thrilled. She'd casually asked her cousin about Jimmy the other day and Sandy couldn't speak of him highly enough. He was a good man, by all accounts, who'd helped nurse his wife right up until her untimely death. But most importantly for Evie, he was one of their own. A Traveller through and through.

Rocky prodded his mother on the thigh, leaving a chocolate fingerprint on her bright pink dress. 'Why you go out again and leave us? Women not meant to go out at night. Only men do.'

'Oh no! Look what's he's done to my dress, Mum. Get over to your granddad's now, Rocky. And you Levi,' bellowed Jolene.

Rocky scowled at his mother and grabbed his younger brother's hand. 'Come, Levi. One more sleep and we get to see Dad again.'

'He been in touch, the gorger?' Evie asked, as she gently rubbed the mark off Jolene's dress.

'Yeah. About an hour ago. Was on his way home. Well, on his way to the airport. He said he'll be round at ten in the morning to pick the boys up, but said me and him need to talk an' all. I'm dreading it. I dislike him even more since I've met Jimmy. But the boys have missed him. He's a good dad if nothing else.'

'Nanna. Nanna. Take,' insisted Romany, handing Evie her favourite doll.

'Thank you, Princess,' Evie smiled, lifting up her wonderful granddaughter. A vision of Psychic Lena popped into Evie's mind. The old lady's last words were never far from her thoughts. 'You need to tell Beau tomorrow it's over for good. But try to be kind to him, 'cause we don't want no trouble. Your dad's getting suspicious an' all. Rocky's right. It ain't normal for a travelling woman to get dolled up and go out of a night. Especially regularly. I think you should tell your dad about Jimmy before he hears it through the grapevine.

I'm sure he'll have your back. But whatever you do, don't tell Beau. He mustn't know. Not for a very long time. You must keep Jimmy a secret from him.'

They were halfway through a game of Scrabble when Sharon decided to confide in her mum about Ray.

Maggie's face lit up. This was just the tonic she needed. 'Oh, Shal. I'm so pleased. Tell me more about him.'

Sharon told her mother all she knew. 'He comes across as such a gentleman and he makes me laugh. I'm sure he really likes me, but after Kenny, ya know, how am I meant to trust any man again?'

'Not all men are womanizing shitbags. Ray sounds wonderful. When can I meet him?' Maggie couldn't contain her excitement.

'It's a bit early for that, Mum. And I definitely don't want Dad meeting him in case he says something to Kenny. I know Dad wouldn't purposely say anything, but Kenny's a slippery sod, he knows how to push Dad's buttons.'

'When you seeing him next?'

'Tomorrow. We're going out for the day. Ray said it's meant to be quite warm and sunny. Dunno where he's taking me, he wouldn't say. But I doubt it'll be drab. He's got a bit of class, ya know. First time I ever went out with him, he picked me up in his Rolls-Royce with a chauffeur driving. I felt a right prat. I've told him under no uncertain terms never to do that again, told him I'd prefer to get in a Del Boy three-wheel van,' chuckled Sharon. 'He is really nice though and I am warming to him.'

'Good.' Maggie squeezed the hands of her beloved only child. 'Nobody deserves to be happy more than you do, and I so want to see you settled with a nice man before I go, love. I'll be able to rest in peace then.'

'Oh, stop it, Mum! You ain't going nowhere for a long while.'

'I don't think I've got years left, darling. We need to face facts.'

Sharon's eyes welled up. 'Please don't talk like that, Mum. You gotta stay positive. We all have.'

'What time's Ray picking you up tomorrow?'

'Nine.'

'Well, you bring him down 'ere for a cuppa first. I'll get rid of your father, like I did tonight.'

'How? The pubs won't be open.'

'I'll send him on an errand.' Maggie turned back to the Scrabble board and laid the words U, N and T under the C.

'You can't have that, Mum. Swear words aren't allowed,' laughed Sharon.

'Yes, I can. Describes Kenny to a tee. And that's another thing, love. Before I die, I want you to divorce that arsehole. I don't want him at my funeral. And if he turns up, you better not let him in. 'Cause if you do, I'll come back and bleedin' well haunt ya.'

In a foul mood, Brett pulled up outside the luxury apartments in Canary Wharf. He'd been ringing Aidan since lunchtime to no avail, had left numerous answerphone messages and now the phone was switched off.

He was about to press the buzzer when a smartly dressed woman left the building and held the door open for him.

With his mother's advice firmly in his mind, Brett got out of the lift and pummelled his fist against Aidan's front door. He could hear music coming from inside, Depeche Mode's 'Just Can't Get Enough'.

Aisling opened the door and quickly pulled it to. 'Aidan's not in, Brett.'

'Where is he?'

'I don't know. He went out with our dad.'

'I'll come in and wait for him then. Only, I ain't seen him for over a week, Aisling, and I was meant to be seeing him tonight.'

'No. You can't come in. I've got some pals round. All lesbians. They won't like it. Aidan's not coming home tonight anyway. He rung earlier, said he was going clubbing and crashing out at a friend's.'

Brett smashed his fist against the wall. 'Oh, so he managed to ring you. Only, he's ignored my fucking calls all day. You tell your brother I ain't no mug, Aisling, and I won't be taken for one by him or any other cunt.'

'I'll be sure to tell him. But don't be too hard on him, Brett. Between you and me, he's had a fall out with our father and that tends to spiral him out of control for a bit. I'm sure he'll be in touch tomorrow.'

When Brett stormed off, Aisling felt sorry for him. She liked Brett. He was a good egg.

In the middle of snorting another line, Aidan looked up with a stupid grin on his face. He was currently enjoying a kitchen party with two gay lads he'd invited round earlier. 'Am I on the naughty step again?'

Aisling grabbed her brother's arm and marched him into the hallway. He was so annoying when blind drunk, especially if he'd been on the kouver too. 'Poor Brett. He looked crestfallen. Please don't feck him about like this, Aidan. It's not fair on him.'

'I'll call him tomorrow. But I got to entertain these two hotties tonight. Be a waste not to. In fact, it's probably best you go out. Don't you think?'

'Oh, I intend to go out, don't you worry about that. I can't be around you when you're like this. I know you like Brett. But you're too scared of Dad to live your own life. Well, more fool you, 'cause I live mine. You need to man the feck up.'

'Brett's a shag. Like all the others. Nothing more, nothing less. Now, I'm feeling the strong urge for a blowjob. So could you leave this very minute, please?'

Aisling grabbed her handbag. For his age, Aidan could be very immature. She liked to party, dance, flaunt herself, have fun. No matter how off her face she was, she didn't act like a retard like her brother.

'Bye, sis. Love you,' laughed Aidan.

Aisling raised her middle finger. 'Go fuck yourself.'

CHAPTER TWENTY

Mad Ginger Daley woke up early, a big grin on his face. *Today* was finally here. Tonight he had a party to look forward to. Then tomorrow, he'd be a free man once again.

Getting banged up for racially abusing a cab driver wasn't exactly the coolest of convictions. Neither was spending time on remand for threatening some old lady outside an AA meeting. But Ginger being Ginger had laughed at it, told fascinating stories about both turnouts. You needed a strong mentality and sense of humour to survive the boredom of prison. That was the key. The abduction charge hadn't stuck, thankfully.

Training helped keep the brain sane too and Ginger had done plenty of that. He'd even got himself a job in the prison gym, such was his cleverness.

Being sent to a different prison than his brother after sentencing had been a downer for Ginger. Yet it had turned out to be a blessing in disguise.

First he had met a funny little Chinese geezer who had told him his friend had made ecstasy tablets in Essex for two men, Mr Tony and Mr Kenny. Then Ginger had hooked up with a female screw who had proved to be an asset to him in more ways than one.

Janey was in her forties, was no looker, but she gave bloody good head, had managed to smuggle in his steroids and, most importantly, had got hold of some vital information for him. Apparently, she had a source who could look up the current whereabouts of anyone on the Criminal Register.

Ginger sat up. He liked Old Lenny his cellmate, even though he could rabbit for England at times. 'Can't wait to get all that lovely fresh air down me lungs, Len.'

'What you doing first? I'd be straight down the Old Kent Road for me pie and mash. Then the bookies. Then the pub.'

'I've got business to sort. I gotta catch up with Mr Kenny and Mr Tony, as they owe me a lot of money. But firstly, I'm off to the seaside to visit another old friend,' chuckled Ginger. 'Mr Johnny.'

Dressed in a baggy linen khaki jumpsuit, Sharon felt good as she continued getting glammed up for her day out with Ray. She was definitely looking slimmer, must've lost a whole dress size since training with Scott and having her appetite suppressed by the new man in her life.

'Morning. You got any headache tablets, please?'

'Bloody hell, Ricky. What you done to your face?' His left cheek was grazed and his eye looked swollen.

'Don't ask, Shal.'

'Tell me. Now! Else, you ain't having no tablets.'

Sighing, Ricky sat at the kitchen table. 'After the

289

Harvester, Candy wanted to go on a pub crawl round Romford town centre. There was an argument and we got into a fight.'

'How? Why?'

Ricky sighed and slapped a hand against his forehead. 'We was a bit drunk, Shal. We drank two bottles of wine in the Harvester to celebrate me passing me test. From what I can remember, Candy was doing her sexy dancing. Then some older man started dancing with her. I had a go at them both. The bloke hit me. Then Candy hit him. Then we got thrown out the pub by the bouncers.'

'Oh, Ricky! Whatever was you thinking, going into Romford town centre? Kenny's told you never to go to the pubs there. He's home today an' all. He'll go mad.'

'Don't tell him, Shal. Please don't tell him. And I won't tell him about your new boyfriend.'

Finding out Ricky had overheard her on the phone to Tina was a shock to Sharon, but nothing could have shocked her more than Ray pulling up on her driveway in a three-wheeled yellow Reliant Robin. 'Oh no!' she gasped.

'It's Del Boy!' shrieked Ricky.

Sharon dashed outside with Ricky in close pursuit. 'I thought he was joking,' mumbled Sharon. 'Oh my God!'

Wearing a sheepskin and a checked flat cap, Ray stepped out of the vehicle with a cheesy grin on his face. 'Your carriage awaits, treacle.'

'Daddy, Daddy,' shrieked Rocky and Levi Bond, bolting outside to greet their father. They'd been sat at their Nan's window for the past half hour awaiting his arrival.

Beau crouched down and held his sons close to him. 'I ain't half missed you two. You missed me?'

'Lots and lots,' beamed Rocky. 'What you bought us?'

Beau took the presents out of his motor. He hadn't been able to find the kids much, but had picked them up some bits and bobs to keep them amused. 'You been good boys for your mum?'

Levi shook his head.

'No. She's been a cow and she's been out lots without us,' added Rocky.

'Has she really?' snarled Beau. The holiday had revitalized him. He looked good, had a bit of a tan and certainly felt more chilled. Until now that was. Jolene rarely went out without the kids. So where was she suddenly swanning off to?

Feeling a nervous wreck, Jolene emerged from her parents' trailer with Romany in her arms. Her dad was at a horse fayre, Sonny had taken Mary-Ann to visit her parents, so apart from herself and her mum, there were no other adults around if Beau were to kick off when she told him the inevitable. 'Say hello to your dad.' Jolene urged her daughter.

Beau held his arms out and felt sad when Romany refused to hug him, and instead buried her head deep in her mother's shoulder. Unlike the boys, Jolene wouldn't let him look after their daughter alone and it was obvious his little princess was rapidly forgetting who he was. She'd adored him before he'd been forced to move out, which was another reason why he was determined to move back in. 'You all right? I got you a present. It's in the car. The kids been good?'

'Erm. Yeah. Not bad. We need to talk, Beau. Mum will look after the chavvies.'

'Sounds ominous,' chuckled Beau.

When Jolene didn't even crack a smile, Beau realized it was probably ominous and in that split second, his blood began to boil.

'Bye, Mum. Love ya. I'll call you later,' grinned Sharon.

'Bye, Maggie. Was lovely to meet you,' waved Ray, as he opened the passenger door for Sharon to clamber inside. His pal Trevor was a market trader and a ringer for Del Boy in more ways than one. He even sounded like him. Hence, Ray and a couple of mutual pals had bought Trev the van as a laugh for his fiftieth. Trevor loved the bloody thing and had creased up when Ray had asked to borrow it to take a woman on a date.

Sharon chuckled as the van crawled slowly down Dark Lane. Her mum had loved Ray, had whispered as much in her ear. She'd said he was handsome, funny, and knocked spots off Kenny. 'I still can't believe you turned up in this. Where did ya get it from?'

'I swapped it for the Roller, just to please you.'

Sharon playfully punched her new man on the arm. 'Don't lie. Where did you really get it from?' Seconds later, as they were just about to turn on the A127, Sharon's amusement turned to shock. She quickly ducked. 'Shit! That was Kenny. I think he saw me!'

Beau Bond wasn't exactly expecting the red-carpet treatment. But neither was he expecting to be dumped like an unwanted dog. 'You never fail to disappoint me, Jolene.

We were so in love, that's why we got hitched. Three beautiful kids later and now you decide marriage ain't for you after all. I wouldn't mind so much if we were struggling, but we ain't. I work my nuts off for you and our chavvies. So, what's changed?'

Remembering her mother's 'Be kind' advice, Jolene chose her words carefully. 'I will always have feelings for you, Beau. You're also a blinding dad and provider. I want us to stay best friends, I honestly do. I just don't want to be married no more. It don't feel the same. Things have changed. And what with Jamie. Too much has happened.'

'Like what?' interrupted Beau. He'd vowed while on holiday never to beg or mug himself off in front of Jolene again. He wasn't stupid either. 'You must think I was born yesterday. You couldn't give a flying fuck about Jamie. He's just your get-out clause. So, what I really want to know, is why you need a get-out clause, Jolene? Only I know you've been swanning off out all the time. Alone, might I add. Got yourself a fresh bit of cock, have ya?'

The snarl on Beau's lips reminded her of an unfriendly stray dog she'd once known while living in Kent. 'How dare you talk to me like that? I'm not a slag. If you must know, I been going out having extra driving lessons with a mate as I passed my test but still don't feel confident enough to drive alone,' lied Jolene. She'd been expecting this question, had guessed Rocky might grass her up, the little shit. 'Best you go now, I think, Beau. You can take the boys with you, but have 'em back 'ere by seven.'

'You don't get to call the shots no more, Jolene. This is as much my home as it is yours. So tonight, I'll be moving back in. I can sleep in the spare room. As for keeping Romany all to yourself, that stops from today an' all. She's coming with me and the boys.'

'No! Brett, no.' Jolene chased after him. 'You can't take Romany. She'll get upset if I'm not with her.'

Evie was cleaning up a milkshake Levi had spilt on her rug when Beau stormed inside and grabbed her granddaughter. 'What you doing? Leave her be,' bellowed Evie, struggling to get up off her hands and knees.

'Keep out of it, you witch. She's my fucking daughter,' yelled Beau, before ordering the boys to get in the motor.

Romany was screaming as her mum tried to unsuccessfully grab her, then began hitting her dad, before losing her footing.

'Quick, Nan got a frying pan,' shrieked Rocky, as his sister was half slung on top of him and Levi in the back of the motor.

As all hell broke loose around him, Beau leapt in the driver's seat, locked the doors and sped away from the Tamplins' at a speed Michael Schumacher would've been proud of.

Aisling Neary tapped on her brother's bedroom door. She knew the two blokes had left, had heard them go. She sat down on Aidan's bed. 'You OK?'

'No. I feel like shit.'

'What happened with Dad?'

Aidan sat up and ran his hands through his dark wavy hair. 'He knows about Brett. Who he is, the works. He brought up Finlay's murder and said I don't want the same happening to Brett.'

Aisling held her brother's hand. 'What you going to do? Only, you owe Brett an explanation at least. Don't mess him around.'

'I know. I'll call him in a bit.'

After spending most of the journey worrying that Kenny had seen her, Sharon decided to put her ex to the back of her mind and enjoy the day ahead. It had been hilarious driving down the A12 in the slow lane. The amount of people who'd peered inside the Reliant Robin and tooted had made Sharon cringe and laugh in equal measures. 'It's very pretty round here, Ray.'

'It's Constable country.'

'What, as in Old Bill?'

'No, ya nutter,' chuckled Ray. 'As in the artist.'

Trouble and strife seemed to follow Kenny around, and the last thing he'd needed this morning was to deal with an irate Jolene and Evie. He'd also had a not-very-happy Bobby on the phone just to add to his angst. Wherever Beau was, he'd switched his bloody phone off, so all Kenny could do was try to appease the Tamplins. 'I can understand why you're angry, Evie. But causing World War Three ain't gonna solve anything. They're his kids and I'd bet me house on it, he'll have 'em back by this evening. He's taken them out for the day, not abducted 'em. He really missed seeing them while on holiday.'

'But he can't just snatch Romany,' snapped Jolene. 'She barely remembers him. She'll be scared and crying without me, the poor baby.'

'No disrespect, but Romany is Beau's daughter an' all. He should be allowed to spend time with her.'

'Your Beau wants to think himself lucky that it's Bobby coming back early from the horse fayre and not my Johnny and Billy. Bobby's told 'em they're not allowed to get involved 'cause he knows they'll beat the granny outta your grandson. And what's all this "he's moving back in" lark? He is not moving back in with Jolene. She don't want him there,' ranted Evie.

Kenny's jaw began twitching. 'Look, let's all calm down. Shouting and bawling at one another isn't the answer. I will speak to Beau. He's bound to call me as soon as he gets my message. In the meantime, try and work out some rota between yous. Only, like it or not, Beau has as much right to spend time with his own flesh and blood as Jolene does.'

Sick of all the arguing, ten-year-old Bobby-Joe had crept away unnoticed from the commotion and knocked at Ricky's door. He didn't see so much of his friend since he'd been with that girl and Bobby-Joe missed him and their chats.

'Hello, Bobby-Joe. What you doing here?'

'Come to see you. What you done to your face?'

'Come in and I'll tell you. You mustn't tell anyone else though. It's a secret. Would you like a burger? I'm just about to make myself lunch.'

The lads ate their burgers and had a good catch-up. Ricky told Bobby-Joe all about passing his driving test and why he wasn't answering the phone to Candy today. 'It was all her fault, honest it was. She acted like a tart. But I didn't even tell Sharon that bit 'cause she would say something to Candy and then there'd be an even bigger fight.'

'If I tell you a big secret, will you promise not to tell either?'

'Of course.'

'I know why Jolene don't love Beau any more. She got a new boyfriend. His name is Jimmy.'

Beau Bond hadn't had any plans to go to Southend, but that's where he'd ended up. As soon as he arrived there, he felt he'd made a big mistake. Romany was still tearful, he had no pushchair to put her in and his head was all over the place. He'd seen the way Jolene had looked at him, heard the way she'd tried to pacify him. She didn't look at him with love any more and that hurt like hell. How could you switch off loving someone just like that? Especially when you'd created three beautiful kids together. He couldn't understand it, which made it all the more difficult to accept. In his heart, he still loved her. He'd forgive her for all this upheaval in an instant if they could only go back to how things used to be.

'Dad, need a wee,' said Levi.

'Wanna go on the rides,' shrieked Rocky.

'Mummy,' grizzled Romany.

Beau took a deep, calming breath. If he drove straight home to drop his daughter off, he'd be admitting defeat – and he was no defeatist. He opened the back door of the Range Rover, lifted Romany into his arms and forced a smile. 'Right, we're gonna have the best day out ever. Who wants an ice-cream?'

*

Having knocked at his own bloody house and got no answer earlier, Kenny drove over to Loughton to visit Jake, then drove back to Dark Lane. He still couldn't get hold of Beau. Brett didn't know where his brother was, he was working up at the garden centre and neither Ricky nor Shal had bothered answering his calls.

Deciding to park at Donny's, in case Sharon was home and purposely ignoring him, Kenny recognized Evie's not-so-dulcet tones and quickly ducked behind a fence on his old neighbour's driveway.

'Hello, Ken. What you doing?' asked old June. She had a set of shears in her hands, was trimming her bush.

Kenny put a finger to his lips to urge June to be quiet and poked his head around the edge. Evie was giving young Bobby-Joe a proper berating, as she physically dragged him up the opposite end of Dark Lane.

'Sorry about that, June. Already had one run-in with Beau's in-laws this morning and I didn't bleedin' fancy another.'

'If you're looking for Sharon, she's not in I don't think, Kenny. I saw her go out earlier.'

'Who was she with, June? Only her car's on the drive and I need to get hold of her. It's pretty urgent.'

Wishing she'd kept her big trap shut, June didn't know what to say or do. She liked Sharon, but missed having Kenny as a neighbour. He'd always been so good to her and George. 'I don't know who she was with, love, but she got into a little yellow van.'

As the penny dropped, Kenny's jaw twitched manically. He stormed up his own drive and smashed his fist against *his* front door. He'd seen that bastard van, well caught a glimpse of it, and its cocky-looking driver, as he'd pulled off the Southend arterial. 'Ricky! I know you're in there. Answer the door, boy,' he bellowed.

Sheepishly, Ricky did as asked. Sharon had rung him in a panic earlier, to tell him she'd just passed Kenny and, if he were to knock, to not answer the door. 'Thank God it's you. I thought it was Evie again. She just went mad at me.'

'Did she do that to your face?'

'No. I got a bit drunk and fell down the stairs.' As Kenny tried to barge past, Ricky put an arm out to stop him. 'You can't come in. Shal's not home.'

'I think you've forgotten something: I own this fucking house.' Kenny pushed past Ricky and sat at the kitchen table. 'We need to talk, me and you, man to man.'

'You gonna buy me a car?'

'Sit yourself down,' ordered Kenny. 'My dear old granddad loved an old saying. A phrase. I'm sure I've told you that before. Well, one of his favourite sayings was "Never forget what side your bread is buttered on".'

'I always butter mine on the top,' replied Ricky earnestly.

'That ain't the true meaning of the saying though, boy. I'll make it simple for you. See us, for instance. Well, I've always been there for you. I kind of promised your dad once that, if anything were to happen to him, I'd take good care of you. And I like to think I've kept that promise.'

'You did. You have.'

'Good. Well, now I need a little something back from you. I wanna know if Sharon's got a boyfriend and who

299

he is. Is he the bloke who was in the yellow van earlier? And what time's she due home? In fact, I want to know everything about what Sharon's been up to lately. And in return for telling me, I will never let on I heard it from you and I'll take you out in the week to pick yourself whatever car you want.'

'Can I have a BMW Sport Convertible?'

'If we can get you insured on it,' lied Kenny. That was a no-go, he knew that much.

Suddenly realizing what side his bread was buttered on really meant, Ricky started to blab.

Unaware that she was currently the topic of conversation back in Essex, Sharon was enjoying an idyllic day out in Suffolk. She'd loved it earlier when Ray had hired a boat along the river, then produced two cans of bitter and a couple of packets of pork scratchings from the pockets of his sheepskin. She'd actually drunk the bitter and ate the pork scratchings. So had he.

They'd then visited a beautiful local church where Sharon had lit a candle and said a prayer for her mum. Ray had lost his own mum to cancer last year and was far more understanding and sympathetic about the illness than Kenny had ever been.

Now they were in a lovely pub and, having tucked into a gorgeous roast, they were sitting in the beer garden that overlooked the river.

'You want another glass of wine, Sharon?'

'I will if you're having another.'

'I better not have no more. Imagine me getting nicked driving that heap of junk back home? My pals would never let me live it down,' chuckled Ray. 'Let me get you one, though. I'll have a Coke.'

When Ray went to the bar, Sharon took her phone out of her handbag. She'd turned it off earlier, just so she could enjoy some peace and quiet for once. 'Oh Jesus,' she mumbled, as she got wind of her messages.

When Ray returned, he sensed something was amiss. 'What's up?'

'Kenny did spot us earlier. Ricky left me a message. So did Kenny, but not to tell me he saw us. He left one to say our grandson had abducted our great-grandchildren and the gypsy in-laws are livid. Oh, and my daughter left one too. She's up at Basildon Hospital. She thinks she's broken her foot.'

Ray squeezed Sharon's hand. 'It never rains, it pours, eh? D'ya want to make a move?'

'No. I'm sick of being at everyone's beck and call. They can survive without me. I dunno what I'm going to say to Kenny though.'

'Just tell him the truth. Tell him we're seeing one another. He's bound to find out at some point anyway.'

'He won't like it, Ray. And believe me, Kenny can be a proper arsehole when he wants to be. I don't want him causing you any grief. I might just say we're good friends for now.'

Ray smiled. 'Entirely up to you. But don't be worrying about me, Sharon. I'm more than capable of looking after meself. And you. Trust me on that one.'

After a crappy start, Beau's trip to Southend with all three of his children had turned out to be a great success.

He'd even managed to find a little pull-along plastic toy in the shape of a ladybird that Romany loved so much, she was reluctant to get out of.

'Who that on the phone, Dad?' enquired Rocky.

'Gramps. I texted your mum an' all. You make sure you tell Mum and Nan what a good day out you've had,' replied Beau. They'd spent time on the beach, gone on lots of rides at Treasure Island, had eaten ice-cream, burgers, chips and candyfloss and were now in an amusement arcade not far from where the car was parked.

'I wanna go ghost train again,' whinged Levi.

'No. I've already told ya, we can't go back there. We've got to leave in a bit.'

'Don't wanna leave,' stomped Levi.

'We have to. I told your mum I'd have you back by six.' Beau glanced at his watch. 'Right, you got another twenty minutes in here, so make the most of it.'

Romany tugged Beau's trousers. 'Dadda,' she shrieked, pointing towards the Two Penny Falls.

Thrilled that in one day, he and his little princess had reconnected as though they'd never been apart, Beau lifted her up to put some coins in the slot. No way was anyone stopping him seeing his girl in future. Jolene and Evie could go fuck themselves.

Jolene arrived home late afternoon. Jimmy Dean had picked her up earlier as pre-planned, but their day had been ruined by Beau's reckless behaviour. Even Demi had been miserable because Romany wasn't around for her to play with.

'Right! I'm dealing with this, Evie. You stay 'ere.' Having been called away early from what would've been

302

a good jolly-up and financially beneficial day for him, Bobby Tamplin was in the foulest of moods. He'd also heard a rumour. One that involved his family.

'Don't you have a go at her. I told you ages ago we should never have agreed to her marrying Beau.'

'Shut your noise for once, woman,' bellowed Bobby, before marching down the dirt track that led to his land.

'All right, Dad? My mate just dropped me off. I rung Mum, told her Beau texted me. He said he'll bring the chavvies home by six. But I wouldn't bet on it. Bang out of order he is.'

'Get indoors,' hissed Bobby. 'We needs to talk.'

Sensing that her father knew something, Jolene felt the colour drain from her face. 'I'll make us a cuppa.'

'Forget the fucking tea. Sit your arse down,' ordered Bobby. 'What's all this I hear about you and Albert Dean's grandson?'

'I take it you mean Jimmy? We're just good friends.'

'I weren't born yesterday. You're a married woman with three chavvies, for God's sake. Talk about give our family a bad name. People ain't long stopped talking about how our Tammy died. Now you're flaunting yourself for all to see, with a man that's only recently been widowed. I take it that was him who dropped you off in the truck? I daren't tell your mother and brothers, they'll bloody disown you. As for Beau, he'd go apeshit – and rightly so.'

'Mum knows me and Jimmy are friends. So does Sonny. I would've told you too, but I knew you'd overreact like this. I ain't no tart, Dad, and Jimmy's grieving his wife. That's why we gets on so well. We're both in the same boat, losing someone so young and so close to us.'

Bobby put his hands on his head and paced up and down. He might've known Evie was aware of the bloody friendship. She hated Beau that much; she was probably encouraging it. 'I gets what you're saying, Jolene. But women can't be good friends with a man. Not if they're married with chavvies.'

'I'm really sorry, Dad, 'cause I know you spent loads of money on the wedding. But I don't want to be married no more. Not to Beau. I don't love him the way I should. And that ain't fair on me or him. I have tried to love him and work things out, but I can't. The only thing I can think of is I married the first boy I met 'cause I was missing Tammy.'

'Bloody hell, Jolene. The lad's going to be devastated. He loves you to bits, and your babbies.'

'I know he does. Which is why I need you on my side. I've made up my mind. I want a divorce.'

CHAPTER TWENTY-ONE

The Reliant Robin turned out to be anything but reliant on the journey back. It conked out along the A12 and the RAC had to tow it back to Chigwell.

Having never seen Ray's home before, Sharon was suitably impressed. 'It's so stylish and modern, Ray. Very tidy as well. You put me to shame, and I like a clean home.'

'I got my cleaner to thank for that, although I do tidy up after meself. I've got a thing about clutter. It does my head in. You in a rush? Or, can I get you a drink? I've got wine, coffee, tea, champagne. In fact, you name it, I've probably got it.'

Sharon smiled. Even though her notright family had done their utmost to ruin her day, they hadn't succeeded. She'd had the best day out in a long time. Even the van breaking down had tickled her pink. 'A glass of wine would be lovely. Thanks, Ray.'

Ricky nervously chewed at his fingernails. Kenny was outside speaking to Sharon on the phone.

Ricky was no snitch; Kenny had personally taught him that grassing was a bad thing. Therefore, he'd tried not to put Sharon in the shit. He had to tell Kenny some scandal though, as he really wanted a nice car, so he'd elaborated about Sharon's friendship with Scott, her personal trainer. He hadn't said a word about overhearing Shal talk to Tina on the phone about Ray, and he'd also been vague about Sharon's movements. He'd had to warn Sharon that Kenny was there waiting for her though. He'd rung her from the toilet and left her a message to say Kenny had barged his way in.

Thinking of Candy, Ricky bit his nails even harder. She'd stopped grovelling, had sent him an abrupt text to say she was going out with her friend Alison in Barking. Ricky didn't like Alison one little bit. She was a dwarf, with a vicious temper and a drink problem. She was also a slag who gave blowjobs to the men in the toilets of her local Wetherspoons pub. 'Everything all right? What did Shal say?'

'Well, she don't wanna talk tonight. But she promised she'd call me tomorrow and arrange a time to hear me out. I made her swear on Donny and Sherry's lives, so I know she won't let me down. Shal's superstitious like that. Fingers crossed,' grinned Kenny, crossing his own, 'things might just be looking up. She certainly sounded like the old Shal on the blower. Not angry, more mellow, like.'

'I'm pleased. Be great if you got back together.'

'Yes. It would. How d'ya fancy going out for a couple of beers? We need to celebrate you passing your driving test, don't we?'

'Yeah. I'd like that. I just need to clean my teeth and change my top.'

'Hurry up then,' smiled Kenny. Ricky's lips tended to loosen after a couple of pints, so not only could he probe him more about Sharon, he also wanted to find out what had really happened to his face. No way had he fallen down stairs. Not on your nelly.

'He's 'ere, the arsehole,' hissed Evie. She was still livid with Beau for snatching Romany earlier, and she was angry with Bobby for being so laid-back about it all.

'You stay here,' Bobby ordered his wife.

Jolene ran outside, grabbed her beloved daughter and held her in her arms. 'Are you OK, darlin'? Mummy missed you so very much.'

'Car, bird,' pointed Romany, shying away from her mother's kisses.

Beau lifted the pull-a-long ladybird out the boot. 'She means this. Loves it, she does,' he smiled. 'Sorry for taking her like that, but she is old enough to spend time with me now. We had a great day, didn't we, kids?'

'The best. We went on big-boy rides,' Rocky informed his mother.

'And ghost train,' added Levi.

'Go tell Nan and Granddad all about it, while I talk to your dad. Take Romany with you. Hold her hand so she don't fall over.' Jolene waited for the kids to be out of earshot before turning back to Beau with a look of hatred on her face. She punched him, hard in the chest. 'Don't you ever fucking drive off like that with 'em again. Worried sick, me and Mum were. Dad weren't happy either. He had to come home early from his horse fayre.'

Beau held his hands up. 'I'm sorry for scaring ya, but I ain't apologizing for wanting to spend time with me own kids, Jolene. They had a ball. Ask 'em, if you don't believe me. Look, I know you ain't ready for us to get back together. Which is fine. But our babies miss me, so I'm gonna move back in. Just for their sake, obviously. I'm quite happy to sleep in the spare room, and you haven't gotta cook for me, not unless you want to. I can always eat at work and grab a takeaway on the way home. Think of me as a babysitter, on tap for whenever you want some *you* time at the bingo or the market. What d'ya say? I think we can make that arrangement work.'

'I don't,' spat Jolene. 'Look, there's no easy way to say this, Beau, but I don't love you any more. I'm sorry. But I can't help the way I feel. It's over. We're over.'

'Nah, nah, nah. You've just got the hump and you're saying that to hurt me. You told me earlier you did still love me, so I know what I believe.'

'I don't, OK! Things haven't been right for ages. I'm not happy with you. Perhaps we got married too young? I don't know. But I think we should get divorced.'

'How can you fucking say that?' Eyes blazing, Beau punched the side of his Range Rover, leaving a dent. '"Soulmates", you always said that's what we were. Why did you marry me if you don't love me?'

'I did love you at the time. Or I thought I did. We were young, Beau. Naive. And I'd just lost Tammy.'

'Don't you dare blame this on your dead sister,' hissed Beau.

'I'm not. But lots has happened since then and I can't get over what you did. You know,' Jolene looked around to check nobody was in earshot, 'to Jamie.'

'You're a cunt, Jolene. D'ya know that? No way are we divorcing though. It ain't right for the kids. They got a mum, and a dad, which is why we stay married. If you honestly want to split up, then fine. But I want the kids three an' a half days a week. They can stay at mine, so I get to see 'em the same amount as you. That's only fucking fair, seeing as we won't all be living together.'

'Don't be ridiculous. You gotta go to work.'

Beau walked towards the stranger who was once his loving wife. 'Don't tell me what I gotta do.' Unable to control the boiling rage inside him, Beau grabbed her by the throat. 'And if I ever find out you've got another geezer, believe me, you'll be fucking sorry.'

'Get off me,' Jolene screamed.

Seconds later, Bobby Tamplin appeared and grabbed Beau in a headlock.

Having received a phone call from an irate Bobby, Kenny didn't get as far as the pub. He asked the cab driver to do a U-turn and head back to Dark Lane.

Beau yanked open the front door, his eyes watery, his knuckles bleeding.

'Bobby's well cheesed off. What was you thinking, grabbing Jolene by the throat? You don't hurt a woman, boy. I've always drummed that into ya.'

Beau gave the wall one final punch. He'd had to release his anger somehow. 'I hate her. The bitch. She's mugged me off proper. No way are my kids coming from a broken family. I won't have it. I'll hire the best brief going if I have to. I got fucking rights an' all,' he seethed.

'Go wash that blood off your hands. You're coming to the pub with me and Ricky. We can talk there and you can explain everything from the beginning.'

'I'm telling you now, if I find out she's got another bloke, I'll kill him. Then I'll do away with her an' all, the dirty rotten whore.'

'Everything all right?' Ray asked Sharon. They were on their way back to Dark Lane, he was dropping her home.

'Yeah. Sherry's foot's not broken, thank God. They reckon it's a bad sprain, have strapped it up for support. She's home now. That'll teach her to get drunk while wearing silly high heels.'

'Like mother, like daughter,' chuckled Ray. 'I remember scraping you and your high heels off the floor once upon a time.'

Sharon playfully punched his leg. 'I reckon you spiked my drink that night so you could have your wicked way with me,' she joked. 'I never behave in that manner as a rule.'

'Yeah, yeah.'

'Seeing as Ricky's down the pub with Kenny and Beau, you can come in for a coffee while the coast is clear.'

'As long as you don't try and have your wicked way with me,' teased Ray.

Sharon laughed. 'You should be so bleedin' lucky.'

Checking the wording once again, Brett finally pressed the send button. He hadn't answered any of Aidan's calls, but had just texted him back saying he wasn't free until Tuesday.

The Brothers

Feeling good for playing it cool, Brett ran the shower. Gramps, Beau and Ricky were all down the Jobber's Rest and he could do with a night out too. Work had been exhausting and a bit boring this past week or so, with only Ricky and the staff around.

Brett's heart leapt as his phone bleeped. But it wasn't Aidan. It was Ricky asking him to bring him a clean shirt as they were going for an Indian later and he'd spilt a drink down his own.

Brett checked the wardrobe to see if Ricky had any shirts there. He didn't. Never mind. He'd get one from his nan's house.

Beau wasn't a good drinker. Therefore, when he started knocking them back like there was no tomorrow, Kenny was worried. That's why he'd suggested they go for an Indian once Brett arrived. He didn't want the lad getting plastered and kicking off.

'Who wants another?' asked Beau.

'We're all right, and you need to make the next one last longer,' replied Kenny.

'I'm a grown man, not a kid,' retaliated Beau.

'I know you are. But I also know what a hothead you can be, especially when you hit the booze. You don't wanna be getting smashed and contacting Jolene again. We've had enough drama for one poxy day.'

'I'll have to contact her tomorrow, as I want to spend time with the kids. She can't stop me. Neither can Evie, Bobby or any other bastard. Those children are as much my flesh and blood as they are hers.'

'A word of advice, Beau. Let things calm down for a

311

day or two, please. In the meantime, I'll speak to Bobby and find out what the hell is going on.'

'She ain't getting one over on me,' ranted Beau. 'I'm not the mug she thinks I am. Loved her to the moon and back, I did. But after today, I hate her with a passion. How could she do this to me?'

Feeling desperately sorry for Beau, Kenny shrugged. He could do without this shit right now. A war with the gypsies was the last thing he needed. Not while he was trying to win Sharon back.

Sharon felt embarrassed. She'd left her kitchen spotless earlier, now it was littered with empty glasses, mugs, plates and it reeked of fried onions. 'Let me just tidy up, Ray. I'll wring Ricky's neck when he gets home. He usually loads the dishwasher, the lazy little sod.'

'Don't be worrying about it on my behalf. Your kitchen is almost as stunning as you.'

'Oh, stop it,' chuckled Sharon. 'Full of old flannel, you are.'

When Ray grabbed her hand and passionately kissed her, Sharon responded with a desire she hadn't felt for a very long time. What the hell was happening to her? She'd gone through the menopause ages ago, yet suddenly felt like a teenager. She pulled away, shocked. 'I really do like you, Ray. But Kenny's the only man I've ever been intimate with and although part of me feels ready to move on, I can't help but worry you might be a bit of a player too.'

At six foot two, Ray towered over Sharon. He cupped her face with his hands. 'Oh, come on. You must know how I feel about you by now? Whatever makes you think I'm a player? I'm anything but.'

'I dunno. Probably 'cause the first time I ever met you was in Palms, then when I bumped into you again, you were in another grab-a-granny venue in Chigwell. I hate places like that, only went 'cause Tina dragged me to them.'

'I can't be drinking in places that are full of youngsters, Shal. That's the only reason I go to venues that are aimed at the over thirties. Believe me, I've no interest in pulling any granny. Some of my pals are like Peter Pan, still think they can pull young birds. A couple of 'em do, regularly. The birds only want them for their money though. Embarrassing.'

If there was a comment to warm Sharon to Ray even more, it was that last one. This time, she initiated the kiss.

'I'll be two more minutes, mate. Don't worry, I'll pay you waiting time,' Brett told the cabbie. 'Just gotta pick something up,' he added, before walking the short distance to his nan's house.

As he approached, Brett heard a bloke's voice. He stopped in his tracks, before ducking and peeping around old June's bush. 'Oh my God!' he quietly exclaimed, barely able to believe his eyes. Gramps was gonna go apeshit.

'It's too small,' complained Ricky. Brett had brought one of his own shirts with him to change into.

'Weren't your nan in?' enquired Kenny.

'Yeah. But she had company.'

'What sort of company?'

'She was saying goodbye to some bloke,' explained Brett.

'What bloke?' asked Beau.

'I dunno.'

Kenny felt his hackles rise. 'Was there a little yellow van on the drive?'

'Nah. There was a dark Porsche.'

'That's Scott's car,' blurted out Ricky.

'Scott who?' asked Beau.

'Shal's fitness trainer. He's ever so nice.'

'Nice!' spat Kenny. He turned to Brett. 'How exactly was she saying goodbye to him?'

Brett wouldn't usually dob anyone in it, especially his own nan. However, Gramps always had his back, therefore Brett couldn't lie to him. 'They looked like they might be kissing. They were deffo in some kind of embrace.'

'Slag,' slurred Beau.

Kenny clumped Beau around the head. 'Don't you dare call your nan that.' Jaw twitching furiously, Kenny turned to Ricky. 'You know this Scott's surname? Where he lives? Where he works?'

Wishing he had kept his big trap shut, as he very much doubted the man Sharon was kissing was Scott, Ricky shrugged. 'I know he's married with three kids and he works as a personal trainer. That's all I know.'

'Well, best you find out more, so I can pay the cunt a visit. Nobody makes a fool out of me, or your nan. I won't fucking stand for it.'

By the time they reached the Indian, Brett wished he'd stayed at home. Beau was drunk, wouldn't stop rambling on about his marriage, and even though Brett felt sorry for his brother, he was sick to the back teeth of hearing about Jolene. 'Can we talk about something else now, please?'

Beau gave his twin a look of daggers. 'Yeah, let's talk about your bird. The one I doubt even exists.'

'Don't talk rubbish. You know Aisling exists. You've met her,' retorted Brett.

'Yeah. Once. Something don't ring true about you and her, if you ask me.'

'Well, no one's asking you. We've not been getting on, if you must know. I ain't seen her since before you went away. We're meeting up on Tuesday, to try and sort things.'

'I've not been getting on with Candy either. We had a big row,' admitted Ricky, before blurting out everything that had happened the previous evening.

'I knew it! I knew you hadn't stacked it down no stairs. Don't you ever go to them pubs in the town centre again, not unless you're with Beau and Brett. As for Candy, there's plenty more fish in the sea, boy. The world's your oyster now you can drive,' replied Kenny.

Ricky downed the rest of his pint, resulting in a loud burp. 'But I love her. I want to marry her one day.'

'Don't ever get married,' seethed Beau. 'They change once you put a ring on their finger. They don't want sex no more and they treat you like shit.'

'Dunno what I'm gonna do about your nan. I'm moving back into *my* house though, I'll tell you that much,' rambled Kenny.

'Don't be too harsh on Nan,' urged Brett. 'She might've just been giving Scott a friendly hug and kiss goodbye. I'm not a hundred per cent sure it was a snog.'

'I know something bad, about Jolene,' blurted out Ricky.

315

'What?' Beau bellowed.

'Ya gotta promise you won't say it came from me. 'Cause I don't wanna get Bobby-Joe in trouble.'

'Promise. Just tell me,' urged Beau.

'I know why Jolene don't love you any more. She's got a new boyfriend called Jimmy.'

Beau's face was a picture of anger. 'You what!'

Enjoying being centre of attention, Ricky now couldn't stop blabbing. 'And she's got a car. Her dad bought it for her. But she hides it behind her mum and dad's home, 'cause she don't want you to see it, in case you follow her.'

Unable to control his fury, Beau threw his glass at the restaurant wall. 'I'll kill her. On my life, I will. She's dead to me. Fucking stone dead.'

CHAPTER TWENTY-TWO

'You ever gonna stop eating? Only, if not, can you do it more quietly?' scowled Baz Daley. He and Ginger were plotted up outside the Cavendish Hotel in Eastbourne.

Mad Ginger stuffed the rest of the McMuffin in his mouth. Five he'd scoffed in total. Three sausage, two bacon and he'd enjoyed every bloody mouthful. 'What's the time?'

'Stop asking me that. He'll be here, OK? I only saw him on Saturday with me own bloody eyes.' Baz had been released a week earlier than his brother and had already put in a bit of detective work.

'Be awful if his old dear's croaked it and he's flown back to Spain, eh?'

'Stop being such a pessimist.'

'I'm winding you up, ya div,' chuckled Ginger. While on remand, Ginger had learned via his brief that Jonathan St Clement was The Scientist's real name. He hadn't pressed charges after the abduction turnout, had instead done a runner. Janey had found out that he was now back in England and residing at this hotel. They also knew that his mother was in a care home nearby.

''Ere we are. Told you he'd show his face around this time, didn't I?' grinned Baz.

'Bosh! Now, drive.'

Kenny Bond turned up at the garden centre mid-morning. 'You made it then. Good lad. You OK?'

Beau shrugged. 'Case of having to be. I got to see the kids last night, took 'em to the Pizza Hut. Romany wouldn't leave me be, bless her. She must've missed me big time.'

'And so she should. You're a blinding father. Did you see Jolene?'

'Nah. Sonny brought Romany out to me, and Bobby came out when we got back. I was gonna say something to him about that Jimmy geezer, but I didn't want to rock the boat. I find it hard to believe they're just friends. I know you trust Bobby, but—'

'I don't think he'd lie to me,' interrupted Kenny. He'd met Bobby alone in the pub on Monday evening for a man-to-man talk, which had resulted in a firm handshake.

'Tell me what you said again and what he said.'

'I just bluffed it, said a pal of mine had seen Jolene out with another geezer, but I hadn't told you as I didn't want to cause any more trouble, in case there was an innocent explanation. Bobby immediately knew who the bloke was, said it was a close friend of the family who'd recently lost his wife. He swore blind nothing untoward was occurring between the fella and Jolene, said they were just friends.'

'Well, he would say that, wouldn't he?' spat Beau.

'Listen, I know we all got on our high horse on Sunday. But a lot of that was the booze talking. As for Ricky and his drunken revelations, ya can take them with a pinch of salt, boy. I wanted to strangle your nan on Sunday, but when I woke up Monday and the cold light of day hit me, I knew no way on earth would your nan be knocking off a married man with three kids. That ain't my Shal. She's got morals. And I'm sure Jolene has too. Ricky hears snippets of things, stores 'em in his nut, then makes a mountain out of a molehill when he's boozed.'

'But it weren't Ricky who saw Nan with her personal trainer. It was Brett.'

'It was probably just a friendly hug goodbye, that's all.' Kenny glanced at his watch. 'I better be making tracks. Best I get there first. I wish she hadn't chosen the Top Oak though. Probably playing mind games. Reminding me of my wrongdoings before she agrees to take me back,' grinned Kenny. Sharon had arranged to meet him in the same pub that Abigail had turned up in many moons ago. Some day that had been, definitely one that Kenny would rather forget.

'Good luck. I'm eating out later, after work. With Mum.'

'Sweet. Say hello to Lori for me. Hopefully, by the time you get home, we'll be neighbours again.'

Sharon arrived at the Top Oak half an hour before she was due to meet Kenny. She hadn't bothered to dress up, was in her work clothes.

'What can I get you, Sharon? You're early today,' smiled the barmaid.

'A large glass of Pinot, please. I'm meeting Donny's dad for lunch,' smiled Sharon. The Top Oak was the nearest pub to the nursery. She and Tina often popped in for lunch, as did Donny. That's why she'd chosen to meet Kenny here. She very much doubted he was going to like what she had to say to him. Therefore, if he kicked off, Donny and Tina were only a few minutes away.

Sharon sat at a corner table and pretended to study the menu. It was weird how her feelings towards Kenny had changed. Once upon a time, she could never have envisaged life without him; now she didn't want him anywhere near her. She would always be grateful to him for her children. She didn't hate him. She no longer loved him though. She could see through him now like a freshly polished pane of glass.

'Hello, you. You're early. What you drinking? It's so good to see ya, Shal. You're looking well.'

Sharon flinched as Kenny bent down to kiss her on the cheek. 'I'll have another glass of Pinot, please.'

Kenny ordered a bottle of plonk, then took off the tan leather jacket Sharon had bought for him many birthdays ago. He was also wearing the black polo shirt and Hugo Boss aftershave she'd given him the last Christmas they'd spent together. 'So, how you been keeping? I really appreciate you agreeing to meet me and hear me out. I get why you were so angry and made me wait so long an' all. But once I explain, I know you'll understand more and I swear on my muvver and Aunt Nell's life, Shal, that there ain't no other skeletons in my closet and there never will be in the future either.'

When Kenny leaned across the table to hold her hands, Sharon snatched them away. Did he honestly think she'd finally agreed to hear him out because she wanted him back? How full of himself and delusional he was. 'I only agreed to hear you out, Kenny. Then I want you to hear me out also.'

'You wanna go first?'

'No. You. Fire away.'

'Not long now,' said Baz Daley. He'd watched Jonathan's movements a few times over the past week. He'd turn up at the care home just after nine, pop out around noon to bring back lunch, probably for himself and his dear old mum. Then he'd leave a couple of hours later and head straight to either the bookies or the casino.

'What we gonna do if he don't blab? Say he just accepts the pain and his fate?'

'For fuck's sake! The man is a gambler. I've done rehab with many. They'd trade in their old granny if the price was right. He'll talk. Trust me. And if he don't, I will personally chop his fingers off. One by one.'

'So, that's about it really, Shal.' Kenny Bond had literally opened his heart to his wife, told her everything he could think of regarding his relationship with Karen and how he'd finally found out Jake existed. 'I truly regret not coming clean with you when we first got back together. You gave me ample opportunity. Had I known there was a chance she might be up the duff, I would've told ya. But I knew how much I'd hurt you with Abigail and I couldn't bear to hurt you even more. How she got pregnant is still a mystery to me as I wore something, ya know, took precautions.'

'How thoughtful of you.' Sharon's voice was laden with sarcasm. 'Donny's getting married. He and Tansey are looking at venues this weekend.'

'He must be mad. Dunno how he's suffered her all these years, do you?'

'He loves her,' Sharon said bluntly. 'I'll have a jacket potato with cheese and chilli,' she handed Kenny the menu. 'Sherry was up the hospital all day on Sunday. She's done her ankle in.'

Kenny rolled his eyes. 'Pissed, I suppose.'

'If you've got nothing nice to say about our kids, it's probably best you don't say anything.'

'I was only messing. Are they both doing all right? I do miss 'em.'

'Yes. They're fine.'

'And what about you? I hear you got yourself a fitness trainer and I clocked you Sunday in a little yellow van.'

'That's right. I went out for the day.'

'Who with?'

'A friend. Not that it's any of your business.'

Kenny leaned forward. There were two nosy bastards on the next table. 'I miss you. You ain't just my wife, you're my best friend. I know I wronged you, but I swear it'll never happen again. Please give us another chance?'

'I'm sorry, Kenny. But not this time. One of the reasons I agreed to see you today was to chat about the future. I don't want it to be filled with hatred and bad feeling. But I do want a divorce.'

With his mother's advice at the forefront of his mind, Brett Bond sauntered into Aidan's apartment, looking far more casual than he felt. 'All right? Sorry I'm late. I had to pop somewhere first,' he lied. He was actually late on purpose.

'No worries. What can I get you to drink? I'm abstaining from alcohol at the moment, but no need for you to.'

Already feeling deflated, because after working his nuts off while Gramps and Beau were away, he'd been hoping to have a nutty day and get right on it, Brett shrugged. 'Just a beer.'

Aidan poured a can of Stella into a glass. He couldn't stand people drinking out of cans, thought it was cheap and nasty. 'There you go, and thanks for coming over. Sorry about the other night. I had words with my dad, then got completely wasted. Hence the health kick. We've got to cool it a bit, me and you. My dad knows we've been hanging out and he's none too happy about it. I can still see you. But we'll have to stay in, until the dust settles at least.'

Brett's face fell. This was not the welcome he'd expected or wanted. 'I ain't gonna spend my life sitting indoors. Surely, you're allowed to have pals? What exactly did he say?'

'That you're young and people are talking. I don't wanna call it a day, but I'll understand if you choose to. It's an awkward situation, I know.'

Brett ran his hands through his gelled-back blond hair and paced up and down the kitchen. He'd expected Aidan to beg forgiveness, not casually try to finish with him. 'You met someone else?'

'Don't be daft. Course not.'

'Where was you the other night then?'

'Getting pissed in a bar.'

'I bet you ended up shagging. You've got guilt written all over your face. Just be fucking honest with me for once. Surely you owe me that much?'

'You want the truth? I can't remember the other night. Aisling said I rolled home early hours, absolutely shit-faced. There's nobody else though, I swear. This is all about my father. I told you before what he was like, said we had to be careful.'

'Bollocks to being careful!' Brett slammed his fist against the kitchen worktop. 'I want us to be together, properly. As in live together. I also wanna go Ireland with ya and meet your boy. I don't look queer and neither do you. So, why is your old man suspecting us in the first place? Especially when you got a son. You told me you had Conor to take the pressure off with your dad.'

'I did. And it did, for a while. But, my dad isn't stupid, Brett. I have no girlfriend, yet I'm seen out all the time with a young handsome blond lad. I still want to see you and be friends, whatever you decide.'

Brett lunged towards Aidan and shoved him hard in the chest. 'Friends! Fucking friends! I don't think so, ya cheeky prick. We're done.'

Kenny Bond felt as though he'd been hit by a ten-tonne truck. So much so, he was temporarily lost for words. A divorce was unthinkable. He and Shal had been as tight as a nun's fanny since the day they'd first met. Apart from the times they'd separated, but that was neither here nor there. Kenny had still financially supported Sharon while they were apart and always knew in his heart, it would only be a matter of time before she forgave him and they were together again.

'What's going on, Shal? You know I love you and I'll always support you. Hand on heart, I will never make another mistake as long as I live. Please, just give me one more chance? You're my world. You always have been.'

Wary of Kenny's unpredictable temper, Sharon chose her words carefully. 'I will always care for you, Kenny. But, I don't love you any more. Not in that way. It's over between us. I'm sorry.'

Jonathan St Clement glanced at his watch. He had a couple of juicy tips today, in the 1.40 and 3.10 at Kempton. 'I've got to make a move now, Mum. I need to get to the bookies to earn us a few bob.'

Geraldine St Clement smiled obliviously. Her Alzheimer's had worsened, leaving her in a muddled-up world of her own.

Jonathan kissed his mother on the forehead. He'd been living out in Benidorm until her illness had become unmanageable. He'd since sold her property to pay for the care she needed and, as an only child, he'd pocketed a nice few bob himself.

'Bring Daddy with you tomorrow. I want to dance with him. We can do the fox-trot like we used to. And the jive.'

Jonathan crouched and squeezed his mother's hand. Robert, his father, had been dead for years. Alzheimer's was a cruel disease, one that seems to erase the present, yet recall the past. 'I think Dad's working. But I'll be here, Mum, whatever.'

'You're a good boy, erm . . . What's your name again?'

Jonathan forced a smile. He hated his mother not knowing who he was, but he was all she had and he was determined to spend as much time as he had left with her as possible. 'Love you, Mum. See you soon.'

Aware that he was cutting it fine, Jonathan walked swiftly. He couldn't miss the first race. That tip was a dead cert, by all accounts. He turned left, then right, then left again. He was just about to do another left when he was grabbed roughly by the arm. 'What the fuck!'

'Hello, me old china,' grinned Mad Ginger. 'Long time no see. Just get in the motor and there'll be no bother. I only wanna talk to ya.'

Jonathan recoiled. He knew coming back from Benidorm to sort out his mother's affairs and spend time with her had been a risk and he suddenly wished he hadn't bothered. He had to stay calm, think on his feet. He couldn't let them abduct him again, pour drink down his throat. He had to get away somehow.

'OK, mate. No worries. I'll tell you whatever you want to know, but can I just put a quick bet on first? It's a dead cert.'

Looking around to make sure there were no onlookers, Ginger gave Jonathan a tidy punch in the ribs. 'No, you fucking can't. Get in the motor. Now!'

By the time the food arrived at the table, Kenny's jaw was twitching far too much for him to eat. Not that he felt hungry any more. He felt hurt, angry and very let down. Yes, he'd made mistakes. But he'd always adored Sharon, worshipped the ground she walked on. 'We can't get divorced, Shal. Not me and you. We're soulmates, we've always been soulmates. You know that as well as I do. Why now? Why say that to me? You've gotta have a new fella on the firm. You must have.'

Sharon could sense how much Kenny was hurting and even though he'd hurt her enormously in the past, she didn't want to rub salt in the wounds by mentioning Ray. It wasn't the right time, nor place. 'There's nobody else, not romantically. I have male friends though. And why shouldn't I? You have no right to tell me what I can do any more, or who I can see, Kenny. A quick divorce is the best thing for both of us. You can do what you like then and so can I.'

The thought of Sharon 'doing what she liked', as she so bluntly put it, was enough to send Kenny over the edge. He slammed his glass against the table so hard the wine flew out the top. 'I ain't signing no divorce papers, and if you force this bollocks, I'll be having my say to a brief an' all. You ain't exactly Saint Sharon. The one time I properly ballsed up, you'd starved me of sex for fuck knows how long beforehand, then you fucked off to Spain to be with your muvver. I had needs too. Hence that nutter Abi. As for Karen, I weren't even with you when I was seeing her. So, what's your grounds for a quick divorce?'

'Shush! You're embarrassing us,' spat Sharon.

Like a roaring lion, Kenny stood up and pointed at the nose-ointments on the next table. 'Fuck them! This is probably the most excitement they've had since they were born. And fuck you, Sharon. 'Cause whether you like it or not, I'm moving back in very shortly. I put in every penny I had at the time to build that gaff. Therefore, if you want a divorce, you move out. That gaff is *mine*. Every single bastard brick of it.'

Lori hated seeing her sons in pain. It made her feel help-less, even though she knew it was a part of life's learning curve. 'I'm so sorry, Beau. But in my opinion, she was never good enough for you anyway. I know you don't see it at the moment, but you are a handsome boy with a beautiful soul. You're also a wonderful father, who deserves to have your children living with you. You will love again.'

'But part of me still loves her, Mum. How can I not? When I first met her, she showed me more love and passion than anyone ever had in my lifetime. Then between us we created three perfect kids. I just want things to go back to how they were between us.'

Lori held her son's hand. 'You can't force somebody to love you if they don't love you any more, Beau. I adored your dad once upon a time and he did something similar to me. The day he walked away and left us all for Tansey absolutely broke my heart. I could perhaps understand him going off of me, but not walking away from you and Brett.'

'Dad's a cunt,' snarled Beau. 'Me and Brett barely hear from him any more, not since he moved to Blackmore. It's like he's left his old family behind to concentrate on his new. Do you think Jolene might try to do the same to me? Only, I've a feeling she's got a new bloke. She must have.'

'What makes you think that?'

Beau explained his reasons. 'I don't trust her any more. And believe me, I will find out the truth,' he added.

Lori leaned forward. She might not have been the perfect mother when her boys were young, therefore she'd move heaven and earth to protect them now. 'Carl knows a brilliant woman. A private detective. She and her team use mainly motorbikes to catch their suspects out. Don't you worry, son. We'll find out the truth. I'll give Carl a call now and we'll pay the cost. It's the least we can do.'

'Thanks, Mum. You're a star.'

By the time they reached their destination, Jonathan's nerves were shot to pieces. He hated heights at the best of times. Yet here he was, halfway up a cliff with two lunatics. 'I beg you not to harm me. I never pressed charges against you last time. You know I can be trusted.'

'Trusted! You,' sneered Baz. 'Don't make me laugh.'

'My mum's seriously ill. I'm all she's got. She needs me,' gabbled Jonathan.

Ginger punched him hard in the back of the head. 'Shut up and walk.'

'Can we just talk here? I can't go near the edge. Heights are my biggest phobia.'

'Oh no!' smirked Baz. 'That's unfortunate, ain't it, Ginge?'

'Very,' chuckled Ginger. 'Right, sit yer arse down and I don't want no old flannel. I want the truth, the whole truth and nothing but the fucking truth. Who were you working for before us?'

'Kenny Bond and Tony Abbott.'

'Well, well, well,' said a shocked Ginger. His hunch had been wrong, although Abbott being involved was no big surprise. 'Bond wasn't a name I was expecting to hear,' he mused. Kenny was spoken about in legendary terms among the criminal fraternity. Killing a copper had seen to that. He wasn't spoken about as some drug-lord though.

'Tony Abbott obviously got Bond at it,' stated Baz. He turned to Jonathan. 'I take it you mean Teddy Abbott's boy?'

'Yeah.'

'What were they? Equal partners?' asked Baz.

'As far as I know. Kenny kept well away. Tony was the more hands on.'

'I wanna know everything,' spat Ginger. 'Where the factory was. Who else worked there. I wanna know every single fucking detail. Then, if I believe ya, I might even give you a lift back to the bookies.'

Feeling totally deflated, Brett opened another beer and flopped on the sofa. He was already missing Aidan, but determined to stick to his guns. What was the point of being in a relationship when they couldn't go out and do things together?

Picking up his phone, Brett called his old friend Alex and was dismayed to find the number discontinued. What the hell was he meant to do now? Alex was the only other gay mate he had, and if he couldn't get hold of him, he had nobody to go to a gay bar with. His love life was over by the looks of it. Kaput.

'Shit,' mumbled Brett as he saw Gramps' motor pull up outside. He really wasn't in the mood for company, just wanted to wallow in self-pity. 'I'll warn you, I'm not in a good mood. Me and Aisling have split up,' he shouted, as the front door opened. His dad would have a fit if he knew Gramps had his own key and came and went as he pleased.

Kenny stormed into the front room like a bull in a china shop. 'You ain't in a good mood! Well, join the club. Seething, I am. Fucking livid.'

'Why? What's happened?'

Kenny paced up and down as he gave a blow-by-blow account of his disastrous lunch-date. 'I want you to ring your dad and find out if your nan's working up the nursery tomorrow. Be a bit discreet like. I mean it, as soon as she goes to work, them locks are being changed and I'm moving back in. I ain't fucking having it no more, Brett. Yeah, I ballsed up once or twice, but what man hasn't? I've been bloody good to your nan. I still give her a lump of money every month and I'm still paying Sherry's mortgage. Sherry don't even talk to me! I gotta be some right mug, me. She wants a divorce, your nan. Well, let her support her fucking self and Sherry. The bank of Kenny is closed.'

'Be quiet then and I'll ring Dad.'

'Go upstairs and ring him. I'm gonna ring Ricky. I want the reg number of Nan's trainer's motor. I'll be finding out where he lives and paying him a little visit, an' all. Nobody puts their mucky paws on my old woman. I won't suffer it.'

'So, that's about it. Hand on heart, I've told you everything I know,' said Jonathan.

'See, there's still something that don't add up to me,' mused Ginger.

'Same 'ere. Who was the rat?' asked Baz.

'What do ya mean?'

Baz crouched down. 'You, Mr Scientist. You're the rat.'

'Nah, nah, nah. This is the first time I've ever ratted on anyone in my life, I can assure you of that.'

When Jonathan tried to scramble up, Ginger pushed him back to the ground. 'You were the only other person who knew where that factory was. Yet the day it got raided you were rather conveniently at a funeral.'

'I was. My uncle's. It was my mum's brother's funeral. You can check my story out, if you like. I haven't got anything to hide.'

'But you did hide, didn't ya?' snarled Baz. 'You went on yer toes, abroad.'

'I didn't. I swear. I only got out the country so I didn't have to testify against you. I was always coming back once the dust settled,' lied Jonathan. He felt ill, flustered, was sweating like a pig.

'You know what I reckon, Baz,' said Ginger. 'I think someone tipped the Old Bill off. I mean, that factory hadn't been up and running for five minutes when it got turned over. Everyone inside it was nicked, which leaves only three people that knew of its existence. Me, you, and our little rat friend, Mr Scientist.'

Jonathan's face drained of colour. 'Oh, no. God no! Lads, I swear. On my dear old mum's life, I never grassed yous up to anyone. I wouldn't do that. I'm respected in my field, trusted. You can ask anyone.'

'You know what I reckon an' all, Ginge. I reckon when the rat didn't take that bit of money we offered him, he went cap in hand snivelling to Kenny and Tony, asking them for the money in exchange for keeping his trap shut.'

'I never. I wouldn't do that,' cried Jonathan.

'We'll find out the truth. We'll ask Bond ourselves. Right, stand up, rat,' ordered Ginger.

Jonathan's legs trembled. 'Nah. Come on, lads. Don't do anything silly. You can't. You won't get away with it,' he shrieked. 'Just take me back to the bookies. Please. I've told you everything I know.'

Taking no notice of his desperate pleas, the Daley brothers dragged Jonathan towards the edge of the cliff.

'God, please no. I'll give you money. I've got plenty. I sold my mum's house recently. Please don't do this. My mum's not well. She needs me. Please,' begged Jonathan.

'Looks like Mummy rat's gonna have to make do without her rat of a son,' chuckled Baz.

Ginger glanced around. The coast was clear. 'Backwards on the count of three. Ready, one . . .'

'Noooo!' shrieked Jonathan.

'Two.'

'Help. Help!'

'Three.'

When Jonathan flew backwards through the air, his scream was phenomenal. A shriek of pure death.

CHAPTER TWENTY-THREE

Sharon wasn't working the following day, so Kenny decided to busy himself and tie up some loose ends. The lease at his flat was due to run out soon, so he gave notice to the landlord. He rang Karen, told her he wanted to spend the day with Jake. Then he rang Aunt Nelly. It was her birthday next week, so he told her to book a table for ten at her favourite restaurant. Since he and Shal had separated, Kenny had spent less quality time with his aunt and mum. That would definitely change once he moved back into his own gaff. He missed the barbecues and his lovely garden. Now summer was approaching, he would organize get-togethers again, whether Sharon was around or not.

'Morning, Gramps. You going up the garden centre?' yawned Brett. He felt shattered and starving. He hadn't eaten all day yesterday.

'Nah. Let your brother pull his weight for once. I'm off to pick Jake up, then I'm gonna take Ricky out to choose a car. I shall stay here until I get back into next-door-but-one. Your dad ain't gonna know, is he?'

'Dad hasn't been round here for months. I dunno what I'm gonna do today, but I need some grub inside me. A full English for starters.'

'Come pick Jake up with me and then help Ricky choose a motor. It's a big moment for him. We can stop off first, get some breakfast. I know you're upset about Aisling, but she weren't exactly a family-orientated girl, was she? We only met her the once, at Sonny's wedding.'

'I know. She didn't want to go out much either, if I'm honest. Staying in got boring in the end.'

Kenny grabbed his grandson around the back of the head. 'Plenty more fish in the sea, lad. Come on. Jake's a good kid. I really want you and Beau to spend more time with him.'

Brett shrugged. He had nothing better to do. 'OK. I'll jump in the shower. Give me ten minutes.'

Up at the Stapleford Abbotts nursery, Sharon was sipping a coffee and reciting what had been said between herself and Kenny the previous day. 'He'll go on the turn now. Good and proper. Part of me wanted to be straight with him and mention Ray. But it's not the right time, Tina. Nobody knows Kenny like I do, and I can sense when he's ready to blow up.'

Shoving the rest of the Kit-Kat in her mouth, Tina shook her head slowly. 'What you gonna do if he moves back in? I'll come and stay with you, if you want? You can't be alone with him.'

'Thanks, mate. But I'm not giving him the satisfaction of having to need backup. I put up with that bastard for years, visiting him in prison, listening to his bollocks, washing his shitty pants etcetera. That house is mine. I've earned it.'

'Good for you, girlie. Now tell me more about Ray. How was your day out?'

'You want the truth; it was the best day out I've had in years. Ray's comical, genuine, cheeky, yet a gentleman at the same time, if that makes sense?'

'Ahh. I'm so pleased for you. You deserve to be happy, Shal.'

'Thanks. I'm shocked at myself, if I'm honest. I don't want to rush things, but I do feel ready to move on with my life now. I never thought I'd want another man after Kenny, but Ray has such a nice way about him. I even fancy him. Mad, ain't it? I mean, I certainly weren't that into him first time round.'

'You didn't really give it a chance the first time. You only went on the one date. I always knew Ray was the one for you. Remember me telling you that when he used to come up the nursery just to see ya. It's fate. Was obviously meant to be all along.'

'Maybe. Who knows? But believe me, Kenny won't like me moving on. He'd never want me to be happy with another man. Not while he's got breath in his body.'

Ricky was like a dog with two tails. Not only was he about to become a man of independence, he and Candy had finally made up. She'd done all the running in the end. After she'd ignored his calls, Ricky had taken Kenny's advice and stopped phoning her. Yesterday she'd called him and told him she missed him. 'Oh, hello, Brett. I didn't know you were coming with us.'

336

'It's a big day for you. I didn't wanna miss it,' lied Brett. He was actually wishing he'd stayed at home now. He'd enjoyed his breakfast, but wasn't in the mood for company. All he could think about was Aidan.

'Oh, hello, Jake. Didn't expect to see you either. We need to pick up Candy, Kenny. She wants to come with us too.'

Kenny slammed his foot on the brake. He was taking Ricky to a couple of pals' car lots. That's all he needed, Nutty Candy flashing her lils and fanny at his friends and his four-year-old son. 'Candy ain't coming. Women are a nuisance when it comes to choosing a car. They can never make up their minds.'

'But I want her to come and I told her she could. You've invited everyone else.'

Kenny gave Ricky a warning look. 'I invited family. Family who've always had your back. Not some tart who's been ignoring you for the past week. Right, I can either drop you at Candy's and you spend the day with her. Or you come get a car with us? Make your mind up.'

Ricky lowered his head. He and Kenny rarely ever had a cross word and he knew Kenny was annoyed with him. 'Come with yous to get the car. Please.'

Seeing her father's Shogun leave, Jolene picked up Romany and dashed over to her mother's. She was running late, for what was probably her most important date with Jimmy Dean yet. It had been Jimmy's idea they have lunch at a nice hotel and he book a room so they could chill and spend some quality time together. 'Please don't think I'm putting it on you, Jolene. I wouldn't do that. I knows you're a decent woman with morals. But we can't even have a proper kiss and cuddle in my truck. All I want to do is snuggle up and watch a film with you and have a proper talk, in private,' was how Jimmy had sold the idea to her, and Jolene had thought of little else since. The thought of spending all afternoon in a hotel room with Jimmy filled her with an excitement she'd thought she would never feel again. 'What took 'em so long to leave, Mum? I'm running late now.' After her father spotted Jimmy dropping her off recently, Jolene had thought it best she meet Jimmy in the car park of Palms Hotel in future. It was only a short drive from her home and she had to get used to driving her car at some point.

'Your dad was faffing about, looking for something. Then Levi shit himself, so I had to change him.' Bobby was driving up to Maldon to look at a horse he fancied buying and, as he often did, he'd taken his grandsons with him. It was his idea of an education for them. He could teach them far more about how to survive in life and be successful than they would at any silly school, was Bobby's view. 'You look beautiful, darling. Stunning, like one of them film stars.'

Since becoming a mum, Jolene had toned down the way she dressed. She no longer wore skimpy, revealing outfits. She liked to look classier, hence the long halter-neck red dress she had on. 'Thanks. Jimmy's taking me somewhere posh for lunch, so I thought I'd make the effort.' Jolene hadn't told her mother about the hotel room. That was private and nobody else's business apart from herself and Jimmy's. 'Right, I'll be off then, Mum.'

'Have a lovely time.'

Having forgotten his phone, Bobby had shot back for it and was shocked to catch his daughter clambering into her car, done up to the nines. 'Where you going?'

Jolene started the engine and wound down the window. 'Dad, I'll have to talk to you later. I'm late, Rosie will be waiting.'

'You must think I was born yesterday. You ain't got all glammed up like that to meet Rosie. You're meeting your fancy man, Jimmy.'

'I'm not. I swear. We're going somewhere posh for Rosie's birthday.'

Bobby pointed a finger. 'Don't fucking lie. I won't have me own flesh and blood lying to me. I don't mind you moving on, girl, even though I thinks you're making a big mistake. But you can't go out hawking your mutton and not expect Beau to find out. Because he will. One way or another. Then I shall look like a dinlo, 'cause I swore blind to Kenny that the man who you got spotted out with is a family friend. You need to tell Beau the truth, so I can look Kenny in the eye and apologize to him man to man for your loose behaviour.'

'There's nothing to apologize for. It's my life and I'll lead it exactly how I want. As for Beau, you don't know him like I do. He's jealous, nasty, with an evil streak. He'll never accept me with another man. He's horrible.' Jolene then drove off at such speed, she nearly ran poor Mary-Ann and baby Lily down in the process.

Unaware that his wife was out hawking her mutton, Beau was helping unload a lorry full of garden furniture when his mum rang him.

'Good news,' Lori told her son. 'The private detective got back to Carl. She's currently got two jobs on but has agreed to helping you. You'll need to meet up with her though. She'll need details of Jolene's movements and a recent photo of her, and stuff. I'll send you her number and you can call her yourself. She's around this afternoon, she said.'

Beau ended the call with a nervousness in the pit of his stomach. He wanted to know if Jolene was up to no good, but if she was, that would spell the end of them forever. No way could he forgive her if another bloke had shoved his cory up there. It wasn't in his nature. Chances were, he'd end up killing her instead.

'There's no nice sports cars here,' stated Ricky.

'You'd never get insured on one of them, lad,' replied Terry Machin. Kenny had rung him up earlier to clue him up on what he should say.

'Why? 'Cause I'm Down's syndrome?'

'No. Course not. No insurance company will insure any new driver on a sports car. It's more than their job's worth,' Terry explained. 'What about this one? It's only done fifteen K on the clock. One owner, full service history. You can take it for a test drive, if you like? Runs like a dream.'

Kenny winked at Terry. 'Nah. That's a Skoda. Only muppets drive them.' Kenny put an arm around Ricky's shoulders. 'That's much cooler, that Fiesta Brett and Jake are looking at.'

'That only came in two days ago. Already had three young fellas trying to buy it, but they couldn't afford it,' lied Terry. 'You want to take it for a test drive, Ricky? Not only cool, but a very sought after car.'

'Yes, please,' grinned Ricky. Candy had given him strict instructions to return home with a cool car, so please her he would.

The lunch was short and sweet. Neither Jimmy nor Jolene were hungry for food. They were ravenous for one another.

'D'ya want a dessert?' Jimmy couldn't take his eyes off Jolene. Her long wavy dark hair glistened in the peeping sunlight, and as for that calf-length red dress, as disloyal as he felt to his dead wife, Alicia, it was sending shivers down his spine.

'No. I'm fine, thanks. Shall we go up to the room and relax?'

Jimmy stood up and held out a hand. His mum was looking after Demi today and she wanted him to move on, be happy again. As would Alicia, if he were honest. No, the timing wasn't great. Lots of people would say it were too soon after his wife's death and he was wrong to break up Jolene's marriage. But it was as though he and Jolene had known one another all their lives, such was their connection.

Within seconds of entering the room, Jimmy and Jolene were ripping one another's clothes off.

Happy as a sandboy, Ricky turned into Dark Lane. 'How did I do, Brett?' He loved his new car to bits, had insisted on driving it home himself.

'Yeah, you did good,' lied Brett. He'd seen his life flash before his eyes a couple of times, none more so than when Ricky had shot out in front of a van at a round-about.

'You made it then?' grinned Kenny. He'd driven on in front, with Jake.

'Just about,' chuckled Brett. He slapped Ricky on the back. 'Nah. Not really. The boy did good.'

'Man,' corrected Ricky. 'Can I drive up to Sharon's now? Can't wait to show her me wheels.'

'Course you can,' replied Kenny. 'So proud of you, Ricky, and so would your dad be. Bet he's looking down beaming with pride, and your mum.'

Tears in his eyes, Ricky grabbed hold of Kenny and hugged him tightly. 'I still love and miss my real mum and dad. But you're my dad now, Kenny.'

Kenny was still feeling a bit choked up when Ricky returned five minutes later. 'That was quick. Weren't Shal in?'

'Yeah. She really liked the car, but she's busy training with Scott. She was out of breath and all hot and sweaty, so I said I'd pop back later.'

'Training my arse,' spat Kenny. 'Did you get his reg number?'

Ricky put a hand over his mouth. 'Oh, shit! I forgot.'

'Don't worry. Brett, you got a minute?' Kenny gestured his grandson to follow him outside. 'You all right to look after Jake for a bit? I'm gonna wait at the bottom of the lane and have it out with that Scott. Who does he think he is, eh? I'm still legally married to your nan. What does he take me for?'

'I'll look after Jake, but don't do anything stupid, Gramps. You don't wanna go back to prison, do ya?'

342

'Nah, I won't. I'll put the frighteners on the cheeky bastard though.'

'OK. See you in a bit.'

Kenny didn't have to wait long. About twenty minutes after he'd plotted up, he saw a grey Porsche heading his way. Kenny blocked the road with his Range Rover and jumped out.

Carjacking was a relatively new thing and that was Scott's first thought. His Porsche was new and was definitely the type of motor that thieves tended to steal. He lowered his window slightly. 'What's up, mate?'

'I ain't your mate. I'm Shal's husband, Kenny. I think me and you need a little chat.'

Relieved his car wasn't about to be nicked, Scott opened the window fully. 'Hello, Kenny. What can I do for you?'

Kenny studied what he thought was his rival. A good-looking bloke with short greying hair, Kenny had already made his mind up about Scott as soon as he'd clocked the number plate. In his opinion, only attention-seeking bellends swanned around with their first name on the front and back of their motors. 'A little birdy tells me you're knocking my old woman off and that makes me not happy, Scott. Not happy at all.'

'Don't be daft!' Scott was alarmed. 'Sharon's just a client. I have plenty of female clients. I'm a happily married man with three young children.'

'Don't fucking lie to me.' Kenny's jaw began twitching. 'You were seen snogging Shal outside my house on Sunday evening.'

Scott was worried now. He was a lover, not a fighter and Kenny was one scary man. 'I can assure you I wasn't. I never work on Sundays. I had family over for dinner and was at home all day with my wife and children.'

Sneering, Kenny grabbed Scott round the back of the neck and smashed his face against the steering wheel. 'You stay away from my wife in future. You don't tell her we've spoken. You just say you've broken your fucking leg, arm or whatever, therefore you can't train her. You understand me?'

Aware that Kenny was still holding the back of his neck, Scott tried to nod. His nose was throbbing. 'Yeah. Whatever you say.'

Unable to stop himself, Kenny thumped Scott's pretty boy face against the steering wheel again. 'And don't even think about involving the Old Bill, 'cause I'm telling you now, you do that or tell Shal, I promise, I will break so many bones in your body, you'll never work as a fucking fitness trainer again. Comprende?'

Scott's nose was splattered, the front of his T-shirt covered in blood. 'Got it,' he mumbled. He was so relieved as he heard a car approach, then toot. Kenny was blocking the lane and the car couldn't get past.

'Hide your mooey, till they pass,' Kenny ordered, before strolling back to his own vehicle. He could see the vehicle was a minicab.

Kenny let Scott go and drove back up the lane grinning. He was confident Sharon wouldn't be seeing Scott again and, in all honesty, he wasn't Shal's type anyway. His Shal liked a proper geezer such as himself. Rough and ready, scarred and hard. Not some pretty boy fitness trainer.

*

'You're back quick,' said Brett. He was out in the garden kicking a football about with Jake. 'Everything all right?'

'Yeah. Sorted. You know that Porsche you saw Sunday night, on my driveway. It was grey, weren't it?'

'Erm, no. Don't think so. It was black. I'm sure it was black.'

'But it could've been grey, couldn't it?'

'Not unless it was the darkest grey ever. It looked jet black to me.'

Kenny crouched and held his head in his hands. 'Shit,' he mumbled to himself.

'Whatta matter, Daddy?' enquired Jake.

Kenny quickly stood up. 'Nothing, son.' He felt a right mug, had probably just pulverized the hooter of the wrong geezer.

The doorbell rang, Kenny answered it and wasn't exactly pleased to see that pest Candy. She was all he needed.

Over-excited, Candy leapt up and down, clapping her hands. 'Where's the car? Where's Ricky?' she squealed.

Kenny felt physically sick as Candy's massive jugs bounced up and down in a tight red vest top. Had her parents never told her she needed to wear a bra? Any normal parents would buy her bras and force her to wear them. 'Ricky's popped out in the car. He'll be back in a bit. Come in and wait. But, erm, button your jacket up 'cause it's cold in ours today.'

Hearing an engine, Candy swung around. 'Noooo! Never! Surely not?'

Ricky put on the handbrake, got out the car and literally ran towards his girlfriend, such was his joy. 'Well? Do you like it?' he beamed.

'No. That isn't a sports car. It's horrible.'

Seeing Ricky's crestfallen expression, Kenny was livid. He laughed falsely, grabbing Ricky's arm. 'Candy's only messing with ya. I told her to wind you up. Go upstairs, Rick. I'll be up in a minute. I need to ask you something in private.'

The moment Ricky was out of earshot, Kenny glared at his dollop of a girlfriend. 'See you, I thought you were good for Ricky at first, but now I'm beginning to wonder. How dare you spoil his joy by slagging off his car. Who do you think you are, eh? You don't work. He does, and I know he pays for everything whenever he takes you out. Who are you to talk down to him?'

Not used to being told off, Candy was a bit taken aback. 'Sorry. I was only disappointed, 'cause he said we were getting a sports car.'

'There is no *we*. That's *his* car. And if it ain't good enough for you, love, then I suggest you go find yourself another geezer with a car that suits you more. Only, you messed Ricky about something chronic last week and I will not see him mucked around. Worse comes to worst, I'll be paying your granddad a visit down the gym, telling him how you've been behaving, then I'll make sure you don't see Ricky no more. You understand?'

Tears welled up in Candy's eyes. 'Don't tell Granddad. I'm sorry. I do love Ricky.'

'Good. Well, start appreciating him a bit more then. Go on, go indoors. Brett's in the garden.'

Kenny ran up the stairs.

'Candy did really like my car, didn't she, Kenny?'

'Course she did. What's not to like?' Kenny sat on the

bed next to Ricky. 'I need to ask you something important, Big Man, and I need you to tell me the truth.'

'OK.'

'Do you know who Sharon's new boyfriend is? You live there, Ricky, you must know something about him. Please tell me. I won't tell Shal, I promise.'

Ricky felt guilty. Kenny was so good to him. 'All I know is he picked her up in Del Boy's yellow van on Sunday and his name is Ray.'

It was at that moment the penny dropped for Kenny. He thought he'd recognized the bloke in the yellow van. It was *him*. The geezer who'd sniffed around Sharon last time they'd split up. Ray fucking Weller.

Not used to being home alone, when Jolene's car pulled up outside, Evie ran out to greet her. Bobby had gone to the pub with Sonny and Bobby-Joe had gone with them. Mary-Ann had taken Lily to visit her mum and the nippers were all with Beau. 'How did it go? Nobody's home, so we can talk.'

'Good. Come in mine then, Mum.' Jolene's day had been absolute perfection. She and Jimmy had made love, then laid lovingly in one another's arms talking about their future. They'd then made love again before leaving the hotel room. Today was the start of something special, both of them knew that.

'So? Tell me everything.' Evie couldn't stop grinning. Jolene looked so happy, radiant in fact.

'Oh, Mum, we had a fantastic day. We really like one another and have already decided we want to be together. I'm sure Tammy has sent Jimmy to me, and he reckons Alicia has sent me to him.'

347

'Ahh, that's lovely, darling. I'm so happy for you. What did Jimmy say about you being together?'

'Well, we both want the same thing, to live together with our children. Obviously, we can't get married. Not yet. We spoke about marriage in the future though. We said how cute Romany and Demi would look as brides-maids, and Rocky and Levi as pageboys. I know Jimmy is *the one*, Mum. I can feel it in my bones.'

'When you know, you know, love. I knew the moment I met your dad that I wanted to marry him. Never regretted it, even though he's driven me doolally over the years,' chuckled Evie.

'I'd move in with Jimmy tomorrow, if I could. Sod Dad and his old-fashioned views. I know Johnny and Billy would be happy for me, and you know how easy-going Sonny is. Romany loves Jimmy and I know the boys would love him in time too. It's just Beau that's the problem. I'd be terrified of his reaction if I told him me and the kids are moving in with another man. He'd burn me alive, I know he would.'

Thoughts of Psychic Lena's last words raced through Evie's mind. She then felt the iciest of chills run down her spine. She clasped Jolene's hands. 'Why don't you run away with Jimmy and the chavvies. Far away. Go to the Scottish Highlands or a remote part of Ireland. Somewhere Beau won't find you.'

Jolene looked at her mother in astonishment. 'Don't be silly! Jimmy's got his business and I could never move far away from you.'

'But you have to, if you want to be happy. We can still talk on the phone every day. Talk to Jimmy, see what he says. Promise me you'll think about it, love.'

Realizing her mother was dead serious, Jolene shrugged. 'OK. But not yet, Mum. We are serious and even though we touched on our future today, we didn't mean we're gonna set up home together tomorrow. Jimmy's in a difficult position too, as he's still close to Alicia's family and they adore Demi. It's an awkward situation all round.'

Evie chewed her already short fingernails. Jolene wasn't a believer in the wonders of the crystal ball. She, Tammy and Sonny used to laugh at her whenever she mentioned Psychic Lena.

'Whassamatter, Mum?'

Evie forced a smile. 'Nothing, sweetheart. I just want you to be happy, that's all.'

Mad Ginger and Baz Daley were knackered. It had been a long old day, collecting debts, giving out a few clumps, dishing out plenty of threats, burning the Ford Mondeo, among other things.

But it had also been a reasonably fruitful day. They were over eleven grand better off, with much more money to be collected over the next week or so. They'd chored a clean-looking white Ford Transit van and already changed the number plates to one that had been written off, but never registered. Having a pal who owned a salvage yard was well handy.

'So, what's first on the agenda tomorrow then, bruv?' asked Baz.

Mad Ginger rubbed the stubble on his chin. 'We'll try Bond's flat first. If he ain't there, you can poke your head in his garden centre. Doubt he knows what you looked like before and he deffo won't recognize you with that longer hair. We'll catch up with him somewhere tomorrow, don't you worry about that. Worst ways, we'll pay his family a visit down Dark Lane and leave a little message for him to contact us.'

Baz rubbed his hands together. 'Kenny Big Bollocks Bond. We're coming for you, sunshine.'

CHAPTER TWENTY-FOUR

The Daley brothers drove out to South Woodham Ferrers early the following morning. It was a nice day, sunny and warm. It felt so good to be out and about again, rather than being stuck in a small cell. Ginger nudged his brother. 'Wakey, wakey. We're 'ere now.'

Baz sat bolt upright and squinted. 'You sure this the right place?' He glanced at the flats. They were newly built, tidy-looking, but you wouldn't expect a man with substance like Kenny Bond to be living there.

'This is deffo the address Janey gave us. Come on, let's see if he's in.' Ginger had promised to visit Janey soon. She was very useful, therefore he would continue giving her a portion of helmet-pie for the foreseeable.

Ginger pressed the buzzer to number seven. There was no reply, so he pressed the other buzzers. Someone let them in. They darted up the flight of stairs and pummelled on what was supposedly Kenny's front door.

Baz crouched and was peering through the letterbox when a woman in the opposite flat said, 'Can you refrain from making such a racket, please? I've only just got my young child to sleep. The man's not there. In fact, I don't even think he lives there any more. I saw him moving his stuff out the other day. I don't even know his name; he was never very sociable. I won't be sorry if he's moved out.'

Baz and Ginger looked at one another. They had no idea how to track down Tony Abbott. He'd gone on his toes over to Spain somewhere. Surely Kenny hadn't got wind they were coming for him? How could he?

'Come on. Let's try the garden centre,' said Ginger. 'Cheers,' he said to the woman.

'Don't reckon he's done a runner, do ya?' said Baz.

'It crossed my mind, but he can't have done. Only two people other than us know we're looking for him. One of them's brown bread and the other's our helpful screw. Just a coincidence, it's gotta be.'

'She's gone,' Ricky informed Kenny via his phone. He felt guilty for betraying Sharon, but if he didn't, he'd be betraying Kenny. He hated being piggy in the middle, wished more than anything they'd just get back together, as he loved them both to bits.

Having dropped Jake back home early this morning, Kenny shot down to the house he should've never left in the first place. He was livid about Ray Weller, had hardly slept a wink last night. Were they at it? Did Shal have feelings for him? He had so many questions, but no answers. 'Cheers, Big Man, and don't worry, I won't dob you in it. If Shal asks, you locked up as normal, then went out, OK?'

'OK. I'm gonna take Candy to Southend for the day.'

'That's a bit of a long journey, Ricky. Why don't you get a bit more practice locally before you start driving that far.'

'But I wanna go there. So does Candy. Please don't stop me.'

'I can't stop you. You're your own man. Please be careful though and ring me when you get there. You leaving now?'

'No. Candy's got to go shopping with her mum first. I'm not staying here in case Shal comes back though. I'll watch TV in Brett and Beau's until Candy's ready.'

'OK. And don't get involved in any more altercations. If Candy starts performing, fucking leave her there.'

Kenny was putting his belongings inside the house when his pal Johnny Long turned up to change the locks. Kenny showed him the patio doors and ordered him to change front and back. ''Ere, you duck and dive in a bit of property. You ever had any dealings with a Ray Weller?'

'I haven't. But a pal of mine has and wished he hadn't. Ray caused him a lot of grief in the end.'

'What happened then?'

'Oh, I don't know the full story,' lied Johnny. 'But, put it this way. Ray's not a bloke you ever want to be in debt to, or upset in any way.'

'Really!' No bastard scared Kenny, but he was bit taken aback, nevertheless. He'd heard Ray's name mentioned over the years, pre-Sharon meeting him, but only ever to do with property. He'd never had him down as a bloke to be wary of, and he bet Shal didn't either. Good job he'd done a bit of digging. Sharon wouldn't be wanting to jump out the frying pan into the fire, that was for sure.

Ginger tapped his fingernails impatiently against the steering wheel. Baz was taking his time. 'What the hell's he doing?' Ginger said to himself as Baz walked out of the garden centre with two big plants, one either side of him.

'Kenny ain't there today, but he does work there some days. They've got a simpleton working there, so I got chatting to him.'

'What are the plants for?'

'I got one for your bird, for getting us the info, and one for Mum.'

'Don't you think that cunt Bond owes us enough money, without you putting more in his pocket? As for Janey, the only plant she'll be getting is my cactus up her. And I wish you'd stop calling her my bird, 'cause she ain't.'

'I could hardly walk out empty-handed, Ginge.'

'Put the poxy plants in the back. Let's take a drive down to Dark Lane.'

'All right, Brett? Beau around?'

'Nah. He had to shoot out, but he shouldn't be too long. What you got for us today then?' enquired Brett. Badger and Mad Dog, as they eloquently called themselves, were two Canvey Island lads who shoplifted for a living. In fairness, they were pretty good thieves. Whatever he or Beau told them they wanted, they usually came back with.

'We got the Gucci sunglasses Beau wanted. We also got a couple of Ralph Lauren shirts in your size, and Nike trainers,' explained Badger.

'We also got some polo shirts and Calvin Klein boxers. We never got them with you in mind, but you can have first dibs,' added Mad Dog.

'OK. Let's have a look then.'

'You got any other orders for us?' asked Badger. They liked dealing with the Bond twins. They paid straight up without any quibbling, usually half of whatever the items were worth. Unless they were electrical, then they'd only pay a third.

A thought suddenly sprang into Brett's mind. Gramps had arranged for them to go out for a meal next weekend for Aunt Nelly's birthday and Brett fancied hitting a club afterwards. 'I tell you what I do need. It ain't for me, like, it's for a pal. Can you get us some cocaine? No crap though. Gotta be decent stuff.'

'I know a good dealer. You won't be getting that half price, mind,' grinned Mad Dog.

'As long as it's decent, that's fine. Get us three grams. But don't say nothing to Beau, 'cause he's really anti-drug and he'll be pissed off with me for helping me mate out.'

'I'll get you an eighth, it'll work out cheaper. And don't worry, me and Badger can be trusted. We won't say jack-shit to anyone.'

'There's a black Range Rover,' pointed Baz. 'That's the son's house. Don't pull on the drive. Park 'ere and we'll both walk up to the door.' Dark Lane was well known in their circles.

The houses had been built by a face and originally sold off to mainly villains, Kenny Bond being one of them.

Ginger pressed the doorbell and it was answered by a Down's syndrome lad. They'd heard through the grapevine years ago, Kenny had sort of adopted the boy. 'Your dad in?'

'My dad's dead,' Ricky replied bluntly. Dark Lane attracted hardly any strangers and these two men looked like weirdos.

'Sorry, lad,' replied Ginger. 'We know you lost your dad. That was a tactless thing to say. We're looking for Kenny. He knows who we are. We got a bit of business to discuss with him, that's all.'

Ricky was wary. The man talking had a shaved head and a gold tooth with a sparkling stone in it. As for the other one, he had longer hair and a beard. Neither looked like any of Kenny's other friends. 'What are your names?'

'You're an' inquisitive little urchin, ain't ya?' smirked Ginger, putting his right foot in the doorway.

'He's only messing with you. We can wait in our motor, if Kenny's due back soon. Is he due back any time soon?'

Wishing the twins or one of them was there, Ricky nervously began chewing on his fingernails. He felt scared and couldn't slam the door to ring Kenny because the shaven-headed man's foot was in it. 'Kenny don't live here. He lives in a flat miles away.'

'Don't lie. We know Kenny's moved out of his flat. He told us.'

'When?'

At that moment, Ricky was relieved as Kenny ran up the driveway. June next door had been pruning her bush and had given him the heads up. 'Get away from him. Whaddya want?' he bellowed. His first thought had been it was something to do with the altercation Ricky had been involved in with Candy last weekend.

'Hello, Kenny,' grinned Ginger. 'How you doing?'

At first Kenny didn't recognize the Daley brothers. He'd never had any dealings with them, and the last image he had of them were their mugshots in the local paper.

'Where's your pal Tony Abbott these days?' enquired Baz. 'Only I think the four of us are overdue a little catch-up, don't you?'

It was only the mention of his one-time partner that made the penny drop. 'You go back inside, Ricky.'

'Are they your friends, Kenny?' Ricky still felt unnerved.

'I know 'em, yeah. Go on, in you go.' Knowing how nosy Ricky was, Kenny gestured his head for the Daley brothers to follow him off the driveway. 'How can I help you?'

'Financially, for a start,' replied Ginger. 'We know everything. We know about your factory, your partnership with Tony Abbott, The Scientist, and the Chinese you employed. Our men got massive long stretches for the cock-up you made with those pills and—'

'Hang on a minute,' interrupted Kenny. He was stunned they knew so much. Even his own family knew sod all about his involvement with those cursed pills. 'What the hell you going on about? Only, you've lost me, lads.' He had little option other than to bluff. It wasn't like Tony was around to help him out.

'Don't take us for mugs, Bond,' spat Baz. 'Your right-hand man, The Scientist, more than spilled his guts.

Our factory was only open for a matter of weeks, yet we got the blame for every fucking thing that went wrong. Someone dobbed us in, they must've done. And that someone was either you or Abbott. Therefore, we're owed compensation, lots of it. For the families of the men you put away, and ourselves. Half a million should see us all right.'

'You're having a laugh, ain't ya? Is this some kind of wind-up?'

Mad Ginger had a strong urge to grab Kenny by the throat and throttle him. That wasn't going to get them their dosh though. He needed to remain calm, for the time being at least. 'You know exactly what we're talking about. You've got a week to come up with some wonga. We want at least half of it by this time next week. We'll meet you at twelve noon next Tuesday, in the Halfway House car park along the A127. Come alone.'

Kenny's jaw twitched repeatedly. 'As I've already told ya, I ain't got a clue what you're going on about. I suggest you go back to whoever your Scientist pal may be, and get him to tell you the fucking truth before you turn up 'ere shouting the odds at me.'

'Too late for that. He had a very unfortunate accident,' blurted out Baz. 'And unless your memory returns sharpish, ya wanna be careful the same don't happen to you, Bond. Next Tuesday. Halfway House, at noon. You either turn up with our dosh. Or live to regret it. Come on, Ginge. Let's go.'

Beau settled up with the shoplifters. 'I'll pay the lot and Brett can square up with me later.' They'd taken a pair of trainers each, the T-shirts and boxer shorts. Plus Beau needed to pay for the sunglasses he'd pre-ordered. 'I can't think of anything else I need offhand. I'll give you a bell if I think of something. Me brain's a bit frazzled today,' explained Beau. He'd shot out earlier to meet the private detective his mum had hired.

Badger handed Mad Dog his half of the money. 'Right, we'll grab some grub and be off then.'

'How'd it go?' Brett asked Beau. He was intrigued by what the private detective might find out, and wondered whether it would be worthwhile him booking her after-wards to follow Aidan. Then again, what was the point? Aidan hadn't contacted him since he'd left his apartment, so obviously wasn't that bothered. Brett had secretly hoped his lover would come crawling back to him, but it was still early days.

'Yeah. It went OK. The woman turned up alone, on a motorbike. She asked me for some details about Jolene and a photo of her. Then she gave me a number to contact her on, which I should imagine is a burner phone, took my number, said she'll be in touch once she has any news. Then she sped off.'

'Weird job for a woman to do, ain't it? I didn't even know women rode motorbikes.'

'She was quite cool as it goes. I couldn't see her prop-erly 'cause she had a crash helmet on. But I could see she had long hair and was about Mum's age.'

'So, is she gonna follow Jolene straight away?'

'No. She's got another job on at present. Jolene's next on her list.'

'What you gonna do if you find out she has got another geezer?'

Beau took a deep breath. Even the thought of his wife mugging him off in such a way made his blood boil to a degree of no return. 'I dunno yet. But I ain't one to be made a fool out of, as you well know. I'll cross that bridge when I come to it.'

Kenny Bond felt good being back in his own home. But this altercation with the Daley brothers had spoiled his triumphant mood somewhat. He'd been so looking forward to Shal coming home and her key not fitting the front door, until those two morons had showed up.

Hearing a car pull onto the drive, Kenny ran over to the window. It wasn't Sharon. It was the minicab he'd ordered to pick him up a cheese and onion French stick and some beers. Shal had very little in the fridge and what was in there was all healthy bollocks. Probably trying to shed some timber so she looked good for Ray, he thought bitterly.

Kenny paid the cabbie, opened the box of Budweiser and poured one into a glass. He'd be fifty-six in a couple of months, was done with unwanted drama in his life. He'd tried to call Tony earlier, but the numbers he had for him were no longer in use. So, he'd called his father, Teddy, who'd promised to get a message to his son. 'They're imbeciles. A pair of rednecks. Who gets banged up in this day and age for racially abusing and assaulting a cabbie? Clowns, mate. Just tell 'em to fuck off. That's what I'd do,' was Teddy Abbott's advice.

Feeling the Bud swill down his gullet, Kenny weighed up the situation. Tony had once warned him the Daley brothers were dangerous, but that was before they'd got banged up for the muggiest of crimes. And he'd trust Teddy's opinion over Tony's; Teddy was old school, like himself. Besides, what proof did that pair of idiots have about anything? One man's word. And in fairness, The Scientist, had approached himself and Tony first. He'd also warned them that if the Daleys were to catch up with him in the long run, he would spill the beans. Which he obviously had. But they still had no proof whatsoever.

Kenny switched the TV on, chomped on his French stick while flicking through the Sky channels. Ricky had texted to inform him he'd arrived in Southend safely with Candy, thank God. Ricky passing his driving test was another worry for Kenny, but like any new driver, only practice would make perfect. He just had to let the lad get on with it and if he had a couple of scrapes in his motor, then so be it.

The news was boring as usual. Who cared if DVDs were replacing video tapes? Or about the poxy Millennium, which was still over eighteen months away. Even worse, Arsenal had a chance of winning the league and had got to the FA Cup Final.

Kenny was searching through the film channels when he heard the sound of Sharon's car. He turned the TV off and crept into the hallway. He heard her trying to put the key in the lock and curse as the door didn't open.

He flung open the door. 'Surprise, treacle!'

Shocked, Sharon dropped her bag of shopping, 'What the hell! Talk about frighten the bloody life out of me.' Sharon picked her shopping up and barged past Kenny. 'Who let you in here? Ricky?'

Kenny followed Sharon out into the kitchen. 'I let meself in, with me new key, that fits the new locks I had fitted earlier. Don't worry. I got you a set cut an' all. You're welcome to stay 'ere – in the spare room, of course. I'm having me old bedroom back.'

'You bastard,' Sharon spat.

'You mug,' Kenny spat back. 'I know all about him, your lover Ray Weller, and he ain't the nice geezer he portrays himself to be. You're making a big mistake, Shal. Mark my words on that.'

'I haven't got a lover. Not everyone moves on as quickly as you. Get out. I don't want you here.'

Kenny opened another beer and chuckled falsely. 'This is *my* home. I bought it. You don't wanna be here, then go and stay with your wrong un boyfriend.'

'Fine. I will.'

When his wife stomped upstairs, Kenny headbutted the fridge in temper. He hadn't expected that response and he didn't like it. Not one little bit.

Maggie Saunders was furious. She'd never forgiven Kenny for the Abigail turnout and never would. All those years her beautiful daughter had stood by that arsehole. Visiting him in prison, having to move home regularly because of the shit she'd got from the supporters of that poor copper Kenny had killed. *And* she'd all but raised Sherry and Donny alone. 'Don't you dare cancel seeing Ray this evening. You go out with him for your meal as planned. Otherwise, Kenny will have won. He's only told you Ray's a wrong un because he's consumed with jealousy. They don't like it, men like him, when the boot's on the other foot, darling.'

'But, say I'm making another mistake, Mum? Let's be honest, I don't know Ray from Adam really and Kenny must have something on him to blurt that out. I wasn't going to give Kenny the satisfaction of asking what he meant. It's left me feeling confused though. I've not even got a home any more and I don't know what I packed. I just chucked a load of stuff in me case in temper. I don't even think I packed any underwear.'

'You can borrow a pair of my drawers.' Maggie got up, walked over to her daughter and put her arms around her. Maggie had found out only yesterday that the chemotherapy had done all it could. The doctor had told her bluntly she had months to live, not years. Her Charlie hadn't dealt with the news well, so she'd urged him to go to the pub today. They'd planned to tell Sharon the awful news together. But she couldn't now. Sharon was upset enough over that bastard changing the locks and moving back in. Her news would have to wait. 'I'm your mum and I'm telling you now that Ray is a good man and he adores you. I know I've only met him the once, but I saw the way he looked at you. The look of love if ever I saw it. Now, you get on the phone to him and ask him to pick you up for your meal.'

'I will on one condition. That you come with us, Mum. I don't care if you're not that hungry and I promise you we'll go local, you can even choose where we go. I just want you to meet Ray properly, without Dad being around. What Kenny said has unnerved me a bit and I need to be sure I'm not jumping out the frying pan into the fire.'

Knowing time was no longer on her side, Maggie forced a smile. 'I'll go get ready, sweetheart.'

*

The Daley brothers were not in the best of moods. They hadn't expected today to go great, but they had expected Kenny to acknowledge them with a bit of respect. Denying all knowledge of why they were visiting him had boiled their piss big time.

'I fancy a drink. Let's go to the pub.'

'Baz, no. Please don't fall off the wagon on me. Once we've got our money, you can sod off to Goa again for as long as you like. Just stay sober until we get it, please. Eh?'

Already sick of the shitty little flat they were now renting in Stanford-Le-Hope, Baz kicked a door before pacing up and down. 'If that cunt don't turn up next week, we need to kidnap one of his family. How old are his grandkids?'

'Sit down. You're making me nervous. I got a similar idea, but a better option.'

'What?'

Mad Ginger smirked. 'I didn't like that mongol one little bit. Cocky bastard, and Bond obviously thinks the world of him. If push comes to shove, he's the one we go for.'

CHAPTER TWENTY-FIVE

'Bloody hell, Shal. You didn't have to bring an entourage. I told you I've got you your own set of keys cut. Surely we're civilized enough to house-share at our age? Even if it is only as mates,' stated Kenny.

Donny glared at his father. 'She don't wanna be your mate, that's the problem. Come on, Mum. Let's get loading.'

'Yeah. Arsehole,' added Sherry, barging past her father. She and her brother were both disgusted at their dad having another kid by some slapper. The least he could have done was let their mum stay in the comfort of her own home. As if she would be stupid enough to live with him again.

'Shal, can we just talk for a minute, please? Alone.' It hurt Kenny that their two children wanted nothing to do with him. However, Sharon was his main priority at present. She'd been staying at her mum's since he'd changed the locks and he was desperate to build some bridges. He could not bear the thought of Shal moving on with Ray Weller, or any other man for that matter.

Sharon told Donny and Sherry what bits she wanted to take. She was only collecting some clothes, make-up, perfume, personal items for now. Anything else would have to wait. 'Be careful with your bad foot, Sherry.' She turned to Kenny. She had things she wanted to say to him also. Stopping at her mum's hadn't been ideal, but it had given her time to think things through. 'Where d'ya wanna talk?'

'Don't be believing any of his old flannel, Mum,' urged Sherry.

'See you,' Kenny pointed to his ungrateful daughter. 'First thing Monday, I'm contacting the mortgage company and cancelling what I pay towards yours. You and that old man of yours can stand on your own two feet from now on.'

Sharon followed Kenny out into the garden. 'She's only sticking up for me.'

'I don't care. I'm sick of it. Why don't you move back in, Shal? Just so we can talk and sort stuff out like adults. I don't wanna chuck you out your own home, but my lease is up on the flat and I need somewhere to live.'

'As do I. Which is why I spoke to my solicitor yesterday. I've started the divorce proceedings and she said half this house is mine and any court of law will say the same. I want you to sell it, as quickly as possible. If you do as I ask, Kenny, then I will leave your garden centre out of the financial equation. But if you don't, I'll want a chunk of that too.'

Kenny kicked the bird tree so hard it fell over. 'You can want what the fuck you like. I ain't selling nothing. So, put that in your nosy brief's pipe and tell her to smoke it.'

*

Beau wasn't having the best of days. He'd picked his kids up early for a trip to Colchester Zoo and only Romany seemed to be enjoying it. Rocky was bored, kept tormenting the animals, and Levi was whingeing because he had a stinking cold.

However, the main reason Beau was peeved was because of the conversation on the journey. He'd gently pumped the boys about Jolene as usual and had been bluntly informed by Rocky that 'Mum don't like us no more. She goes out on her own all the time and leaves us with Nan.'

'Dad, want an ice-cream,' shrieked Levi, pointing at some woman's cornet.

'Let's go this way then,' gestured Beau. That bitch must be seeing another geezer. She had to be. Probably too scared that if she took the kids with her, they'd drop her in it, he fumed.

It was just as he reached the front of the queue that Beau's phone rang. It was the private detective asking to meet him. She had news.

Aunt Nelly hated foreign food, said it did terrible things to her insides, so she'd chosen a steak house in Stratford for her birthday meal. The demographics of the East End had changed immensely in recent years. Gone were a lot of the old English eating haunts, replaced with Indian, Turkish and Jamaican restaurants. Fast food outlets had taken over as well. There seemed to be one on every corner. Especially chicken shops.

'The garden centre was rammed today, Gramps. We took over three grand more than last Saturday. I sold some of that new garden furniture an' all. Took two lots of deposits on it,' Brett said, trying to sound upbeat. Aidan was on his mind constantly and he'd yet to hear from him. Part of him wished he hadn't jumped the gun and ended things so abruptly. He missed him.

'Great stuff.' Kenny was still seething with Sharon. Over his dead body was he selling the house. He loved that gaff. He'd had it built from scratch and helped design the place himself. Worst ways, he'd have to get it valued and pay Shal half. It was probably worth around a million and even though he wasn't short of a few bob, he didn't have half a mill lying around. He'd hang it out as long as possible. No way was he being blackmailed by Sharon, or those two numpties who'd turned up at his door in the week. He'd heard nothing from the Daley brothers since, but guessed they'd try their luck again when he didn't show to meet them. 'You all right, Ricky?'

'Yes and no. I really wanted Candy to come tonight and I can't understand why she wasn't allowed.'

'I already told ya, it's family only.' Kenny could only imagine his mum and aunt's reaction if Candy had turned up with her lils and snatch on show.

Kenny pulled up outside Karen's and Jake excitedly ran out to greet him. He'd wanted to keep his son overnight, but Karen was taking him to Chessington World of Adventure early tomorrow. He was paying for it as per usual, mind.

'I starving, Dad. Will they have burgers?' enquired Jake.

'Yeah. Nice big thick ones. Ring Beau, Brett. See what

time he's gonna meet us.' Beau had decided last minute he was going to bring his motor too.

'No answer,' Brett lied. His brother didn't want Gramps to know he was having Jolene followed. That's where Beau had gone. To meet the private detective.

Beau was sat stationary in the car park of the Little Chef in Brentwood. Instinct told him whatever news he was about to be told was going to be bad. He'd had a horrible feeling in the pit of his stomach since he'd woken up this morning.

Beau's stomach somersaulted as the motorbike pulled up next to him. He couldn't remember if she'd told him her name or not, but he'd spoken to his mum and Carl earlier and Carl had informed him her name was Gloria. 'All right? Just hit me with it. I know it ain't gonna be great.'

Gloria handed Beau an envelope. 'Not good news, I'm afraid, but it rarely is in my job. These were taken yesterday. Jolene ate lunch with a companion, then they rented a room in Ye Olde Plough House in Bulphan. The last photo is of them leaving the hotel, at approximately ten past seven in the evening. Oh, and we managed to find out his name. It's Jimmy Dean.'

Beau felt anger surging through his veins. She looked so happy, the whore. Like she used to be with him. As for Jimmy Dean, he was dark, tall, but not as good-looking as himself. How could she do this to him? To their kids? 'Thanks for this. What do I owe you?'

Gloria waved a leather-cladded hand. 'It's fine. Carl's sorting it. You've got my number. Anything else you need, just give me a call. Good luck.'

Beau had never felt so wronged as he did right now. Enraged, he put his foot on the accelerator. She would pay for this, that slag. Big time.

Vera Bond tapped her fingers against the table and pursed her thin lips. She was yet to forgive her son for the despicable way he'd treated Sharon and couldn't believe he'd turned up with *the* bastard child in tow. Surely, he didn't expect her to be nice to it?

Jake looked at Vera's beehive with interest. He'd never seen anybody with so much hair on the top of their head. 'Are you really my nan?'

'No, I bleedin' well ain't.'

'Vee,' Nelly nudged her miserable sibling, then smiled at Jake. He was a cute little boy, reminded her of Donny when he was young. 'Yes, love. She is your nan and you already know me, your Aunt Nelly. I'm your nan's sister.'

'Is Nan lots older than you, Aunt Nelly?'

'Right, that's it,' hissed Vera. 'I'm off over there to say hello to Queenie Butler. What a good son her Vinny is to her,' she added, as a knock at Kenny. She'd barely seen Kenny since he'd split up with Sharon and when he did pop in, it was brief.

'Is that Vinny Butler?' Brett asked his grandfather. Vinny was a notorious name out in the East End.

'Yeah. Don't look over,' urged Kenny. He knew who Vinny was, everybody who mixed in his circles did. But he'd never had any personal dealings with him and neither did he wish to. Vinny was another lunatic by all accounts. 'He's part owner of this gaff, along with Nick, the geezer who runs it.' Kenny informed his grandson.

'He's coming over, I think.'

Kenny stood up as Vinny held out his right hand. 'Good to finally meet you, Kenny. Don't think we've ever crossed paths, but we have a mutual friend. Eddie Mitchell. I didn't realize it was your aunt's birthday until your mum just said. I've told the waiters to bring over a couple of bottles of bubbly. On the house, of course.'

Kenny shook the man's hand. 'Cheers, Vinny. Yeah, I know Eddie well. Top bloke. I'll let me aunt know what you're sending over. Very kind of you.'

Kenny and Vinny's conversation was cut short by the arrival of an irate Beau, who promptly prodded his granddad in the shoulder. 'See that cunt, Bobby, he's been lying to ya. Wrong uns that family, the fucking lot of 'em. I want my kids living with me.'

Sharon Bond was over at Ray's house, eating popcorn in his cinema room. It had been pre-arranged that she meet Ray's friends and their partners tonight for a birthday meal for one of them, but after the stressful week Sharon had endured, she hadn't been able to face it.

'You all right, girl?' Ray kissed Sharon on the forehead. He'd sat through *Titanic* with her and now they were watching *Donnie Brasco*.

Sharon moved her head off Ray's shoulder and smiled up at him. He was so understanding, so nice, the more she saw of him, the more she felt at ease. 'I can't understand how no woman has snapped you up before, Ray Weller.'

'Because I'm a fussy fucker probably. And from the moment I met one particular woman, I didn't have eyes for any other. Even though she got very drunk on me, stacked it and nearly spewed up in me Roller,' chuckled Ray.

Knowing Ray was referring to her, Sharon rolled up, before locking lips with him. She then began to feel urges she hadn't felt for donkey's years.

Unaware his wife was about to bed another man, Kenny was having a shit time anyway. Beau was drinking heavily and in a worrying mood, and his mother hadn't stopped moaning.

Having had a couple of lines in the toilet, Brett arrived back at the table full of beans. He grabbed Beau's arm. 'Let's go to a club somewhere eh, bro? I ain't had much to drink, so I'll drive your motor.'

'Yeah. Let's. I could do with a shag meself, now I know what that slag's been up to.'

Kenny cringed as he clocked the Butlers looking their way. He'd never known Beau to be so loud, or act so silly. 'Go on. Off you go, lads.' Kenny grabbed Brett's arm. 'You look after him and make sure you drive home an' all.'

As the twins said their goodbyes, nobody at the table realized what carnage they would cause. If they had, they'd have stopped them from leaving.

Sharon Bond rolled over and held Ray's handsome face in her hands. She'd never *come* with Kenny, not since he'd got out of prison. She'd faked it, as most women probably had to. But Ray was different gravy, and even though it had taken some time, she'd managed an orgasm for the first time in years.

Ray kissed Sharon on the tip of her nose. 'I know it's early days, Shal, but neither of us are getting no younger. Why don't you just move in with me? It's the answer to all the grief you're going through at present, and I know a really good brief who can get you what you're owed off Kenny. Not that I'm bothered about that side of things. You can walk away with nothing as far as I'm concerned. But I get you want what's rightfully yours.'

Sharon took a deep breath before flopping back onto the pillow. Her head was mashed, gone. Her mum had absolutely loved Ray when they'd gone out for a meal in the week and had urged her afterwards to take things further. 'I want you to be happy before I die, Sharon. Ray is the one for you, I know he is.'

'What you thinking?' asked Ray.

Sharon ran her fingers through his hair. Ricky was an adult now and as much as she'd miss him, she wouldn't miss bloody Candy. Kenny might be an arsehole, but he was more than capable of being Ricky's guardian again. 'You're right, I suppose. We've got nothing to lose, giving it a go, have we?'

Ray smiled. 'That's my girl.'

Beau and Brett were in the Ilford Palais, on completely different levels. Beau was pissed as a fart and Brett as high as a kite.

'You're handsome, you.' Brett cringed as an older blonde bird stroked his face. She looked repulsive; a real mutton-done-up-as-lamb type. 'Where's your handsome twin gone? Only my sister likes him and I like you,' she slurred.

Relieved as he spotted Beau return from the bog, Brett removed her sweaty hand from his face.

Having already been accosted by the sister, Beau staggered towards Brett and punched him on the shoulder. 'We're well in. Been invited back to theirs. Let's grab a couple of bottles of wine and get out of ere.'

'I don't wanna go back to theirs.'

'Why not? They're offering it on a plate. What's wrong with ya?'

'They're minging, that's what. Let's just go home, Beau. You're steaming and I've gotta drive your motor.'

'Nah. I need to empty me ball-bags before they burst. Come on, it'll be a laugh.'

Brett sighed. 'I ain't shagging either of them. You can have 'em both.'

Grinning stupidly, Beau staggered back over to the sisters.

Leanne and Chantelle Cooper couldn't believe their luck. The twins were gorgeous and obviously wealthy. Their Range Rover was the best motor they'd ever been in.

As the older sister sidled up next to him on the sofa, Brett gulped at his wine. He didn't even know what area they were in. Some council estate near Ilford. 'Leave it out, will ya?' he hissed, as she tried to kiss him. Her breath stank of stale cigarettes, as did the flat.

'Oh, come on. Don't be so boring. Your brother's enjoying himself.' Beau was in the bedroom with Chantelle.

'He's pissed. I ain't. Anyway, I got a girlfriend,' lied Brett, before topping up his glass. The quicker Beau shot his load and they got out of here, the better.

When the bird brazenly put her hand on his cock, Brett leapt up. 'Look, I ain't fucking interested, OK? Go in there with them two. Ask me brother to shag you an' all.'

'Fine. I will.'

'Turn that down, Beau. I can't think straight and I dunno where we are.'

'We're in Newbury Park and ya can't beat a bit of Kiss FM.' Beau turned the volume up even higher.

'Drink don't suit you. It turns you into an annoying arsehole.'

Beau turned the stereo down. 'You need to let your hair down more, you. I did. So funny when the other one came in and sucked me off. That's legendary,' Beau laughed. 'I bet you've never had a threesome, have ya?'

'Yeah. With Aisling.'

'Hmmm. The mysterious Aisling,' mocked Beau. 'I don't even reckon you and her were a couple. I reckon you bat for the other side, you.'

'Shut up, ya cunt,' spat Brett.

'Iron, iron, iron,' Beau repeatedly poked Brett in the arm.

'Give it a rest. I'm trying to drive.'

In a strangely irritating mood, Beau grabbed his brother in a playful headlock.

Brett took his eyes off the road for no more than a couple of seconds. 'Fuck! Nooooo!' he shrieked. He tried to swerve out the way, but it was too late. The Range Rover hit the small car with such force, it sent it somersaulting through the air.

Beau leapt out to check the damage. 'Shit! Look what you done. Me bumper's hanging off and me front light's smashed.'

Brett ran over to the small red car that was lying on its roof with smoke coming out the engine. He knelt down. 'Jesus Christ!' The motor was a Volkswagen Golf and the impact had all but flattened it. 'Give me hand, will ya? We need to try and get whoever's in this out.'

'Leave 'em. Let someone else deal with it. Come on. We gotta go,' urged Beau. They were in a quiet road, all fields, no houses or other cars in sight.

Fear and paranoia swept over Brett. No way would he pass a breathalyser. He had both drink and drugs in his system, would be looking at prison, especially if someone was seriously hurt, or worse still, died.

'Come on, ya dinlo,' bellowed Beau. 'I'll drive.'

Brett took a quick look around the other side of the vehicle, before running back to the safety of the Range Rover. 'There's a girl in the passenger seat,' he gabbled. 'She's got blood pouring out of her mouth. I think she's a goner.'

'Fuck!' Beau swerved, narrowly missing a car pulling out of the Dick Turpin car park. The accident had affected the steering, it was veering to the right. 'We'll plot this up somewhere, then ring Gramps. He'll know what to do.'

CHAPTER TWENTY-SIX

'Brett, wake up.' Beau shook his brother. 'That was Gramps on the phone. We gotta meet him.'

Remembering what he had done, Brett pulled the quilt over his head. Whatever had he been thinking, turning up at Aidan's in the middle of the night like that? 'I don't feel well. You go meet Gramps.'

'He's got the right hump and said we both gotta go. Don't make me deal with this on me own, bruv. I got enough going on with Jolene betraying me.'

As memories of the girl covered in claret in the passenger seat came flooding back, Brett put his hand over his mouth and bolted to the en suite.

Kenny Bond was sat in Leo's café sipping a strong mug of tea and reading the *Sun*. One of his all-time heroes had sadly died. 'Ol' Blue Eyes'. He loved a bit of Sinatra, wanted 'My Way' and 'Fly Me to the Moon' played at his funeral. Not that he planned on kicking the bucket any time soon. But when your time was up, it was up, just like it had been for his pal Alan Davey, Ricky's real dad.

Kenny chucked the newspaper on the table. He hadn't appreciated being woken at two in the morning, but was pleased the boys had used their brains to call him. His first thought had been to report Beau's Range Rover as stolen, pretend someone had taken it off the drive late last night. But the twins had reassured him that nobody had seen the accident or passed by when they'd got out of the vehicle.

Kenny had a pal who was a sound geezer and a decent mechanic. Mick had his own garage on an industrial estate in Chadwell Heath, so Kenny had met the boys, led them there, plotted the motor up, then he'd driven the drunken pair home. Kenny had belled Mick first thing this morning, before opening up at work. The Range Rover was already out of sight and would be repaired professionally, but most importantly, on the quiet.

Looking at his watch, Kenny sighed. He'd told the boys to be on time, yet they were already twenty minutes late. Beau and Brett were his pride and joy, his protégés. They had the world at their feet with his guidance, which is why he would give them a hard time today. He was determined they wouldn't make the same mistakes in life that he had. It was no fun spending years sat in some poky bastard cell, that was for sure.

About to ring the twins and bollock them, Beau walked in the café, alone. 'Sorry I'm late, but Brett ain't well. He's in bed still, so I had to get a cab.'

Kenny leapt up. 'He ain't shirking his responsibilities,

no matter how ill he is. Come on. I'll drag him out of bed if I have to.'

Another two waking up with raging hangovers were Mad Ginger and Baz Daley. All their good intentions had gone out the window on Friday afternoon when they'd been confronted by Eddie Irons' henchman. They owed Eddie money, they knew that, but hadn't expected him to put the pressure on them so quickly. That had led to them having a couple of drinks, which turned into an all-day binge. They'd caught up with old friends, got bang on the gear, partied half the night and then ended up in a brothel miles away. Feeling rough yesterday morning, they'd then stupidly decided to get on it again and pressed the repeat button, minus the brasses.

'Baz, wake up.' Ginger, who wasn't known for his patience, filled up a glass of water and chucked it all over his comatose brother's head.

'What the fuck!' blinked Baz. It took him a moment to even realize where he was. At their mother's gaff.

'Get up. We need to go home, get freshened up. We have to bring things forward now Irons is on our back.'

'How?'

'Pay Bond another visit. Only I got a horrible feeling he's not gonna turn up on Tuesday with our dosh and we need to make sure he does.'

'How?'

'Stop saying "How", you sound like a fucking Red Indian. By kidnapping the mongol, ya melt. Now come on. Move.'

*

Feeling like death warmed up, Brett sat in the back of Gramp's Range Rover trying to recall what he'd said to Aidan. He had no idea what time Gramps had dropped them off, but he remembered needing another drink and finding some whisky in his dad's cabinet, which he'd started downing to get over the shock. Then he'd snorted the rest of that crap cocaine the shoplifters had got him, before phoning Aidan. Christ knows what he'd said, but he remembered Aidan humouring him in his drunken state for a bit before abruptly ending the call. Aidan had then ignored his next couple of calls before turning his phone off completely, which is when Brett had convinced himself Aidan had another boyfriend indoors, had ordered a cab, finished the rest of the whisky on the journey, before probably creating havoc. He didn't even know how he'd got home, but he obviously had somehow.

A vision suddenly flashed through Brett's mind. He'd had an argument up at Aidan's. With a woman. Was it a neighbour? Only, he couldn't remember seeing Aisling. But then, he couldn't really remember anything at that point. But he could recall Aidan in his navy dressing gown outside the apartments. The reality of what a show he'd made of himself suddenly hit Brett big time. 'Pull over. Quick. I'm gonna be sick.'

Sharon felt awkward waking up in the cold light of day in Ray's bed. She was busting for a wee, but only Kenny had seen her naked before and she couldn't bear for Ray to witness her saggy breasts and lumps and bumps as she did the walk of shame towards the bathroom. Not that she regretted last night. It had been lovely at the time. But only having ever slept with Kenny before, this was all new to her.

Aware of Sharon stirring, Ray leaned over and stroked the back of her neck, before kissing it. 'Good morning, sweetheart. How did you sleep?'

'Not great. But your bed's ever so comfy. I suppose it's gonna take me time getting used to sharing a bed with a man again. Since I split up with Kenny, I tend to lay in the middle of mine, face down, like a big fat starfish.'

'You're not fat, Sharon. You're perfect. Every woman should have curves. Imagine snuggling up to someone who feels like a skeleton. Sod that.'

Feeling more at ease, Sharon turned over and smiled. She stroked Ray's handsome face. 'You're lovely you are, and I do wanna move in with you. But not immediately.'

Ray held Sharon's face in his hands, pecked her on the nose and chuckled. 'I get it. I was tossing and turning all night an' all, 'cause I'm used to sleeping alone. But I then had an idea. I dunno about you, but I'm long overdue a bit of sun. Apart from a couple of golfing weekends away with the lads, I haven't been on a proper holiday for ages. How about I book us somewhere? Somewhere really special, where we can just chill out and get to know one another a bit better. You have a think about it while I make us a cup of tea and a bit of breakfast. There's a dressing gown hanging up in the en suite and fresh towels if you want a shower.'

Feeling more at ease, Sharon couldn't wipe the smile off

her face. 'That all sounds bloody perfect, Ray. The cup of tea, the breakfast, but especially the holiday. Let's do it.'

Kenny drove the twins up to the garden centre. He'd searched the local news stories on Ceefax and there'd been no mention of a car accident. It was better to be safe than sorry though, and for Beau and Brett to show their faces at work, acting normal so to speak. 'Go sit in the portacabin. I'll grab us some sandwiches and coffee. Then I wanna know everything that happened last night. So think carefully.'

Brett looked at Beau. 'We gonna tell him we went back to those birds' flat?'

'Yeah. We better. Why did we go back there? They weren't even nice.'

'I did try and tell you that. But you were insistent on getting laid. Knowing your luck, you've probably got one of the mingers up the duff.'

'Shut it,' snapped Beau. 'Don't joke about shit like that. It ain't funny. I only shagged the younger one, I think.'

'You said the other one sucked your cock an' all.'

Beau shrugged. 'I honestly can't remember much. What were their names?'

'Chantelle and Leanne.'

'Best you tell Gramps you sodded off out in the middle of the night an' all. What happened there?'

'I can't remember much either. I think Aisling shoved me in a cab and sent me packing. I remember that girl's face in the passenger seat though. The blood pouring out of her mouth.' Brett put his head in his hands. 'She looked dead to me.'

Kenny came back with the coffees. 'They're bringing the grub over to us. Right, we need to get a story straight just in case. If the Old Bill come sniffing around, our story is, the Range Rover's been stolen and we didn't bother reporting it, 'cause the Old Bill fucking hate me. We'll say we put the feelers out ourselves and were confident of getting it back, which is why we ain't reported it to the insurance company yet.'

'Where did it get stolen from?' asked Beau.

'You went Ilford Palais, didn't ya? You can say you left it there 'cause you'd had a drink and it was gone when we went to pick it up today.'

'We gave two birds a lift after the Palais and went back to their flat,' Brett informed his grandfather.

Kenny paced up and down the portacabin. 'Don't do anything by halves you two, do ya? Now think carefully, are you sure nobody saw the accident or passed by when you stopped?' The crash had happened in Aldborough Road North, which was thankfully pretty desolate late at night.

'I was more sober than him and no way did anyone see us,' Brett replied confidently.

Unfortunately for the twins, neither recalled the car Beau had swerved to avoid shortly after the incident.

After a fruitless trip to Dark Lane, the Daley brothers headed back up the A127. They'd done a bit of digging over the weekend, had found out Kenny also had a young son and that his Mrs and eldest son ran another garden centre up at Stapleford Abbotts.

'Don't open another can. We're there now,' scolded Ginger. Baz had made him stop at an off-licence. He'd had the DTs.

'Bingo!' Ginger said as he clocked Kenny's motor. 'Right, I'll do all the talking. Ready?'

'Yep.'

Seeing a woman serving, Ginger walked over to her. 'Kenny around, love?'

'In the office,' she pointed at the portacabin.

Ginger yanked open the door of the portacabin. Kenny was inside alone. 'Morning, Mr Bond.'

Kenny leapt up off the chair. 'It's afternoon now. What the fuck do you want?'

'No need to be rude. Just a social visit to check all's in place for our little meet on Tuesday?'

'I told yous last week, I don't know what the hell you're going on about. Now get outta my face before I lose my bastard rag.'

Ginger pointed at Kenny. 'I'm telling you now, you don't pay up, you'll regret it big time.'

Kenny picked up the convector heater and slung it at the two imbeciles' heads. Ginger ducked, but it clipped Baz and sent him flying. 'Do your worst, ya pair of fucking mugs.'

'Oh, we will,' spat Ginger. 'Don't you worry about that. Then we'll see who the mug is. Come on, Baz. We're going.'

Across the other side of the garden centre, Beau was sitting in the shoplifter's car. He hadn't told anyone about his plan, he doubted even Brett would be agreeable. The less people that knew, the better. 'Whaddya reckon then, lads? Five grand in cash as soon as the job's done. But, it has to look like a mugging. You nick her bag, phone, whatever she's got on her. She wears a lot of Tom usually, earrings, necklaces. Take it all if you can. But don't be flogging it in boozers or anything like that. You need to get rid of whatever you nick off her, sharpish. Throw it in the fucking river or somewhere it won't be found. Don't sling the wedding and engagement ring though. I'll have them as a keepsake.'

Badger and Mad Dog glanced at one another. Neither were comfortable with what they'd been asked to do. Neither was Beau offering enough money. Not for that. 'I'm not sure it's our thing if I'm honest, Beau,' said Badger.

'Not for five grand,' added Mad Dog. 'We'll be looking at a proper long stretch if we get caught. Not being funny, Beau, but we can earn that in a good week, thieving,' he lied.

'All right. Ten grand. But you don't tell a soul. This is between us only. Even Brett mustn't know, and you gotta get her when she's on her own. I can trust yous, can't I?'

Mad Dog and Badger looked at one another again. They'd often spoken about spending a month in Thailand, but never seemed to be flush enough to do so. 'Twenty grand and you got yourself a deal.' Mad Dog knew that Beau was rich.

'Fifteen,' bartered Beau.

With visions of shagging pretty Thai birds and basking in some serious sunshine, Badger could barely keep the smile off his face. 'OK. We're in. But we want half up front.'

*

Back at Dark Lane, Brett's hangover had finally started to wear off. He'd sicked up the bacon sandwich Gramps had forced him to eat earlier, then got one of the lads to drop him off home.

Brett flicked through the regional headlines on Teletext again. 'No news is good news' as Gramps often said. He then tried Aidan once more. He'd already left two messages. Brett's heart sank as this time it went straight to answerphone rather than ringing first. Aidan had obviously switched his phone off.

Not knowing what he'd said or done was pure torture for Brett. No way could he leave things like that. He needed to speak to Aidan. In person.

Ricky was treating Candy to lunch at their favourite restaurant, The Harvester. It had been Kenny's idea he take a couple of weeks off work, so he could enjoy his new-found freedom. It was great, as he was still getting all of his wages too.

Candy picked up a rack of ribs and chomped noisily around them. 'So, what we gonna do next week? You taking me somewhere tomorrow?'

About to put a lump of steak in his mouth, Ricky instead grinned broadly. His beautiful girlfriend looked stunning in her tight green minidress. So much so, everyone in the restaurant had looked their way when they'd arrived. 'Of course, treacle. I will take you wherever you want to go.'

Candy grinned then went back to scoffing her ribs. She'd got a bit bored recently, which is why she'd had a fling with one of her exes. Steve drank in the Barking Dog, but after spending two nights at his grotty flat, she'd soon realized the grass wasn't greener. Steve lived on benefits, like herself, but he never seemed to have any money. She'd had to pay for the cider and their kebabs two days in a row. 'I've been thinking. What would you say, Ricky, if I asked you to marry me?'

'What!' Ricky dropped his fork in shock, then did his best to sound cool. 'I thought it was the man's duty to ask the lady?'

'Not always. My mate has asked lots of men to marry her.'

'Oh, right. Well, are you asking me then?'

'Might be. Might not.' Candy ate the rest of her meal deep in thought. It was frustrating living with her parents, and she'd never had a boyfriend as generous as Ricky before. He paid for absolutely everything, which allowed her to spend her benefit money on herself. Also, Kenny was really rich, so surely if they got married, he'd send them on a fabulous honeymoon and buy them a lovely house? Ricky was like a son to him after all. Maybe they could even have their own swimming pool? And a cleaner. Candy hated cleaning. 'OK. I am asking you. Will you marry me, Ricky?'

'Dad, this is Ray,' smiled Sharon.

Charlie Saunders felt awkward as he shook hands with the man but remained polite. He'd only found out his daughter was courting an hour ago when Maggie had informed him Sharon was bringing her new beau round. Kenny most certainly would not be happy with this situation. Charlie dreaded to think of the outcome.

'Ray wants to take me on holiday, Mum, and I really could do with one, if I'm honest. But I'm worried about leaving you. We'll probably be away for a few weeks.'

'Isn't it a bit soon to be going away together?' piped up Charlie.

Maggie punched her husband in the leg. 'No. It isn't. They've been courting for a while. We just didn't tell you because we know what an old fuddy-duddy you are. Don't you be worrying about me, darling.' Maggie smiled at her daughter. 'Nothing would make me happier than you two going on holiday. Do you know where you're going yet?'

'We quite fancy Hawaii or the Maldives. Ray's friend's daughter works as a travel agent, so we're going to see her tomorrow to book it.'

'Oh, how lovely,' gushed Maggie. 'Your dad used to love that programme *Hawaii Five-O*. Steve Garrett, weren't it, Charlie?'

'Steve McGarrett,' corrected Charlie. 'Maggs, come into the kitchen for a minute. I just need a quick word with you.'

Maggie winced as she stood up, but tried not to show it. The pain had worsened lately. 'Whassamatter with you? Can't you be happy for her?' she hissed, once out of earshot. 'Our girl deserves some happiness after spending most of her life with that cheating arsehole.'

'You need to tell her the truth, love. That you haven't got, you know, long left. She'd never forgive herself if something happened to you while she was away.'

Maggie wagged her finger in her husband's face. 'I will not spoil that girl's holiday and neither will you. I'll still be here when she gets home. I'll make bloody sure of it. Then I'll tell her.'

'Hello, son. Not seen you for a while,' said the jolly old security guard that checked who was coming to and from the posh apartments where Aidan lived.

Grateful that the man obviously hadn't been working when he'd caused mayhem, Brett raised his eyebrows. 'I've been busy, working. You know how it is.'

'I most certainly do. "Gotta keep the wolf from the door" as my old dad used to say. If you're looking for your mate, he's gone out to that new restaurant that's opened round the corner. Well, it's not exactly round the corner. You go right, left, then right again. Italian, it is. No parking there though, so you might want to walk it.'

'Cheers, mate. I'll park this up 'ere then.'

Brett didn't have a clue where he was walking to, but asked a couple of people and soon found the restaurant. He walked in.

'Can I help you, sir?' asked a man dressed in a pinstripe waistcoat.

'I'm looking for my friend. He booked a table here, I think. Aidan. Aidan Neary.'

'Ah, Mr Neary. This way,' gestured the chap.

Aidan was horrified as he saw Brett heading his way. Face draining rapidly of colour, he spilled his wine before shooting out of his seat. 'Won't be a tick, Dad.' He roughly grabbed Brett by the arm. 'Outside.'

'Sorry if I disturbed you, but I had to see you to explain. I'm so sorry—'

Snarling like a rabid dog, Aidan grabbed Brett by the neck and slammed him against a nearby wall. 'You fucking idiot. That's my father I'm eating with. What's the matter with you? You're a fool that's what. I thought last night was bad enough and now this. Go home, Brett, and don't ever call me again. We're over. Done, dusted, fucking finished.'

Tears sprung in Brett's eyes as the reality of Aidan's harsh words hit home.

As Aidan turned to leave a humiliated Brett standing in the cold, he hadn't noticed his father watching from afar. Cormac Neary was not a happy man.

Unaware that his wife was in the vicinity with her new lover, Kenny was debating whether to ring his pal Big Dave to get hold of a gun for him.

Once upon a time, Kenny had always had a shooter around, didn't feel safe without one. But times had changed. He was older now, wiser. Aware of the strength of his own temper, he was frightened that if those morons the Chuckle Brothers, as he'd now nicknamed them, turned up at his door, he'd lose it and blow both their heads off.

'Don't do it. Don't do it,' Kenny mumbled, trying to convince himself. He had the usual tools a man had to protect his home, a machete, baseball bat, a cosh. He didn't fancy doing another lump of bird, not at his age. He'd spent far too long behind bars as it was.

Hearing a car pull up, Kenny ran over to the window. It was Ricky. 'Oh, for fuck's sake,' he cursed, as he realized that notright Candy was with him. As if his day hadn't been bad enough.

'Kenny, where are you?' bellowed Ricky.

'In 'ere, Big Man.'

Excited as a kid at Christmas, Ricky bounded into the kitchen, grasping Candy's hand. 'You'll never guess what.'

'What?'

'Candy proposed to me. I'm getting married.'

'You all right? Where you been?' Beau asked Brett.

After crying most of the way home because he felt so hurt and such a fool, Brett's anguish had turned to anger. 'To see that cunt, Aisling. I fucking hate women. We're done, me and her. For good.'

Secretly pleased that Brett was in the same boat as him, Beau handed his brother one of the beers he'd bought on the way home. 'Slags,' he hissed. 'The lot of 'em. Apart from the older ones like Mum and Nan. The only thing the younger ones are good for is having our kids. I felt like shit earlier. Rocky and Levi were well upset 'cause I had to let 'em down today. I'm taking 'em out tomorrow instead.'

The conversation was cut short by Ricky and Candy bursting in. 'We're getting married,' they said in unison.

Kenny felt weighed down with worry as he flopped onto the sofa, an extra large brandy in hand. The twins were both at home, thank God. He'd checked. Ricky and his not-so-beautiful bride-to-be were staying at Donny's too. That was where they did all their bonking, apparently. The way his luck was going, Ricky would probably get her up the spout next. That was all he needed to add to his woes. Miniature Candys running around. As for the

Daley brothers, they were a pain in the proverbial. One he'd probably have to deal with at some point. But not now. He had too much other grief on his plate.

Feeling absolutely shattered, Kenny decided to have one last check through the local news before retiring to bed. His complexion went deathly white as he spotted the headline: THREE TEENAGERS DEAD AND ONE CRITICAL IN HORROR CAR CRASH.

CHAPTER TWENTY-SEVEN

Kenny woke the twins at dawn the following morning, having decided against telling them the news the previous night. He hadn't wanted to risk them hitting the booze again, would rather them get a good night's kip. He needed them to have their wits about them.

'Oh my God! Why me?' Brett gently headbutted the kitchen wall. Helping Beau kill Jamie had been bad enough. But now he'd killed three more, possibly four. He'd only taken his eyes off the road for a few seconds. His luck was well poxed.

'Come on, bruv. Nobody saw us. We'll be fine,' re-assured Beau. He didn't feel any guilt whatsoever. It was an accident and accidents happen.

'Get off me, you fucking idiot.' Brett pushed his brother hard in the chest. 'This is all your fault. Piss-balling about, grabbing me in a headlock. It was you that made me take me fucking eyes off the road. You made us crash.'

When the boys started wildly arguing, Kenny separated them. 'Behave, the pair of ya. Now's not the time to be falling out, is it? Sit your arses down and I'll tell ya exactly what we're gonna do.'

'Right, act normal, happy, you know what we spoke about,' urged Kenny, as they pulled up at the garden centre. 'Make sure you have a laugh and joke with the staff before you shoot off with the van, Beau.' His grandson was taking his kids out for the day. Kenny had urged him to use a work van, rather than borrow his motor, so as to avoid suspicion. 'Just tell the kids you had a big delivery to do on the way if they ask,' he'd told Beau. He very much doubted the Old Bill would question the staff at the garden centre if they got wind of the boys' involvement. But they were slippery bastards, the police, and you couldn't rule anything out. Some of 'em would sell their own grandmother down the river to get a decent conviction.

Beau looked at his watch. He'd have to be swift. He'd arranged to meet Badger and Mad Dog at ten.

Ian Dodge, AKA Dodger, was a small-time drug-dealer who lived in a council flat on Marks Gate Estate. He'd done a bit of graft for the Daley brothers in the past, looked up to them like idols. 'I cleaned it up as much as I could for ya. TV works, stereo is decent. There's nothing much in the fridge, but there's soup and some other tins in the cupboard. If you get peckish, just help yourselves,' grinned Dodger. He actually felt honoured that they'd asked for his help. They needed to hole up a geezer on the run for a couple of days, maybe more. Not only did it prove Baz and Mad Ginger trusted him implicitly, they were also paying him two hundred and fifty quid a day to vacate his property. Easy money.

Mad Ginger looked out the window. Dodger's flat was at the bottom of a quiet no through road. They hadn't wanted to hide Ricky around their own neck of the woods, as they knew that would be the first place Kenny would come looking. 'Whaddya reckon, Baz?'

'Spot on for what we need.'

Ginger took a wad of money out of his pocket. 'There's five hundred up front, 'cause we'll deffo need to be 'ere today and tomorrow. I'll settle up the rest with you at the end, OK?'

Dodger grinned like a Cheshire cat. 'No worries, lads. You know I'm sound. Your fugitive secret's safe with me.'

'We're all sorted then, yeah?' Beau had met Mad Dog and Badger at a quiet spot in Wickford. He'd provided them with a burner phone and precise instructions of what to do. He'd also given them a list of Jolene's known movements, her car registration and a recent photo.

'Well, sort of. We ain't really happy with just a grand up front though, Beau,' complained Mad Dog. 'We settled on half.'

'No. We didn't. You two settled on half. Not saying I don't trust you, lads, because I wouldn't be asking yous to do this if I didn't. But seven an' half grand is a hell of a lot of dosh to be parting with before a job is done. Not only that, I ain't got that amount of cash around me at short notice. You know me well enough, where I work, my family. As if I would screw you over. Get the job done and I promise ya, the other fourteen grand will be with you the following day.'

Badger looked at Mad Dog, who shrugged, then nodded. 'All right then. We'll get everything organized today, then start work on the job first thing tomorrow.'

Still feeling like shit over Aidan, his life in general, but mostly over the accident, Brett was sitting in the porta-cabin alone. He'd done what Gramps had ordered, acted jovial and normal. It had been a struggle though, just like it had when Jamie had died.

Brett glanced at his watch. The local news was on soon. He'd been flicking the radio stations between Essex Radio and Radio London for the past hour or so.

Unfortunately for Brett, the latest news bulletin wasn't good: '*Police are asking for witnesses to come forward after three teenage girls died and a fourth remains in a critical condition . . .*'

Unable to listen to any more, Brett ran out the porta-cabin and leapt into his car. He needed to talk to his mum. She was the only one who could help him now.

Undeterred by recent events, Beau had taken his children to a new restaurant, Frankie and Benny's. 'Enjoying your burgers, boys?' Rocky and Levi were good eaters, so he'd bought them an adult meal. They weren't going to get through it all though, especially Levi.

'Dadda, eat,' smiled Romany, as she pushed a chip into his mouth. She loved sitting on her father's lap while scoffing her own food.

'We'll go the toy shop next, eh?' grinned Beau, stroking the face of his little princess.

'Yeah,' shrieked Rocky, who stood up to high-five his dad.

Levi tried to do the same but couldn't reach.

'Daddy needs to go to the toilet, darling. You sit in between your brothers for a minute.'

'We look after her, Dad,' said Rocky.

Beau walked towards the Men's with a spring in his step. Thank God when he'd turned up at Aunt Nelly's birthday bash, Gramps had been talking to Vinny Butler. He'd very nearly blurted out about the private detective, the works. But he'd had the brains to play it down afterwards, saying he was upset with Jolene going out all the time. Only Brett knew about Gloria and, with what was about to go down, that's the way he wanted it to stay.

Checking the cubicle to make sure nobody was inside, Beau smirked as he pulled out his own burner phone. He'd gently pumped the boys on the journey and, as usual, Rocky in particular had been more than informative.

The Daley brothers couldn't believe their luck. They'd been plotted up in the lay-by for no more than twenty minutes, when Ricky came along in his car. Only downside was, he had a bird with him. They hadn't stopped laughing since they'd followed them into Romford, mind. The bird was a right mess, dressed up in a short, emerald-green number, and she was giving their intended victim a hard time by the looks of it. She was a hefty lump and was literally dragging him from one jeweller's shop to the next.

'Oh, hang on, she's just clumped him. No, wait a minute, he's grabbed her hand and he's dragging her in the boozer,' laughed Baz.

Ginger grabbed his brother's arm. 'Stay well back and stop laughing. We don't want him looking around and spotting us.'

'What do we do now?' Baz asked, as the couple entered the Golden Lion.

'You stand against the wall for a minute, so we know they don't leave, while I move the van closer. Then we wait. Bit of luck, he might pop out the boozer alone, to surprise the fucking moose with whatever she wanted in the jewellers.'

Lori held her distraught son in her arms. Even though her sons were identical twins, they were very different on an emotional level. Apart from Jolene, nothing fazed Beau, he was tough as old boots, like his father. Whereas Brett was more like her, hard on the outside, soft on the inside. Her heart went out to him. 'I know you're hurting, son, but we're going to sort this. OK? There isn't much I can do about Aidan. You're just going to have to put that down to experience, like I had to with your dad. But Carl and I will help you with the crash. We'll give you an alibi. You and Beau were here all evening with us.'

'Nah. You don't understand, Mum. Let me start from the beginning.'

Lori listened intently as Brett outlined everything that had happened that night. Therapy had taught her not to judge or butt in when others wanted to get things off their chest. She even felt partly responsible. Donny had never suffered with problems relating to addiction, so her beloved sons had obviously inherited her dysfunctional genes.

'What am I gonna do, Mum? It'll be me who spends years in prison. Beau won't. If only he hadn't grabbed me. I told him to stop.'

Lori stroked Brett's handsome face. 'I promise you; you will not end up in prison. Carl knows people. Important people. Let me speak to him. See what he can do.'

Brett managed a watery smile. 'Thanks, Mum. You're a star.'

Ricky took a gulp of his shandy. It was thirsty work this shopping lark. 'You made a decision yet?' Candy must have tried on about twenty engagement rings so far.

'I only like that one. That one you told the man was "Too dear". Talk about embarrassing me,' sulked Candy. 'If you love someone, nothing's too dear.'

'I'm sorry and I didn't mean that you're not worth it. You are. But, I haven't got that amount of money saved up, Candy. If I'd known you were thinking of proposing to me, I'd have saved harder.'

'Ask Kenny to buy it. He's got loads of money.'

'Kenny won't pay for it. I asked him if he was going to pay for the wedding earlier, like you told me to, and he said it's your parents' duty to pay, 'cause you're the bride.'

Bordering on furious, Candy downed her cider and slammed the bottle against the table. 'Bloody cheek!

My parents haven't got no money. Not being funny, Ricky, but if any woman is worth a real diamond, then I am.'

'I know you are and I will get you one. I promise.'

'When?'

'I don't know. We'll have to stay in more, so I can save up for it.'

'Boring,' Candy rolled her eyes. 'I'm going home. I feel smelly in these clothes. I've had them on since yesterday morning.'

Ricky stood up. 'I'll drive you.'

'No. You stay here. I'd rather get the bus. Ring me later when you've spoken to Kenny again, about the wedding and the ring, 'cause if no one's gonna pay for them, we might as well not bother getting married.'

'Hang on. We have lift off. The bird's stormed out,' said an excited Baz.

'Open the back doors. This is the best chance we're gonna get.' They were parked in the marketplace, nigh on outside the Golden Lion. It was a non-market day and even though there were shoppers milling about, there weren't too many. Both men were dressed in hard hats and boiler suits in an attempt to pass themselves off as workmen.

Baz leaned against the passenger side window, pretending to be having a conversation with his brother. 'What we gonna do if he walks in front of the van? Wouldn't you be better reversing it, so the back doors are facing the pub?'

Ginger grinned, his diamond-studded gold tooth glinting in the sun. 'Good thinking, Batman.'

*

Ricky tilted back his head and emptied the packet of peanuts inside his mouth. Being in love, he'd wanted to run after his fiancée, make everything all right again. But Kenny had given him a good talking-to recently. 'Don't you be making the same mistakes with Candy that me and Beau have with women. The more you give in to 'em, the more they mess you around,' Kenny insisted.

Ricky sighed. Yesterday, he'd been so happy, yet today he felt sad. That was women for you, he supposed. No wonder all the men in his family were single again now.

Ricky stood up, stretched, then slowly walked out of the pub. Should he have a mooch round the shops? Or should he go straight home?

Regrettably for Ricky, getting grabbed, then bundled into the back of a van, kind of took the decision away from him.

'Fuck me, he's strong as an ox, Ginge,' panted Baz, trying to restrain their victim once more. Ricky was rolling around the back of the van like a big fat eel, yet throwing his weight about with enormous strength at the same time. He'd even bitten Baz on the arm.

'Fucking clump him. We gotta get him inside the flat quietly, and we'll be there soon.' Marks Gate Estate was only a ten-minute drive from Romford market.

Baz grabbed the lad by the throat and smashed the back of his head against the van's interior. 'Look, we don't want to hurt you. Just calm down and I promise ya, you'll be fine. It ain't you we got the hump with.'

Rubbing the back of his sore head, Ricky didn't know if he was coming or going. 'I don't understand. What did I do wrong?'

'Nothing,' replied Baz. 'Kenny did. He owes us money. Lots of it. Once he pays up, you can go home. But you gotta behave yourself, 'cause if you keep kicking off, we'll have no option but to hurt you badly. You don't want that, do you?'

Feeling a bit nervous, Ricky weighed up his options. He recognized the men now. They were the ones who'd knocked at Donny's last week asking for Kenny. The problem was, he hadn't been down the gym much, not since he'd met Candy, and both these men were double his size. Not in a fat way. They were scary looking and had really big muscles. 'OK. I won't kick off. But I don't want anybody to steal my car. I parked it in Romford, near The Bull pub.'

Nearing Dodger's flat, Ginger put his foot on the brake and glanced around, 'You put that yellow jacket and hat on, Ricky, and as soon as we're inside the flat, you can speak to Kenny and sort your car out. You gotta be quiet though. No making any noise as we go up the stairs. Deal?'

Ricky didn't trust the men one iota, but had little option other than to play along with them. 'OK. Deal.'

Kenny let himself into his son's house. 'What you laughing at? I thought you had company.'

Beau paused the programme. '*Harry Enfield and Chums*. Some of the characters are well funny. You wanna watch it with me?'

'Not really in the mood for comedy today, Beau, and neither should you be. Turn it over to ITV. We need to watch the local news. The fucking radio's full of the crash now. The police know another car was involved. You better be right that nobody saw you, 'cause you and Brett are bang in trouble if not. Your brother not back yet?' asked Kenny. After disappearing from the garden centre, Brett had rung him to say he was with Lori.

'No. But he's OK. Mum's doing him dinner. Nobody saw us, I promise. So stop worrying.'

'Someone must've seen you driving along afterwards with a smashed light and half the bumper hanging off. And what about them two tarts you took home? How'd you know they won't put two and two together once they hear about the crash? That's if they ain't already heard. It's headline news now on every fucking local radio station. For all you know those tarts could be sat down at the cop shop as we speak, giving a blow-by-blow account. I take it you gave 'em your real names?'

Beau shrugged. 'Can't remember. But we had no reason to lie to 'em at the time.'

Kenny's jaw began to twitch. 'The filth'll be under pressure to get some answers to this. Three brown-bread teenagers and one on death's door is one of them stories that becomes national news. I can't believe Brett didn't see the people in the back. He said there was only two of 'em.'

'I think the roof was all squashed. Like when you stamp on an empty fag packet, ya know.'

'What a pleasant description. Right, I'm gonna ring a pal of mine. Get a plan in place. You and Brett might be better off abroad until the dust settles.'

'I can't just swan off and leave me kids.'

Kenny went out into the back garden. After he'd got in touch with Teddy, Tony Abbott had rung him back regarding the Daley brothers. 'Be careful, Kenny, 'cause I told you before, they can be unpredictable. You've done the right thing though, denying all knowledge of their grievances. The Scientist has obviously spilled the beans, but they can't prove sod all. And they never will be able to. It's one man's word against another.'

Kenny had been a bit pissed off with Tony's weak response. If the boot had been on the other foot, he'd have jumped on the first plane home to help out his old partner in crime. Tony was living a quiet life now in the Costa del Sol, with a bird and a couple of young kiddies.

Lighting up a cigar, Kenny took a deep drag. He would rather the boys be in Spain if the shit hit the fan. Tony owed him. The least he could do was help him hole the boys up somewhere for a bit. He had a fair few pals that were on their toes out there, on the run from the British police. The extradition laws might have changed back in the eighties, but Spain was still a far easier country to hide in. Be invisible, so to speak. In certain areas especially, ex-pats had a habit of looking out for one another.

When his phone rang, Kenny didn't answer. He hated unknown callers and it was the same number that had rung him twice while driving. Why didn't they just leave a message? Because it wasn't important, that's why. Unlike weighing up the pros and cons of sending his grandsons away for a while. It was vital he made the correct decision. He could not bear the boys' lives being ruined, like his had.

'Gramps! Come quick,' yelled Beau.

Kenny dashed into the front room. It was on the TV, the crash. An officer was standing there in the exact spot, a sombre expression on his mooey. Behind him on the grass verge lay bouquets, cards, teddy bears.

Then they rolled a witness out. Some grey-haired geezer in his fifties who said as he was about to leave work at approximately 1.55 a.m. on Sunday morning, he narrowly avoided being another victim of what he described as 'the killer's vehicle'.

'Drama king,' spat Kenny. 'Do or say anything to get themselves on TV, some people. He looks like a nonce an' all.'

'Shush,' urged Beau.

When the witness gave a vague description of Beau and a decent description of the Range Rover, Kenny's anger reverted to his grandson, whom he promptly clumped around the head. 'You fucking idiot. You swore blind nobody had clocked you, ya moron.'

Beau put his head in his hands. He remembered it now. He'd swerved to avoid that car pulling out of the Dick Turpin car park.

Over in Mark's Gate, Ginger had started running out of patience. He'd got the numbers of Kenny, Beau and Brett off Ricky, yet not one of them had answered his calls. No way was he leaving any answerphone messages, just in case it implicated him and Baz in any way. He'd also rung the garden centre, but none of the family were there.

Feeling scared and uncomfortable, Ricky was tied to a wooden chair in the middle of the front room. His arms were hurting because they'd been forced behind his back, and his ankles were sore, as the thick rope was far too tight. 'Can you untie me, please? I need to use the toilet.'

'Number ones? Or number twos?' smirked Baz.

'You ain't going nowhere, sunshine,' snarled Ginger. Not until we've made contact with a family member. What other numbers you got on your phone for me to try?'

Ricky's first thought was Sharon, but he didn't want her to be frightened like he was. It wasn't a nice feeling. 'Look under D, then ring Donny.'

Life was currently good for Donny Bond. Moving away from Dark Lane had been the making of him and Tansey. Living in Blackmore suited them down to the ground. Their kids had flourished too. Harry had landed himself a decent job up town and Bluebell went to a wonderful local school where she'd made lots of nice little friends. Even Alfie had managed to stay out of trouble for the past nine months or so and that was a miracle alone.

Yawning as he neared the end of counting up the day's takings, Donny answered his phone without even looking at the screen. 'Hello.'

'Hello, Donny. Now listen to what I have to say and listen very carefully. I've got a message for your wrong un of a father. Tell him Ginger called and if he wants Ricky back, he needs to pay me the money he owes me. I'll be calling him at six on the dot, you tell him.'

'You what! Who is this? And how'd you get my personal number?'

'I haven't got time for small talk, Donny. Say hello, Ricky. Tell him what's happened to you. Go on.' Ginger held the phone to Ricky's ear.

'Donny, I got kidnapped and I'm worried about my car 'cause I left it in Romford market. You need to ring Kenny and tell him to pay the men the money 'cause otherwise they won't let me go home.'

Donny went cold. 'I will. You just be strong until this gets sorted, OK? Put that Ginger back on, Big Man.'

Ginger put the phone to his own ear. 'Oh, and tell your father, if he involves the Old Bill, the next time he'll see Ricky, he'll be lying on a cold slab in the mortuary.'

Determined to protect his mother and his own brood, Donny worded his reply carefully. 'I don't have nothing to do with my old man any more, neither does my mum or sister. But I'll make sure he gets the message. One question though – and obviously, you don't have to answer it if you don't want to. But, what does he owe you money for?'

'You remember all them deaths due to a bad batch of ecstasy pills a few years ago?'

'Yeah. I remember.' Donny could hardly forget, not when Tammy Tamplin was one of the victims.

'Your cunt of a father and his mucker Tony Abbott were the supplier of those pills. But it was my men who got stitched up, blamed, then banged up. The money is compensation for those men and their families.'

'OK, thanks.' Donny felt sick as he ended the call. He'd had a feeling way back when his father was knocking about with Tony Abbott that he was up to no good again. He'd even asked him outright about it once. Now this.

Poor Ricky. Thank God he'd moved his family away. Because they'd be bang in the firing line if not. As for his father, he never failed to disappoint him.

Kenny paced up and down the front room like a lunatic. Donny had given him a right earful. His heart went out to Ricky, that lad was as good as his own flesh and blood. He'd underestimated the Chuckle Brothers, but over his dead body would they get away with a stunt like this. They were dead men walking once he got Ricky back safe and sound. He'd already rung his pal, Big Dave, who was picking a gun up first thing tomorrow.

Kenny glanced at his watch again, willing it to quickly turn six. He was yet to tell Beau and Brett what had happened. They had enough going on with the crash and he didn't want to cause them additional worry and upset.

At six on the dot, Kenny's phone burst into life. It was that unknown number from earlier. 'Hello, Mr Bond,' said Ginger.

'I'm telling you now, you harm one hair on that lad's head and I'll kill you and your brother stone dead.'

'Calm down, calm down,' mocked Ginger. 'I'm calling the shots now, Kenny. Not you.'

'Put Ricky on the phone. I need to know he's all right.'

'Hold your horses. I want my money. All five hundred grand of it. When can you have it by?'

'I dunno. Ain't got that type of money lying around. But I'll get it. It might take me a day or two. You gotta let the boy go though. He ain't used to being away from home.'

'Yeah, right. And pigs might fly. I'll call you same time tomorrow, see if you've got the wonga.'

'Put Ricky on to me. Please.'

Ginger put the phone to Ricky's ear. 'Say hello to Kenny.'

'Hello, Kenny. Please hurry up and pay the men their money. I don't like it here. I want to come home.'

'Where are ya?'

'I'm in a flat and I'm . . .'

Doubting Ricky knew their location, Ginger snatched the phone away, just in case. 'And he's tied up is what he was gonna say. You get us the money, Bond. Then you get the boy back. Laters.'

When Ginger ended the call, Kenny punched the wall with frustration. Ricky's safety was paramount; therefore he would get the money together somehow. Then he'd do away with the Chuckle Brothers and hopefully get every penny back.

Beau watched the local news on ITV, then turned the telly off. There were no more updates. They'd shown the same witness from earlier and asked for more witnesses to come forward, then shown a phone number to call. The other girl, who was apparently the driver, was still in a critical condition with possible life-changing injuries.

Beau got himself a beer from the fridge and debated whether to order himself a takeaway. Brett was staying at their mum's overnight. Thinking of his kids, Beau smiled. They'd had a great day today. He'd bought them whatever they wanted out of Toys R Us. Money was no issue. All that mattered was his children's happiness, which is why he needed Mad Dog and Badger to come up trumps. It was weird, because he surprisingly felt little hatred towards Jimmy Dean. It probably helped that he didn't know the bloke, but if it hadn't been him, that slag would've got her claws into some other unsuspecting mug. Just like she had with him. She'd reeled him in like a fish, flashing her big breasts in her low-cut tops, wiggling her perfect little arse in those hotpants and skimpy denim shorts. She'd then chewed him up and spat him out like a bit of unwanted chewing gum.

Anger surging through his veins, Beau downed his beer and opened another. He'd married a slut, a fucking whore. But she would pay the price for what she'd done. No man would want her after what he had planned. Fact.

Having sifted through Dodger's record collection, Ginger and Baz had opted for Pink Floyd's *Dark Side of the Moon.*

'I'm hungry. Are we going to have any dinner?' asked Ricky. It was uncomfortable being tied up, but the men hadn't been too horrible to him. They'd allowed him to go the toilet and they hadn't hit or kicked him.

'This ain't a restaurant,' snapped Ginger. 'But if you behave yourself, I'll go to the chippy in a bit. Sausage and chips OK for ya?'

'Yes, please. Can you put lots of salt and vinegar on the chips? And get me some tomato ketchup?'

'Fuck me! Cheeky bastard. Don't want much does he, Baz?' Ginger laughed.

Singing along to 'Money', Baz was feeling that uncomfortable urge start to play on his mind. 'Can't you see if you can get us some puff from somewhere, Ginge? These tunes make me want to chill, man.'

'No, I bloody well can't. We need our wits about us. I'll grab us a few beers though.'

'Can I have a beer too, please?' enquired Ricky. He wasn't feeling quite as scared any more. Not now Kenny knew. He trusted Kenny to rescue him somehow.

'You'll get what you're given, ya saucy bastard.' Ginger grabbed his coat. 'Don't untie him for any reason until I'm back.'

As soon as Ginger left, Baz ran into the kitchen searching through cupboards and drawers. Dodger sold drugs; he must have something lying about somewhere.

Having no joy, Baz ransacked the bedroom next and was just about to give up when he looked in a shoe box and struck gold. Acid tabs.

'Can I go to the toilet, please? I need a poo,' shouted out Ricky.

A terrible thought popped into Baz's mind and he couldn't resist the fun he would have. He walked back into the front room. 'Open your mouth, Ricky. I got a present for ya.'

CHAPTER TWENTY-EIGHT

'Stop fucking fidgeting. What's the matter with ya?' snarled Mad Ginger. 'You've been fed and watered. Now behave.'

Ricky stopped rocking the chair backwards and forwards, then closed his eyes in the hope it might help him compose himself. He felt weird and it was freaking him out. The lights were hurting his eyes, they were way too bright and the brown curtains seemed to have things crawling on them, like big insects. But it was the Daley brothers that were really weirding him out. Their faces had changed for the worst. They literally looked like big scary monsters.

Enjoying watching Ricky come up on his trip, Baz smirked. He was yet to take one himself as he didn't want Ginger to know what he'd done. This was funny though and would only get better. A proper bit of entertainment for the long evening ahead. 'Chuck us another beer.'

Averting his eyes from Ricky, Ginger handed Baz a can of Stella. 'You didn't do anything to him while I was out, did ya?'

412

Baz acted shocked. 'Don't be daft. Like what?'

'I dunno. Like threaten him or give him a dig?'

'Course not. Whaddya think I am?' Ricky wouldn't have a clue he'd given him anything untoward, as he shoved a square of Yorkie Bar in his gob at the same time as the tab.

'He ain't half acting like an oddball now.'

'Well, he is one, let's be honest. You only gotta look at him to see that. I reckon he's just tired after all that grub. He didn't half scoff it fast. Give him a can of Stella to wash it down. That'll soon liven him up.'

Having been let down by Big Dave, Kenny got in contact with Teddy Abbott. Teddy was in his late sixties now, but was still a big name within the underworld. He was also the father of Kenny's ex partner in crime, Tony.

'Come in, son,' smiled Teddy. 'We'll go in the games room. The wife's in the lounge watching her shit TV programmes.'

Kenny followed Teddy and gladly accepted the large glass of brandy handed to him. He couldn't stop thinking about poor Ricky, prayed the lad was keeping it together.

Teddy offered Kenny a Montecristo cigar and lit one up himself. 'So, what can I do for you, Kenny?'

'I need a shooter, ASAP. My pal was meant to be sorting me one, but he's had to bolt up to Liverpool on a bit of urgent business.'

'I take it this has something to do with the Daley brothers?'

Kenny trusted Teddy and desperately needed to spill his guts to someone. 'Them cunts have kidnapped my Ricky.

Demanding half a mill for his safe return. I'm up to my neck in it and your son's nowhere to be seen in me hour of need. I need help, mate. Proper help.'

His wrists now tied more loosely in front of him, Ricky lifted up his can to have a gulp of lager. He still felt odd, couldn't shake the feeling off. Perhaps he'd caught food poisoning off that sausage? Whatever it was, it was making him paranoid. 'Could you untie my feet, please? The rope's bothering me. I won't try to run away, I promise.'

'Whaddya reckon, Ginge? Can we trust him?' grinned Baz.

''Ere a minute,' gestured Ginger. He slung a small see-through bag of white powder onto the kitchen worktop. 'Charlie, left over from the other night. Want a line?'

'Does the Pope pray?' chuckled Baz, snatching the rolled-up tenner out of his brother's hand.

Ginger did a couple of fat lines, then dragged his brother back into the front room. 'We've decided to untie ya, on one condition, Ricky.'

'What?'

'That you entertain us. Know any songs or dance moves, do ya?'

Desperate to be untied, Ricky would have agreed to most things. 'Erm, yeah. I'm a good dancer.'

'Wonderful,' chuckled Ginger. 'I'll pop out, stock up on the beers. Then as soon as I return, we'll untie ya. You better be bloody good though, Ricky, as me and Baz don't suffer fools lightly. Oh, and a word of warning, if you try to do a runner, I'll chop both your big toes off. Understand?'

When the brothers started laughing at him, Ricky started to panic again. Ginger's diamond-studded gold tooth was freaking him out and Baz looked like a were-wolf with his shoulder-length wavy brown hair and beard. He shut his eyes again. Why was this happening to him? He just wanted to go home.

Deep in thought, Teddy Abbott paced up and down his games room. He liked Kenny. They went back years. However, he could understand his son not wanting to get involved. That business with the ecstasy pills was old news and Tony had since built a new life for himself in sunny Spain. He also had two young children to look out for. Which is why Teddy had decided to offer Kenny the best help he could. 'I know a couple of men who run the doors out Basildon way. Proper geezers. Trustworthy. Let me speak to them, see if they can find out where the Daley brothers have taken your boy. In the meantime though, I can get you a piece, but do you really want to take that chance? You have no idea where they want you to drop the money off yet. If it's somewhere public, ya can't just start firing a gun, and if it's somewhere remote, chances are they'll be armed or have some form of backup.'

'So, what do I do? I ain't gonna be able to get me hands on half a mill in cash by six tomorrow. A few hundred grand, maybe. But, there's no way I want them walking away with a penny. Me and Tony never grassed those cunts. It was just bad luck their men took the rap. The Old Bill needed a conviction and they obviously weren't careful enough. End of. But it's the boy, ain't it? They've got me by the bollocks by snatching Ricky. I love

415

that lad. I can't bear to think of him being with those two arseholes. I want 'em dead, Teddy. Whatever the outcome, I want them dead.'

'Get it done professionally then. You can afford it, and it saves you spending the rest of your life in prison. I know of a good hitman. Hire him to do your dirty work.'

Kenny put his head in his hands. He might not have contact with Donny and Sherry now, but they were adults, had their own families and lives. The twins still needed him though, as did Ricky and Jake. Teddy was right. Why would he want to go back to prison when he could get a professional to do his dirty work? 'Can you ring the hitman for me? It'd be handy if he turns up when I'm dropping off the dosh. As long as I've got Ricky back at that point, of course.'

'Oh, come on, Ken. You're a man of the world. You know as well as I do, professional hitmen don't work like that. I don't even know the bloke personally. All I know is he is referred to as "The Assassin" and who to go through to make contact. But that's neither 'ere nor there at present. You gotta get your Ricky back first. Why don't you let me chat to the other blokes? If anyone knows where your boy is being held, they will.'

'Do "Oops Up Side Your Head" – you must know the rowing song?' laughed Baz.

'I do.' Ricky sat on the stained carpet, swaying from side to side.

'Nah. Stand up, Ricky,' ordered Ginger. 'You ain't very good at that one. What about "Night Fever"? You must remember those Travolta moves?'

'Not really.' Ricky put his hands on his knees. He felt hot and out of breath. 'I know "YMCA" though.'

'Nah. Fuck that. You're boring me now,' replied Ginger. 'Tell us about that bird in the green dress. The one you were with today.'

'That's my fiancée. We're getting married.'

Baz burst out laughing. 'Fuck me, imagine standing up the aisle and seeing that walk towards ya. You'd run a mile.'

Ricky sat back down on the wooden chair and closed his eyes. He still felt weird, could see shapes and everything seemed so bright. Apart from Ginger and Baz. They were just horrible. He knew they were taking the mickey out of him too. Yet, he would continue dancing to their tune, literally, if that meant they wouldn't chop his big toes off.

'You shagged her yet?' enquired Baz.

'Course. We bonk all the time.'

'Bonk!' Ginger laughed out loud. 'I ain't heard that expression since the eighties. She suck your knob, does she?'

'Yes.' Ricky wasn't particularly happy discussing his and Candy's sex life, but what choice did he have?

'I bet you like licking her fanny, don't ya?' Baz chuckled.

'No. I don't actually. I tried it once and it tasted like fish. I don't like fish much.'

When the Daley brothers rolled around the floor laughing, Ricky had no idea what he'd said that was so funny.

Ginger handed Ricky another Stella. 'Funny fucker you are. What's her name? Your fishy-smelling bird.'

'Candy.'

'Nah. You're having a laugh. You gotta be,' shrieked Baz. 'That can't be her real name.'

'It is. I swear.'

'Fuck me,' laughed Baz. 'The parents must be complete notrights, worse than her. If they had any sense they'd have called her Rover. What a dog! And that's a bit of an insult to dogs, if I'm truthful. Most of them are far better looking.'

Ginger was rolling around the carpet in stitches. 'He's right, Ricky. Candy ain't much of a looker is she, lad? In fact, she's that ugly, if she were a dog, her owners would shave her arse and walk her backwards.'

'What was that song? I'm sure it was called Candy. It had a dance to it,' said Baz.

'Candy Girl?'

'Nah. Later than that. More recent. The same band that sang, "Word Up".'

Ginger leapt up. 'Cameo! And I remember the dance. Stand up, Ricky. This is gonna be your wedding moves and song, when you marry the rottweiler.'

By early hours of the morning, Ricky was flagging. He looked at his watch. It was gone five a.m. He never stayed up this late. Thankfully, all the weird visions and paranoia he'd been feeling earlier had mainly worn off. But it had left him feeling very tired. He'd also been urged to drink numerous cans of Stella, which had only added to his fatigue.

Out in the kitchen, Ginger and Baz were snorting the last of the cocaine. 'Can't you call someone? Shout us up some more,' suggested Baz.

'Don't talk daft. We're holding a geezer hostage, ya plonker. We need to be back on the ball by the time Bond rings us later. What we'll do is wait until these last lines have worn off, then take it in turns to get our nut down. One stays guard, while the other has a kip on Dodger's bed.'

Baz's mind turned to the actual tabs in the shoe box. No way would Ginger know if he took one now and Ricky could do with another, just for the comedy value.

'I need a crap. That gear's going straight through me,' Ginger informed his brother.

Baz acted swiftly. He swiped two tabs, put one on his tongue, grabbed a Stella from the fridge and dropped the other inside the can. He then handed it to Ricky. 'Drink that. It'll liven you up, I promise.'

'I need food, not more drink. I'm hungry.'

'Drink that quickly and I'll make sure you get a nice fry-up for breakfast. Go on.'

Stomach rumbling like mad, Ricky downed the lager.

'Morning. Did you sleep? I've checked the local news. Nothing else been reported,' Kenny informed Beau. With everything going on, he'd hardly slept a wink. He couldn't stop thinking about Ricky.

Beau sat up in bed and squinted at the alarm clock. 'Bloody hell, Gramps. You shit the bed?'

'I woke up early 'cause I need you to open up the garden centre today. I got some running around to do.'

'No worries. I was going to work anyway.' Beau felt a mixture of excitement and trepidation. Today was the day when karma would hopefully be shoved into Jolene's face, literally. She deserved everything coming her way, that bitch. But he still had slight concerns that Mad Dog and Badger might balls things up. 'Ricky all right?'

'Yeah. He stayed round Candy's. Her parents are away,' lied Kenny. He was hopeful the blokes Teddy Abbott knew would come up trumps for him. They'd agreed to help out last night when Teddy had called them.

'I was thinking, be nice for me, you and Brett to go out for an Indian or something tonight, seeing as we ain't got a woman between us to cook for us,' suggested Beau.

'I can't. I promised Jake I'd visit him later.' Kenny hated lying to his grandson, Beau especially. 'You go out with Brett. Don't get bladdered though, please. Just in case another witness comes forward or something. You need to have your wits about you all the time.'

Beau nodded. He had his wits about him all right. He would make damn sure he was acting normally and around numerous people when Jolene got her comeuppance. Hence his decision to work all day and go out for an Indian afterwards.

Back on Marks Gate estate, Ricky had started to panic again. Those horrid visions and feelings had returned and they were much worse than before. He could see big spiders now, they were crawling all over the curtains too and some were coming towards him across the laminated floor. 'I need a poo,' he panted.

'In a minute,' chuckled Ginger. 'You need to perfect this wedding dance first.' It had been hilarious when Baz had sorted through Dodger's CD collection and found the Cameo song on a compilation. 'Ready? Come on. One, two, three.'

Ricky began the dance. 'Just like Candy,' he said.

'Sing it. Don't just say it,' ordered Baz.

'Oh no!' Feeling the excrement leak from his backside, Ricky burst into tears. He'd shit himself, and it was a runny one.

'You dirty bastard.' Baz held his nose.

'Don't just stand there,' scolded Ginger. 'Get your kecks off quick, then go clean yourself up.'

As Ricky pulled his trousers down, his penis fell out of his pants.

'Fuck me! Size of that. That ain't a cock. It's a button mushroom,' laughed Baz.

Praying Kenny would turn up soon, an embarrassed Ricky just wanted to die of shame.

'Good morning, darling. How you feeling?' asked Lori. She'd loved having Brett stay over last night, even though the circumstances surrounding his visit left a lot to be desired.

Brett sat up. 'I feel better than I did and I've been thinking about what you said, about Cyprus. I want to go with you. I doubt Beau will come, 'cause he won't want to leave his kids. But he's had a holiday this year, with Gramps. I need one too, Mum.'

Lori stroked her son's blond hair. Carl had a friend in the music business that owned a villa in Northern Cyprus and had kindly said they could stay there. 'Have a word with your brother; try to convince him to come too. We'll book the flights later today. But first things first, you need feeding. What would you like for breakfast?'

Brett smirked. His mum was so calming and even

though life wasn't great at present, he knew she would help him get back on track. 'You decide. I'll ring Beau.'

'Hurry up,' urged Mad Dog. 'We don't wanna be late.'

'I don't know why we gotta get there so early. Beau said she was meeting her cousin this afternoon, not this morning.' complained Badger. He hadn't got up at this unearthly hour for years.

'Yeah. But, she's meeting her cousin in Lakeside. How'd you know she ain't gonna get there early and go shopping first?'

'Well, I don't.'

'Exactly! Listen, the quicker we get this job done, the quicker we'll be living it up in Thailand. Imagine all the drugs we'll consume and the birds we'll pump.'

Badger grinned. 'It's gonna be cosmic.'

Jolene waited for her father to leave before running over to her mum's with Romany in her arms. 'Can you do me a big, big favour?'

'What?'

'Jimmy just rang me. He's not working today 'cause of the wind and rain. Can you have the kids all day instead of just this afternoon? I can meet him first then before I go to Lakeside.'

Evie sighed. She desperately wanted her daughter to be happy, but not if it were affecting the chavvies. 'This can't continue, love, all this underhandedness. Your dad really ain't happy with you flitting off all the time. Rocky said something to him the other day about you not being a proper mum any more.'

'I know and if I could take the chavvies with me, I would. But I can't for obvious reasons.' Romany was saying and understanding certain words now, so Jolene even had to be careful what she said in front of her.

'Beau's gonna find out at some point, Jolene. I bet the boys have already told him you don't take them out with you any more.'

'Oh, don't exaggerate, Mum. I took all three out yesterday.'

'I'll have 'em today, but I don't want you driving all the way to and from Lakeside alone. It's too far and I'll worry.'

'No. It isn't. I drove there last week with Jimmy. He showed me the back way to go, so I hardly have to touch any main roads.'

Evie sighed again, this time more deeply. She'd been woken up by a lone magpie smashing its beak against her window this morning. Never a good sign. 'Promise me you'll drive carefully.'

Jolene grinned. 'I promise to drive as slowly as a snail crawls.'

'Good morning.'

'There she is!' Tina grabbed Sharon's arm. 'I've been dying to know all the goss. Why didn't you call me back?'

'Because I stayed at Ray's over the weekend and last night.'

'Oh my God!' Tina put her hand over her mouth. 'You've finally done the deed with him, haven't you?'

Sharon could barely wipe the smile off her face. Apart from her mum's poor health, she felt the happiest she had in a long time. 'I did, and yesterday we booked the holiday of a lifetime in Hawaii. We're going in July for a whole month.'

'Bloody hell! You got a keeper there, mate.' Even though Tina was thrilled for her friend, she couldn't help but feel a tad envious. She had no luck with men whatsoever, only attracted life's losers.

'He's even mentioned me moving in with him and part of me is tempted. I feel it would be good for me now to get away from Dark Lane and not having to see Kenny any more. But, I'm worried it's a bit too soon. Let's be honest, I barely know the man.'

About to reply, the conversation was cut short by Donny. 'Mum, I need a word. In private.'

Sharon followed her son into the nursery office. 'What's up, love?'

'I had a disturbing phone call 'ere yesterday when I was counting up the takings. To do with Dad. He's upset the wrong people, put it that way.' His father had begged him not to tell his mother that Ricky had been abducted, reckoned the shock might give her a heart attack.

Sharon's rosy cheeks faded to white. 'Is he OK, your dad? He's not hurt, is he?'

'Nah. I was just told to give him a message. But, I fear the situation is serious. I let the caller know that me and you had nothing to do with Dad, as I don't want us being targeted next.'

'Next! Who's being targeted then?'

'Nobody. Only him, I should imagine,' lied Donny. 'I think it's best you stay away from Dark Lane though, until all this is sorted. Can you stay at Ray's?'

'Well, yeah. But I still need to visit your nan. I pop in to see her all the time. What's your father done, Donny? I need to know.'

Donny flopped onto the office chair and held his head in his hands. 'That turnout that time, those ecstasy pills, where people were dropping like flies, including Tammy. Dad was the one making 'em, Mum. He was the main man, the supplier. Him and Tony Abbott.'

Being held hostage was the worst thing that had ever happened to Ricky in his lifetime. He'd thought losing his parents in a car crash was bad enough, yet the situation he was now in suddenly seemed far worse. The Daley brothers looked like scary monsters, the spiders were breeding like flies, his heart was beating like a drum and he truly feared he was about to die. He also stank of shit.

Ginger had gone to bed in the other room with a very stern warning. 'I'll leave you untied, but believe me, you try to creep out that front door and down them stairs, I will catch ya and I'll chop your button mushroom off.'

As for Baz, he was dancing around the front room, making Ricky even more anxious. Every time he closed his eyes to block out the spiders, Baz would poke him, then appear in front of him resembling a giant werewolf.

Having already planned his escape route, Ricky was just waiting for the right moment. That moment finally came when Baz decided he was hungry and began raiding the kitchen cupboard.

Ricky felt no fear as he moved the wooden chair and opened the big window. Seconds later, he jumped.

CHAPTER TWENTY-NINE

Baz ran into the bedroom and shook Ginger. 'Wake up. He's gone. He fucking jumped.'

'You what?'

'Out the window. I only went into the kitchen. What we gonna do?'

Wondering if his brother had lost the plot, Ginger looked out of the window. 'Shit! You idiot. I told you not to take your eyes off him.' Dodger's flat was on the third floor, which was the top floor. Down below was a big patch of grass with a small brick wall around the outside of it. Thankfully, Ricky had landed in the centre of the grass. 'Come on, we need to get him back. Quick.'

Ginger bolted down the stairs and kneeled on the grass. 'You all right? Come on, get up.' Ricky didn't reply or move, just looked at him glassy-eyed.

A woman who'd been walking her dog ran over. 'I'll go home, call an ambulance.' She pointed upwards. 'I heard a loud thud. I think he fell out of one of those windows.'

'Nah, nah. We saw it,' bluffed Ginger. 'He was walking on that wall and fell. That's all.'

The Nigerian man who lived in the ground-floor flat appeared. 'I hear noise too, but he not live here.'

Totally out of his nut, Baz was as unresponsive as Ricky until his brother roughly grabbed him by the arm. A couple more people had appeared now. This wasn't looking good. 'Go upstairs; get our phones and his phone. I put his in the bedroom. Oh, and our jackets and keys. We need to get away from 'ere,' he hissed. 'Meet me where we parked the van and don't forget nothing,' he added.

When an elderly man appeared saying, 'It's OK. My wife's called an ambulance,' Ginger knew his luck was poxed.

'Is he breathing?' asked someone else.

Sensing his moment, Ginger knelt back down next to Ricky. 'You got an ambulance coming,' he hissed in his ear. 'You don't mention our names, what happened or being in that flat to anyone. You got drunk and fell off that wall. Say anything wrong and we'll come back and kill Candy.'

Having no idea she was being followed, Jolene pulled into the Palms Hotel off the A127. Usually, Jimmy would pick her up from there and drive them to what they now joked was their 'Love Nest' in Bulphan. But today, they were short on time, so Jimmy had booked them a room at Palms.

Observing the situation, Badger turned to Mad Dog. 'No wonder he wants her disfigured. She's obviously shagging that geezer.'

'He wants her blinded,' Mad Dog reminded his partner in crime.

As a big gust of wind rocked the stolen van, Badger said the obvious. 'We're gonna have to get right close up to her unless this wind dies down.'

'Yeah. Too bloody close for my liking.'

Inwardly fuming, because he'd heard from the lads that Jolene was currently getting her end away in that seedy hotel along the A127, Beau plastered a fake smile on his face as he turned up at his mother's house to pick up his brother's car.

Brett greeted Beau at the front door. 'You OK with me going on holiday with Mum? I don't wanna leave you in the shit, but we've been checking the news and if anything, the crash story seems to have died down. I so need to get away, get a bit of sun, like you did with Gramps.'

'Yeah. I get it. That's fine. Where is Mum?'

'In the kitchen.'

Beau gave his mother a hug and wished her a lovely time. 'I might come out there at some point, surprise the pair of ya. Give me the address of where you're staying, Mum?'

'Come with me, Beau, and I'll get it for you. Brett, could you make me another Cappuccino please, darling?'

Carl had taken Hope out to visit his mum at the luxurious care home she was residing in, so Lori dragged Beau into Carl's music studio. 'I'll give you the address, write it down in some kind of code. Think of something only you will understand. I haven't said this to your brother because he's not as strong as you, but the reason

428

Carl and I thought Northern Cyprus was best, is because the police won't be able to touch you there. There are no extradition laws. I mean, I'm not saying any more witnesses will come forward. But three teenagers dying and one still in intensive care probably means the investigation will continue for quite a while. The family are bound to demand answers. I know I would.'

For the first time that day, Beau's smile was genuine. 'Do you know what, you're a star, muvver. Not just any old star. A fucking superstar!'

Unable to concentrate on anything other than getting Ricky home, Kenny was going out of his mind. He didn't even care about the money any more. Teddy Abbott had given him fifty grand towards the ransom and he'd managed to come up with the bulk himself. All in all, he had over three hundred and fifty grand stuffed in two sports holders, which if worse came to worst, should be enough to get Ricky back home.

Kenny snatched at his phone as it rang. Surprisingly, it was Sharon. Surely Donny hadn't told her about Ricky? 'All right, Shal? What's happening?'

'Don't you all right me, you no-good arsehole. I know about the pills. I know everything. Disgusted ain't the word. You truly are a despicable man, Kenny. Don't you ever contact me again. You're dead as far as I'm concerned, and when you do die, no way will God allow you in heaven. He'll leave you to rot in hell.'

When Sharon cut him off, Kenny sank to his knees. His life was doomed. Well and truly.

*

Ricky was still lying in the same spot when the ambulance arrived. He was cold, soaked through to the skin, but that was the least of his worries. He was still getting those bad visions. He couldn't see spiders any more, but all the people looked scary, their faces distorted, their noses enormous. He couldn't move his head or legs either, both felt as though they were weighed down, too heavy to lift up.

When two men in green uniform knelt either side of him, gently asking questions, Ricky tried to answer. But he couldn't. His mouth was opening, but no words would come out of it. It was at that point, an even bigger panic started to set in.

Stuffing the rest of the Esso egg mayonnaise sandwich in his gob, Mad Dog nudged Badger. 'She's coming out. Look! And she's on her own.'

Badger sat bolt upright. There was no CCTV where their vehicle was parked, or Jolene's. There were quite a few cars parked up nearby, but no occupants inside them. 'Get ready, yeah.' It had been decided by Badger that Mad Dog perform the actual deed. He was a far better shot than him at football, darts and snooker. It made sense.

'Shit! He's coming out now and he's following her over to her car.'

'Oh, bollocks! But at least they look like they're leaving separately. Fingers crossed she heads to Lakeside now, like Beau reckoned she would. Be better to do it there anyway, will look more like a mugging at Lakey. I bet nobody's ever been mugged 'ere before.'

'Yeah. You're right. Best to be safe than sorry.'

*

'What you doing now?' Baz asked his brother. He was still tripping out of his nut, yet trying his best to disguise it.

'Trying to work out how to sort out your mess, you twat.' In turmoil, Ginger had driven straight back to their own flat after the incident. They were now sharing a two-bed flat, having had their house in Stanford-le-Hope repossessed while in prison.

'I only went in the kitchen to make a pot noodle. How was I to know he'd try to commit hurry curry?'

'Go pack some clothes. We ain't staying 'ere.'

'Why?'

'Just do as I say. I'm gonna ring Bond, see if I can salvage something outta this fucking shambles.'

'You what!' spat Kenny. He was finding it hard to comprehend what was being said to him.

'It weren't our fault, I swear. We did the right thing and called the ambulance,' lied Ginger. 'Look, I've been thinking all this has got a bit out of hand. You meet us today with three hundred grand and we'll call it quits.'

'Where'd the ambulance take him? Where is he now?' bellowed Kenny. He'd thought Ginger was on a wind-up at first.

'We dunno. We couldn't hang around, could we? But we did a good thing, the right thing, we got the lad help. We could've left him there or kept him holed up. Three hundred grand and I swear you'll never hear from us again.'

'You ain't getting a penny outta me and you wanna hope that boy ain't badly hurt. 'Cause if he is, I'll be putting a bullet straight through your fucking skulls.'

*

'Shall we do it now?' Mad Dog suggested. 'She's got a handbag that we can snatch.' They'd followed Jolene to Lakeside Shopping Centre.

Badger looked around. 'Nah. There's way too many people about. 'We'll do it when she comes out. As soon as one of them motors moves in front of where she's parked, I'll move the van so our back doors are facing the front of her motor. When she returns, you can be in the back of the van and ya just jump out, do her in the eyes, grab the handbag, then we go.'

'What about her jewellery? Beau said to snatch some of that.'

'It's too public 'ere to faff around. I couldn't see if she had a necklace on, but just go for that if she has, and the bag.'

Mad Dog chewed at his already sore fingernails. 'Can't I be the getaway driver and you do the deed?'

'No. We already decided, you've a better shot than me.'

Out of his mind with worry, Kenny dashed into the A&E Department of Oldchurch Hospital. 'Move, move,' he shouted, as he barged his way to the front of the queue. 'I had a phone call from a pal whose wife is a nurse 'ere,' Kenny explained to the miserable-looking receptionist. 'My son, he's Down's syndrome; he's been rushed in 'ere.'

'There is a queue, sir,' pointed the receptionist.

'Yes. I know there's a fucking queue. I can see it. But this is extremely urgent. Jeanette Barry is the nurse. I need you to get her, so she can take me to my boy. She said to ask for her.'

'What's your name, sir?'

'Kenny Bond.'

'Stand over there, Mr Bond, away from the queue, and I'll try to locate Nurse Barry for you.'

Kenny paced up and down, his mind playing tricks with him. The phone call from his pal, David Barry, had come straight after Ginger's. David had informed him that a lad matching Ricky's description had arrived at the hospital via ambulance, but had no identification on him and he wasn't speaking. 'I know Jeanette's only met Ricky a couple of times, but she's sure it's him because of his dyed blond hair.'

Kenny said a silent prayer. Why wasn't Ricky talking? He didn't stop rabbiting as a rule. Something had to be badly wrong.

'Kenny.'

'Hello, Jeanette. Thanks so much for calling David. How is he? I've been worried sick about him.'

'He's not good, Kenny. We have no idea what's happened to him because he's unable to tell us. It seems he'd been drinking alcohol and may also have consumed some kind of drug. We're waiting for the blood tests to come back.'

'Nah, nah, nah. Ricky would never take drugs. I promise ya that much. Can I see him? He'll talk to me. Tell me everything.'

Jeanette led Kenny to a cubicle with the curtains drawn around it.

One look at Ricky confirmed Kenny's worst fears. 'Oh, boy. My boy.' Tears rolled down Kenny's face as he stroked Ricky's deathly white cheek. He had a neck brace on and a terrified expression in his eyes. An expression that would haunt Kenny until his dying day.

*

433

'Jolene,' beamed her cousin, Kirsty. Jolene had been unable to make her big birthday meal in Swanley on Saturday, so they'd arranged to meet today at the little Italian restaurant in Lakeside.

'How you been? Feels like ages since I've seen ya.'

A waiter appeared handing the girls two menus.

Kirsty waved her hand. 'We're not ready to order yet, but we'll have two pints of coke.' She clasped Jolene's hands. 'A little birdy tells me you and Jimmy Dean are erm, getting very friendly.'

'Who said that?'

'Jimmy's mum to my mother-in-law. They're mates. So come on, spill the beans.'

Every time she thought of Jimmy, Jolene couldn't stop smiling and today was no exception. 'If I tell ya, you promise me you say nothing to no one?'

'Hand on heart.'

'I was with Jimmy earlier. I'm in love, Kirst, and he feels the same. So much so, we've decided to take the plunge and move in together.'

'Bloody hell!' chuckled Kirsty. 'Yous don't hang about, do ya? Nah, seriously, Jimmy's a good un. A decent man. Does his dead wife's family know?'

'No. And neither does Beau. That's the problem we got.'

'Life's too short not to be happy. And true love's hard to find, so you need to grasp it, if you find it. What was his wife's name? I forget.'

'Alicia.'

'Alicia's family are about to be a bit peeved 'cause she ain't been dead long. But, they'll come round. Gonna have to if they want to see their granddaughter, ain't they? As for Beau, he's a bellend. All mouth no action, those gorgers. Don't worry about him. What's he gonna do?'

Kenny sat in the corridor sipping a vile-coloured, pissy-tasting plastic cup of coffee. Had his sins from the past come back to haunt him? Only, nothing else could possibly go wrong. Everything already had. God must have some proper grudge against him. But he'd rather the bad things be happening to him, personally. Not via his loved ones whom he'd fought so hard all his life to protect.

'You all right, Kenny?' Jeanette sat down beside her husband's distraught friend.

'What's going on? What do the doctors really think's wrong? Please tell me. I'd rather know now, so I can prepare for the worst.'

'Nobody's sure at present. They want to do an MRI scan. It does seem as though he's been traumatized in some way. That would account for him being unable to speak. Once Ricky's coherent, I should imagine the police will want to interview him to find out what happened.'

'He won't wanna talk to no Old Bill. He's shit-scared of 'em. You make sure the police are kept away from him, Jeanette.'

'My shift finishes soon, but I'll let my colleagues know.'

'I heard a doctor say something about his legs and toes. That they weren't moving. What's that all about?'

'I don't know much about that,' lied Jeanette. She knew her colleagues feared Ricky had suffered a broken neck. She squeezed Kenny's hand. 'I've got to go now, but let's keep in touch via David. I'll say a prayer for him tonight.'

435

'You don't think he's gonna die, do ya?'

'His condition doesn't seem to be life-threatening. Life-changing, perhaps. But fingers crossed that isn't the case.'

Kenny put his mangled head in his hands. He'd picked Ricky's car up from Romford market with the spare key. It was waiting on the drive for him. Say he could never drive it again? Ricky had worked so hard to pass that test; he'd never be able to cope if his licence got snatched away from him.

Knowing he had to pull himself together, Kenny stood up. 'Is there a call box in 'ere, mate?' he asked a porter.

'Do a left at the bottom of the corridor, walk straight down the end and there's one on your right.'

Kenny picked up the phone. The receiver stank of a mixture of bad breath and fags. He stared at his mobile and punched in Teddy Abbott's number. If the Daley brothers were capable of doing this to Ricky, they were capable of anything. 'Ted, it's me. That geezer, The Assassin, I want you to get in contact with him. I don't care how much it costs; I want them Daley brothers dead. As soon as humanly possible.'

Still fuming over his Sunday lunch being ruined, Cormac Neary lay in wait. The problem with his Aidan was that he was easily led and immature, seemed to prefer the company of younger males, rather than knocking around with friends of his own age. That's what Cormac had convinced himself anyway.

Finding out what car Brett drove was easy. After his Italian meal had been so rudely interrupted, Cormac had headed straight to Aidan's apartment and got the car details off the old cockney security guard. Those apartments were incredibly expensive to purchase; anybody who came through security had their registration taken.

Having been watching the garden centre all afternoon, Cormac knew that Brett was the last to leave. He'd seen the work vans being parked up and the rest of the staff leave one by one.

Getting a bit impatient, Cormac rubbed the barrel of his gun. Every man needed friends, including Aidan. But when they became what Cormac referred to as a 'Special Friend', problems arose. The last time Aidan had a special friend was back in Ireland. Another young lad. Another nuisance. Which had unfortunately ended with Finlay's head being blown off in front of his son. A lesson learned. Or so you'd think.

Cormac sighed. Such a waste of a young life, Finlay's death. It also could have been avoided, if only Aidan had listened to his warnings.

Beau locked up the portacabin with half a smile on his face. He'd spoken to Badger, who'd reassured him all was going to plan. The police had no more leads or witnesses to the accident. In fact, the crash was kind of yesterday's news. It hadn't been mentioned on any local news all day.

As he strolled towards Brett's car, Beau was stunned, literally, as he was smashed across the back of the head by something hard. He fell to the ground in a daze. 'What the hell!' The man glaring at him was menacing-looking yet smartly dressed in a white shirt, grey slacks and an ox-blood leather jacket. He also had a tasty type of gun in his hand.

Cormac bent over and roughly shoved the barrel of the gun deep inside Beau's mouth. 'You ever go near my son again, I will blow your fucking brains out. I know what you are and he's not like you. He has a child and a wife back in Ireland. He's a happily married man.'

His life flashing before him, all Beau could think about was his kids. He had no idea who the mad Irishman was, or what he was talking about. Instinct told him to stay schtum and not ask questions.

As the man walked out the gates, Beau lay still, trying to compose his erratic breathing. Seconds later, he heard a vehicle roar away.

Jolene paid for the boots in Top Shop, then glanced at the time. 'I'm gonna have to go now, Kirst. Mum's had the chavvies all day and I don't wanna leave it no later in case it starts getting dark. I've not driven in the dark yet.'

'I need to get going too. Been lovely to see ya, and don't forget to keep me updated about lover boy. I needs to know when to buy a hat,' Kirsty joked.

Jolene rolled her eyes. 'I got to get a divorce first. Where you parked?'

'Debenhams end. You?'

'The other end. I'll call you soon.'

Jolene left her cousin and made her way back to her vehicle. It was still a bit windy, but not as bad as earlier. The rain had thankfully stopped now too.

When her phone rang, Jolene put down her shopping to pull it from her handbag. 'What now, Mum?' Her mother had already rung her three bloody times.

'You left there yet? Only I got one of me bad feelings, Jolene. Had it all day, I have.'

'For Christ's sake! Will you stop it, Mum. I'll be fine. I'll drive slowly and I'll be home soon. I'm just leaving 'ere now.'

'You be extra careful.'

Jolene picked up her bags and walked towards her car. Seconds later, a man in a dark hoodie appeared and she was squirted with a liquid. A liquid so potent, she could literally feel her skin bubbling and burning. 'Help! Help me. Help!' she screamed desperately. The pain was horrendous, torture. Was her neck on fire? Her shoulder? Her face?

The agony proved that severe; Jolene's body could not bear it any longer. It was at that point, she fainted.

Feeling too shaky to drive and desperately needing a stiff drink, Beau called a cab and left Brett's car at work.

It took a lot to jangle his nerves, but that Irish nutter had managed it. 'How much do I owe you, mate?' he asked the cabbie. He wasn't one bit hungry, but had got dropped at the Indian Gramps liked. The staff knew him and Brett in there and most importantly, could tell the difference between the two of them.

'Ahh, Mr Beau. No Mr Brett today?' smiled Darsh, the owner.

'Nah. He's swanning off on holiday, him. Lucky sod,' joked Beau, desperately trying to sound and act normal. 'Can you get me a large brandy and a bottle of Tiger beer please, mate? Had to deal with the customers from hell today.'

As Darsh walked away, Beau's burner phone rang. 'All right?'

'It's done,' Mad Dog informed Beau.

'You away from there?'

'Yep.'

'Any issues?'

'Not really. Couldn't get any gold. Couldn't see any on her. Got the handbag though and I grabbed her shopping bags just to make it look more real.'

'You need to torch everything.'

'Will do. As soon as it gets proper dark.'

'Good lads. Give me a couple of days and I'll sort yous the rest of the wonga out.'

'You said we could have it the following day,' Mad Dog reminded Beau.

'You can have it, as soon as I can get me hands on it. I have got it. It's stashed away though. You get her bang in the eyes?'

'Erm. Yeah. I think so.'

'Whaddya mean by think so?'

'As I did it, there was a big gust of wind. She went down like a sack of shit though, screaming for England.'

'Good. I'll call you on *that* phone tomorrow. Whatever you do, don't call me on your normal phone, OK?' Beau ended the call. He would have loved to have witnessed Jolene rolling about the ground in terrible distress. What comes around goes around, he smirked.

By the time he'd eaten and had a couple more beers, Beau felt much more like his old self. He knew he must tell Gramps about the Irishman though. Perhaps Gramps might know who he was?

Still down the hospital and in absolute bits, Kenny

walked outside to take the call. They'd just informed him they'd found LSD in Ricky's bloodstream and he was not only stunned, he was livid. How could anybody be that cruel? To drug a lad with Down's. It was incomprehensible.

'What's up?' Beau asked. He could tell immediately something was very wrong. Surely Gramps hadn't already found out about Jolene? But how?

'I want you to stay at your mother's tonight. Do not come back to Dark Lane.'

'Why?'

'Because I got problems. Big problems. Go to your mum's and I'll pop over later and explain all.'

'Something bad happened to me today too, at work.' Beau then went onto explain about the Irishman.

Kenny smashed his fist against a nearby wall. 'Where are ya now?'

'In the Indian we like near Rayleigh. I was so shaken up; I had to get a cab 'ere.'

'Good. I don't want you driving. Ask Darsh to book you another cab and I'll meet you at your mother's in say, an hour.'

'Is this about the other thing? Ya know, what was on the news?'

'No. Speak in a bit.'

Another one in pieces was Evie. Jolene should have been home by now and she wasn't answering her calls.

'Sit down, woman. You'll wear the bloody carpet out,' demanded Bobby.

'Something's happened to her, Bobby. Something bad. I can feel it in me bones.'

Young Bobby-Joe turned around. 'Don't say that, Mum. You're scaring me.'

'You talking about my mum?' enquired Rocky.

'No. She's not.' Bobby fired a warning look Evie's way.

Levi put his hands on his hips. 'Where is Mum? We not seen her all day.'

'Go and look for her, Bobby. Please,' begged Evie. 'She said she was taking the back way wherever that is.'

'I know the way she means. Give it another fifteen minutes and if she's still not home, I'll go look for her.'

'Go now. He's done something to her, I knows he has. He's found out about her friendship with Jimmy Dean. I bets ya.'

'Rein it in. You're a bloody curse you are, woman.'

'How can you say that? I was right about Tammy. I knew something bad had happened to that girl that night. I told you it had. Nobody knows their own daughters like a mother does, Bobby Tamplin. I gave birth to them and I feels their pain. I always have.'

Starting to feel on edge himself, Bobby pulled his dealer boots on. Seconds later, a police car pulled up outside.

'The gavvers. The gavvers!' shrieked Evie. 'Not again. Not my baby. Not my beautiful Jolene.' Evie fell to her knees and prayed to the good Lord above.

When Bobby-Joe burst into tears, Bobby ordered Evie to stay inside with the chavvies. A minute later, Bobby was back with a face like thunder. 'Get your coat. We've gotta go to the hospital in Chelmsford. She's all right though. The gavvers said she'll be OK.'

Tears streaming down her cheeks, Evie pummelled her fists against her husband's broad chest. 'What's happened to her, Bobby? You tell me what's happened,' she cried. 'Cuntsmouth! I'll kill him, may God be my judge I will.'

'They says it looks like a mugging. But I'm not so sure. They threw acid at her, Evie, tried to burn her face.'

As reality hit home, Evie grabbed the table to support herself. That was the last of Psychic Lena's visions to come true. 'Heat', she'd said she'd seen. 'A burning, vicious heat.' Her poor baby.

Kenny turned up at Lori's, his face drawn, his skin ashen. He sat the boys down, told them about the Daley brothers and what had happened to Ricky.

The boys were stunned. 'Poor Ricky. Fucking hell! Where were they holding him hostage?' asked Brett.

'In some flat. He must've been so scared, the poor little sod, he chucked himself out of the window. My heart bleeds for him, it honestly does. What kind of monster gives a Down's lad LSD? Strokes like that are unheard of in my world. That's no different than forcing drugs down a little kiddie's throat. Wrong uns. Scum of the earth.'

'Wicked cunts,' spat Beau. 'They can't get away with this. We need to do something.'

'Believe me, they're dead men walking,' replied Kenny. He was yet to hear back from Teddy regarding The Assassin, but was hoping he would soon.

'He will talk again though, Ricky, won't he?' asked Brett.

'Doctor seems hopeful he will, reckons his speech loss is more to do with the trauma and extreme shock he's suffered. It's his movement they're more concerned about. They reckon he might've broken his neck.'

443

'Oh God!' exclaimed Beau. 'That's terrible.'

'They're doing more scans and tests tomorrow, so we'll know more then. They couldn't do much today in the end 'cause of the shit them cunts put in his system.'

'I honestly can't believe it,' mumbled Brett.

'Never rains it pours, don't it?' added Beau.

Kenny took his phone out of his pocket. It kept ringing, then stopping, then ringing again. Five missed calls he'd had, all from Bobby Tamplin. 'Hang on, I need to make a call. I'll go outside. I could do with a bit of fresh air.'

Lori comforted her sons when Kenny left the kitchen. Hope was upstairs being bathed by Carl. 'The surgeons and doctors can do marvellous things these days. I'm sure Ricky will recover in there.'

'Not with a broken neck, I doubt,' replied Beau bluntly.

'Kenny said they need to do more scans and tests yet. Let's say a prayer for Ricky. All of us.'

'All right,' Brett replied.

Lori sat on a stool in the middle of her beloved sons and held their hands. 'O Lord, the oil of your healing flows through me like a living stream. I choose to—'

The prayer was rudely interrupted by an irate Kenny grabbing Beau by the throat and forcing him up against the kitchen wall. 'Please tell me you ain't, but I already know that you have. You fucking clown. What were you thinking? We'll have murders now. As if we ain't got enough on our plate, you imbecile.'

'Kenny, put him down, please. Violence isn't the answer to any problem,' pleaded Lori.

'Best you teach your dumbass son that, not me,' seethed Kenny. 'Bobby Tamplin's going apeshit. He knows it was you. You'll never see those kids of yours. Not now, you fool.'

'I ain't done nothing,' shrieked Beau. 'What am I meant to have done?'

Kenny let go of Beau's neck and sank to his haunches. 'Jolene had acid thrown at her today, by someone who obviously had reason to want her maimed. The only person that's got that reason is you, Beau. Why did you do it?'

'I've been at work all day. I didn't do it,' Beau shouted.

His life in absolute tatters, Kenny stood up and faced Lori. 'You need to book another flight for Beau. Where you going? And when you flying?'

'Kyrenia. Northern Cyprus. Mine and Brett's flights are booked for tomorrow.'

'I can't go away. What about my kids?' panicked Beau. 'I can't just up and leave them.'

Kenny looked at his grandson and shook his head in despair. 'If you don't go away, I guarantee you'll be dead within a week. The Tamplins are raging, baying for your blood. You gotta go, Beau. You got no choice. It's either Northern Cyprus or a coffin. Take your pick.'

CHAPTER THIRTY

Three Months Later

Ricky Davey lay flat on his back, his eyes staring at the ceiling. He tried his hardest not to sleep these days, as he couldn't stand the nightmares, the terrors. He would dream he was back in that flat with the Daley brothers, their ugly faces distorted as they mocked him and forced him to sing and dance.

Thinking of how his life used to be, tears ran down Ricky's cheeks. He missed his job, had loved working at the garden centre, having a bit of banter with the lads and customers. His car he refused to even think about. That hurt far too much. He wished he could be at the gym again, lifting weights and running on the treadmill. He missed having his independence, going shopping for hours on end or popping out for meals. Then there was Candy. His beautiful fiancée, who no longer wanted to marry him. He didn't blame her, of course. If he was her he wouldn't want to marry him either. Not now.

'Morning, Big Man,' smiled Kenny. 'Did you manage to get much sleep?'

'A bit.'

Kenny opened the curtains and windows. Due to a broken neck, Ricky had spent over eight weeks in hospital. Once discharged, Kenny had brought him over to the Costa del Sol in a camper van he'd purchased especially for the journey. He didn't even want Sharon knowing where he was, so they'd travelled out on false passports. 'The boys have landed. They'll be 'ere soon. Let's get you bathed and all spruced up. They can't wait to see ya.'

'OK.' Ricky tried to smile, but his lip quivered. The last time he'd seen Beau and Brett, he'd been normal. He'd been him. He wasn't now. He was a paralysed, incontinent cripple and he hated himself.

Sharon Bond lay on a sun lounger reading a Martina Cole book. It was gripping, set in areas she knew well and the main character was a right arsehole who reminded her of Kenny.

Ray propped himself up on his elbow. 'You blanking me, or what?'

Smiling, Sharon put her book down and sat up. She'd had the best holiday ever in Hawaii. It was a beautiful place, idyllic. 'I wish we had another week left. Although I can't wait to see my mum.'

Ray stroked Sharon's face. 'We can always come back 'ere again. Or anywhere else you wanna go. I love travelling, seeing new places, experiencing new cultures. That's what life's all about. Especially with the woman of your dreams.'

Sharon laughed. Ray was so handsome, funny, kind, unselfish. All the things that Kenny wasn't. 'You're a bloody smoothie. I'm sure you must be too good to be true at times. Seriously though, I'd love to go on more holidays, see a bit of the world. Kenny never wanted to go away much. What about your work though?'

'I don't hardly work any more. Semi-retired. Couple of bits and bobs pop up 'ere and there. But, I did the sensible thing years ago. Got into the property game at the right time and earned meself a nice few quid.'

'I'll have money too for holidays. Once my divorce is settled. That's if that bastard ever shows his face again.' Sharon rolled her eyes. Kenny had disappeared recently and taken Ricky with him. The twins had disappeared too. Abroad no doubt, after what had happened to Jolene. Her poor Donny had suffered the brunt of that. The gypsies had driven a bulldozer into his house in Dark Lane and trashed the gaff. It was Donny's house that Beau and Brett had been living in before they'd fled the country.

'Your money's all yours, Shal. Where'd you reckon they are? Spain?'

Sharon shrugged. 'Probably. Partying in the sun some-where fancy, amongst a load of fellow criminal ex-pats, I should imagine. Be right up Kenny's street that. A legend in his own lunchtime,' she laughed.

Hearing his phone bleep, Ray read the message and smirked. Speak of the devil and it appears, he thought. He still hadn't decided what to do about this yet. But he would. By the time he got back to England anyway. He grabbed Sharon's hand. 'Let's go get some grub. I'm starving.'

*

'Rocky, Levi, stop that now,' shouted Jolene. Her sons were chucking all their toys out of the boxes she'd packed them in.

Rocky angrily stamped his foot. 'No. Don't wanna move. 'Dad won't know where to find us.'

'Your father is a shitcunt,' bellowed Evie. 'You know what he did to your mother. You should be ashamed of yourself for even mentioning him.'

'You the shitcunt,' scowled Rocky.

'Go wash your mouth out with soap,' bellowed Evie. 'He's the devil in disguise, your dad, and best you remember that.'

Levi put his hands on his hips. 'Don't care. Still our dad.'

Unable to stop herself, Evie clouted Levi around the head. 'He's evil. And you'll end up just like him if you're not careful. Now get out my sight.'

When Romany burst into tears, Bobby Tamplin picked up his granddaughter and led his wife away. 'I know you're angry and I get it. But keep arguing with those boys and they will turn against you, Evie. Let's have a break from the packing. Make us all a cup of tea. That'll calm you down.'

'Is that it, love? You got everything?' asked Geoffrey Bamber.

Karen glanced around at her beautiful home in Loughton for the very last time. She and the children had been so happy here, until Kenny had disappeared off the face of the earth and left her potless, unable to pay the rent. Overcome by a mixture of anger and sadness, Karen shut the door for the very last time. She had little savings, so was temporarily moving back in with her parents.

Jake clung to his mother as she got in the back of his grandparents' car.

'What's wrong, Jake?'

'Nanny said that Dad might be dead or in prison,' Jake sobbed.

Karen glared at the back of her mother's permed hair. 'What a charming thing to say to him. Thanks, Mum.'

Marjory Bamber pursed her lips. 'Well, it's true. Told you not to get involved in the first place. A married man and a gangster. What did you bloody expect?'

Seeing Tony pull up outside with the boys, Kenny ran outside the villa to greet his favourite grandsons. It was three months since he'd last seen Beau or Brett and he'd missed them big time. 'Go inside, lads, have a look round your new home. And try not to act shocked when you see Ricky. He ain't the way you'd remember him at all, but just act normal.'

Tony Abbott got out the car. He'd been glad when he'd been able to help out Kenny in the end. There'd been no way he would risk his partner and his two nippers' happiness by going back to England. He led a much simpler, quiet life now. But he'd felt terribly guilty over what those bastards had done to Ricky, as did his dad, Teddy. Which is why, when Kenny had contacted him, he'd pulled out all the stops. The villa he'd found Kenny was superb, the absolute nuts, and he'd got it at such a cheap price to rent. He'd also sorted out everything for today. He knew the score and would have his pal's back in whatever he needed from now on. But only in Spain.

'Cheers for picking up the boys and for everything else,' said Kenny.

Tony grabbed hold of Kenny and hugged him close. 'Everything's sorted onboard. I just want you to know I think you're doing the right thing, if you know what I mean?'

'I know exactly what you mean, mate. Thanks again.'

'Conor, help me carry these shopping bags in,' said Aidan Neary.

Aware that her men were home, Brianna Neary opened the front door, a big smile on her face. 'What did you get, Conor? Did you spend all your father's money? All those bags! So many,' she chuckled.

Aidan strolled indoors and kissed his loving wife on the cheek. Brianna was a good-looking woman. An ex-Irish beauty queen. 'He's worse than you to take shopping. Never again,' joked Aidan.

'Sit down, boys. I have some exciting news to tell you.'

Aidan obediently sat on the sofa. After the turnout with Brett, his father had ordered him to return to his family home in Dundalk until further notice. He was still getting paid for doing nothing, but was missing London. Life in Dundalk was so slow in comparison.

'Tell us then, Mam,' urged Conor.

'You're going to have a little brother or sister,' beamed Brianna, looking at Aidan's reaction. She hated her husband working away in London, hoped her news might keep him at home more.

451

'Oh wow! How'd that happen? I thought you were taking precautions.' Aidan didn't know if he were coming or going. He loved Conor, but he was a teenager now. Aidan wasn't a baby person.

'I was,' Brianna fibbed. 'Must be God's work.'

Feeling like an animal trapped in a cage, Aidan excused himself to use the bathroom. Masturbating, he thought of Brett. Blond, beautiful, handsome Brett.

Evie looked forlornly out of the window as Jimmy Dean, Bobby and Sonny loaded Jolene's belongings into the van. Jolene didn't want to keep the beautiful home she'd shared with Beau, said it brought back too many bad memories.

Even though Jolene had needed a skin graft on her neck and shoulder and had been in a hell of a lot of pain, she'd been relatively lucky. She didn't remember much about the attack, said it had happened so quickly, but she recalled a lad in a dark hoodie and knew that he'd aimed for her eyes, face, or both. It was only a gust of wind that had saved her whole life from being ruined.

Watching Rocky and Levi playing up again, Evie cursed the little sods. She loved them dearly, but they were still part of *him*, had *his* wicked blood running through their veins. Her Johnny and Billy had gone ballistic over Jolene's injuries, had hunted high and low for Beau, but been unable to find him. So they'd driven a bulldozer through the front of his house as a warning of what was in store for him if he ever dared show his face again. As for the gavvers, they were useless, had put it down as a mugging, the fools.

Evie had been even more livid when Kenny Bond had insisted his grandson was innocent, had alibis as to where he'd been all that day. As if that proved his innocence. Beau might be the devil in disguise, but he wasn't bloody daft. He'd obviously hired somebody else to do his dirty work.

A lone tear rolled down Evie's face. Jolene was moving onto a site over in Kent. Jimmy's family all lived there, and her cousin Kirsty lived nearby. Jolene was going away and for the first time in her life, Evie would be waking up tomorrow to neither of her beautiful daughters. How she loathed that Bond family. Even her Bobby had seen the light, had no more to do with Kenny. Rumour had it, Kenny had disappeared too. Probably too scared of the repercussions, the coward. Evie wished them all dead. The whole lot of them.

Evie smiled as Jimmy Dean put a strong arm around her daughter and kissed her on the forehead. That was the only saviour. Jimmy was lovely, the type of lad her Jolene should have married in the first place. Bobby had now accepted their relationship, as had all Jolene's brothers. Jimmy's family had all welcomed Jolene with open arms too. Apparently, there was a bit of friction with his previous in-laws, but nothing that couldn't be smoothed over in time.

Seeing Jolene walk her way, Evie pulled herself together. 'You all packed?'

'Nearly, I'm leaving the rest to the men now.' Jolene adjusted the cotton scarf around her neck. She never left her home without one now, unless she was wearing a rollneck. She was way too conscious of her scars.

She had also been left with a couple of minuscule burns on her face, but did her best to cover those with make-up. 'You OK, Mum?'

It was at that point Evie broke down. 'I'm gonna miss you so much and the chavvies. I want to move to Kent too, but your father won't hear of it. I hate it here. The land's cursed.'

'Oh, Mum,' Jolene hugged Evie close to her chest. 'Kent's not that far and you can visit us all the time. I'm so sorry for leaving you, but I desperately need a fresh start. You won't be bored here. Billy and Johnny are moving back 'ere with all their chavvies and you got Sonny and Mary-Ann and Lily. You'll be rushed off your feet.'

'I suppose so. And I do want you to be happy somewhere safe. 'Cause *he* will return one day, Jolene, and try to snatch those chavvies. I just know he will.'

'Welcome aboard,' grinned Tony Abbott.

'Cor, this is nice, ain't it, Ricky?' Kenny wheeled Ricky onboard.

'Bloody hell!' Brett said, as he spotted the balloons and banner that read HAPPY 21ST, BOYS. 'We didn't realize it was a party for us. We thought you'd forgotten,' he chuckled. The twins had spent their actual birthday in Northern Cyprus with their mother.

'It was Ricky's idea,' smiled Kenny. 'He was upset he'd missed your big birthday. We both were.'

'Cheers, Ricky. We love it,' smiled Beau.

'Top man.' Brett bent down to give Ricky a hug. It was horrible seeing him like this, a shadow of his former bubbly self.

'Right, champagne's over there in ice,' pointed Tony. 'There's beers in the fridge and soft drinks. Spirits are next to the champers and there's plenty of Guinness for Ricky. I'll bring the hors d'oeuvres up, then set sail. We got loads of lovely grub for later, but you'll want to chill a bit first. Enjoy.'

'Look at the Jacuzzi, Ricky. You'll have to get in that later. We all will. Right, let's get you out that chair and on a sun lounger. Then I'll get you a Guinness.'

'Thanks, Kenny. But I need changing first. I think I shit myself.'

Badger and Mad Dog were livid. Not only had their trip of a lifetime to Thailand gone up the Swanee, Beau was on the missing list and he owed them fourteen grand.

'There must be a way we can find out where Beau is. Someone must know,' said Badger.

Mad Dog folded his arms. 'We've asked everyone up the garden centre and nobody knows. Or so they say.'

'Brett's obviously with him wherever they are, and Kenny, I reckon. Something must have happened for them all to do a runner at the same time. D'ya think it's 'cause of what we did to Jolene?'

Mad Dog shrugged.

'I wonder who cashes up the takings now at the garden centre? Perhaps we can rob 'em, get our money that way?' suggested Badger.

'Yeah. Especially if it's one of the old birds. I ain't gonna forgive Beau for this though. We trusted him and he ripped us right off. No wonder he only parted with a grand up front. Geezer's a cunt and if he shows his face round 'ere again and don't pay up, it'll be him getting acid in his face next time.'

It was the perfect day to be out on a luxury yacht. The weather was beautiful, as was the clear blue ocean. The atmosphere jovial, yet with a tinge of sadness.

'This is the life, eh?' said Kenny, tilting his head towards the sun.

'It certainly beats your old banger of a boat, Gramps,' joked Beau.

'Don't you knock *The Duchess*. We had some good times on her, me and your dad.' Kenny had once bought a boat for himself and Donny to make a living from. They'd hired it out for parties along the Thames and it held lots of personal memories. They'd had some great family parties on there too. Things had turned sour after firstly witnessing the *Marchioness* disaster, then Tammy Tamplin collapsing at the twins' sixteenth birthday party. Kenny sold the boat shortly after that. 'So, tell me about Northern Cyprus, lads. Did your mum look after you well?'

'Yeah. Mum's well cool, Gramps. She was great,' replied Brett. 'I really enjoyed spending lots of time with her.'

'She looked after us well. But she don't half bible-bash sometimes,' chuckled Beau.

'No, she don't. I think that's just stuff Mum learned from rehab. It's all part of her recovery. I think she's done brilliant to stay clean.' Brett had grown to truly love his mother, wouldn't have a word said against her.

'Right, let's get this party properly started. I'll open the bubbly and put some music on. Tony made up a couple of CDs for us, of all our favourite songs. There's lots of yours on there, Ricky.'

Ricky smiled, yet inwardly felt dreadfully sad. He had loved dancing to music, now he couldn't even do that.

Back in Hawaii, Ray and Sharon were drinking rum cocktails out of coconut shells.

'Blimey, these ain't half strong, Ray. I feel a bit light-headed.'

'They are a bit potent,' chuckled Ray. He'd purposely asked for them to be made strong, as he was hoping it might loosen Sharon's tongue a bit. 'You know we're gonna be living together, like, properly now, as in you moving all your stuff in and that?'

'Yeah.'

'Well, I don't think we should have any secrets. Especially recent ones. My ex was really secretive, and it ended up causing many a row between us. I don't want that to happen to me and you.'

'I agree. I hate arguing and keeping secrets. It still baffles me how many Kenny kept. I must have been so bloody thick.'

'No. You're not.' Ray propped himself up on his elbow. 'Tell me what happened with Kenny. I know he did or said something bad to you not long before we came away. What was it?'

Sharon sighed. 'I can't. It's too awful, Ray, but it was nothing to do with me, just something I found out about him.' Sharon still had no idea Ricky had been abducted, neither was she aware of his injuries. She just thought he'd gone abroad to live with Kenny without telling her.

457

'You don't have to tell me if you don't want to.'

'It's not that. I'm just ashamed of him and ashamed I was married to him.'

'Christ! It must be *bad*. Did he kill someone? I would never repeat anything, you know that.'

'God no. He wouldn't kill anyone. Not intentionally, anyway,' Sharon sighed. She owed Kenny nothing now. Her allegiance lay with Ray. 'You remember that scandal a while back, a load of youngsters died after taking a bad batch of ecstasy pills?'

'Yeah. It was plastered across the news and you told me about Tammy.'

'I found out Kenny was responsible. He set up a factory to make the pills and that bad batch were down to him and a partner. I didn't have a clue what he was up to, Ray, honestly. Makes me wonder now if I ever really knew him at all.'

Ray sat up, squeezed Sharon's hands and looked deep into her eyes. 'None of that's your fault, darling. Kenny's a shark. There's plenty of them out there.'

'Don't you ever turn out to be one, will you?'

'What you see is what you get with me, Shal, always. I'll go get us another drink.'

Ray sauntered up to the beach bar. *That* decision, the one he'd been toing and froing over, was now solved. All he had to do now was make the phone call.

After a lunch fit for Kings, Kenny, the boys and Ricky were all chilling inside the Jacuzzi, reminiscing.

Beau grinned. 'God, we used to love this tune, didn't

we, bro?' The song was Black Box's 'Ride on Time'. 'You remember us singing it at karaoke?'

'Yeah. 'Ere, Ricky, remember that time you cut Nanny Vera's beehive off at Gramp's barbecue? That was one of the funniest things ever,' laughed Brett.

'Yes.' Ricky said solemnly. Thinking of the past depressed him. He would never be that fun-loving person again.

Kenny put an arm around Ricky's shoulders. He'd brightened up a bit today, but not much. The light had gone out of his eyes. 'Hang on, I just remembered something.' Kenny jumped out the Jacuzzi and ran down to the lower deck. 'Tone, you got a pen and a bit of paper?'

'Yeah. Hang on. I'll get you one.'

Kenny returned minutes later and stood by the side of the Jacuzzi, letter in hand. 'This got sent to Tony yesterday, Ricky. I reckon it must've been delivered to Sharon.'

'What is it?' asked Ricky.

'A letter. I'll read it for you, Big Man. It says: "Dear Ricky, I'm so sorry that I couldn't get to the hospital to see you, but my mum and dad moved away to Norfolk and I had to go with them. I miss you loads and often think of the great times we had. I hope to see you again one day. Love always, Your fiancée, Candy."

'And she's put five kisses at the bottom,' added Kenny.

The light did momentarily return to Ricky's eyes until he remembered something. 'Candy couldn't have written that. She couldn't read or write!'

In a flat in Basildon, the Daley brothers were weighing up rocks of crack cocaine. After failing to get any money out of Kenny, they'd had to get back to work and earn some dosh somehow. They had debts to pay themselves.

The radio on in the background, both brothers burst out laughing as Cameo's 'Candy' came over the airwaves.

'I wonder how he's doing, our mate, Ricky?' chuckled Ginger. They'd not heard a peep from Kenny Bond, so guessed the lad had fully recovered from his little jump.

'I know it all went Pete Tong in the end, but that was a funny night. I got a confession to make an' all.'

'What?'

'I found some LSD in Dodger's flat and put a tab in Ricky's Stella,' laughed Baz.

Ginger stopped what he was doing. 'You wanna hope the hospital never blood-tested him, yer dickhead. Only, no way will Kenny Bond let that one go. Not a cat in hell's chance.'

'Look! There's a reward now. Ten thousand pound!' shrieked Leanne Cooper, while waving a copy of the *Ilford Recorder* at her sister. 'We gotta go to the police. It's them. I know it's them. We could be rich, Charlene.'

Charlene Cooper grabbed the paper and threw it in the pedal bin. They'd not seen hide nor hair of Beau and Brett again, even though they'd been stalking the Ilford Palais every weekend. 'We can't grass them up, and we don't know for sure if it was them any way.'

'Oh, come on. Even you agreed you thought it was them. The time they left here, the dark Range Rover, the description of the driver. It all adds up. Ten grand! Don't you want to go to Turkey? Find ourselves a nice handsome waiter. Or Greece? We could go anywhere with that kind of money.'

'Not really. I can't anyway. I'm pregnant, Leanne. And it's Beau's.'

'Where you going?' Sharon asked Ray.

'To stretch me legs. Want another cocktail?'

'No. Christ! You'll have to carry me back to the room.'

'Wouldn't be the first time.'

Sharon laughed. 'Get me lemonade please, Ray. A pint.'

Ray walked towards the bar but took a little detour to ring his business partner. 'All right? It's me. That job. The Bond job. I don't wanna do it. Let the man know and we'll catch up properly when I get home.'

Feeling on top of the world, Ray continued his journey to the bar. His unusual choice of career had earned him a hell of a lot of money over the years, but he was very careful whom he dealt with and he never dealt with certified wrong uns. In his eyes, Bond and the Daley brothers were both just that, so let them fight their battles out between them. Bit of luck, they'd all shoot one another at the same time.

'You all right, Ray?' asked a northern bloke he and Shal had been chatting to the previous evening.

Ray grinned, showing off his glowing white teeth. He was more than all right. Sharon was the woman of his dreams, he was absolutely cake-o, and apart from his business partner, nobody knew who he really was or what he really did. Ray was clever. 'The Assassin' might be his nickname, but nobody knew that was him.

'Can you get that away from me? I hate the smell. It reminds me of *them*,' panicked Ricky. Every time he'd caught a whiff of lager since that fateful night, it took Ricky back to being inside *that* flat with those two monsters leering at him.

'Beau, Brett,' gestured Kenny. He'd done all he could and now it was time.

'Don't leave me here in case I drown,' shouted Ricky.

'We're not. We're just behind you,' Kenny replied.

'You ready?' asked Beau.

'Yeah. It's time. Go stand in front of him with Brett. Tell him a funny story about when he was a little boy, something to make him laugh. I want him to have a smile on his face.'

Beau and Brett stood on the edge of the Jacuzzi opposite to where Ricky was sitting. ''Ere, Ricky, do you remember that time when we went to McDonald's and that tosser threw a chip at you, then you offered him one and he shit himself?' asked Beau.

Ricky smiled.

'God bless you, Big Man,' Kenny whispered, before pulling the trigger.

The bullet landed in the back of Ricky's skull. He flopped face down in the Jacuzzi, with part of his brains floating separately beside him.

'He was smiling, Gramps,' said Beau.

'Yeah. He looked happy,' added Brett.

Tony helped Kenny clean up. They wrapped Ricky up in a black sleeping bag, put heavy weights inside, then zipped it up. His favourite teddy bear that his parents had bought him as a small child was put inside the bag with him.

Tony had come well prepared with all the correct professional cleaning products. The boat belonged to him anyway, not that anybody knew Ricky in Spain. Since moving into their villa, Kenny hadn't taken the lad out.

It was a sad ending for Ricky, but an essential one, nevertheless. The lad had no quality of life left, neither was there any chance of him recovering from the traumatic injuries and experience he'd suffered.

'Right, we ready?' Beau gestured towards the sleeping bag.

'Hang on. I wanna put one of his favourite songs on,' replied Kenny. He'd got on his hands and knees earlier on the lower deck, had begged his pal Alan Davey for forgiveness. He was sure Alan would understand why he'd done what he did though. Kenny had given Ricky the best life since Alan's death and Kenny knew in his heart that Alan wouldn't want to see his bright, bubbly son now living as some miserable, incontinent vegetable.

Ricky was a big fan of George Michael, so Kenny chose 'Club Tropicana' as his send-off song. It seemed fitting, seeing as they were on a boat. A happy song, rather than sad.

'Ready, Gramps?' asked Brett.

'Ready as I'll ever be.' Kenny picked up one end of the sleeping bag. The boys picked up the other. 'After three. One, two, three . . .'

Ricky's body made an enormous splash as it hit the ocean, which seemed apt, as he'd made an enormous impact on all throughout his life. Not many Down's syndrome sufferers learned how to drive and pass their test, reckoned Kenny. Ricky had achieved so much. He truly was the best.

'Bye, Ricky,' said Brett, as the body disappeared under the clear ocean waters. 'Love ya, mate.'

'Bye, Ricky. You were a top lad,' said Beau. 'Life ain't gonna be the same without you, bro.'

'God bless you, Ricky.' Tears streamed down Kenny's face as he peered over the side of the yacht. 'We love you and we'll never forget ya. Until we meet again, Big Man. You fucking legend, you.'

EPILOGUE

We sat on the balcony in silence, the Spanish night air hot and sticky.

I top up our brandies. 'I don't arf miss my kids. I miss 'em so fucking bad, I get pains in my gut even thinking about 'em,' I admit.

Brett lights up one of Gramp's cigars. 'I feel for you, but what did you expect? I know you was behind what happened to Jolene, so you might as well just admit it. When have we ever kept secrets from one another?'

'You have. You've kept a whopper for years.'

'Nah. Never.' Brett's in denial, no surprise there.

'Liar!' I spit. 'And do you know what, I think I've known it all along. Even as far back as Compton House. I got no issues with it, ya know. Apart from I'm hurt you couldn't tell me. You're my brother, the one person I'm more closer to than anyone. Don't you think I'd love and support you whatever?'

'Ain't got a clue what you're rambling on about,' lies Brett.

'OK. I'll go first,' I hiss. 'Yeah. I did organize that attack on Jolene. I wanted her blinded, so she couldn't run off with another geezer and take my kids away from me, the fucking slag.'

Brett softens, squeezes my hand. 'You'll get your kids back one day.'

'How?' I snap. 'Our lives in England are over. Kaput! We can't go back there. Probably got bounties on our heads, the pair of us.'

'I ain't,' Brett mumbles.

Pissed off, I leap up and grab him by the shoulders, give 'em a good shake. I hate being lied to, especially by Brett. 'Don't you think I know it was Aidan's dad who shoved that gun down the back of my throat? And don't you think I clocked your reaction when I told ya? White as a sheet you went. You even had to grab hold of Mum's table for support. Stop taking me for a mug, bro, 'cause you're seriously winding me up now. There was never any you and Aisling. You were with Aidan all along, weren't you?'

Brett falls into my arms. 'I didn't know how to tell you. I never thought you'd understand. I thought you'd hate me, disown me.'

I hold him close. 'I could never hate you. You're the other half of me.'

Tears run down Brett's cheeks. 'You can't tell Gramps. I don't want him knowing. He's too old school.'

'I won't say a word. I promise. Shall we go back inside? Put them CDs on from earlier? Cheer ourselves up a bit,' I suggest.

Brett nods.

The Brothers

I switch the music on and turn up the volume. The song is The Hollies, 'He's My Brother'.

Me and Brett hold each other tightly as we sway side to side, singing the words to one another, meaningfully.

'We might have fucked our lives up, but at least we got each other,' Brett says.

I hold Brett's face, look deep into his eyes. 'We're only twenty-one, got our whole lives ahead of us. Nothing keeps us Bonds down for long. This is just a blip. We'll be back. Mark my words. Back with a fucking vengeance.'

The Bond family's story isn't over...

Don't miss the gripping new novel, *Essex Wives*,
from No.1 *Sunday Times* bestselling author
Kimberley Chambers

COMING SOON